DREAM OF EDEN

A novel of Old Hawaii

*

Sandol Stoddard

Big Island Press
Kailua-Kona, Hawaii

Cover design by Ali Abbas.

ISBN: 0692569316
ISBN-13: 978-0692569313
LCCN: 2015919025

ALSO BY SANDOL STODDARD

The Thinking Book (1960), Atlantic Monthly Press
Keep It Like a Secret (1962), Atlantic Monthly Press
Saint George and the Dragon (Adaptation) (1963), Houghton Mifflin
Curl Up Small (1964), Houghton Mifflin
My Very Own Special Particular Private and Personal Cat (1965),
        Houghton Mifflin
 I Like You (1965), Houghton Mifflin
From Ambledee To Zumbledee: An A.B.C. of Rather Special Bugs (1968),
        Houghton Mifflin
Growing Time (1969), Houghton Mifflin
Hooray For Us (1970), Houghton Mifflin
On the Way Home (1973), Houghton Mifflin
Free (1976), Houghton Mifflin
The Hospice Movement: A Better Way of Caring for the Dying (1978),
        Random House
Five Who Found the Kingdom (1979), Doubleday
Bedtime Mouse (1981), Houghton Mifflin
The Doubleday Illustrated Children's Bible (1983), Doubleday and The
        Literary Guild
Bedtime for Bear (1985) Houghton Mifflin
God's Little House (1985), Paulist Press
The Rules And Mysteries Of Brother Solomon (1987), Paulist Press
A Child's First Bible (1990) Doubleday and The Literary Guild
The Hospice Movement: Updated and Enlarged Edition (1992), Random
        House/Vintage
Prayers, Praises and Thanksgivings (Ed.) (1992), Dial/Penguin, Literary
        Guild
Turtle Time (1995), Houghton Mifflin
What are Roses For? (1996), Houghton Mifflin
The Eloquence of Silence (2008), Castle Press

(Prior to 1976, by Sandol Stoddard Warburg)

To my remarkable sons
Anthony, Peter, Gerald and Jason Warburg

and

to my beloved companion
Michael J. Walsh

CONTENTS

ACKNOWLEDGMENTS

Heartfelt gratitude to the following for support and counsel during the preparation of this book: Peter Randall Goethals, John Phillips, Deborah and Leonard Wolf, John Engelcke, Bill Lamers, Maynard Mack, Cynthia Salley, Carol Jung, Stacy Puhala, Pualani Gillespie, Curtis Tyler, Brad and Meris Farwell, Gordon and Fiona Menzies, Daniel Morrissey, and Robin Straus.

I would also like to thank the helpful people I met over several years of research for this book in various archives in the U.S. and abroad, especially at the Bishop Museum, Honolulu; the Bodleian Library, Oxford; the Borneo Research Council of Phillips, Maine; the Fondren Library at Rice University, Houston; the Hawaiian Historical Society, Honolulu; the Kona Historical Society, Kealakekua, Hawaii; the Lambeth Palace Library, London; the Rhodes Library, Oxford; and the library of St. Augustine's Missionary School in Canterbury.

Sandol Stoddard
Holualoa, Hawaii
December 2015

AUTHOR'S NOTE

DREAM OF EDEN is a work of fiction, although each of the major public events recounted actually happened and the lives of leading characters are closely based upon those of real people. A few names and personal descriptions have been changed in courtesy to the guilty as well as the innocent.

The imagination may be compared to Adam's dream –

he awoke and found it truth.

– John Keats, 1817

BOOK ONE: YOUTH

1

The children playing by the shore could see at first only an inch or so of darkness just below the horizon: something that looked like an empty space or scar on the glittering surface of the ocean. They watched it for a time, then stored the memory away. It had been very hot that afternoon, and they had caught a great many fish. Laughing and splashing now through the shallows, they set most of their captives free, since this was only a game, though an important one: a way of teaching themselves what they would be doing later in all seriousness.

A chosen few they placed in tidal pools among the shore-bound lava rocks, but however many they trapped in their woven baskets, more came swarming to feed in the warm, transparent waters. Iridescent, striped and motley, in every imaginable hue, they had names like *manini*, *kupipi* and *moi*.

At the end of the afternoon each player in the old familiar game would choose several to bring to the family meal, and an equal number to give away. The rest would be lifted carefully from the tide-pools and given back to the sea, for this was the way it had always been done in their village.

It was late in the day now, time to begin the final choosing. The sun, partially masked by low clouds, cast shafts of golden light obliquely over the water. Soon darkness would descend at this latitude. It was only a brief trek back to their seaside village, and yet at this hour, and in the dazzling radiance of the sunset light, time seemed suddenly suspended. One by one the children fell silent. It was not the silence of fatigue, for all of their senses were now at their keenest. It was the heat of the day, the perfect silken softness of the sand, the fragrance of the gleaming green and golden tide-pools, that all at once became mesmerizing, brimming with mystery.

They sat down on the sand now or stood quietly at the water's edge as they listened consciously, for the first time in many hours, to the thrust and boom of surf against the barrier reef. They looked out to the sea that flashed its silver fire beyond the reef, except in the one place without form: the dark scar or wound on the surface of the water that was gradually growing larger.

Still their reverie continued, until a small breeze came to skim the water, lifting the hair from their hot faces and stirring the row of coconut palms that fringed the curving shore. Those wading in the water felt the wind as a sudden chill against their wet skin, and they began to study the horizon more carefully, shielding their eyes with slim brown hands.

Nothing. Only bright water, mile after mile. "What was that?" asked one of the younger boys. "I saw something. It was out there this morning too. Did you see it, Kimo?"

"No."

"Kualani?"

"No. What did you see?"

Then they all saw it. Shapeless and contorted, something was approaching the barrier reef. A moment more, and it was lifted over the reef on a long, sinuous, resounding wave, rushing directly toward the children for an instant, then sliding sideways, and dipping again from view.

"Canoe," said Kimo, the eldest. "Some kind of boat. Broke down, I think. Watch when it comes again."

They watched in silence. "See that," said Kimo. "How it moves. No one steering."

He waded into the water, calling to the others, "Something wrong. I'm going out there!" Kimo could swim as well as he could walk, yet for a time he hesitated.

Then a young girl called Noni shouted, "Don't go, Kimo! Look! *Mano* out there too – see, behind the boat!"

"That's no *mano*. Can't be. Shark never come in here!"

"It is! I see it – a big one! Look, it's white, a white one! Maybe *Akua!* That means – oh, it is the Shark God I know, coming here! Kualani, what shall we do?" Hiding her face, she turned to the older girl.

"Shark God!" shouted Kimo scornfully. "That is bad to say. Don't let Mister Shadbolt hear you!"

"I don't care!"

"*Akua?* Shark God! Shame! You want big trouble? That what you want, stupid?"

"It's the Americans make trouble," said Noni, weeping now. "Maile says so! Shadbolt is a bad man, I hate him! But he's gone now, never coming back."

It was true that, after nine years of impassioned preaching about the angry God he had brought with him from Connecticut, the Reverend Lemuel T. Shadbolt had been overcome at last by illness and exhaustion. He, his bone-weary wife and their five sickly children were now on indefinite leave, and the little church by the waterfront had been empty for many months when a violent storm came in and demolished it.

Kualani put her arms around the younger girl. "Hush, Noni. It will be all right. *Akua* won't hurt us. No! Kimo, wait! Stay here! I will run get Papa – he will bring chicken, or something good for *Akua* to eat." But it was too late for that. The glistening fin had cut an arc on the surface of the bay and plunged back toward the reef. There it vanished into the distance, heading out to sea.

During the hour that followed, the sun dropped slowly at first, then swiftly to the horizon, and the silver sea dimmed gradually toward gray. Clouds towered above the water, turning gold and crimson, violet, and finally a pale, smoky blue. The breeze quickened. The evening star appeared, and under a

3

lemon-tinted sky the children continued to wait, stamping their feet impatiently from time to time while the crippled boat drifted and wallowed its solitary way toward shore. It was nearly 7 p.m. when they decided to swim the last few yards together and pull it in. By then it was dark enough so they could not see that it trailed behind it a viscous, spreading stain.

*

Soon after sunset, all the dogs in the village began to bark. At the top of a cliff above the native settlement, David Wilkinson consulted his watch and remarked aloud, "Something is wrong. " As the clamor continued, the young Anglican priest made a note about it in his diary, followed by a question mark. It was eight o'clock on the evening of June 17th, 1867. His diary, which he kept with him at all times, was a small leather-bound booklet with filmy, gold-edged pages and a blue silk ribbon to mark his place.

Nursing painfully blistered hands, the young Englishman sat alone in the hut, newly built, that would serve as his parsonage. His missionary college at Canterbury had taught him the principles of simple carpentry, but as an amateur, he had managed to build little more than accommodation for a hermit crab. It was twelve feet by fourteen, give or take a little, and its charm, if any, lay in the window he had laboriously carved, glazed and hinged, so that he could invite the breeze and look out over the sea. This humble outpost represented the first missionary home of the Anglican Church on Hawaii's "Big Island."

The day had been blazing hot, utterly still and silent. In fact, the Kona Coast was often so at that time of year. Wilkinson had been nailing shingles to his roof all morning, hoping to stop some leaks. Later, he had hauled in his sea chest and set it up as a miniature dining table with storage underneath. He had attached a pair of shelves to the seaward wall, and there he arranged six silver forks and spoons, four china plates from his grandparents' dispensation, his mother's second best

Wedgwood teapot, a battered silver candlestick, a box of beeswax candles, and a dozen books. His crystal wine glasses had been broken in transit, and so, at the sunset hour, he raised a toast to first to Queen Victoria of England, then to Queen Emma of Hawaii, in a tin cupful of Spanish sherry. He dined on cold, leftover rice with a sauce made from the pulp of the wild guavas that grew by his door; and later, after reading Evening Prayer aloud, stepped outside in the dark to look up at the vast night sky that was filled with blazing stars. Then, with a quick, silent prayer of his own, he pulled on a nightshirt and blew his candle out.

Moments later he began to hear horses' hooves, and the shout of a man urging them forward. He listened. Not one but two horses were cantering toward him, threading their way between lava rocks of the kind called by the natives "a'a". An ordinary animal's leg might be broken easily in this terrain, but local mounts seemed to have a sixth sense in the matter.

"Something <u>was</u> wrong," he said aloud. Hastily dressing again, he lit his kerosene lantern, tucked a clean handkerchief into his breast pocket, and stood at the door. A single rider soon appeared, portly, red-haired and sweating: Richard Cornwall, the local storekeeper and fellow Yorkshireman. Another horse trailed close by, on a lead.

"Hullo there! Come in!" said Wilkinson. "I have a second chair now in my parlor."

"House all finished?" asked Cornwall without dismounting.

"More or less. I hope to do better when I build my church."

"Sorry to bother you, sir, at such an hour."

"No bother. You look like a thirsty man. May I offer you something to drink?"

"Water, please, if you have it." The storekeeper drank greedily, still pouring sweat, and Wilkinson noticed that he was even a bit more fragrant than usual this evening.

"The fact is," said Cornwall, wiping his face on his sleeve, "I am sorry, but you are needed down at the native village. I

5

don't like it. Don't want to be the bearer of bad news. But there has been some trouble."

"What sort of trouble?" Wilkinson slipped his prayer book into his pocket and shut the door behind him. "Is anyone hurt?"

"Disagreeable business, yes. I'll show you the way. I've brought my old mare. She's slow, but kindly. She'll see you safe down the *pali*."

The priest lifted his lantern to study his visitor's face, and said, "We'd better go then. Perhaps you can tell me more about it on the way." He swung himself easily onto the mare's back, took up her reins, and freed the lead-line. But now Cornwall suddenly became talkative. Droplets of perspiration stood out on his face again, and again he wiped it. "Not very nice, I am afraid. Not nice at all. I'm sure that the Church and the Law are both needed. I've sent for the sheriff, but before we go down there, sir, I want you to know that I've been here nigh onto fifteen years and never seen anything like this. Never!" They began riding slowly now, side by side over the dark field.

"What has happened, Mr. Cornwall?"

"A boat came in," he replied, evidently struggling for words. "Two men in a boat. One dead and one alive, but only just."

"I am sorry to hear it. What sort of men?"

"Not good. Both *haoles* - white men, that is to say. Both of them quite without clothing. Derelict! Badly burned by the sun. Burned, sick, infected, festering, waterlogged, the foulest kind of mess. Blood all down in the bilges, leaking, and a shark alongside. God only knows how long they have been out there. Terrible business for the youngsters that found them."

"*Children* found them?"

"Yes, sir. Playing in the tide-pools. They saw the boat first, then the shark."

They rode on in silence and then Wilkinson said, "I will talk with them about it. But surely, Hawaiian children know that

6

such things happen. It's a brutal coastline here, and the currents are treacherous."

"True," said Cornwall. Then he added, "They are saying that the shark was an *akua* , one of their gods. A powerful one – the Shark God. So the children were going to find some food for him, but he disappeared. Strange business, this! I mean, I never heard of sharks inside that reef."

"*Akua*?"

"Well, either that or else an *amakua* – guardian spirit of sorts. Helpful sort of creature. Nothing to worry about."

"Stop a minute, Mr. Cornwall," said Wilkinson, and they both stopped. "I am at a loss here, and I see that I shall need your advice. If I understand you correctly, the people in this village still believe in pagan gods and spirits. But I was told before coming here that they had been Christianized already by the Americans. My task was simply to improve on that beginning."

"Oh my," said Cornwall. "Well, let's see. Christianized, yes, and many are quite devout. They love Jesus, that is to say, and pray to him. They love the Bible, and try their best to read it. But they keep some of their wicked old ways as well, and I for one truthfully can't blame them. They didn't care for Shadbolt, the American missionary. You saw where his church was washed away, but that wasn't why he left Hawaii. Fact is, he had to."

"Oh. And why was that?"

"Rebellion, sir. The whole village up in arms. In a manner of speaking, that is. Ungrateful of them, you might think. After all, they were ignorant savages when he came. Didn't know right from wrong, you see. T'was Mr. Shadbolt that made them put on clothes and begin to act decent."

"I see," said the priest, although he did not. They rode on in silence for a time, turning back and forth on the sharply declining path across the face of the cliff. The lantern soon went out, and Wilkinson was grateful for the surprising radiance of the blazing stars. As they reached the narrow shoreline below, Cornwall remarked, "I notice you've been on a horse before."

"Somewhat," said Wilkinson, pronouncing it *summaht*. "Will they speak English here?"

"*Summaht*," said Cornwall. "They'll understand you."

"And what of the shipwrecked men? Does anyone know them?"

"No sir," said Cornwall with a sigh. "All I can say, Mr. Wilkinson, these are not the sort of people I would introduce to my wife. And I am extremely sorry, because you being a new priest, and this your first parish and you just coming to the Islands, it really is not nice. I fear it will give you a nasty impression. but what can we do? I very much regret to tell you, sir – the disagreeable fact is – one of these two miserable white men has gone and eaten quite a bit of the other."

2

The two men rode on through a fine grove of coconut trees, and soon caught sight of a bonfire among rocks ahead, and several smoking torches. Grass-roofed huts were scattered about on raised platforms of lava rock near the sea. A dozen canoes lay on the sand, drawn up from the water's edge. Children of all ages were awake and running about, even at this late hour, while men sat together eating and drinking. Only a few of them glanced at the newcomers or rose to acknowledge their presence. It was the women who moved slowly toward them, one by one.

The most distinguished of these was an immense dark figure wrapped in tapa cloth, with a necklace of shells about her throat, and a wreath of foliage drawn low on her brow. She came forward without hesitation, and stood in the moonlight facing the men, expressionless, evidently waiting for them to speak.

"Peace be to this place and all that dwell in it," said Wilkinson. There was no response. He dismounted, and continued cheerfully, "My name is Wilkinson. I am a priest. I am sorry to hear of your trouble. I shall be glad to help you if I can."

The vast personage ignored his outstretched hand and

turned to Cornwall, questioning him in Hawaiian too rapid for Wilkinson to comprehend. Cornwall replied more slowly, in the same language. He gestured toward Wilkinson, repeatedly using the word "Pelekane," and causing the young priest to wonder why they were discussing a rare variety of shore bird.

"Excuse me – what is this about?" he queried, and the storekeeper stopped to explain that *Pelekane* in Hawaiian means "British," or "Englishman."

The enormous female turned to the young priest and stated firmly, "Pelekane!"

"Yes indeed, " he replied as firmly, " I am Pelekane." But where, he wondered, was the boat? And the two men? The dogs were quiet now, though they moved about restlessly. A circle of dark faces surrounded him, impassively staring.

"So you be no America, no French?" she continued.

"No, I am a Yorkshireman, from the north of England. But Madam, about the shipwrecked men, I must – "

She interrupted, as the children began to grin and whisper among themselves, and said, "I give you my name. I am Mailelani."

"Thank you, Mailelani. May I be permitted to see the –"

She interrupted again. "Pelekane! You say you are priest. No French kine, no Catholic, yes? So, are you for Jesus?"

"Of course I am! England is a civilized country. Now, if you please, may I be allowed to see the two men?"

She shrugged a huge shoulder and said in her low, powerful voice, "Two *haoles* come here. What kind? Rubbish kind, I think. English, maybe. Or American. The children find them, and that is too bad. One man dead, the other like a baby crying. He say he sorry now, but that is no good. This thing is abomination. This man will burn in Hell. God will not forgive him."

Those miserable American missionaries! thought Wilkinson, and said "Is that what you learned from the American? Is that the sort of thing Mr. Shadbolt taught you?" He knew that his tone was much too sharp, and regretted it immediately. Mailelani did not reply, and no one else stirred. They simply looked at him, until Wilkinson thought that he would like very much to be back in Yorkshire. Still, he insisted that he must see the man who was still alive.

"Look first what he done!" said a tall, silver-haired man standing near Mailelani. "See that, then see the one who done this thing."

Obediently, Wilkinson followed the elderly man across the clearing. The body had been wrapped in a grass or fiber mat and suspended on ropes from the roof of an open shed, where dogs and vermin could not reach it. The stench, as they approached the shed, was terrific. The body was taken down by two powerful young men and unwrapped for the priest's inspection. He knelt beside it.

The dead man was bearded, dark-haired, evidently of European stock, perhaps 35 or 40 years of age. The expression on his face was curiously peaceful. At first, in the flickering torchlight, Wilkinson could see only that his body was naked, mutilated, dark red with blood that had escaped and dried, and blackish-red with sunburn peeling and ulcerated. The flesh was surprisingly warm, partly gelatinous, but no longer suppurating. The throat had been savagely sliced along one side. The liver, and other organs perhaps, had been removed from the body. The remaining flesh in that area was covered with thickly curling and matted hair. One buttock had been deeply carved away. The private parts were missing.

He covered the body and stood. They were all watching him now, crowding close and studying his face for every fleeting expression. Even so, Wilkinson felt that he was standing there alone, with only a shocking corpse in all the world as his companion. Nocturnal insects fluttered about the shed, one so large that he wondered idly if it were actually a bird or a bat.

Auwe! cried one child, and then another. He could not see where Cornwall was. *"Christ have mercy,"* were the only words that came to him, and he spoke them aloud. To his surprise, several voices responded *Amene! Amene!*

He reached for his prayer book and began, before opening

11

it, "I am the resurrection and the life, saith the Lord: he that believeth in me, though he were dead, yet he shall live…"

Amene, amene, said many eager voices. A young girl came to stand beside him holding a burning *kukui* nut candle which helped him read. Wilkinson was well into the burial service before he realized that he was doing this wrong – after all, this was not a burial. *What a fool I am,* he thought, and ended abruptly with the words of comfort he himself needed to hear: "O Lord Jesus Christ, who by thy death didst take away the sting of death, grant unto us thy servants so to follow in faith where thou hast led the way…" After that, he felt tremendously tired, and wondered how long it would be before he could lie down somewhere.

But the people still looked at him, and waited. It was obvious that they wanted more. What was he to do? The Americans, he knew, habitually preached for hours on end. That was very far from his own style, and he did not intend to do the same. Surely, he thought, these people must know at least the Lord's Prayer. He led them in the familiar words, some speaking English, some Hawaiian, and that seemed to him a pleasant mingling. What need for more? He drew a deep breath, then did his best to preach the shortest sermon he had ever uttered.

"Good people, we have met in a dark hour, but surely there are brighter days to come. In the meantime, let us not judge what we do not understand. We do not know these men, or how long they may have been lost at sea, or what their suffering may have been. We can be sure only that they – and we – are all children of God, equally cared for by our loving Father. Jesus has taught us to care for one another, and so, if no one else claims this unfortunate stranger, I shall bury him near my own dwelling. That is the new little house on the hill above, and you are all welcome to visit me there. I hope you may also come to my church when it is built. In the meantime I shall continue to pray for this poor soul, whoever he may be, and I ask you to do the same. In the name of the Father, the Son and the Holy Ghost, Amen."

"That is wrong!" cried a hard young voice. Wilkinson looked up and saw a slim man-child of 13 or 14 years staring at him with contempt. "You tell us pray for a dead man. This is bad - this is evil, *Catholic* thing to do! Mister Shadbolt say only filthy Papist pray for the dead."

"I am not Mr. Shadbolt," said Wilkinson shortly, and put his prayer book into his pocket.

"*Shut your mouth, Kimo!*" To the young priest's surprise, this was said in commanding tones by the handsome, silver-haired elder. "You so big, what you know? Listen to this one! – This is *Pelekane!* Different man, same Jesus."

Wilkinson was grateful for the elder's support; he wanted to get on with his duties, and he also needed very badly just then to wash his hands. Richard Cornwall reappeared and walked with him to the water's edge. There he stood as if on guard while the priest cleaned his hands and face, scouring his blistered fingers by massaging them as gently as possible with wet sand.

"Not a pretty sight," Cornwall remarked.

"True," said David Wilkinson.

"What sort of person would do a thing like that?"

"I don't know. Someone very hungry, I suppose."

The coconut trees tossed their fronds high above them, and the fresh evening breeze from the sea was a blessing. There in the shallows, the water was very nearly as warm as human blood. Wilkinson's thoughts fled from the scene, out as far as the white-crested waves breaking in the moonlight against the reef. In Honolulu a month earlier he had ridden such waves on a long board in the native fashion, for the Hawaiian king himself had taught him how to do it, at his own fine beach called Waikiki.

"The other chap is awake now," Cornwall remarked. "Appears to be doing rather well. Marvelous gift for medicine these people have. Healing, that is - nothing scientific, of course."

Wilkinson smiled. "My Yorkshire mother has that same gift. And I'll wager yours does too."

"Did, yes. She was from Lewis in the Hebrides. Out there in the Isles they keep to the old ways. Now, sir, will you be speaking to the culprit before the sheriff comes?"

"Yes, I'll do that next."

Cornwall hesitated. "I've been wondering. You don't imagine he's any sort of demon?"

"No. Merely human, I suppose."

"Human," said Cornwall. "Well, I'll wait of course. You won't be long?"

"That depends," Wilkinson told him. Cornwall began to walk away, then turned back. "If you don't mind me asking, Mr. Wilkinson, how long since you was ordained?"

"Deacon, five months. Priest, three weeks and two days."

"Oh my," said Cornwall. "Well, never mind. It's plain enough that you know what you're doing."

"Thank you. But I see now that I should have come to visit these people much sooner. And I don't look forward to the next bit. Pray for me."

"Oh my," said Cornwall again. "Well then, Vicar, I shall just do that," and he ambled off into the darkness.

*

To Richard Cornwall, born and bred in England, manners were an integral part of his religion. He was aware that the gravest of matters should be addressed in private, and so he moved away quietly. However, among many indigenous peoples, the need for privacy is relatively unknown. It has been reported, for example, that when the crews of European trading ships first landed on certain Polynesian shores, they found it expected that their amorous exertions with the local maidens would be conducted in public, for the entertainment of large audiences. Apparently the men got used to it, but that, of course, was before the missionaries came.

The entire population of the native village came along now with the Reverend David Wilkinson as he went to meet the guilty cannibal. The hut where the man had been placed was set a little apart from the others. Its roof, made of *pili* grass, was tall and sloping, with an opening at the front so low that a man of Wilkinson's height had to fold himself up like a measuring stick to enter. Several of the villagers pressed in with him, and through cracks in the walls he could hear the voices of many more.

Inside the hut he found an extraordinary scene. His first impression was that this was not a living white man, but a mummy out of Egypt. A young native girl sat beside him, fanning insects away, while the object of her care lay on a *lau hala* mat, with a pillow under his head made of some soft stuff from the base of forest ferns that was known as *pulu*. The man himself was wrapped from head to foot with broad green leaves that were moist and glistening, as if soaked in some ointment or oil.

Kneeling beside the patient, David Wilkinson explained that he was a clergyman and asked the man his name, which was Billy Smith, or so he claimed; the police, later, had a different opinion. Next David asked if he were a Christian, but the mummy did not answer this, except to nod his head and begin bawling.

"Are you in pain?" Wilkinson asked. The reply was, "Oh, oh, oh, I am lost, I am damned. Don't let me die! Oh, oh, what have I done," and so forth, with many groans and great sniffling. His pulse was fast, but strong and steady, and his lungs sounded to be in good condition. "You are not dying," said Wilkinson. "At least, not just now." Only a part of the sunburned face was visible, and from that it was impossible to guess at the man's age, character, or nationality.

Now the mummy began to wail and cry out that his arm was broken. "Oh! The pain! The pain!" Wilkinson unwrapped the arm, but found no sign of a fracture. Still the man continued to weep and moan. "See here," said Wilkinson firmly, "I have <u>looked</u> at your arm, and it is <u>not</u> broken!" Around them in the hut, people began to murmur excitedly, and he heard his new name spoken: *Pelekane! Pelekane!* Evidently they thought he had just performed a miraculous healing.

"Listen to me, people," he told them firmly, "I must pray and visit with this man quietly. Be kind enough to leave us now, and go to your homes." No one moved.

He tried a softer method. "It is very late," he said to the girl with the fan. "You must be tired. Here, let me do this for you." He took the fan and said, "Please, all of you, go to your own dwellings now and rest. Soon it will be morning. I will stay here and care for Mr. Smith." There was loud chattering, but only a few people departed. Squatting beside Wilkinson now was Harold Lopaka, the elder who had spoken on his behalf.

"Has this man been given nourishment?" Wilkinson asked.

"Water," Lopaka replied. "Some *poi*. Too much now is no good."

"Right you are. Who has done this splendid bandaging? And what is this medicine?"

"This is nothing," said Lopaka. "Only to cover him."

"But surely this is a medicinal oil or ointment of some sort?"

"You think?" Harold Lopaka, wrinkling his dark forehead, was a portrait of innocence.

"Yes, I have studied a little doctoring. What is this called? Apparently it is something for burns, and perhaps to help the pain?"

"You say," the Hawaiian remarked calmly, and looked away. Wilkinson turned to the others and told them, "I am sorry I do not speak your language yet, but listen! You will understand me. This man is a stranger. He comes here in bad trouble, very bad. You do not know him, yet you care for him. You take the part of the Good Samaritan. You carry him to a safe place, and you pour oil on his wounds. This is what Jesus teaches. Surely you know the story?"

The men and women in the hut, and the children who clung to them, all looked at one another, seemingly in alarm. Smith once more shed copious tears, while Lopaka considered the last statement. At length, the elder said, "I know one thing. No good, this old Kanaka medicine."

"Kanaka! Why, that means Hawaiian, does it not? Are you saying that your own traditional way of healing is bad? Who told you so? Did Mr. Shadbolt say that too?" David Wilkinson was growing angrier by the minute. Lopaka replied impassively, "The man was naked when he came. That is not right. Now he is covered. This is all."

Then a small, piping voice entered the discussion. It came from the child called Noni, the same who had held up a candle for him. "Mailelani did it," she said, "and I help her. I always do. Maile knows every kine medicine for heal."

"And I thank you both," said Wilkinson. "That was very good of you." He turned to the invalid, who lay quiet. "Did you hear that, my poor miserable friend? These people think that you are worth saving. Take heart! If strangers do this much for you, how much more do you think your Heavenly Father will do?"

The mummy made no reply, but hiccupped several times and gave a huge yawn. "Look here," said Wilkinson, "all of you. Pay attention now. It is nearly three o'clock in the morning. Go to your homes now and sleep. I must speak and pray with Mr. Smith about private matters. Do you understand? Now, I insist that you go!"

At this, most of the crowd reluctantly departed. Wilkinson called after the last of them, "I will be here as long as I am needed, and I will speak to the sheriff as soon as he..." But at the sound of the word *sheriff*, the bandaged mummy suddenly leapt up like a dead man hearing the trump at Resurrection, and began roaring, thrashing, and striking out with astonishing force in all directions. The leaves flew from his flesh, he showed his teeth like a raving animal, and actually growled.

Wilkinson reached out with the vain thought of trying to reason with the madman, and was greeted by a heavy calabash that struck him in the face. He fell to the ground beside the doorway. Two or three powerful young native men came running and thrust their way into the hut. During the next few minutes, each one had the crazed invalid briefly in his grasp. However, Smith was so desperate, and his naked body was so slippery from the oil in which he had been marinated, that he managed to escape them every time.

Now the dogs began barking again, and the mayhem increased. David Wilkinson began searching for the watch that had been in his hand minutes earlier. It was gone! He needed it badly in this outpost; it had belonged to his father, that beloved parent's parting gift to him as he left England . Crawling about the ground in semi-darkness, he searched frantically for it while Smith threw calabashes, jugs, hampers, fish nets – anything that came to hand. *Mirabele dictu*, his arm now showed no sign of injury! A moment later the wildman discovered a stout length of bamboo, and with this weapon struck brutal blows at anyone who approached him, all the while continuing to howl and growl and caper like a lunatic.

The watch was found at last, with the help of a single remaining source of light - a small jar of oil with a twisted rag serving as wick. Three Hawaiian lads were circling the villain, grinning with delight in the fray, although all of their faces were bloodied. Wilkinson held up the lamp now and began to shout, warning Smith that he would certainly go to jail for this. Then he lunged at the man and nearly succeeded in bringing him down, but Smith at the same time delivered a blow to Wilkinson's knees that would leave them aching in damp weather for the next fifty years.

The burning wick fell onto the invalid's pallet, and bright flames sprang up immediately. Wilkinson turned to smother them, and when he turned back, Billy Smith had vanished. Gasping and coughing, the four remaining men crept out to the cool night. Perfect stillness had descended upon the village. The huts were dark, the dogs were silent, and there was no sign of the fugitive.

After walking about aimlessly for a time, Wilkinson lay down on the sand, that was blessedly cool after many hours of darkness. What had become of Cornwall? He decided that the sensible soul must have gone home long ago. Where on earth was the mad, ungrateful criminal? The village lads who had tried and failed to subdue him were now treating it all as a great joke. Laughing and chattering among themselves, they wandered down the beach and disappeared.

The young priest fell suddenly asleep then – perhaps, as he thought, for only a minute or two. When he awakened, it was with the strong sense that an unfamiliar presence was quite nearby. Opening his eyes, he saw a lantern on the ground beside him, and looked up to see a man in a wide-brimmed rancher's hat standing over him, with a large revolver in his hand.

3

"Father Wilkinson, is it?"

"Yes?" he replied, not in a mood to quibble over ecclesiastical titles.

"Do not be alarmed. I am Kevin Kildare, sheriff of the district."

"How d'ye do, sir?" said David, not moving an inch.

"Thank you, Father, very well indeed this lovely evening. But I must inquire, do you by chance find yourself in any sort of personal difficulty just now?"

So gracious and courtly was his manner, and so rich the Irish melody of his voice, that Wilkinson suddenly found himself helpless with laughter. Kildare waited patiently until he could speak, and heard him explain that he was not inconvenienced just now, either by drink or by injury. Then the Sheriff helped him to his feet, and insisted on seeing him walk a few paces, after which, he took a silver flask from his pocket, and poured a bracing draught into its cap. "A small nip for fellowship," he said, "and for the time of day."

*

Richard Cornwall reappeared as the moon slipped into the

ocean, while the glow in the east began to promise a glorious dawn. Cornwall had found some bananas, and the three men breakfasted gratefully on them. "I thought you must have gone home," said Wilkinson. Cornwall looked astonished, and replied in hurt tones, "But I promised to wait for you! I went for a walk. Then I heard a noise and came back, but I couldn't find you. What happened?"

My question," said Kevin Kildare, "is this. I am told that a bucket of blood was found in the boat, and that the survivor had been drinking it. But I need to know whether or not the blood will run freely from a man after his death, and happen to fall into a convenient container. And if it will, then how much will come forth from the body, and for how long? Assuming of course that the poor soul has already died of natural causes. Assuming in fact that his thirsty comrade has not murdered him. Yes, 'tis a puzzle, 'tis a conundrum. Alas, I expect that we shall have to consult the experts in Honolulu – always a disagreeable task.

"And now," he continued cheerfully, "in sum, what have we here? A melancholy set of events, to be sure. One man dead, of unknown identity, with time, place and manner of death unknown. And if that were not enough, we have a second man, himself badly damaged, and not in the best of spirits, running around the place without a thread of clothes on. I do not believe that the second man can have gone far. What say you?"

Birds twittered in the palms and small waves tumbled at the brink of the shore, while the gray of the sea was gradually transformed into pale, transparent green, golden and lavender. Beyond the reef, deeper waters now began to blaze sapphire blue. A solitary figure stood on a point of land some fifty yards to the north, fishing net in hand. As long as they watched, waiting to see him fling his net, he remained there motionless, gazing at the broad reaches of the new day's horizon.

"The Lord is in his holy temple," said Wilkinson. "Let all the earth keep silence before him."

Cornwall cleared his throat loudly and said, "Ah-men."

"Ay-men" said Kildare. "Yes indeed, sir. And will you believe, from this very spot last Christmas week I saw a pair of whales just there, in surprisingly shallow water, celebrating the glory of God and the everlasting nature of things – yes, Father? Life! Life! Indeed, I myself had often wondered how they do it. But the female apparently knows exactly what she is after, and the male has an exceedingly large member, all of which makes for festivity on a grand and glorious scale. What a world! What a world! One miracle after another, and the joy, the beauty, the sheer extravagance of it all! I ask you, Father, is there no limit to His goodness? Does His generosity never cease? I recall that we had quite a handsome little earthquake up *mauka* that very same day.

"Which reminds me," he continued blithely, although Richard Cornwall by now was quite pink, "I believe I know the identity of our fugitive. A disagreeable fellow. Wanders about one place to another, has a way of turning up now and again, always bringing trouble. Whenever he's out of the lunatic asylum, that is. At times, he has managed to attract quite a following. "Prophet" – yes, that was it – "Greatest of all Prophets" he was calling himself last time we met. Over on Maui that was, where people are not always sensible. I had a warning that he might be paying us a visit here. But the name is not Smith – no, not Smith by any means. I cannot recall it just now, but it will come to me." He drew the revolver from its holster, and checked its preparedness.

"I'll stay if needed," said Cornwall. "The shop can look after itself for a day."

"Most considerate of you, sir," said the sheriff. "Very gracious indeed. But having viewed the remains, I think it best for you and Father to tend to the – ah – sooner rather than later. A Christian burial – least we can do for the poor soul, very least we can do."

Wilkinson turned to Kildare. "Are you sure you want to pursue this alone? The man is violent, and sure to be in a desperate mood."

"Yes, yes." He smiled. "We'll just see what develops. I

venture to suppose that he's stopped at the moment for a wee nap some place nearby. So I'll just be having a bit of a lie-down here, where I can watch the path. Fear not, all shall be well! Good day, gentlemen!"

The remaining two strapped the remains of the desecrated body to the back of the patient mare, and Cornwall set off with her on a lead toward the base of the cliff. David Wilkinson had volunteered to bring up the rear of this mournful procession on foot; however, as soon as the others had vanished into the coconut grove, he heard a familiar voice calling, "Pelekane!"

There on the outskirts of the village stood Mailelani, even taller, darker and more majestic in the morning sunlight than she had been the night before. Her great glistening shoulders were bare today, but adorned with a wide lei, or wreath, of leaves intertwined with blossoms. Struck anew with admiration, Wilkinson approached her. "I want to thank you again, Mailelani. The man turned out to be a bad one, but your medicine was excellent."

"I tole you that was one rubbish *haole*," said she.

"Yes, and you were right. But tell me, if you will, why did you nurse him? Why did you trouble to do that?" She shrugged, but did not reply.

"I need to know," Wilkinson persisted. "Please help me to understand. Was it because you are a healer in the old Hawaiian way? What I believe is called, a *kahuna* – yes? Or did you do it for Jesus' sake, since you are a Christian – that is to say, I am assuming that you were baptized by the Americans?"

She tossed her head back and gazed at the young priest coquettishly, through lowered eyelids. Then she said, "I tell you something later, maybe. Not today. Bye 'n bye you come back here, Pelekane. I like you, so come over my place, then we talk more."

"I'll do that, yes. Also, I mean to speak to the children after I bury this man. Please tell them that I will come back in a day or two." As an afterthought, he added, "In the meantime, see that they take care, will you? The madman may still be nearby, and he is dangerous."

"Yes he is," she said. "So I got him."

"Excuse me?"

"What I say."

"I'm afraid I don't understand."

"No?" She laughed. "You not so smart, I think."

"Indeed," he replied, "you are quite right about that."

"Take easy. I tell you all," she said with a glorious smile, and then began to explain at some length. The gist of the matter was that the fugitive had made the mistake of arriving in a nasty mood at Mailelani's dwelling shortly before dawn. At that time she was enjoying a splendid dream about her grandfather's grandfather, of whom she was very fond, who had lived in this village before the English came, and whose spiritual presence, or image, or *aumakua*, came frequently to talk with her, and especially to comfort and advise her at that time of night, always in the form of a large green sea-turtle. At such a hallowed moment, the lady was not pleased to receive an uninvited visitor.

So, as she explained, she rose from her sleep, overpowered Mr. Smith, rolled him up in a mat and tied it securely. Next, having attached the bundle by another length of hemp to her own ankle, this astonishing person lay down again, prayed to Jesus Christ for the second time that night, and went back to sleep. She dreamed no more of her *aumakua*, which was a great disappointment, and did not awaken again until morning, when the sun struck her face. Smith was alive today, she said, though despondent. She had given him water and coconut milk, but not his freedom. Then she had spoken to the sheriff, before coming after David.

"You disappeared again," said Cornwall when David Wilkinson caught up with him. "Are you all right? Did they find Smith?" But the heat was so intense by now, and the young priest was so lamed by the blows he had suffered, that he could only nod by way of answer. At this, Cornwall insisted that David must ride while he himself climbed the *pali* on foot.

When they reached the little parsonage nearly an hour later, Richard Cornwall helped to build, load and close the coffin.

Then he dug the main part of the grave himself, in hard ground, while Wilkinson sat nursing his wounds in the scanty shade of a young mango tree. After that, tenderly as any woman, Cornwall bathed the priest's swollen bruises and wrapped them in cool, wet cloths. This time Wilkinson read the Burial Service from beginning to end, while Cornwall stood up as his entire congregation, and brought forth the right responses from the depths of his memory.

Cornwall's aid was a notable deed of kindness, for David Wilkinson was in great need just then of human help and fellowship. The events of the previous night had been deeply troubling. He had begun to imagine that there was something inauspicious and unhealthy in the plot of land where he had settled, after seeing such beauty and promise there at first. Was there something, after all, so wicked as to be demonic in the death of the mutilated stranger? And, why had he brought the ghastly remains to lie beside his own home?

These were foolish thoughts, he knew — mere nerves and superstition. The coffin, after all, contained only a ruined man's physical remains. Yet David felt soiled by all he had witnessed, and asked himself why he had chosen to bring any sign or remembrance of it to the site of a new Anglican mission. It had occurred to him that primitive tradition in these islands, as in many other places, might have called for human sacrifice to insure the success of a significant new venture. This, however, was such an unsettling thought that he refused to pursue it. Cornwall had declined his offer of food and drink, saying, "I'd better get back to my wife. She's expecting, you know."

David had not known. New life! Especially on this isolated, thinly populated coast, a cause for rejoicing. The two men shook hands and walked out together along the dry weeds and grasses of the hillside. After a few words about the gallantry of the female sex in their times of travail, Wilkinson said, "It has been a pleasure and a privilege for me to meet Mailelani. When I left her this morning standing by the shore, I thought she looked like the very soul of Hawaii. The strangeness, the darkness, the mystery were there; also the beauty, the grandeur and dignity. I see independence of spirit in her, he said, together with courage, intelligence and compassion. What a magnificent woman!"

"Oh my," said Cornwall. "Well, now."

"What? Don't you agree?"

"Well, Mr. Wilkinson, you see…"

"See what?"

"Actually, ah –"

"Well – ?"

"I thought you knew. Mailelani isn't a woman."

"What is she, then?" Wilkinson thought he could not be serious.

"Maile is a man. Maile is what they call a *mahu*. Didn't you know? There are quite a few of them around. Certainly in Honolulu you must have… Did you never see a *mahu* before?"

"Excuse me. A part of my education seems to be lacking."

"Men who dress as women, live as women. Here it's traditional, goes back centuries. Harmless enough, I'm sure. They are different, yes, but generally accepted. Usually artists, healers, people of that sort. Valuable to the neighbors, you see – and they rarely disturb or upset anyone. Quite the contrary. Certainly, not Mailelani. She's a treasure. But Shadbolt couldn't abide the very thought, had fits about it. Told people she was an abomination – *kapu*, forbidden. Preached about hellfire, damnation, all that. One time in a fury actually declared that Maile ought to be stoned to death! The people rose up, wouldn't stand for it. After that, you see, Shadbolt fell into a fever. Stricken, waked up paralyzed. A brave man, but his nerves finally gave way. The wife and chilldren were gone already. I saw him carried on a litter to the ship."

Wilkinson was trying to digest all this. Cornwall looked at him anxiously. "But tell me now, sir, you won't… condemn Maile? At least, not pass judgment until you know her more? It's hard for me to explain, but there's no harm in it, do you think? I mean to say, I hope you don't <u>strongly</u> disapprove?"

"I have no opinion on the subject," said Wilkinson. "I

haven't earned one. I've simply been a fool, as usual."

"Not so bad as all that," said Cornwall. Then, while the two men stood together, the sun slipped behind a cloud and the landscape around them glowed more vividly than ever, as if lit from within. At the same time, with most of the sky quite clear, a soft, misting rain came out of nowhere and gently touched their faces.

"Here's a touch of the Islands," said Cornwall. "This is a message, I always think, from the spirit of the place. Of course, I've missed dear old England all these years, and this land is not, strictly speaking, nearly so civilized. However, I would have to say there is something powerfully sacred about it."

"Sacred?"

"Well, it's different of course, but what's happening now , for instance.– we call it a Hawaiian blessing when it comes like this -- water from heaven, just as a drift in the air. Happens all the time here in Kona."

"Evidently a good place to plant a garden," said Wilkinson.

"Yes indeed. Most of us have some fruits, some vegetables in our yards. And the people – well, I suppose people are the same everywhere. But in these Islands, I'm sure you will find an extra touch of kindness."

After mounting his horse, he added, "Look for a rainbow soon! You'll likely see one. I hope you sleep well, Mr. Wilkinson. Not easy for you, all this, just at the start."

*

David Wilkinson did see a rainbow later, one that arched through heaven in hues of such splendor that it seemed very nearly substantial. Then the light shifted, the wind freshened, clouds gathered, and the glorious vision was gone. And indeed, he did sleep well that night. So soundly, in fact, that he did not notice the hot red light that was flickering below, or the smoke that filtered and billowed up the *pali* toward his dwelling. He had not managed, after all, to put out the fire in the native hut. Its embers had been concealed by the mossy pillow that cradled the criminal's head. He learned later that the people of the village stood in silence, watching the building while it burned to the ground. No one raised a hand to save it, for they felt that the place had been desecrated by the evil it had sheltered. Therefore, they concluded, it was of no further use to them.

4

David Wilkinson had been born on May 16, 1846. He arrived laughing – or so it was said – early one morning in his parents' vast four-poster bed. The event took place at *Green Gardens*, a modest estate among apple orchards in the village of Bromley Crossing, Yorkshire. His infant memories were all of a softness and a sweetness, with kisses and custards, bathings and powderings, milky puddings with sugar in them, and all such manner of agreeable things. An only child with a ferocious appetite, he clung first to his mother and then to a doting nurse who rocked him to sleep every night on her vast bosom while singing gentle songs about Jesus. One day in the kitchen, when he was ten months old, he suddenly stood upright., and the jolly Irish cook cheered him on while he launched himself across the floor to her waiting arms.

When little David learned to walk, and to speak a few words, he became infatuated with an old rag doll that someone had left at the house, and carried it around, chattering to it incessantly in a private language. This habit, alas, did not meet with adult approval; the doll was taken away from him, and he wept bitterly. A year later he howled louder when his baby smocks were removed and he was put into trousers. At the age of four he taught himself to read, and soon after that developed a passionate interest in climbing trees, kicking stones, and concealing himself in secret places – under his mother's dressing table, behind the harmonium in the parlor, or high on a shelf at the back of the potting shed. He particularly liked being alone in his private fort, among the branches of an old oak tree beside the kitchen garden. There he ate wind-fallen apples, or bread saved secretly from the dining table, or fresh-picked berries pilfered from the cook.

There in the tree he heard the voice of an angel one day when he was seven, and it was an experience that stayed with him far into the future, causing him to listen intently to sounds of the natural world when he was alone. The angel had spoken to him in an ancient language that he could not understand, and yet he felt certain that there was an important message in it. A loathsome tutor was hired when he was ten years old to teach him Latin and Greek, and he was bitterly disappointed when neither of those languages turned out to be the one he longed to hear again. Unlike most boys in prosperous families at the time, David was not sent away to a boarding school, for his parents believed that boys were badly treated in such places, and learned nasty habits there.

When he was eight, David discovered a thrilling volume called *The Adventures of Captain Cook* in his father's library, and devoured it in a fever of excitement. Danger! Storms and shipwrecks! Cannibals! Barbarians! Beautiful brown maidens wearing nothing but leaves and flowers! Here he learned for the first time that England's venerated hero, Captain James Cook, had grown up not far from Bromley Crossing. In fact, Cook had set sail for his adventures in the Pacific from the seaside town of Whitby, where David had once gone on holiday with his mother.

It had been a joyous time for both of them – a whole week all to themselves while a seamstress who lived there stitched up new gowns for his mother and shirts for him. Whitby on the map was a neat little spot with a harbor, a river and an ancient church, but when one was actually there, it became a huge, vertical place with steep stone steps, fierce winds, and a looming sky that was now dark, now blazing bright. When they walked there together in the ruins of Saint Hilda's Abbey, his mother's parasol suddenly flew over the cliff and vanished, but she only smiled, and then laughed aloud as her long black hair escaped from its chignon and flew about her shoulders. Then, at a nearby teashop, they bought scones that were still warm from the oven and ate them together, sitting on a bench.

How wonderfully, magically strange it was that the immortal Captain Cook had sailed from that very place to the Sandwich Islands, half a world away! The thrilling book had told David what no one had mentioned to him before: that Cook had met a terrible end. At Kealakekua Bay, on the wild volcanic island of Hawaii, he was slaughtered by savages, and then his body was dismembered and roasted – though not, apparently, eaten. After learning that, David put the book carefully away where he had found it, and went back to his fort by the kitchen-garden. There he began making a large collection of dead beetles, while drawing complicated maps of imaginary islands.

During the following year he suddenly grew nearly five inches taller, fell asleep at the dinner table, and developed pale blue circles under his eyes. Katherine Wilkinson dosed him with rhubarb and garden herbs, but finding no improvement, consulted his father. At this, the Hon. Charles Wilkinson announced that he would soon be going on a journey to London and desired little Davey's company. They would have a fine holiday together! They would see where the Queen lived, and watch the soldiers marching outside her house; they would visit the Tower, and feed the ducks in St. James Park. Before coming home they would pay a visit to Canterbury Cathedral, which he assured his son was the grandest, most beautiful building in England, and in some mysterious way, the most important place on earth.

David later remembered almost nothing of this excursion, except for an incident that took place in the cathedral. During an interminable service with echoing music, strange silences and faraway voices, he noticed that the steps inside the building appeared to be dangerously soft. They were made of stone, but all curved down and sunken in their middles. Perhaps the whole vast structure was in danger of collapse, and if so, when would it begin? When he complained to his parent, "Hush my dear!" was the response, "We must take this matter under advisement."

After the final hymn, while a great procession was still making its way out of the cathedral, Charles Wilkinson knelt down beside the inner steps in his best frock coat. Ignoring the stares of people around him, he took out a small folding ruler of silver that he always carried, and began measuring the height of the stone steps, first at their sides, and then in their centers. He showed his son that there was a three-inch difference, and then said, "See here, lad, put your hand to it. The stone is not soft, it only appears so. The middle part has been worn down this way over centuries by the feet of pilgrims. Thousands of people come from all over the world to this holy place for comfort and healing. It's the pain of history, it's the sorrow of humanity that you see here."

As David considered this, a grand old man stopped beside them, carrying a shepherd's crook. His robes were so fine that David wondered at first if he might be Jesus. But his father quickly rose and said, "Your Grace!" The tall man greeted him courteously, then smiled at David and said, "Having a history lesson, are we?" Awestruck, the boy nodded.

"Very good, son, and I hope that in a few more years you may study theology," said the Archbishop.

"Yes sir," said David, in some doubt.

"Indeed, Your Grace, he'll be going up to Oxford!" said his father, beaming with pride. The two men spoke quietly together while the boy gazed up at the colored light streaming from stained glass windows. A moment later, he felt a large, warm hand resting on his head, and heard angelic powers and heavenly hosts called upon to aid, succor and protect David Charles Pierpont Wilkinson, both in body and in soul, throughout all the days of his life, in the name of the Father and of the Son, and of the Holy Ghost, Amen.

With that, David's childhood came to a sudden end. Thus far he had dutifully said his prayers each night, and had rather enjoyed going to the village church on Sundays, but this was an experience of a different sort. In an instant he had sensed the power, the majesty and the magnanimity of the Church of England, and from that day forward, he considered himself a man and a churchman.

*

By the late 1850s, all England was in a missionary fever. Earnest young Christians across the country dreamed of going abroad, carrying the Gospel to the world's uncivilized pagan masses. David lay awake at night imagining that he was a missionary priest in faraway places. He saw himself saying a brave farewell to his parents, then standing at the prow of a great clipper ship with all sails set, silently speeding over the wild Pacific. Once on the Isle of Hawaii, he would plant a flag for England at Kealakekua Bay, and there with his own hands he would raise a church consecrated to the glorious memory of Captain Cook.

As time went by, he began to fancy that he might be a very successful priest – one who would win over the minds and hearts of all the natives. Perhaps they were not really wicked, he thought, only ignorant. He imagined teaching them to read, and telling them his favorite Bible stories. He would befriend them, heal their illnesses, bind up their wounds. He would show them by his own example what it was to be decent and honorable, chaste and devout. Yet God help me, he thought. If this is my destiny, then I will surely live and die in great danger, alone and far from home.

*

At last he was fourteen, and almost ready for Oxford. Spring came early that year, bringing blossoms to the hawthorn and honeysuckle in the hedgerows, and larks caroling over the meadows, and nights that were finished before they had fairly begun. It was in the month of May when a winsome little Scottish housemaid called Jenny Miller came to work at Green Gardens, and quickly won every heart there. Not only that, but found her way quite soon into the young master's bed. Jenny had been folding clean sheets from the clothesline in the kitchen-garden one day when, with a mischievous glance and a curious little smile, she asked David to help her. The two were nearly the same height, and their eyes met easily. After that, their fingers touched once, twice, three times - and next, their lips. His did not know quite what to do at first, but he managed to take delight in the taste of her, and his hand soon strayed of its own accord to her soft young breast. Soon after that, she took his hand in hers, led him upstairs, and introduced him (most sweetly, most tenderly) to certain astonishing mysteries.

During the weeks that followed, young David Wilkinson lived in glory. Past and future vanished entirely; the incandescent joy of the moment was all. The entire month of May went by unnoticed; June followed; but in July, sweet Jenny Miller was suddenly dismissed. No word of explanation would be given to him, but David knew then for the first time the foul taste of guilt. What would become of her? And what of himself? He was no criminal – no liar, no thief or murderer. Yet he had sinned, and he wanted desperately to sin a great deal more. To be fifteen and celibate again was agony.

*

"Children of light, children of air, children of nature's bounty!" cried Samuel Wilberforce, Bishop of Oxford, addressing a large audience in the Yorkshire town of Leeds. A grim, penitential David Wilkinson was in the audience that day. Famed far and wide as England's great "missionary bishop," Wilberforce did not go abroad himself, but traveled the home country delivering silver-tongued oratory on behalf of the

Anglican Church and Queen Victoria's foreign interests. The Bishop's face was kindly, but his message about the Hawaiian people was stern: "They are children," he said, "with every imaginable solace and comfort – yet, how pitiable are these natives of the Hawaiian archipelago, since all that they need comes to them freely, without effort! They are like unruly infants, spoiled by overindulgence and excess. Nature has given them perfect ease, and the fatal gift of beauty. Exotic fruits fall from the trees into their hands; plentiful, sweet-fleshed fish are easily caught in the warm, clear waters that surround them. Idling their lives away in the soft, delicious meadows of Eden, they are morally weak, prey to every vile desire and animal impulse. Singing and dancing all the day, forever indulging in low, sensual pleasures, they lack the discipline of labor and deprivation that alone builds character. Think of it, my friends: England would have no empire today if we did not have the strength that comes only from work and hardship, struggle and self-denial."

And by the way, he added, these islands were critically important to England's future. In Honolulu, at the crossroads of the vast Pacific Ocean, lay one of the world's finest harbors. America wanted that harbor, and so did France. Both countries had missionaries in place, spreading their evil influence while promoting heretical versions of Christianity. The innocent Hawaiians, he said, were in desperate need of conversion to England's finer, purer version of the faith. Only a determined effort on our part would save them from the American Protestants – those greedy, cold-hearted people – on the one hand, and the evil, idolatrous Roman Catholics of France on the other. It was our clear duty to send Her Majesty's own missionaries as soon as possible out to the rescue of those endangered Hawaiian Islanders!

His presence here today, the Bishop concluded, was in part a plea for funds, but it was also a call and a challenge to the fine young men of England who might choose to leave their homes and live a life of service and sacrifice abroad. In such primitive lands. The dangers to foreign missionaries were many, and the rewards but few. Great indeed were the perils of travel abroad, of disease, injury, and of violence done to them by angry natives in distant places. He would freely admit that British casualties in this field had been shockingly high. However, we Christians know that God has a special love for those who serve Him at great personal cost. This is a cause in which devotion to God and England can win for its brave supporters an immortal crown; and the plate would now be passed for donations to the cause, that the natives of Hawaii might be blessed with the knowledge of our true religion, the patronage of our gracious Queen, and the saving power and might of the Anglican Church.

David's decision was made before Wilberforce finished speaking. He had come to Leeds that day in the back of a farmer's cart, by way of a jolting three-hour journey amidst leeks and cabbages. However, Bishop Wilberforce was an old friend of his mother's, and so David rode swiftly home under a fur-lined lap-robe, in a carriage emblazoned with a coat of arms and drawn by a handsome pair of chestnut bays.

5

The house had been swept and dusted; the silver and brass had been polished, the finest of the linens were freshly laundered, and Katherine Wilkinson had sent David to fetch the ancestral rubies from the buttery. There on a high shelf, hidden behind a loose brick, lay the family's finest heirloom: three rubies the size and shape of plover's eggs, hung on a golden chain. The jewels had been awarded to a valiant forbear five generations earlier for loyal service to the Crown. The Wilkinsons had always been Royalists, and under Cromwell's bitter reign, they had been made to suffer for it.

The Bishop was graciously welcomed by his hostess, who was a distant cousin as well as a treasured friend. Seated at once in the most comfortable chair in the parlor, he was served various delicacies of a medicinal sort: hot tea with sherry in it for nervous fatigue, dainty sandwiches of fresh garden watercress against chills and catarrh, sweet biscuits sprinkled with nutmeg for the digestion. Katherine Wilkinson generally assumed that her guests were fragile and unwell, since it was her pleasure to indulge them. Wilberforce sighed with delight, devoured her offerings, and told her at length about his sciatica, after remarking fondly that she was looking more beautiful than ever. Charles Wilkinson arrived soon after in stocking feet, having left muddy boots at the scullery door. A youthful mare had foaled successfully during the night, and he himself had supervised the delivery. He raised a fist in triumph, then tossed off a large tumbler of ale. "A fine little filly!" he cried. "A perfect beauty! Great long legs, and she's standing on them already. With any luck at all, she'll burn up the track one day! What shall we name her, Davey? Something about her tells me her name ought to be *Twilight*. What do you think of that?" But his son could not think of a sensible reply; he was suddenly struck by the full weight of his dilemma. How could he explain his decision to his parents? His father would be bitterly disappointed; his mother would be horrified. Their only son, their only child, to be a ragged, exhausted and endangered foreign missionary? Should he, perhaps, have spoken first to the Bishop, and asked for his support? Listening to Wilberforce, he had known that he could not fulfill his parents' expectations. He could not go up to Oxford after all; he would refuse to take on the role of a traditional country gentleman with an elegant house, plenty of servants and a stable of fast horses. He had a higher calling - he was sure of it – to a far lower station in life: one of poverty, service, and hardship. Not only that, but he must prepare himself, and soon, by going to a missionary school.

*

The rubies had been brought to Katherine Wilkinson's dressing table, so as to be worn at a dinner party in honor of Samuel Wilberforce. In later years David returned many times to the memory of that gathering, coming as it did at a time when he had made his fateful decision and was nearly bursting with the urge to confess it. During his years in the Islands, he would often go to bed in his tiny parsonage still hungry after a cold supper, with none but the wind and the stars for company; and then he would reach for comfort to the memory of this evening. At other times he had no supper at all, but lay shivering on the ground in some high mountain bivouac, with the earth shaking beneath him and the scent of burning forests in the air. Then he would hold fast to thoughts of that clear summer eve that was warm, windless and fragrant with scents of his mother's flower garden.

At the center of the oval dining table, Katherine had placed a silver bowl filled with large, peach-colored roses, to which she had whimsically added stalks of mint. As the guests took their places, a dozen beeswax candles surrounded the party with a sheltering glow.

Charles Wilkinson was stationed at the head of the table as usual, and the rubies glowed royally on Katherine's breast as she smiled at her husband across the way. Baynes the loathsome tutor sat opposite David looking far more agreeable than usual, with a handsome monocle in his eye and a bright pink spot on each cheek from his recent trek across the moors. Their near neighbor Mrs. Violet Potts, ordinarily the primmest, shyest of widows, had arrived this time in apricot velvet, with a look of toothsome, creamy satisfaction that aroused David's keen curiosity. The timid, stammering young vicar from the village church sat halfway down the table in his best suit, with his pretty wife smiling beside him. Aunt Elizabeth and Uncle George Merryman were there, both large and rosy, laughing a great deal and making their usual outrageous remarks. Across from Uncle George, in the place of honor beside his hostess, sat Bishop Wilberforce in formal regalia, gazing about him with the look of a hungry man who knows that he will soon get a splendid dinner.

The Bishop said a speedy grace, and then, amid great conversational gaiety, several dozen oysters were consumed. While the shells were carried away, David was recruited to pour the best of their wine into the family's finest crystal, while his father performed a ritual sharpening of the bone-handled carving knife. A splendid joint of mutton lay on the trencher before him. When his knife was ready, Charles Wilkinson raised it alongside its matching fork, then paused and sat still for a long moment, gazing at his son. A lifetime of fierce devotion went into the look; their eyes met, and David clenched his jaw to hold back sudden tears. Studying the familiar, smiling faces around the table, he told himself: *Remember this moment always!*

Wide slices of lamb fell one by one, steaming under the knife. A bird cried out in the garden. Glass window-panes rattled suddenly in a wayward gust of wind, and the fireplace quietly began to smoke. Aunt Elizabeth tried to speak, but sneezed into her napkin instead, and said "Damn!" quite loudly, at which the vicar, in a startled gesture, spilled red wine over the white linen tablecloth. David came to the rescue with salt and kitchen cloths, but the timid clergyman would not be consoled, and spoke scarcely at all for the rest of the evening.

Bishop Wilberforce began now to expound at some length upon the Hawaiian royal family and their interest in forming a political and military alliance with Britain. The two countries, he said, should get on well together, since they were both monarchies. After a pair of revolutions, neither France nor America would be so compatible.

"But are these people educated, Your Lordship?" the tutor asked. "Oh my yes," Wilberforce replied, "That is, if you're speaking of the royals and their set. Queen Emma has even been to this country, and I myself had the pleasant duty of looking after her while she was here. A new widow then, sister-in-law to the present king. Handsome young woman, elegant in her way. Splendid eyes. Somewhat dark of skin, but not objectionably so. She is part   English, you see, actually granddaughter of an Englishman. Her Majesty had her out for tea at Windsor, says she behaved beautifully. Perfect manners, knows how to dress, what to say, which fork to use, and so forth. Knows more Shakespeare than most of our own people. Agreeable soul, too – brought us a priceless gift, a cloak of her late husband's, all made of feathers. Can you believe it? Hundreds of tiny red and yellow feathers from Hawaiian birds – rare ones they find only far up in the mountains. Extraordinary thing." Having conveyed all of this to his satisfaction, he retired to his plate and began to chew vigorously. A total silence suddenly descended upon the table.

Katherine finally spoke up brightly, "All made of feathers, did you say? Goodness gracious, how remarkable." Half a minute or more went by in silence. Then Violet Potts drew her shawl over her shapely white bosom and remarked that an angel must be passing by. "A devil more likely," said George Merryman, "given the state of the world these days. You won't believe it, of course, but a man I know was actually robbed on the high road only last week of his trousers."

"No!" said his wife Elizabeth. "George, you are not serious!"

"On the high road," he insisted, "Just beyond the village, in broad daylight."

"I don't believe a word of it," said Elizabeth.

"Suit yourself my dear, but it's true."

"What exactly was he doing at the time, I wonder?" asked Violet Potts, with a glint in her eye that David found interesting.

Silence again, and the sound of chewing reigned until Baynes said hastily, "I believe that such an extended silence in company is often taken as a sign that someone has died nearby."

The Bishop frowned and wagged a fork at him. "Superstition!"

"Well, Your Lordship, it's only what I've heard."

Katherine quickly added, "I'm sure I have heard something of the sort myself, but after all, we aren't obliged to believe it. People like to believe the most extraordinary things these days, don't they? David dear, open another bottle of wine for us, if you please. And when that's done" – in a low voice, to him alone – "please go and tell Cook the scullery door is banging in the wind again, and she must close it."

"Rather like, step on a crack, break your grandmother's back," said Elizabeth suddenly, and sneezed again. Her husband handed her a clean handkerchief from his vest pocket, saying, "Someone else's back please – not dear old Granny's."

After yet more silence, punctuated only by the pop of a cork, Wilberforce remarked, "If you want to see the feathered cloak, you must visit the missionary college at Canterbury. She left it there. They have a little museum for such oddities."

"Missionary college? At Canterbury, did you say?" David inquired, pouring red wine very carefully.

"Saint Columba's, yes. They've sent some of their lads out to serve in Hawaii, so Emma favors them. The cloak unfortunately was attacked by moth and had to be treated with poison."

"Poison? Oh dear," said the Vicar's wife, troubled. "Oh my, so dangerous. And who was it who died? Who was that?"

"No one," said her silent husband rather sharply.

"No one, darling," said Katherine Wilkinson. "Don't worry. No one at all has died. It was only an old saying, a myth, a legend. No one can possibly die while I am having such a lovely dinner party. I absolutely won't allow it."

6

David Wilkinson drew a breath that caught in his throat when he saw Canterbury Cathedral for the first time several years later. Now it was glittering in the distance, on a wintry day of the year 1864. Snow lay on the fields that afternoon, blinding white with a wind-scrubbed icy crust under the sun, while in shadow, softer coverlets were tinted with mauve and palest blue. Several miles away, like an imaginary citadel or the palace of a great magician, the Cathedral rose against the sky, garnished with the storm's icy fretwork of silver and gold.

After stepping from the train he walked slowly toward the old city walls, then entered the narrow, cobbled streets of the medieval village. The vast power and weight of the Cathedral seemed to speak directly to him even when he could not see it. If he forgot it or lost it for a few moments, then as soon as he turned a new corner it would be there again, towering and brooding above him – a tremendous, man-made forest of stone and glass – a place of refuge, a fortress and a stronghold.

His interview with the Warden of St. Columba's Missionary College went well, and thus, at the age of eighteen, he qualified for admission as a student there. He was assigned to a room of his own, and that pleased him, especially since he did not know anyone at all, either in the school or in the town. Then, somewhat to his surprise, he found that before attending classes, he must sign a paper stating his submission to the following:

RULES AND REGULATIONS
St. Columba's Missionary College

1. No student is at liberty to contract any matrimonial engagement, or to conduct himself in a way likely to result in such an engagement, during his three years of study here.

2. No matrimonial engagement or undertaking leading thereto is, *under any circumstances*, to be formed by any student with anyone belonging to the town or neighborhood of Canterbury.

3. The College does not send out married men to the Colonies or the Mission Field. Men going out to the Field must be free from all ties, and may not marry until they have worked for at least three years in the Mission where they have been sent.

Signature _____ Date_____

---

*

"Did you know about this? It's uncivilized, positively obscene!" said a cheerful voice beside him as David emerged from the Warden's office. He turned to see an elegantly dressed young man near his own age, with a head full of untidy blond hair and a merry smile. The two shook hands, compared notes, laughed together, and were friends for years to come from that moment on. Through their college days they were looked upon as an odd combination: Scott Partridge was city-bred, gregarious, short, fair and tending toward the stout, while David the silent North-countryman was taller, leaner and so much darker that Scotty sometimes accused him of being Italian – a wicked, spying Papist in disguise.

Scott was bright and witty, though a somewhat careless student who often left things until the last minute, and never earned the academic awards that he should have done. David worked seriously, steadily, systematically, and came away in three years with a double first in Mathematics and Old Testament, as well as a pair of notable prizes: one in Church History, and the other for the best theological essay of his final year.

Theology, dogma and religious practice were pressing matters in that time and place, for Evangelical Christians were locked into battle with the old guard, the Anglo-Catholics of nineteenth century England. David Wilkinson admired the beauty of the "High Church," Anglo-Catholic services at Saint Columba's, and had no objection to the vestments, the candles, the incense and the music involved. Still, he managed to avoid Confession, which had not been a part of his experience in the far more Protestant parish of Bromley Crossing. Sinner that he was, he still did not believe that only a priest had power to grant him God's forgiveness. Scotty as usual had a different point of view, but refused to discuss the question at all.

The maidens of Canterbury town were not as a rule great beauties, but some were pleasant to look at, and nearly every one that David saw had some charm or grace that made him want to linger and learn more. From time to time his dreams were riotous, and the physical pain of frustration often made him irritable. He and Scotty made bitter jokes about it, but David had not realized how deeply troubled his new friend was on the question of sexuality until one day during their final year of study. Scotty came to him, flushed and stammering, and said, "I have found something – someone, that is, who – I think - can help, truly help with – you know, *the worst of it all.* Will you come and meet him?"

Together they walked through the village until they came to a small, shabby house tucked away on an outlying street. "He lives here," said Scott. "He is a Dominican friar. His name is Father Jeremiah."

"Roman Catholic?"

"Yes. Do you mind terribly?"

"No, but the authorities will."

"Please," said Scotty. "This is important."

They stayed for the rest of the afternoon in the parlor of a house where Father Jeremiah lived with several other friars, near to a tiny Catholic Chapel. The topic of their conversation was carnal woe, and the maddening allure of the female sex. While neither of the young men made a formal confession, it was plain that they needed help. The holy man listened warmly, sympathized tenderly, and spoke to them passionately of the evil charms indwelling in the female body, mind and soul. The fallen state of man, he said, was caused by Eve, and although the fruit of Eden was not named in Scripture, the sin it caused was definitely *copulation.* He would pray for them to the Blessed Virgin and Saint Joseph, and he would give them each a small token that would help. The Virgin herself, he told them, had given this same gift in a vision to the great medieval Catholic theologian, Thomas Aquinas, with the promise that he would no longer be tormented by sensual desires.

They prayed together, and after another hour, the two younger men came away grim and resolved, each carrying a cord with small knots in it. These instruments were to be worn about the waist, drawn tightly enough so as to be consistently painful, although without breaking skin. Each knot honored one of the fifteen mysteries of the life of Jesus, as recalled in the Roman Catholic rosary devotion. The constant discomfort, said the friar, would remind them of their near and present danger, and the symbolism involved would give them power to resist. If this should fail, he promised to provide them with a special whip for self-flagellation.

David found the belt somewhat helpful at first, but Scotty gave it up in a fit of fury after less than a week, saying that it made him think of nothing day and night but the act it was supposed to prevent.

Soon after this, the Reverend Theobald Eggelstone, Headmaster, (privately known, of course, as "Eggy"), called a special assembly of the school. Standing up before them pale and trembling, he announced that a most shocking event had taken place. Several students of the Missionary College had been seen going into the local Catholic Friary. What were they doing there? The answer to this question was at first unclear On the following day – yesterday! – two of those young men had told college authorities that they could not remain in good conscience in the Church of England. Both of them were going over to Rome! They had left brief letters of resignation and departed without another word. "We are wholly in the dark," said Eggy, "as to what treachery has thus beguiled them. In our ignorance and great distress," he said, "we refrain from further comment at present, except to say that a crime has been committed. A ravening wolf has found its way into our fold!" David and Scotty did not look at one another as they left the hall, and a few days later, David sent his knotted cord, hidden and well wrapped, out with the rubbish.

*

At last it was time: the two young friends were ordained as deacons, and by apparent coincidence, both were assigned to the Honolulu Mission. First Scotty, then David performed the wrenching duty of bidding farewell to their families, perhaps never to see them again. Together they embarked on a storm-swept Atlantic, and the ensuing voyage was miserable. New York seemed to them a raw and bleak, unlovely place, filled with a bewildering lot of noisy foreigners who did not even try to speak English. Continuing south along the American sea-coast, they found many views to admire; their spirits rose and their excitement and impatience grew. The two spoke of little else now but their curiosity about the people of the Islands and their high hopes for the work they wished to do. First of all, they knew, they must learn to speak and understand the Hawaiian language – and how best to manage that? They knew that American missionaries had created a written language for Hawaii, yet they had never heard it spoken or seen it in print.

"How lucky it is that we are able to go out there together!" David remarked one morning.

"Luck had nothing to do with it," Scotty replied, with a grin.

"Well, then, what?

"Arrangements were made, with some help from Slippery Sam."

"What do you mean?"

"Simple. Samuel Wilberforce, after all, is head of the Missionary Committee. That's where the money is. So, naturally, he can tell Honolulu what to do."

"But surely he wouldn't…"

"Of course he would. Why not? Obviously, it was a help in that he knows your family, but the deciding factor – forgive me – was that my Aunt Lavinia is married to a Duke."

"What has that to do with anything?"

"Come now! Wilberforce likes money, Wilberforce likes power, and he also likes Duchesses. That's why they call him Slippery Sam."

"Do you mean that your relative spoke to Bishop Wilberforce… and that you…?

"Why, of course. That's how things are done."

"Even in the Church?"

"My dear chum, especially in the Church. You're the one who made such a brilliant splash in that course on Church History. Didn't you notice?"

"No," said David slowly. "I didn't. Perhaps that's the sort of thing the history books tend to leave out."

*

At last they were on land again, dizzied by the heat of Central America and reeling on their sea-legs. It was time now to board a miniature train belonging to the Panamanian Trans-Isthmus Railway. A narrow track had been wrested recently from the jungle between Colon and Portobello, so that travelers might be spared the dangers and miseries of a voyage around Cape Horn. The car Scott and David entered, furnished with chairs done up in soiled red plush, was crammed with sweltering people of all descriptions, together with various animals, birds, baskets and toppling mountains of luggage. One passenger carried a cage with a rooster in it, and another was accompanied by a large and stinking goat. Insects of every description, including some very large cockroaches, apparently lived in the train and would be traveling with them. The heat and the dampness were appalling.

At the genteel speed of eleven miles per hour, the trip from Atlantic to Pacific took a little more than four hours. As the train began to move, Scott Partridge promptly dozed off; he could sleep anywhere. David, gazing out at steaming, shimmering miles of green, was far too excited even to sit still. All that is soft and tranquil in an English countryside was writhing and roiling here, blazing with emerald fire. On either side of the track were strange growths, tremendous ferns and bulging tree forms that he did not recognize, some twined about one another with aerial roots flung out; and all of this alien vegetation was overgrown, bearing vines, pods, leaves, fruits and blossoms that he had never seen or dreamed of before. Monster butterflies, some larger than birds, floated through the forests on brilliant wings that might have been made of silk or stained glass. A red and yellow parrot flew by the open window beside him, shrieking, just as he discovered a spider under his shirt.

At one turning of the track, David saw an alligator haul himself out of the swamp just as the train approached, and then the creature opened his hideous jaws, as if to greet the travelers. At another turn, a row of entirely naked, very black children stood and waved, one of them eating a huge banana with the skin peeled back. Banana trees held up their leaves like swords while their great pendant blossoms dangled below in crude, sensual display. The air was fever-hot, and the odor of the jungle was both rank and voluptuous. David wondered, with pounding heart, whether Hawaii would be anything like this.

"Wake up, Scotty!" he said. "You don't know what you are missing!" But his companion, swaying with the motion of the train, continued to doze.

*

Three weeks later, under a pale half-moon, their ship swayed at its mooring amid the cool gray mists of San Francisco. Alas, it was not the grand old clipper ship of David's childhood dreams, but a relatively charmless conveyance of the latest design: a 2,000 ton screw-propeller steamer named the *Hermes*. The two young men had come aboard that evening for the final segment of their journey to Hawaii. Fascinated by the gaudy, teeming little town where they had stopped for a week, they had risen early each morning to stretch their sea-weary legs in climbing its nearly perpendicular hills. They had strolled the waterfronts, dodging pickpockets, confidence men and painted ladies; and they had talked in taverns late at night with sailors and poets, drifters and adventurers, carpenters and tycoons: a jumble of humanity they had never expected to see under one roof. On Sunday they attended an Episcopal service at Grace Church on Stockton Street, surprised to find that it was dignified and devout, with apparently respectable people in attendance, and a liturgy nearly identical to their own. Scott had firmly believed that all Americans were uncouth ignoramuses, and Baynes the loathsome tutor had taught David that he should regard them as distant relations of a particularly unattractive sort.

In the cabin now, as they awaited the turning of the tide, a glint of moonlight slanted across their porthole, while small waves lapped gently against the sides of the ship. Scott lay in the lower berth and David in the upper, in a space that was large enough for two only if they had brought almost no luggage and did not try to unpack.

"Wilks, are you awake?"

"More or less."

"Did you know that the hull of this ship is made of iron? I can't think of a single reason why it won't sink to the bottom of the sea."

"Yes," said David. "That thought has occurred to me."

"On the other hand, we can't have come this far only to be drowned!"

"There I fear I must disagree."

"You are no help. Another thing, this outlandish contraption we are in is called the *Hermes*. I find that troubling.

"A Greek god. Why troubling?"

"He was a tricky creature, an agent of surprise . And he was a god, after all, not a goddess. Is it not true that ships have always been considered female, and are spoken of as "she"?

"I suppose," said David vaguely, and after that, there was no more conversation. Soon they were both fast asleep, and David was dreaming of a meadow in May with someone close beside him – a female someone, soft in the hollow of his arm. Then, in the depths of the night he stirred, imagining that he had heard a voice in the meadow, so close by that it was clearly speaking to him. "There's a good lad!" it said. But what had he done? Nothing forbidden, he hoped. The lilting tone and the Scottish accent were disturbing. What was this? Was he awake or asleep? A girl had spoken to him, sounding like Jenny Miller. But no, that could not be! Then he was suddenly wide awake, and heard the same voice speak again: "Aye, just there – yes, yes! Thank you so very much! Here's something for your trouble. Goodnight and good luck to you." A door closed softly across the way and a lock was vigorously turned. Then, silence.

Impossible! He sat up suddenly, giving his head a vicious blow on the berth above him. Tears rushed to his eyes – tears of pain, tears of remorse for all that had happened between sweet Jenny Miller and the eager boy he had been so long ago. The entire history, geography and anatomy of their love were laid out before him again in an instant. It was unbearable, insufferable. He called upon God, who surely knew that he had done penance for those sins of his time and time again, as the long years passed. He had tried, failed and tried again to be entirely pure, and yet, here the old memory was again, rising up to torment him! David was angry, aghast, mortified and deeply ashamed. At the same time he craved another touch and taste of her so fiercely that he groaned aloud.

Near dawn he finally slept again and dreamed of a silken nightdress with rows of tiny buttons that were all but impossible to undo. She was young and beautiful as ever, with the same fragrance that he remembered, and her dark hair fell in a shining cloud around her shoulders. Her small, soft breasts were still a perfect fit for his hands. She was trying to undo the buttons of her nightgown, and she could not. After a time she sighed, and sighed again, and then gazed at him in such a way that he knew he must help.

*

The following morning, as the sun plunged into clouds above a bruise-colored sea, they made their way through the tumultuous passage known as the Golden Gate. As they entered the open ocean, the weather turned wholly foul. The ship pitched and tossed so mercilessly that, for the first few days of the voyage, almost none of the passengers appeared in public. A silent, red-turbaned Indian busied himself bringing tea and toast to the passengers' quarters. Albert Coldwell, Anglican Bishop of Hawaii, had come aboard at the last moment with a large entourage, including a personal secretary, a private chaplain and a new governess for his children in Honolulu; but after greeting his two new missionaries on the dock, he was not seen again for several days.

Scott Partridge was being violently seasick in the cabin, and wanted only to be left alone. David's stomach was steady enough, but his spirits were low, and he paced about the ship for hours at a time, contemplating his many follies and failures. The mechanics in the engine room were a friendly lot who explained to him at great length how burning coal is used to propel a ship, and how a compound engine works, using its steam not once but twice, in order to save fuel. All that, however, failed to improve his mood very much. Back and forth he paced on deck, trying to see how far he could go without being thrown down. Then one day, unexpectedly, he found himself standing before the owner of a painfully familiar voice.

It was early in the morning just before the breakfast bell sounded, and David was shocked to see how inaccurate his imagination had been. This was not a playful young housemaid; this was a personage: a lady of uncertain age, tall, pale and strangely elegant. She wore a grand sort of garment, something between a cape and a coat, that extended from her ugly woolen bonnet to her well-worn dark leather boots. Her face was refined, but so weary and pale as to suggest the presence of serious illness. The ship was still floundering when they met, and she was moving with great care upon the arm of a man David had not seen before. "Good morning!" she said quietly in her clear Scottish lilt, adding that her name was Julia Stuart. "And this is Mr. Clemens," she said of her companion, an American with large, drooping moustaches and a melancholy air. David bowed to her, offered his hand to Clemens, and managed to tell them his own name.

"We have been improving our health," the lady continued, "with a bit of exercise. It seems somewhat brighter today, though I must say that the weather is far from tropical. Have you been quite well thus far, Mr. Wilkinson?"

"Quite," he replied, and for the moment, could say no more.

"Then shall we look for breakfast?" she asked.

"Quite," said Clemens, gazing disagreeably at David. After this, although the two men came to like one another quite well, he never used David's proper name, but always referred to him either as "Mr. Quite" or else as "The Deacon."

7

"What a pretty ring you are wearing!" said Bishop Coldwell as soon as he had exchanged greetings with Miss Julia Stuart. He was stationed at the head of a table where she and Clemens had settled, along with David Wilkinson. They were in the ship's well-appointed little dining salon, with hanging lanterns of polished brass and gimbaled tables with rims to save sliding crockery. More passengers were becoming visible now, although Scott Partridge was still among the missing.

The Bishop, smiling benignly, pronounced a rapid blessing on the meal and turned again to Miss Stuart. "Is it an emerald? Of course it is. Oh, what a large one. An heirloom, no doubt. So beautifully cut! Such splendid depth, such color! You'll pardon me, I'm sure. I adore jewels. Gracious, I'd be surprised if the Queen herself had anything finer. Or the Archbishop, for that matter."

Julia Stuart drew her hand away and put it beneath the table, but Bishop Coldwell continued, "You are a member of our Church? No? Scottish? Oh, Scottish. Well, I see. I have not been much in the North, but of course I know Edinburgh. Everyone knows Edinburgh. Pretty old castle there. Bagpipes. History. I trust our ancient quarrels have been forgotten?"

At this, Miss Stuart simply looked at him and said not a word. Reaching to spear a pat of butter the Bishop continued cheerfully, "Sensible people in the North, not like the Irish – a nation of thieves and ruffians. I have never been in Ireland, and have no wish to go there. America of course is fast filling up with refugees from that dreadful country, and some day they will regret it. I was never in such a vulgar place as San Francisco. Never saw so many ugly women in my life, nor so many Jews, either."

To this, Miss Julia Stuart replied not a word. Helping himself to a large spoonful of marmalade, Coldwell continued in softer tones, "Well, my dear, you have chosen the right table. Look there!" Across the way, an American missionary was still praising the Lord while the porridge grew cold. "We Anglicans know how to do things with dispatch. Ah me, traveling is so tiresome these days. Miles and miles ahead of us. Do you play cards? Dominoes? No? I myself am a man of action – ordinarily, that is, but in circumstances such as this, ha-ha! – packed in like cargo – I shall require some distraction. I shall in fact demand that you allow me to teach you how to play dominoes. I was, you see, for many years a schoolmaster, so I am accustomed to being obeyed. Also, I expect that you shall always be here beside me at meal-times, for it will cheer me immensely to look at that pretty face of yours, and listen to your charming voice."

At the next meal Julia Stuart sat at the opposite end of the table, and never again moved from that position. Thus the seats of honor beside the Bishop were left to his secretary, C. J. Truckle, who lacked something of charm, and a tottering old planter from Singapore named Foxe-Henley, who was deaf as a stone and habitually reeking of gin.

Their other companions included the sharp-nosed prospective governess, Miss Geraldine Prosser, and the Bishop's chaplain, a pretty youth by the name of Peregrin White. Clemens and Wilkinson sat together, and beside David, an empty space was reserved for Scott when he should recover. Across the room, the aged American missionary held forth in an atmosphere of rigorous gloom alongside his silent, white-haired wife.

Early in the midday meal the following day Bishop Coldwell said, "I see that you are here, Mr. Wilkinson, but where, may I ask, is Mr. Partridge?"

"Unfortunately, he is still unable to join us," David replied.

"Ah! Lying about feeling sorry for himself, is he?"

"He is quite unwell, Your Lordship."

"Refuses to take nourishment, I suppose. That is foolish. Weakening, weakening. I trust he will improve upon this sorry performance when we reach the Islands. I have not brought him – and you – all this distance only to be disappointed." David, who had paid for his own ticket, did not respond, but glanced at Julia Stuart across the way, and found her looking curiously at him.

"I have had enough disappointments already, in Honolulu," said the Bishop.

"Far too many," said C.J. Truckle.

"Yes indeed," said Miss Prosser. "'Tis a shame."

"One after another, from the very start. Did you know, Miss Prosser, I was to have been private tutor to the little Hawaiian Prince. Then just as I arrived in the Islands, he suddenly died. At one moment he was alive, and at the next, dead. Imagine that! What a disagreeable position that left me in! Of course, it is sad to lose a child, but life must go on."

"Quite," said Miss Prosser, touching the tip of her nose with one finger.

"Then too," the Bishop continued, "my tenure in Hawaii has been constantly interrupted by travel – during which, of course, I do important work abroad for the Church. But each time I return, I find the people of Honolulu more disloyal than ever. The foreigners there are largely unsympathetic to our cause, and the natives are a primitive folk, ignorant, lost in superstition. Still, I begin to believe that there is something else at work here, something definitely wicked."

"Disgraceful," murmured C.J. Truckle, soft and smiling. "But it's surely due to the American newspapers, Your

Lordship. They turned against you early on. These days they never find a kind word to say about you, or about the Church, either."

"Impertinent rabble!" said the Bishop. "I consider it my duty to ignore them." His hands trembled as he folded his napkin. Preparing to leave the table, he spoke disdainfully to David Wilkinson, "You may tell your friend Mr. Partridge that I expect to see him here at dinner this evening. He is not on holiday! And I assure you, I do not look for laziness or dereliction of duty in my missionaries."

Samuel Clemens had taken a small notebook from his pocket, and was scribbling into it. Bishop Coldwell stared at him for a moment, then said sharply, "Look here, sir, what are you doing?"

Clemens thrashed rather oddly in his chair for a moment before replying, "Well now, Your Highness – excuse me, Your Holiness – I was just making a little note here, reminding myself to go back to the cabin and beat up on my no-good, worthless servant Billy Brown. Any of you folks met Brown yet?

"We do not meet servants," said Miss Prosser.

"Lucky you," said Clemens. "This one aint much of a treat. In fact, he's a low down specimen of humanity if ever there was one. Yes indeed. Low down, ugly, ignorant, heathen, the worst kind of waterfront scum. Which is where I found him to begin with, drunk under a dock in Mississippi. And I've been stuck with him ever since, trying to make a decent Christian out of him. So what is my reward? Believe me, Your Highness, I sympathize deeply with your sad, undeserved disappointment. It happens to me all the time." The Bishop began to interrupt, but was quickly overtaken by Clemens, who continued, "Why, would you believe, sir, Brown stole a bottle of my best brandy last night, drank every drop of it. Went up on deck afterward and threw it all overboard. Now, if that aint a waste! Not only that, but back in the cabin this morning I caught him draining the dregs. Would've eaten the cork for breakfast if I'd let him. Matter of fact, had his knife and fork out to do it when I came in. Napkin under his chin, too. I rapped his knuckles with a ruler, and made him kneel down while I read the entire Book of Leviticus aloud to him. "

Here Miss Stuart glanced with merry eyes at David Wilkinson, and he quickly looked away, trying his best not to laugh. But the Bishop loudly interrupted the torrent of words, saying "Mr. Clemens, if that is your name, I assure you, we have all heard quite enough. Brown is your servant, not mine. And as for Partridge, mind you, I have not said a word against him, but if he neglects his duties as a missionary in my service, that is nothing to smile about. Put away that notebook of yours, and let me warn you! If you fancy yourself some sort of spying journalist, then I shall see that you regret it."

"By my sainted mother's bunions!" cried Clemens. "That poor seasick boy! Another missionary for poor old Hawaii? Another, you say? Tell me, how many does that make these days, per capita? Come on now, aint you fellas about runnin' out of natives to convert?"

"You do not strike me, sir, as a gentleman," said the Bishop with steel in his voice, as he drew himself up and left the table.

*

Scott Partridge came at the Bishop's bidding that evening looking wretched, and still unable to eat, but this time Clemens settled himself beside Ezekiel Calhoun, the American missionary across the way. This table had been joined by two other Americans, a Dutchman from Java, a Viking-sized Norwegian, and a pair of handsome Italian lads in military uniforms. All in all, it appeared to be a far more interesting group than the one surrounding the Anglican Bishop. Clemens took out his notebook and asked a number of odd questions before he was heard to say, "Reverend, I hope you have some advice for me. It's about my man Brown. He's a heathen, Brown is, a no-good, unrepentant sinner and I can't do a dang thing with him. Fact is, whenever I make him read the Bible, he starts up with Genesis fine and dandy, frisky as a frog on a hot stove; swears up and down that he loves the Lord and all His works, especially the part about the snake. Yessir, he gets real teary-eyed over the garden and the lady with the snake, and he weeps over the sad way that story ends. But right after that he starts to kind of run down, and hard as I push, I never can get him past the Book of Deuteronomy. You see, this here Brown is a tender-hearted sinner, and he claims there's too much blood and mayhem in that book. He gets upset over the way people treat their friends and relations there, and those poor old bullocks being slaughtered every other day so's the Israelites can drip their blood on some altar. I never know what to tell him, so can you explain to me, sir, what in tarnation they want to do that for? It don't seem right to me. What kind of an altar is that, anyhow? Aint that kind of a messy proposition for an altar?"

Mr. Calhoun's response was to stare past Samuel Clemens as if he did not exist, and go on calmly eating his dinner. When the mad Mr. Clemens returned to the Bishop's table, Miss Stuart remarked that she was glad to see him even-handed in his troublemaking. "Troublemaking?" he replied. "I couldn't trouble that one if I tried. Ezekiel Calhoun is a hero." He looked across the table at Bishop Coldwell and said loudly, "Fine fellow, that old Calvinist. He's a warrior. He's coming back now from the first holiday he's had in 22 years. Built his church in Hawaii with his own hands. Heals the sick, tends the suffering, buries the dead, comforts the orphan and the widow. Prays up a storm, even on weekdays! Now there's a man that believes in working for a living."

8

One bright morning David came on deck to find Miss Julia Stuart wrapped in a great, gray woolen shawl. She was seated alone in a sheltered place on the ship's lee side, and her eyes were closed as David approached. When his shadow fell across her face, she opened them and smiled. "David Wilkinson! Take this chair if you like. Mr. Clemens had it earlier, but he seems to have vanished. Not overboard, I trust."

"I won't disturb you?"

"No, I was just resting my eyes. It is all such a dazzle." And it was, indeed, a day so brilliant as to be almost blinding.

"I hate missing things," she said, shielding her face with a fragile hand. "Tell me please if there is anything I should notice, You are still good at noticing, I trust?"

"Still good...?

"After so much academic training," she said. "It has been known to blunt the intellect. I rather think that is not true in your case. Correct me if I am wrong." The sea around them winked and glittered like a hoard of jewels. He considered replying, "I have noticed that you no longer wear your emerald," but thought better of it, and told her, "You're not missing anything just now. No ships, that is, no whales, not even a seabird following us at the moment."

"Oh, did you see them earlier? The whales, I mean, leaping and playing? Wasn't it bliss? But I was afraid you'd missed them, waiting upon your Bishop. I don't know how you can bear to sit with him in that stuffy place downstairs."

David thought of correcting the lady's nautical terminology, but decided against that, too. "Downstairs," she continued, "or whatever one is supposed to call it on a ship. It's a terrible thing to breathe the same air over and over again. That batch has been down there since California. And the windows don't open properly. The portholes, that is to say. But do you actually enjoy it? Playing dominoes, I mean."

"Enjoy? Actually, not."

"But he is your Bishop, therefore you must obey him, cosset and flatter him, see that he is pleased? Pray, Mr. Wilkinson, tell me no more about it."

"David, please, if you wish," he said somewhat distractedly, for he had told her nothing as yet, so how could he tell her more?

"Well then, down with formality. Julia, by all means" she said, without moving.

"Thank you. A lovely name. But English usually, isn't it?"

"It was my mother's. She was English. But you may as well know, there are more. I have five names in a row, including all sorts of MacIntoshes and Camerons. Quite an encumbrance, yes? But I am in a shedding mood these days, and so I shall probably drop most of them over the side before we reach Honolulu."

He laughed and closed his eyes against the brilliance. But at the next moment, something strange happened. It came to him all at once that the lady Julia herself might fall one day from the ship, either deliberately, or in the act of throwing something overboard. He saw her floating, encumbered by her shawl, just below the surface of the water, while her long black hair spread out like seaweed floating with the tide. He turned his head quickly to study the person beside him and discovered that her hair, which was confined in a netted chignon, was not black like his mother's, nor gray as might have been expected at her age, but a pale reddish-gold. Her eyes were still closed, and now he saw a sudden look of anguish cross her face. Was present suffering reflected there, or something from the past? Was her pain physical, mental, or both? He wondered, but did not dare to ask.

The spell was broken when she said with sharp impatience, "Dominoes, really!"

"Dominoes? Well, Mr. Calhoun disapproves of all such amusements. But then, as you must know, we of the Church of England are not Puritans."

"Deary me, you don't say. But it's a child's game. Counting up all those wee dots,

how could you?"

"Perhaps I might explain. We Anglicans are not Protestants in the Scottish mode, nor the New England mode either. We are not Roman Catholics, but something more moderate – something at the center of all that. Theologically speaking, I believe it is the right place for us to be."

"All well and good, but I'd have thought chess at least, for a man like His Lordship. Hah! There's a pleasant pastime. All those kings and queens, knights and bishops scheming and plotting how best to destroy one another! They wait and they watch – then, they strike! Morally enlightening. Socially uplifting, too, don't you think? That is, if one cares to be socially uplifted." The words were whimsical enough, but the bitterness of her tone was actually wounding. He allowed a small silence to fall between them, and then it occurred to him to ask her if she had ever played chess.

To his surprise, she replied in a low, impassioned voice, "Aye, with my uncle, in prison. And I can tell you, I dearly hope never to see a chessboard again."

"In prison, did you say?"

"Prison. Gaol. Some might have called it a castle. So it was, long ago. By now, the next thing to a ruin. An old, cold, crumbling fortress of a place, with a moat on one side and a loch on the other that is bottomless, or may as well be, and black as pitch. Iron bars on the windows, iron stakes in the moat, iron pots rusting on the battlements. That was from the time not long ago when my honorable forbears poured down boiling oil upon the enemy. Who was usually, by the way, either a near relative of ours, or else an Englishman."

A patch of nettles, he thought. *Bitter. Difficult.* As if she had heard him, she said, "I know, I am being difficult."

"Perhaps you have reason to be."

"Not at all. It is simply a decision I have made. I have been agreeable, and amenable, and pliant and obedient for the past – well, over twenty five years, and I have decided that is enough. More than enough. And so I am going to be – well, difficult, from now on. Perhaps, if all goes well, I shall even learn in time to be outrageous."

The last was said with such sweet, earnest dignity that he could not find it in his heart either to laugh, or chide, or trespass in any way. Instead, he sent up a quick, silent prayer of thanks for the sudden, unearned intimacy that sometimes arises between travelers. Then he said, "If I may ask, since you have left Scotland, who is now playing chess with your uncle?"

"The devil, I trust. He died last year." She thought for a moment, and added, "But I did not kill him."

Before David could respond to this astonishing remark, Julia Stuart turned abruptly to face him. "Have you ever been poor?" she asked politely, in a tone of mild curiosity, as if inviting a discussion of the weather.

He considered for a time, then replied, "Only in the sense of not having any money."

"Ah!" she said, and smiled down at her hands, that were now without ornament.

"And you?" he ventured.

"I have already told you quite enough about myself!" They sat side by side in silence for a time, looking out at the glittering sea. Then she said quietly, "But you are obviously a gentleman. Why have you had no money?"

He could feel his face growing hot, and said only, "A family matter."

"Someone stole it!" she said instantly.

They smiled at one another. Hers was a strong, level glance, from eyes so dark as to be nearly black in the shade of her ugly, old-fashioned bonnet. In a face so marked by fatigue and suffering as hers, their effect was remarkable. Because of that face, and the eyes, he told her what was never mentioned at home. The fact was, his father had given most of their money away.

"He did *what?*"

David explained that he had done it for what seemed to him at the time, a good reason.

"What on earth reason?"

He pondered. "Matter of honor between gentlemen."

"Oh my God!" she said. She stared at him for a moment, then turned away with such a sad, angry expression that he decided to amuse her with his ludicrous history. Shortly after David's fifteenth birthday, a former schoolmate of his father's had come round one day in a terrible state. Wept like a waterfall, spun a brilliant tale of woe. Desperately needed to borrow – well, a very large sum of money – but only for seven days. Then the entire amount would be repaid in full. The man swore on the Bible, on the Cross, on his Sacred Honor, on their Ancient Friendship, and on his own Extremely Distinguished Family Tree that included royalty.

The loan was made, and on the following day the visitor packed up the money, took his wife's jewels from the bank, and fled to Liverpool with his children's delightful young governess. They were last seen boarding a ship for Australia, and no one has heard from them since. "So you see, at fifteen, instead of going up to Oxford as planned, I went out to work as a bank clerk at Leeds. Most of my salary was needed at home. So I was – yes, very poor indeed."

None of this, apparently, surprised Miss Stuart. Frowning slightly, she said only, "Then, you were unable to continue your education."

"True and untrue. Consider it this way. I had never seen a slum or a tenement before. I didn't know that little children were forced to work in factories, or sent out into the streets as rag-pickers, beggars or worse. I had never seen fallen women selling their bodies, or old people starving and abused. I knew intellectually that there was such a thing as evil, but not that it could enter into my world. I knew nothing beyond an idyllic little corner of Paradise, a bit of Eden called *Green Gardens*, safely tucked away in the Yorkshire fields and woods. So it was my privilege, you see, during the years at Leeds when I had no money, to be given a liberal education free of charge."

She sighed, and sighed again. "Oh, David. Yes, I see. For how long was this?"

"A lifetime. Three years, nearly four." He laughed, but Julia Stuart did not. Instead, looking down at her hands again, she said softly, "Of course that is a lifetime, if you think it will never end." She stirred in her chair, wrapped the shawl more closely around herself, and closed her eyes once more.

The thrill of revealing himself to a stranger had set David's heart to pounding. Finance was the most sternly forbidden of all topics at *Green Gardens*, where an interest in money was considered so vulgar that no civilized person would dream of mentioning it. He wanted to tell her a great deal more, but made a quick vow to bury the financial topic.

Then she said, "But how did you manage the cost of your missionary college? St. Columba's, did you say? That must have come dear."

He hesitated for only a moment before replying, "An angel intervened."

She frowned. "An angel? Gave you money?"

"An angel named George Merryman, my uncle – my mother's brother. Money? That was the least of it. He gave me back my life."

She thought about this, and watching her, he knew that she was not debating the existence or non-existence of angels. "You want to know," he said, "how, where and when my uncle George got his money. And how much."

She laughed heartily, but did not deny it. "I am being most unmannerly. Unforgivable, I know. But you see, I am obliged to have a serious interest in the subject. I am on my own now - my parents died many years ago - I shall never marry, and so there is a great deal that I need to learn about finances, now that my uncle and guardian is gone. Sensible management, that is. How to avoid taking undue risks, how not to be foolish or wasteful. I feel it a serious responsibility."

"I see. Well, my brilliant uncle won it on the horses."

Julia Stuart clapped her hands and shouted, "Oh! Oh! How perfectly splendid!"

"Yes, my entire training as a priest in the Church of England was provided by the winnings of a fast little filly called Twilight.

"*Twilight!* I've heard of her!"

"She was born in our stables - *Green Gardens*. Uncle George is the owner."

"Ah!" Uttered softly, with a radiant smile, it was a benediction.

Another silence fell between the two, but this time he felt her becoming distant and withdrawn. She said after a time that she "must go downstairs and collapse for a bit" and allowed David to help her to her cabin, that was just across the corridor from his. It was plain to see, and to feel in the icy grip of her hand, that Julia Stuart was in pain. However, she said nothing about it, but thanked David Wilkinson courteously, and then quietly closed her door.

A valiant lady, he thought, and clenched his teeth in shame for all that he had dreamed earlier about fragrant flesh, a silken nightdress and rows of tiny buttons.

*

That same evening David won three games of dominoes in a row from the Bishop, and His Lordship was not pleased. He put the tiles away and, sadly shaking his head, poured the last of the champagne into his glass. "Ah," he said, "the blessed vines of France, how well they do provide! You have not been to France, I suppose, Mr. Wilkinson."

"No sir."

"Nasty people, the French. Sharp tongued, quarrelsome. No respect for authority. Still, it must also be said that their food and wine are excellent, especially their champagnes. I always avail myself of several cases when I am there, and have them shipped home to me in London. Of course, if you want good sherry or brandy, you must go to Spain. By the way, you were at my table, were you not, when that American made a fool of himself?"

"Mr. Clemens?"

"Then you should know that he is not what he pretends. I spoke to the Captain about him. The man is traveling under an assumed name. One may easily imagine why. His name is not Clemens, it is something else I have forgot. As for his disgusting servant Brown, he has no servant with him at all, and there is no one on this ship by the name of Brown. It was all a lie. The entire story, apparently, was the product of his diseased imagination. Watch out for him! He will cause trouble."

"Oh," said David. "I see."

"And as for the Stuart woman, it seems that she has several other names as well. Therefore she fancies herself to be of some great importance, or else she has been married several times, which would not surprise me. It seems the Scottish royals may indeed be relatives of hers – but not necessarily by blood. I thought as much when I saw that extraordinary ring she wore. Still, no reason for her to play Miss Haughty! I know that sort of Scots nobility. They are all penniless, ragged and rude. I'll wager her father is one of those Highland lairds that runs barefoot in the hills and eats his meat from a knife."

"Thank you, sir. It is very late, your Lordship. May I be excused?"

"Very well," said the Bishop. "But I saw you speaking with the Stuart woman on the deck, and that was unwise. She is of no use to us, and she cannot be a good influence. Mr. Wilkinson, you are still wet behind the ears, you and Mr. Partridge both. There is a great deal about the world that you don't know."

"Thank you, sir," said David. "And goodnight."

9

As they neared the Hawaiian Isles, the wind came roaring out of the southeast with tremendous force, accompanied by deluges of rain. The *Hermes* lay helplessly rolling, tossing and heaving, while decks went awash and chairs slid to and fro in the public rooms. On the first night of the storm, the cook's henhouse was swept away, together with all of its unfortunate residents. On the second, a torrent of cold salt water poured into the dining saloon. Shy young Peregrin White, the Bishop's chaplain, was the champion that night. Singing operatic arias as he worked, he led a human chain for bailing that included the Italian adventurers, the Dutchman (who for once shed his pipe), Samuel Clemens, and the two young Anglican deacons. Bishop Coldwell had retired to his berth, and few of the other passengers appeared during the storm, which the Captain declared was not a typhoon, but only something near it.

The steward, impassive as ever in his red turban, carried tea to the indisposed and served cold rations. David knocked at Miss Stuart's cabin each morning and evening to make certain that she was safe, and she always answered cheerfully, but never opened her door to him. Finally, after three tumultuous days, the skies cleared, the seas grew calm, and there was a faint new fragrance in the air suggesting the existence of something warm, green and promising not far away.

"Oh give thanks to the Lord!" said old Ezekiel Calhoun, when he met David in the corridor. "For He is gracious, and His mercy endureth forever," David added more or less automatically, although he was surprised to be addressed by the stern old man who had never before acknowledged his existence. The top of Calhoun's white head did not reach David's shoulder, but he fixed the younger man with a canny stare. Then a thought came to David: *Blessed are the peacemakers*, and he said that, too, aloud. Surely, this was a good time for a service of General Thanksgiving? Thus far the Calvinists had gone to services on the starboard deck at 7 a.m., while the Anglicans met portside at 11. Julia Stuart came to neither of these events, but Clemens came with great enthusiasm to both; a sinner like him, he said, needed all the help he could get. The more David saw of Clemens, the more he liked the man, and sought his company.

He went to the Bishop now, who was incensed by his suggestion. The Reverend Ezekiel Calhoun, he said, was a traitor. None of these American missionaries were ministers of the One True Faith. None had any right to lead Christian services, and furthermore, there was not a gentleman among them. Despite what they claimed, they were born working class men and tradesmen of the lowest sort. "It has long been my wife's desire," he said, "to send them to the back door when they call upon us in Honolulu, and I do not fault her for it. Americans lack distinction in any case, but they have been sending their dregs out to Hawaii." He ordered David to speak to Ezekiel Calhoun, if at all, only of two separate Thanksgiving services.

Wearily, David obeyed, and then ventured to tell the American that he was sorry they could not worship together. Calhoun snorted derisively and muttered "Papist folderol!" Next he demanded in scalding tones to know if it was "Rome or the British Foreign Office" that was paying their way across the sea, so that Britain might take over Pearl Harbor, after having ruined the morals of the natives.

David replied somewhat sharply. "It has been my impression, sir, that the natives have no morals, but that we hope to bring them some. Furthermore, I for one have no interest whatever in collecting pearls. Have you?"

This set the old man to shouting until the veins stood out on his freckled forehead about the wicked, blaspheming Popery of the British coming to Hawaii at the eleventh hour to destroy his life's work with their Lordships and their Thrones and their Pagan Images in Holy Places, and their Candles and their Burning of Incense that stank to Heaven; not to mention the example they put before the natives, claiming to be Christians while gallivanting around through the Islands behaving like Barbarians and Heathen Savages.

Pointing a long finger at David's ribs, he claimed that clergymen of the Church of England robbed the Royal Hawaiian Treasury to line their own pockets, that they regularly indulged in the Seven Deadly Sins while inventing some new ones, what with their Games of Chance, their Smoking of Filthy Tobacco, their Imbibing of Spiritous Liquors, their Approval of the Lewd Indecency of the Hawaiian Hula-Hula, and their looking away from every other pagan form of Sin and Lechery! The long and short of it was that, in the Gospel According to Calhoun, all Anglican priests and members of the English Church were Bound for Perdition, and could not get there fast enough to suit him.

Why, this is a Borders man, thought David. *The accent, the freckles, the hair that was surely once red. His kin have been in America for a few generations and so he thinks of himself as American, but he is still a cranky, fiery, intractable, horse-trading Scotsman all the same. Which is not so far, after all, from being a cranky, fiery, intractable, horse-trading Yorkshireman!*

"Come, sir," he said, holding out his hand. "I have reason to believe that our forebears were neighbors not so very long ago. Peace! Let there be peace between us for their sake, and for the sake of the beloved Book and the sovereign Lord we both love." Calhoun looked down at David's hand, then looked him in the eye with a glance as hard and cold as lapis lazuli. After another moment, he turned on his heel and walked away.

*

They had been aboard the *Hermes* for a little more than two weeks when the cry came at dawn one morning, "Land! Land ho!" Passengers rushed to the decks. They could see nothing except blue water and far away, a smudged horizon; yet, after this they suddenly began laughing and chattering with one another in a friendly way, and making themselves known to those who had remained strangers. Even so, by mid-morning David Wilkinson wondered whether a cruel trick had been played upon them all. Since childhood he had known what to expect when he finally reached Hawaii. Here he was, just off the coast, but where were the exotic, palm-fringed shorelines, the quaint little native huts by the sea? Where were the verdant forests filled with tropical vines and fruits, and the rivers, the pools and the leaping cataracts? All he could see before him now was a barren coast where a gloomy diadem of cloud hovered over a raw, red hill that appeared to be made of clay, with its rough slopes absorbing the glow of early sunlight. Gradually the ship reduced its speed until there was no breeze to cool them. Perspiration bathed his forehead as the sun blazed down with the promise of a February day like none he had ever known before. He smiled as they turned south-westerly, past the point of Diamond Head. After all, he had not really believed that it would be made of diamonds – or, had he?

And now, without a hint of foretaste or warning, an entirely new landscape spread itself suddenly before him. Sheer blue mountain slopes in the distance folded rhythmically into one another, falling swiftly to rich, blue-shadowed valley deeps. The soft green verdancies of the foreground appeared to breathe, like the body of a sleeping woman, plumed and feathered with golden light. All this beauty was first hidden, then revealed, by roiling, tumbling mists of silver, blue and rose, while in the full sunlight directly ahead, the arc of a white-rimmed bay embraced a small forest of ships.

David was nearly stunned by joy and wonder, but then turned to speak to the person standing at the rail beside him. He had thought it was Scotty, but it was not, it was Samuel Clemens, wearing a long brown linen coat that looked as if he had slept in it. "Glorious!' Clemens pronounced, and David agreed. Soon after that, they both glimpsed a rainbow arching from peak to peak above the little port. "Look at that!" they said simultaneously, and Clemens began to hum the opening bars of *Glorious Things of Thee are Spoken.*

"That is one of my favorite hymns!" said David.

"Mmm" said Clemens, stroking his moustache. "Too bad. I only know one hymn, and far as I recollect, that's not it."

The softest, lightest of rain showers touched them, and then withdrew, as the little town by the bay unveiled itself. Here and there a miniature church steeple rose above its mantling greenery; then the tops of several other small buildings appeared, and tiny figures could be seen moving along the waterfront. It was Sunday morning; David noted that there were a great many churches for such a small town, and wondered how many among the general population would be worshipping at services today.

"Glorious things of thee are spoken, Sion city of our God," Clemens sang now, surprisingly well for a man who had claimed musical imbecility. David wondered only for a moment whether the Bishop would approve, then decided that God would not mind, and joined in. Between the two of them, they managed to do a creditable job of it; and when they came to *"Round each habitation hov'ring/ See the cloud and fire appear,"* a cannon came awake on a highland near the port, and began to salute their ship. Clemens and Wilkinson grinned at each other as if it had been all their doing.

Then the *Hermes* uttered a booming riposte, while between explosions they could hear the chime and clamor of more and more church bells, adding their notes to the general jubilee.

David suddenly found himself wild with joy and relief, so much so that he felt tempted to tear off his coat, for lack of a hat, and launch it into the air. Thus he was not surprised when Miss Julia Stuart came to stand beside him and cried, "Oh my God, how glorious!" and then, a moment later, stripped off her ugly woolen bonnet and hurled it over the rail.

As he watched the little object floating away, he thought better of their mutual impulse. "See here!" he said. "You may want that!" and turned to look at her. She was flushed and wide-eyed, with a rainbow of emotions sweeping over her face.

"See here yourself!" she answered. "I think – just possibly – that I may never want it again!" Then she gave a little laugh, drew a deep breath, and burst into tears.

"Oh but you may," said David. Then, knowing that it was an idiotic thing to say,

he added, "Shall I try to get it for you?"

"Don't be an idiot," said she. "My dear. Excuse me. Give me a handkerchief."

He gave her one of his own, which as usual was clean and neatly folded in a breast pocket. Clemens had moved away by now, but David could see the Bishop and Scott Partridge at a distance, and knew that he ought to go to them.

"But Miss Julia, are you quite all right?"

"Of course," she said, "only I'll not be Julia Stuart in the future. I have decided that I shall simply be Fiona Cameron from now on."

"I see,"

"You don't – you couldn't possibly, but thank you," she said as she tucked his handkerchief into her pocket. Then she turned away from him rather quickly, so that the vivid red paisley shawl she was wearing slipped from her shoulders, and one side of it fell to the deck. Before either of them could retrieve it, David Wilkinson caught a glimpse of her back that was somehow deformed, unnaturally shaped from the hips to the shoulders. Her waist was thick and ungainly, all ribbed around with a bulky, supporting or concealing structure of some sort that lay in ridges and creases, straining the fabric of her gown.

She snatched the shawl, hastily wrapped herself in it, and turned to confront him with a look that stayed with him all the years of his life. In that one long glance a Highland lady bound him soul upon soul to her forever, in a way that had nothing to do with romance or sexual congress between man and woman. He saw her inmost being then and saw it whole: her fear, her shame, her pain, her overweening pride, her courage that had finally grown reckless, and the fierce, virgin spirit that sustained her.

BOOK TWO: GARDEN

10

A burly brown Hawaiian man in an open shirt and a large straw hat was sitting on a barrel, fishing from the pier. The day was yet young, but the sun shone down like thunder, and the air was so damp that their clothing clung to them like a second skin. The Bishop and the rest of his party went on ahead while C.J. Truckle and the two young deacons stayed at the waterfront with orders to collect the luggage. Fiona Cameron, meantime, was nowhere to be seen.

It was an entertainment to watch the astonishing amount and variety of cargo that emerged from the *Hermes*. Across the Pacific in its capacious hold had come every imaginable product of civilization, from pianos to sewing machines, from chandeliers to corsets, from butter packed in ice to firearms, tobacco, candles, wines and brandy, apples, books and magazines, farming tools, crystal and silverware. At the end of it all, the captain carried away a large mail-bag made of canvas and fastened with a chain.

It was late afternoon when their hired carriage threaded its dusty way through the town, where here a dark face, there a lighter one smiled to them as they passed. It was a jolly scene: ordinary people, both men and women, wore garlands of flowers as if going to a festival. The shops were apparently prosperous, and the residential district was surprisingly grand. While the sun blazed down from a stainless heaven, families sat together on their deeply shadowed verandahs, looking as serene as if they were praying or reading Scripture. Perhaps, indeed, they were.

Threading its way through tunnels of hot green shade, the carriage tumbled along, soon climbing uphill past native houses that were all but buried in vines, and crowned here and there with blossoms bright as fire. David and Scotty perched on the toppling luggage while, across the way, Mr. Truckle nodded, uttering a gentle snore from time to time.

"Oh – oh – oh, my brains are melting!" Scotty groaned, after a great yawn. "If this weather continues, I am going to be useless among the noble savages!"

"I haven't seen a savage yet," said David, "noble or otherwise. Thus far, Honolulu looks to me like a charming outdoor Sunday School."

"It is no such thing," said C. J. Truckle, without opening his eyes. "Be warned, lads! You must guard your virtue here in town on a Saturday night."

The road rose steeply now into the green cleft of the Nu'uanu Valley, where the moist air embraced them with a dreamlike softness, and a subtle fragrance that was poignant as an invisible caress. A broad silver stream meandered beside the road, crossing it here and there, while patches of unfamiliar vegetation grew in irrigated fields, tended by pigtailed Chinese workers under conical hats. Taro? Not rice, thought David. Here and there he could see a grass-roofed native hut tucked under vine-draped trees, or a mansion all but concealed by green luxuriance.

"But Scotty, have you wondered, seriously, whether we are needed here? Perhaps Hawaii has more than enough missionaries already." David was remembering Samuel Clemens' remarks.

"Needed?" said Scott, after a drowsy interval. "Depends upon the point of view. Consider, for example, that!" He nodded toward the snorting Truckle, whose head now rolled helplessly back and forth with the motion of the carriage. "Did you know that His Lordship plans to ordain him?"

"No!"

"Verily."

"Not so, Scotty. I won't believe it."

"Suit yourself. The horrid fact is true."

"Who told you such a thing?"

"Himself. Coldwell. You and I are to be raised from deacon to priest at the same time. Any day now. In fact, I predict that as soon as the Bish has unpacked that stunning cope and mitre of his, we'll be off to the races."

"But we're not ready. We don't even know the language."

"He doesn't mind. We'll serve his purpose. And at the same time, he'll make up a pair of deacons to take our places – the Reverend Sleeping Beauty here, and little Peregrin White, who is not yet through school."

Here the driver stopped at a crossing of the stream to water the horses. Truckle was apparently still sleeping while Scott and David walked a short distance away, and stopped amid the whine of mosquitoes in dappled shade.

"Why, Scott? I don't understand."

"Wilks, I'm sorry, but there it is, as usual – money. Our bishop loves it so much that he has run himself out of funds. They pay him back in London by the head – by the number of missionaries working for him. Well, don't break your heart over it. This is no reflection on you, or on me either. It's just, the man is desperate."

"Unbelievable. Out of funds? With so many sources? What about the Wilberforce committee? And the Gospel Society? Not to mention the Hawaiian royals. Wilberforce always said they wanted us, and would be generous with finances. And the Hopkins book about Hawaii certainly implied... You did read it, didn't you??"

"Should have. Sorry, never got around to it. But the fact remains, the money's gone.

According to our foolish leader there was never enough, and now disaster looms. The former king, Emma's husband, promised to help. Then, of course, he died. It seems the present monarch doesn't like us much, probably isn't even a

Christian. Queen Emma will do what she can, but she herself is in debt. Very badly."

"Queen Emma in debt? How can that be?"

"Yes! To the point of trying to borrow large amounts. I didn't like to tell you after you fell in love with that photograph of her, and the amazing feathered cloak. But the truth is, while she was in England, she begged a huge sum from a rather plush cousin of mine, Beresford-Hope by name. The word was soon out; they all know each other in those circles. He couldn't, or else wouldn't give it to her. It was all very embarrassing."

"Not our business."

"No - and yes, unfortunately. The point is – according to Coldwell, who surely ought to know – that the royals here in Hawaii live far beyond their means. Yachts, retinues, receptions, elaborate gifts, clothes, carriages, jewels and so forth. And our bishop, being a thorough parvenu, believes he must keep up with them. 'Show the flag' as he says – but it's not the flag, of course. It's his own ambition, trying to climb here socially in a way he knows he could never do at home."

"I've never understood that sort of thing. But what does all this have to do with –"

"With the One True Faith? Nothing. Absolutely nil. Zero."

"Scott, he told me that even the Americans have given him money. The people in Philadelphia – ?"

"Those were Episcopalians, yes. Next thing to Anglican. But there aren't many of them, and they may not want to do it again. Can you imagine his behavior there?"

"Yes." They were both silent for a time.

"Well, don't give up on the old boy entirely." Scott began to laugh. " Perhaps we can help him to improve. Tell you what, I'll teach him to stop snatching food with his knife and talking with his mouth full. Give him some lessons in polite conversation, etcetera. Then you work on the old ancestral bit. Train him to stiffen the spine, play the proud role of the impoverished aristocrat. You know that one well enough!"

"I admit," said David, "that a few people have tried to warn me. I heard some rather discouraging remarks at home about the so-called Hawaiian adventure. And it occurred to me recently that the only current book I could find about Hawaii before we left was written by a man who has never been there. Yes – that's a fact. Manley Hopkins, the British consul is the author, and the introduction was written by our old friend Samuel Wilberforce."

Scott yawned before replying, "This will be an adventure, yes, but not the one we looked for. Of course, the official story is that our clergymen come out here, and then either fall ill or misbehave or else go mad, and so are shipped home again. *White man cannot stand heat* is the contention. Balderdash! Look at what we've done in India, and a dozen other colonies," He yawned again. "Just give me a week or two of uninterrupted sleep, and then you'll see manly British vigor!"

David paced in a small circle, then returned. "Scotty, do you honestly mean that a certain amount of money goes into the Bishop's pocket per missionary?" Scott nodded. "And he controls it all, even though he is constantly traveling abroad?"

"That's it. But of course he's not the only one. There are others who make their underlings do all the work while they preen in the House of Lords and visit the European spas. The problem for Coldwell is that if there aren't enough of us out here, the rather solemn Gospel Society chaps will refuse to pay him at all. They're a tight-fisted lot."

The coachman hailed them, and they waved to him, but for the moment did not move toward the carriage. Scott wiped his face with a crumpled handkerchief, and David began to scratch his neck and wrists, realizing suddenly that he had been stung by a great many insects. "Scotty," he said, "How did you learn all this?"

"One night we were talking – the Bish and I. It was after the storm. He had been terrified, and that made him cross. Then quite a bit of champagne after dinner, and so forth. I was sympathetic. By the end of it, the poor man was nearly weeping."

"Poor man nearly weeping!" said David bitterly.

"Champagne after dinner! The entourage! The secretary, the chaplain, the governess! All this, and children starve in Leeds! What are we doing here?" For this, Scott had no reply, and as they climbed back into the carriage, David told him, "Please to remember, Partridge, that Hawaii is <u>not</u> one of our colonies. It's an independent monarchy, and we'd both do well to keep that in mind."

"But really," said Scott. "He was quite pathetic. I actually felt sorry for him."

*

A concourse of coconut trees formed a grand entrance to the Bishop's house, which was made of wood, once painted white, that was now peeling. A verandah lay open at the front of the house under broad eaves, with a few scattered pieces of straw and bamboo furniture. A disappointing fringe of garden had gone mostly to weed, and monster geraniums eight and ten feet tall straggled toward a wooden tank that served to collect rainwater. As soon as they entered the house, Scotty and David knew that they must not stay. Mrs. Coldwell was in a towering rage, declining even to speak to the latest arrivals.

At the first sight of their new governess, the three Coldwell children had fled from the house and could not be found. The Chinese servant had also vanished, and it was unclear whether or not he would return. Vivid discussions of a domestic nature were taking place behind closed doors; the two young deacons did their best not to hear them, but sat on the porch steps swatting more mosquitoes while Truckle fell into the nearest chair and apparently went asleep again. As soon as the Bishop reappeared, Scott and David asked permission to depart. Permission was given, and the Bishop walked out with them as far as the driveway.

David had decided that one question, at least, must be asked. "Your Lordship, when, sir – if I may inquire – may I expect my stipend?"

The Bishop gazed at him, and said nothing.

"My promised stipend of £60 annually. To draw upon, that is. I was assured that you would have it in hand by now, from the GSBE. And the fact is, that I shall soon be having some expenses."

The Bishop's face was still entirely blank.

"The Gospel Society," David added.

"Gospel Society?" He did not seem to have heard of it.

"Of the British Empire," said Scott. "In London, in Marlborough Street."

"Quite," said the Bishop. "Arrangements, yes, must be made. But gracious! So much as £60? I believe the others have made do with much less. In any case, we have only just arrived. There is a reception at the Palace tomorrow evening. Best prepare yourselves for that." He turned away as if to leave them, then turned back and said, "That suit of yours, Mr. Wilkinson. See a tailor! I recommend cashmere, for this climate."

David's reply was more vigorous than he intended. "I am not in the habit, sir, of buying things that I cannot afford. If others care to do so, then that is their concern."

The Bishop regarded him now with a light in his eyes that David mistook for approval. In courteous tones, he reminded Coldwell that he had paid his own way to the Islands, and had also raised money for the Hawaiian Mission by speaking to the public about it at home. As the result, a fund of £68 was now in the hands of the Wilberforce Committee, where it was held for a splendid cause: the building of a memorial church in honor of Captain Cook. Only gradually did it come to him that the look on his bishop's face was not what he had imagined.

"Excuse me," Scott interjected. "My Lord Bishop, this is not the best time, I think, for – that is – I pray you, sir, convey our greetings to Mrs. Coldwell. And now, Wilkinson, come along. We must depart."

David bowed to the Bishop in silence and the two young men turned away, but Bishop Coldwell followed them. Clapping a hand to David's shoulder, he spun him around and shouted, "You! You will stop this insolence! Both of you! This is outrageous! Insupportable! Do not smile at me, Mr. Partridge! It is time you both learned to appreciate your situation. You are under my rule here. You'll do as I say. You wish to quarrel with me, do you Wilkinson? Challenge me, make yourself obnoxious to me over a matter of £70? Call me dishonorable, will you? For shame! You know nothing about the situation here, nothing at all. You are a pair of ignorant fools. A memorial for Captain Cook? That is the least of my concerns. I shall decide what is done with the funds in my See. You shall make no decisions whatever. None! Keep your opinions to yourself! They are of no possible interest to me." He started to walk away, but turned back again, and in low tones of scarcely suppressed violence, continued: "You place yourself too high, Mr. Wilkinson. You assume that you are a person of some importance! Evidently you believe that Samuel Wilberforce is your friend. He is not. He is mine. He will not hear you. London will not hear you, and for good reason. You are not to be heard! No! Not without my permission! It is I who rule here. Learn that! Learn obedience to me!"

Since he had reached his full height, no man had dared to lay hands upon David Wilkinson. So shocked was he by the Bishop's behavior that he thrust his fists into his pockets to keep himself from striking back, and stood quite still. The Bishop was breathing so harshly and rapidly that David wondered for a moment whether he might collapse. But he only turned away and walked quickly back to the house.

"Wilks old boy," said Scott with a shrug, "I've heard better in my time, and had a thrashing to go with it. What about you? "David did not answer, for he was thinking of the Bishop's words, "Call me dishonorable!" That most certainly he had not done. He reflected, too, that the hard-won £68 for the Cook memorial had suddenly become £70 of the Bishop's own to spend. He remembered the spectral blaze in Coldwell's eyes as he raged, and told himself that something was seriously wrong here, morally askew.

"This is all very strange," he said at last to Scott. "For some reason, our bishop is not in control of himself. In fact, I wonder whether his mind may have suffered some injury." Scott refused to take it seriously. "It's just that the man has no *style*, David. All in all, I find him disappointing."

"We had better pray for him. I know if I don't, I may knock him down one day."

"Get your money back first," said Scott.

"It's not my money, nor his either. It came from my friends and neighbors, some of whom could ill afford it, and it was given specifically for the Cook Memorial. Bishop Wilberforce knew that and told me that he approved. Now, to my everlasting shame, I suppose it will go for cashmere! Cashmere and champagne." In silence they retraced their path through the sylvan beauties of the Nu'uanu Valley to Honolulu, where they found rooms at a modest pension on Fort Street, near the waterfront.

11

D*arling Bethy,*

If you were not the kindest of sisters you would hate me– I know you must have worried. Please forgive. I've been here 9 days, quite safe, but simply too weak & stupid to write. Brother Hal won't mind, I'm sure, if I delay Australia – I simply cannot go on just now. As for Borneo & the White Rajahs – they too must wait, for I begin to think I may never go that far.

I trust you rec'd my note from New York – a dirty place, I did not like it. San Francisco had splendid views & fascinating people. Silks & gold on miners, poets in gems & elaborate whiskers. Not many women about, but several I was told received in the politest parlors after careers unmentionable! What tales those old dears must know & will never tell – alas – to the likes of me & thee. I begin to think this voyage an opportunity for me to become completely anonymous. The voyage to Hawaii was not very nice – our ship so crammed with crooks & missionaries that it fairly reeked of deception, greed & piety.

It was called the <u>Hermes</u> *– well-named, a vessel obviously determined to toss us about for the fun of it. The females aboard were not interesting, but happily, of the other sex there were some – a mad journalist, American, who was good enough to squire me about – and a very kind, solemn young priest from Yorkshire who was astonishingly handsome. Almost too beautiful, although entirely unaware of it – and so shy I*

86

thought he might jump from the ship when I spoke to him. An odious little English Bishop tried at our first meeting to make love to me – or rather to Nana's emerald – so I have it now on a chain around my neck. You were right, of course, it was foolish of me to wear it – should have left it with Wm. at the bank.

As we neared the Isles we were struck by a terrific storm & I lay abed 3 days deciding that I was a fool to have undertaken this journey. Now that it's over I confess – darling, don't fret – that I shed a good many tears, for I was exhausted & could not in that chaos undress without help – or even unhook the damned Tormenter that was harder than ever to endure, for fear of being thrown naked across the cabin and dashed to pieces. Fortunately I had saved some grapes plus cheese and crackers that kept me alive while I fairly wallowed in self pity – dismal performance, but God be thanked, no witnesses.

Speaking of God, the storm was actually a blessing in a way – to survive it and then to rise up with that added lift of joy & relief – to see the land before us all soft with rainbows – and the sweetest, wildest blue mountains, peak beyond dale for miles. Near to the harbor as we came in I could see women on horseback dashing about – & thought, can it be true that I will never ride again? More tears, alas, but only a few this time – & I borrowed a handkerchief from the young Adonis – one that I now see I neglected to return. Truly, I must change my habits!

Thanks to dear Angela's letter of intro. I am staying now with the King's sister in law, Queen Emma. I planned at first to rest here only a week – but am apparently adopted. She seems really to want me & I am too shaken – or lacking in character – to resist. Emma (Hawaiian name Kaleleonalani) is dowager Queen royal, widow of the King's brother & matriarch of a large clan – I never know quite who is living here & who not. She herself is a darling – merry, sweet & sensible – beautifully educated – amazingly, unspeakably kind. I am allowed to do nothing whatever but sleep, eat, dress myself with the help of Her Majesty's own maid, who does my hair beautifully – walk in the garden for a bit, eat more & then ride about in a carriage looking at views. My appetite here is outrageous!

So do not worry please – truly I am better, safe as can be – and receiving the best of care. Only keep yourself well – embrace dear William for me – and as for the bairns, tell them their wretched, unworthy aunt has not caught a single monkey for them yet, nor has she seen either a cannibal or a pirate. However she sends at least a hundred kisses to each, and for you — dear girl, as ever — a thousand.

Later: Missed the packet, sorry — could not get to the harbour in time. Came back — slept more — yet wonder, will I find the energy to sit under a palm tree at sundown, watching croquet? The heat and the strangeness of it all have destroyed me — removed every trace of ambition. It's confusing too because the customs here of course are so different to our own.

Her Maj. rises early — walks in her garden before breakfast in bare feet — tends her own flowers ad lib, caressing & whispering to her favorites — she is a marvelous gardener. Also, she appears with her hair down whenever she pleases — now there is royal privilege worth having! Yet she is entirely a lady — treats every soul with utmost courtesy & spends most of her waking hours on Good Works.

Matters of health & moral education for women are the Q's passions. Also of course the Anglican Religion — she slips away to church 4+ mornings a week & often takes tea with Sisters of Mercy. Sews for the poor as well — and performs various labors in aid of a hospital she & her late husband founded. Above all she is indomitable in the protection of Hawaiian children who are badly used or otherwise in need — simply adopts them — makes them her protégés. It's a beautiful example to her people — also helps I think with the terrible loss of her own — her only wee lad, who died suddenly at the age of 4. Her eyes fill with tears when she speaks of him...

I'm amazed to discover how much E. has read and traveled — not just to Britain, but the Continent — America, even. She spoke last eve at dinner with shining eyes about the South of France — the beauty, the quietude of it, the charm of the people — the simple seaside villages she so loved because they reminded her of home. They used to cook there sometimes on the beach — holding sticks to the fire & she thought that was glorious!

Here we have everything from English tea with all the trimmings to an occasional dejeuner sur l'herbe, Polynesian style, crouching on straw mats (I with a cushion) & consume such exotic stuff as mangoes bananas & cocoa nut milk — passion fruit & raw fish — not to mention, shrimp so fresh they are sometimes still wriggling. At this sort of feast we all put fingers into a common bowl for the native dish called poi – revolting to look at but actually not bad – a sticky, porridgey sort of stuff, nicely tart and said to be nourishing. It is made from a purple root that they smash – I hope no one chews it for us too, in the kitchen – & the result is fermented. Oh, how pleasant it is to lick one's fingers at table without criticism!

The passion fruit I hasten to say is not the scandal you might suspect, but an innocent little yellow orb filled with the most exquisitely delicious flesh (Hawaiian name, lilikoi). The designation I was told has something to do with the Passion of Christ – a cross shaped pattern somewhere inside – though I have yet to discover it.

As for cleanliness, they all bathe constantly in the sea – & I have heard them say that there are pools in the volcanic mountains here quite as warm as a bath. But also some natives – & foreigners too – have lovely fresh-water bathing rooms especially made for the purpose, pleasantly cool on a torrid day. All this washing seems to be taken frankly as sensual pleasure – an approved one. Not a sour-faced Scottish parson in sight! Still, I'm told that the American missionary party does its part in disapproving most everything. The Queen's town house – elegant in an unpretentious way – is called the Winter Palace, since she has various other dwellings in the Islands & visits them at different seasons. This one has airy rooms painted white, furnishings cosy and comforting a l'Anglaise – bowls of flowers & fruits everywhere – ranks of French doors opening onto balconies & verandahs both above and below, welcoming the breeze. Winters here are actually warmer than summers in Scotland!

The clothes in Honolulu – you will crave to know – are a bit of everything from the nearly naught – to the practical – to the fanciful – to the height of European convention! The Queen is beautiful, although she thinks too stout – dresses sensibly for the climate as a rule, but feels that she must be fashionable too, so her finest gowns now have skirts drawn up in the new French manner, showing yards of troublesome petticoats. People do laundering here every day – and often the ironing out of doors, under the trees. Emma insists on wearing white kid gloves upon occasion & has trouble getting them from abroad – her size like my own is 7+3/4" so I've given her half a dozen pair. We two had a great fit of laughter yesterday – saw an old Hawaiian man on the street, very drunk, very *dignified, wearing a long ruffled shirt made of fine linen, but no sign of trousers. I looked the other way – so as not to cause royal embarrassment, but the Queen whispered in my ear, "Now I know what a Scotsman wears under his kilt!"*

Bethy dear – I am trying to think how to describe to you another form of recreation considered quite respectable – a healing sort of regimen – whether or not one is an invalid. It is so comical, I am helpless with laughter thinking of it. Even the name is silly – it's called lomilomi. Can you guess? Never in the world. Imagine then a huge Hawaiian woman – I don't know if men do it – stripping the victim bare, pouring on cocoa nut oil, arranging the slimy outcome on a pile of straw mats – then furiously assaulting it! Rolling – pummeling – pushing & pulling, kneading the poor, bare, forked human carapace for an hour or more – like so much dough for baking! One is supposed to say a prayer before this treatment – to what god, I wonder? Though I should pray ecumenically as necessary to survive. Q.E. is a devout Christian, but rises up when it is over like Venus from the foam – garbed only in her own magnificence – saying that she is reborn – resurrected!

So of course the dear, benevolent lady wishes the same for me, ruined as I am – oh yes, has begged me many times to try it – can you imagine? And her women are willing – she has two at once working on her – they smile and beckon to me seductively. Her Maj. insists that this rash procedure could heal me of my trouble – Lord! I am coward enough as you know, about letting anyone touch me – let alone strip me bare and maul & pummel! But even worse – absolutely – is the fact that I could not bear to fail her hopes & disappoint dear Emma. So I have no choice but to flee, make every excuse I can think of – and now must end this quickly, another ship leaving. But oh Beth, I am so very tired of the person I have been for so long – poor old crippled Julia and all her trouble, I need to shed her! Dear sister mine, can you possibly think of me from now on as plain & simple Fiona? It is one of my names already, after all, and you know Mum always liked to call me that…So, would you mind terribly? Tell me you don't, darling please.

Love ever from your own Julia/ Fiona

12

as lamps were lit at sunset in downtown Honolulu, while garland-decked native riders dashed on horseback up and down the boulevards. The Hawaiian women rode astride like the Amazons of old, with their long hair flying and their brilliantly colored riding skirts streaming out behind them. On the night of a royal reception, all the doors of the palace were thrown open. Torches blazed within and without; chairs and tables were carried to be placed under the trees; paper lanterns were set aglow in the gardens. At eight o'clock in the evening, dozens of eager citizens approached the palace on foot, or else descended in evening dress from their carriages.

The royal palace of the 1860s was a charming, unpretentious place, with an open, breezy aspect becoming to the Islands. It was simply constructed on classical lines out of coral blocks carved from the sea, with broad eaves descending from a sloping roof, and a balcony above that served as a lookout. Set like a jewel in the midst of its great park with magnificent flowers and foliage, the building served the royal family for all public purposes, while footpaths led to grass-thatched cottages that were hidden away for domestic use.

*

"There you are!" cried a jovial voice as David and Scott approached the palace entrance. The Bishop and his wife stood at the door as if this were their own home, and their duty to welcome all visitors. Mrs. Coldwell was resplendent in a white gown of silk brocade and a tiara of diamonds with an ostrich plume attached. "Come in, come in!" said His Lordship, without so much as a glance at David's old black suit. Bright-eyed and flushed, he seemed in the best of spirits, as if there had never been any trouble between them. Abandoning his wife at the door, he hastily led the two young deacons to the reception room, where the monarch of Hawaii sat enthroned.

King Lot Kamehameha was a splendid figure: a large, swarthy, swashbuckling sort of man with the look, David thought, of an amiable pirate. He wore no crown, merely a plain, dark uniform with a heraldic ribbon across his chest, yet it was clear at once that he was accustomed to rule, and meant to continue in that pleasant habit. In a quiet, intelligent way he asked Partridge and Wilkinson a number of questions about England, about their homes and families, their education, their hopes for the future. Then, after listening intently to their replies, he asked whether they cared either for fishing or for boating. Both answered immediately that they cared for whatever might please him. The King smiled, and invited them to visit him two days hence in his seaside cottage at Waikiki.

At that moment it came to David Wilkinson that he had seen this man somewhere before. But where? And when? It was a puzzle, a vexing one, that would trouble him for the rest of the evening. As they moved away from the throne, he heard Bishop Coldwell muttering beside him, "… never said a word about the Church!" And then David, who had never in his life been sick at sea, became gradually aware of a strange disturbance to his equilibrium. It seemed that the floor of the palace was rocking ever so gently beneath him, rising and falling in the wayward rhythms of the ocean. He himself, he realized, was swaying slightly as he walked; he was not imagining it. What was the meaning of this? Was his body confused, remembering the motion of the long voyage? Or was the palace itself actually moving? Perhaps a volcano was beginning to stir nearby?

Fashionably dressed people around him seemed undisturbed, and continued to greet one another, conversing in a Babel of accents and languages. The heat was extraordinary. Even in the soft tropical darkness, with a breeze moving through the palace, men of many nations were perspiring freely in stiff collars and woolen suits. The ladies, encased in corsets beneath their satins and velvets, presented faces that sometimes glistened wetly from the effort to speak or move. He watched as one dignified granddame took a handkerchief from her sleeve in the midst of polite conversation, and used it to dry her dripping forehead.

The Bishop was looking for his wife, and Scotty had drifted away, chatting easily, as usual, with everyone he met. Great silver epergnes had been placed on the side-tables, overflowing with unfamiliar fruits. Enormous platters held row after row of dainty sandwiches, and pastries of every tempting sort. Soon an invisible orchestra began to play a lively European tune, then stopped for a brief time as if to reconsider, then started up again. David had been thirsty all day, and was glad to see a liveried attendant dipping claret sangaree for the guests from a crystal bowl. Another was stationed nearby, serving sweet lemonade. He would have preferred a tall glass of water, but David chose lemonade. As he raised his cup, he heard loud laughter behind him, and turned to see a portly Englishman who immediately introduced himself as Henry Chatham, peering at him curiously.

"Ho ho!" Chatham shouted. "What on earth are you drinking? Lemonade? Come, laddie, you can do better than that. You're an Anglican clergyman, aren't you? Well then, don't drink like a damned Puritan. Where ever did you find that suit of yours – washed up on the beach, or did you inherit it?" A handsome half-caste girl in a red dress leaned affectionately on Chatham's arm, but he did not introduce her.

In his foghorn voice, Chatham now announced to all within hearing that he had sailed to Hawaii in his private yacht, which was the only civilized way to travel. What is more, he said, he had brought a splendid new flag for the Bishop of Hawaii, one bearing the coat-of-arms of the Church. "What do you think of that?" he asked David. Without waiting for an answer, he continued, "And your Bishop said to me 'Now that I have a flag,' he said, 'I shall want a yacht to go with it.' A yacht to go with it! What do you think of <u>that</u>, young man? He wants a yacht! Do you suppose Queen Emma will give him one?" The girl in the red dress leaned against Lord Henry shaking with laughter, and hid her face against his chest.

Through all this, David stood silent, looking about him in hopes of rescue or relief. In the distance he glimpsed a tall, bent figure wrapped in a paisley shawl. Julia Stuart? Fiona? He began to move in her direction, but was halted by the pleasant words, "Welcome to Honolulu!" Beside him now were two smiling clergymen, one white haired, with a long untidy beard and a ruddy complexion, the other young, clean-shaven and very pale. "You are Mr. Partridge?" said the elder.

"No sir, Wilkinson here. How do you do?"

"Russell and Riggs," said the elder, who was evidently Riggs. "Of the Anglican Mission. Here for the past three years. Just the two of us remaining."

"We are unspeakably glad to see you," said Russell. "The others have all left. Where is Mr. Partridge? We have prayed for your safe arrival. Father Riggs must be on his way home to London soon, and I shall follow him as soon as possible."

Riggs stroked his beard. "Wilkinson, is it? Well then, keep in good health, young man. That above all. Honolulu has a way of making men old before their time. Stay out of the sun – that is my recommendation. And be advised that the ocean is treacherous here. Bathing in Hawaiian waters is not wise. Sharks, you see, and poisonous jellyfish. All sorts of creatures you don't want to meet. And don't spend your money traveling to the outer islands – Maui and so forth. Nothing to see out there – nothing but more of the same. Especially to be avoided is the Big Island, so-called, where there is a nasty brute of a volcano, a devilish big hole in the ground. I saw it once. You don't want to be there when it erupts. Best to stay here in town and live quietly. Do your best for the heathen, of course, but make it a habit to take naps during the heat of the day. Study your scriptures and write your sermons at night. Have you brought a mosquito net? You'll need one."

"Philip! You will frighten him away," chided the younger.

"Ah!" said Riggs, "Not my intention. Good sir, I apologize. Very well, consider instead, if you will, the new cathedral. Not yet built, of course, but it will be splendid, splendid! We Anglicans are forced to worship now in a wretched place, no better than a country barn. But you may judge for yourself how grand the new structure will be when I tell you that the stone for its adornment alone has arrived from England, and it cost no less than £3,000. Pounds sterling, that is! Far more valuable than the American dollar."

"Yes," said Russell. "And lovely stone it is. But it turns out there was no money here to pay the import dues. So the stone in question is put away now in a warehouse and cannot be used."

In response, David intended to say something polite about English stone, or else something much less polite about the cost of it. Instead, he heard himself say, "Actually, I am thinking of going on to Japan." A sudden silence followed. The two priests stared at him in astonishment, as he stood blinking, slightly off-balance, holding a cup of warm lemonade. Elves, or pixies perhaps, must be in charge of a man's life at such times; the guardian angel has been caught napping. Until that moment, David Wilkinson had never thought of going to Japan. He had no reason to go to Japan. Also, he knew that a great number of Christian missionaries had been crucified there, after trying to win converts. David had no interest whatever in being crucified. In fact, he began at that moment to wonder in all seriousness who he was, and what on earth he was doing here. What indeed? And Miss Julia Stuart, where was she? And Samuel Clemens? And the King? That familiar face, those familiar, bulky shoulders! *Where have I seen him before?*

"Excuse me, sir," said a gentle voice nearby, in a strong German accent. "Did you say that you go to Japan? My name is Hillebrand. How do you do?" A small gray person stood beside him, shyly peering through his spectacles: this was William Hillebrand, chief physician at the Queen's hospital, a learned botanist, and a member of the King's privy council. "Japan!" he was saying. "Soon myself I shall go there, for the recruiting of the plantation labor. In China I have already done the same. I should be pleased to have a clergyman to help me, for the rights of the working man." David murmured that they should talk more on the subject soon. But other introductions followed, for it seemed that Hillebrand knew everyone present, and that they all knew and respected him. David's journal devoted several pages the following day to a newcomer's first impressions of that company:

Theophilus Davies: from Liverpool. Keen-eyed, spirited. Tall forehead, short chin with whiskers. Much involved w. Church. Said to be merchant of great skill.

Wm. Green: British Consul. Amateur scientist, business man, experimental planter (sugar cane) on Kona Coast. Says poor soil there & not enough rain. Going over soon to see crops, take volcano measurements.

Archibald Cleghorn: Scottish, Pres. of Queen's Hospital, Park Commissioner, several Boards & civic Orgs. Close friend of royals. Here since age 16.

Charles Bishop: (banker, not clergy: American). Member of King's Council. Orphaned, left home at 15. Sat on high stool doing ledgers same age I did. Married H'waiian princess, Bernice Pauahi (descendant of Kamehameha I). She – kind & lovely lady.

Chun Afong: Born China, here since 1840s. Large family, many daughters. Sells fine silks, brocades. Operating ships Hawaii to China + back. Partner in several plantations – sugar, coffee, etc.

Samuel Damon: American, intelligent, outspoken. Strict missionary party man, but also polite, fair-minded – actually welcomed me. Editor & pub. of "The Friend."(seamen's journal), Chaplain at Bethel Church, Honolulu. Wife Julia.

When a clock struck ten, Samuel Damon and David were speaking privately at a small table in the garden. At the sound of the last chime, Damon stood and remarked that it was time for him to leave, for now the dancing would begin; of this, he and his party unfortunately could not approve. David was astonished. What was coming next, Damon explained, was a *quadrille*, cousin to the minuet. This, David knew, meant that some of the guests were about to face one another and touch hands from time to time in the course of bowing, curtseying, and moving gracefully about to the accompaniment of some extremely formal and stately music. To David's amazement, the entire American missionary party rose up now and began to stream as if in panic away from the palace. Puritans by the dozens, fleeing from the sight of a genteel dance and the sound of decorous music!! Years later, David was still unable to understand it. After all, was the first miracle of Jesus not performed at a Jewish wedding? And was no one dancing there?

He was disappointed to lose the intelligent companionship of Samuel Damon, who had been particularly courteous to him. David liked a vigorous country reel well enough, but he was not so fond of mincing and prancing about in the antique European manner. He decided to walk for a time alone in the garden, and then, as he glanced back into the open palace, he caught a glimpse of the Hawaiian king still seated on his throne. The monarch was leaning forward now, with a shadow fallen on his forehead that looked at first rather like the brim of a hat. In a thunderclap it came to David where he had seen the man before. This was the person he had observed when they first arrived in the harbor: the burly brown Hawaiian sitting on a barrel, fishing from the pier.

The air was cooler under the trees, and the grass was velvet-soft as he wandered slowly about, wishing that he might abandon dignity and go barefoot. Feeling somehow lighter than usual, and still not quite sure of his balance, David began to notice that the night sky over these Islands was luminous in an unfamiliar way. Evidently, he must learn a new heaven now, as well as a new earth. The stars here did not twinkle or glow in the firmament; they burned and flamed wondrously, mysteriously, as if an enchanted orchard was offering down its fruits. The moon had risen almost full, and he saw that it too was different here: not a silver disk lying flat against the sky, but a mighty being, sculptured and rounded, a world unto itself, suspended in the vacancy of space. Vacancy? He had never thought it so before. Now he understood fully for the first time that he was standing on a spinning orb in the midst of black, enormous emptiness; and he felt that he was a frail and paltry, vulnerable thing.

"What am I doing here?" he asked himself. "Why did I come to this place? And how ever did I come into this world that is so vast and curious, so wholly incomprehensible?" In another moment, he allowed himself to wonder whether there was any God, whether Jesus of Nazareth had really lived and died, whether Christianity had any truth in it, whether human life itself had any meaning. Had Darwin been right after all, in the book he had published when David was a schoolboy? They had scorned it then. Samuel Wilberforce himself had attacked it brilliantly in public debate, but the general opinion was that he had lost that argument. Perhaps we had all lost some treasured illusions that day. Were we, David asked himself, after all is said and done, merely clever animals in human finery? Was he even now a poor sort of whimsical-clerical ape or baboon staring up at the moon – not by God's grace, but by the whims and vagaries of Natural Selection?

The low, insinuating laughter of a woman sounded nearby. A quick patter of footsteps brought into view the girl in the red dress, closely followed by the stout, perspiring figure of Lord Henry Chatham. Both were laughing, and they took no notice of David. When they had passed by, he stood where he was and listened. It seemed suddenly now that all the shrubbery around him was filled with whispers, that the scented silence of the night was interrupted by the crackling of twigs, the rustling of leaves, petals and branches. He began to understand that there were many other people in this garden, and that their purpose here might be quite different from his own.

Enough! he thought. *Enough! This is all a waste, a fraud, a mockery. It has nothing to do with my faith, my soul, my dreams, my hopes and sacred intentions. I cannot stay here! I'll go to Japan! I'll do it! Hillebrand will surely let me accompany him!* Youth is wonderful this way; decisions are made with so little trouble. He did not even stop for the parting courtesies that night, but walked directly from the royal garden to Fort Street, where he began to sort his belongings. Most he would leave for Scotty, bringing only the bare necessities: a change or two of clothing, a few books and medical supplies. Hillebrand would surely provide his passage, and after serving him for a time, David would be on his own, free to seek either his salvation in good works, or his wretched undoing.

Was he moon-struck? Land-sick? Temporarily insane? He would never know, for as he was searching through his luggage, he came across an envelope that his mother had given him as he left home. "Take care of this, but don't open it," she begged him, "until you are safely there. Promise me!" He opened the envelope now and found a bank note for the stunning amount of £500 folded inside a letter:

Dearest Boy,

The great joy of my life is now accomplisht, for I am able to help you with your dream of Capt. Cook and the monument you've always wanted. Oh, I know it will be beautiful. All England will thank you for it + I shall be so proud. This "bit of paper" by way of an offering comes from a lucky investment with Uncle George.

Davey, you worked so hard, you sacrificed so much for us those hard years, but all that is changed now, we have plenty with your help and George's management, so there is nothing left to wish for except to see you satisfied.

Darling, be well, be safe, be happy – and know each day that I am thinking of you and thanking you for your goodness. With all my heart I remain

always and ever

Your Loving Mama

He sat on the floor after reading this, torn between tears and laughter. It was not difficult to guess the story of that "lucky investment." On his last visit home, his mother had been frightened by a rumor she had heard – perhaps from Wilberforce himself – that the Hawaii Mission was close to bankruptcy. David had told her not to believe it. Later, he noticed that her rubies were missing from the buttery. When he asked, she said they were in London for mending of the chain. Something about her tone of voice, and the expression on her face, had made him wonder. His mother never lied – or did she?

The pelican, he thought, is said to tear its breast with its beak and feed its own blood to a hungry fledgling. Alas and alack and welladay! Farewell to the glorious sign and symbol of our noble heritage that came to us long before Cromwell's time.

13

B ethy dearest,

How I do miss you! I realize now more than ever that the remains of our little family – you and dear Hal before he fled to Australia – have been my only refuge & release all these years from that terrible – splendid & furious isolation! But you most of all darling – else it would have been for me one pit of darkness.

Here in the Islands, to the contrary, light & more light – almost too much of it – very little privacy indeed. People visit one another every day – one never knows, for ex. how many to luncheon or dinner. Gossip is ubiquitous – not unkind as a general rule, but incessant, reporting arrivals & departures, deaths – births – illnesses, recoveries, marriages & engagements—who has won or lost a fortune since yesterday, what liaisons or alliances impend. Beyond this, everyone sings, plays the piano, dances, rides on horseback – appears frequently at one church or another – and knows the intimate business of everyone else in town. Heavens! I should be terrified by it all – might have retreated by now to some silent cave in the mountains – if it were not for the Queen, who is so delicately sympathetic.

A fortnight ago, for ex. there was a great Reception at the Palace, where the current monarch is her late husband's brother. Obviously we were obliged to go, along with the rest of Honolulu society – especially to *"receive" with him because the King has no wife. I trembled & shook at the thought of evening dress – in this heat! – and strangers peering, expecting me to dance.*

That morning began the old blinding headache misery that turns things black with blazing wheels – followed as usual by violent pain & nausea. So of course, I expected the worst & thought I would be ruined for 2 days. But Emma herself brought me a splendid little brew made from some herbs in her garden & told me she did not want to go to the Palace either. Instead, we should rest until dark and then have a nice, quiet little party here at home.

Oh my dear – if only you could have been there, to witness that quiet little party! But first – how I wish we could have a gossip & a nestle just now – for there is one thing I simply cannot discuss with dear Emma. The dreadful little Bishop I mentioned earlier – he of the covetous eye – is to my amazement a frequent visitor to this household! Comes trotting up the path at all odd hours as if he owns it. Closets himself with the Queen – an hour passes – silence & murmuring – then he grimly departs & she goes back to her quarters looking like thunder. She tells me that he comes to provide spiritual counsel – I've already told you how devout she is, Church of England, and it seems that he, the miserable sycophant toad, fancies himself as her "Confessor."

Why "Confessor" darling I ask you – isn't that only for Papists? Not the approved Ch. of E. style at all. In fact, didn't they fight a war or two – and burn some rather nice people to death – over that issue, not long ago? So far away as this, of course, Coldwell is free of supervision & I wonder if the Q. does not know any better, out here a widow alone in the mid-Pacific. A sailor is supposed to have said there is no God west of Cape Horn – and at times I am tempted to believe it.

But you see I sense that His Toadship uses the sanctified spiritual thing to pry at her privacy – insinuate himself & try to manage her for his own purposes. If true, I am furious. If untrue, I am furious anyway, seeing her unhappy. It's maddening to find Christianity used so – a remark that may surprise you. But thank God we all left the church when we did – makes it possible for us at least to take it seriously.

It all reminds me rather of a chess game here, viz: the Bishop with a fistful of pawns from England – & his Knights lurking nearby with their warships. Emma has lost her King, poor soul – has Knights & pawns aplenty, for she is greatly loved by her people – but lacks a Castle. Brother-in-law has Castle – but not being properly pious, must make do without a Bishop.

So, like it or not, the royal two must cooperate in order to save themselves – from what? From seeing their country devoured, I suppose – if not by England, then by America, France or even Russia – who knows? There are even some Italians here in soldier's costumes, looking eager. Why oh why is it that people – even in supposedly civilized countries – must behave like thieves and cannibals? Why do they always want more of other people's substance – and still claim their own moral purity?

The American warship Lackawanna looms in the harbor now, "keeping an eye on things" – as their dreadful Captain Reynolds says – a crosseyed wretch of a man with the rudest manners. But the English have a man-o-war & the French have a corvette – keeping an eye on the Lackawanna! What next? Are we to be entertained with battle in the harbor? If so, I shall not watch – I'll read a really good book or else take a good long nap instead. My own opinion, since the Americans here appear to have the most money & energy – is that one day they'll simply tip the whole board over & put all the players into their pockets.

This tells you, I suppose dear, that there is not an overly large supply of _trust_ here at the highest levels. To an extent this affects me – I wonder myself at times what to say safely – which way to turn. Meantime, with politics intruding upon her religion, darling Emma must suffer – exactly what, I am not sure – have not lowered myself yet, to listening at keyholes.

But as for Emma's believing, as she obviously does – that England will support the Hawaiian monarchy at all costs, simply because it is a Monarchy – Hah! God in heaven! I sometimes want to say to her, dear lovely Emma – sweet Kaleleonalani – I lift my glass and I give you a toast to Flodden Field, where 12,000 of my kinsmen – nobles, princes, priests – and my cousin the learned King – were butchered like animals by these same savages – these English! And I give you the slaughter at Culloden & the things they did to our helpless survivors after that. By this time – even imagining it now, I grow warm – I may finish by lifting the bottle entire & after taking a goodly swig from it, stand up and sing all 6 verses of "Scots Wha Hae Wi' Wallace Bled!" Of course, I must learn to rise without help, before this can be effective.

Later: About the eyes – my sight cleared in twenty minutes that day

& no headache afterward - but a sense of bliss quite infinite. I must discover what herbs those were and try to keep some with me at all times. But Emma's party – I meant to tell you about that. I couldn't think at first who might be coming – not the King, to be sure, nor the Bishop either. They would be busy preening at the palace. So much the better! The King's Christian name – incidentally – is "Lot" which seems rather unpromising for any future wife he may have, but no sign of one as yet. In the old Hebrew system – of course – he would have been required to marry Queen Emma since she is his brother's widow. He is not bad really – and obviously likes me well enough – but makes me uneasy. Emma is not her usual self with him – tends to chatter nervously when he is near.

Still, I'm growing fond of her other friends – Archibald Cleghorn, a rather rough and hairy old dear from Edinburgh – actually, not so old as all that – & a shy little Prussian doctor named Hillebrand who knows everything about trees. Louise de Varigny, wife of the Foreign Minister, is also a sweetie – but I know they must all be going to the Palace. So who would come here? I needn't have worried! It was all very easy, beginning with the arrival of Emma's mother – her sweet Hawaiian one, Fanny – the Queen was raised by an English family – not unusual here, where babies are frequently passed along quite casually from one family to another. Can you imagine? No, of course not – but I am assured they don't mind. It's a custom here, they call it "ohana."

But a bevy of smiling natives came to the party – relatives of the Queen's, plus many of the young Hawaiian girls she cares for. The feasting was even more extensive than usual – including raw fish, very fresh & delicious – various succulencies wrapped in leaves – a very sweet cocoa nut jelly – and something they said was pig, although tasting to me more like roast goose. They cook it in a hole in the ground with hot stones, and I won't spoil your appetite with further details. "Long pig" I'm told actually refers to a cooked person, but I'm sure they don't do that here – so be a good girl and forget that I mentioned it. Twas all very festive – the prettiest blossoms everywhere – the fragrance of the night – torchlight in the garden – much noise & laughter, with little children tumbling merrily about.

Rather late in the evening, after the moon had risen, a troupe of dancers came in – 15 or 16 of them, both men and women – modestly clad & adorned with garlands plus bracelets & anklets of leaves and flowers Their music was made with rattling gourds & sticks plus 2 large drums & a small one made from a cocoa nut shell. Much chanting ensued, in a somewhat fierce & prophetic vein, though relatively cheerful, compared to what we hear from the monks at home. I of course did not understand the words – but it was all so expressive, I felt that did not matter. Truly it was a solemn, joyous thing - & indeed the hula (as Emma tells me) has been much misunderstood & maligned by American missionaries – who with prurient eyes see it only as lustful & lascivious. Which of course is a large reason for the Queen's lack of affection toward that country. It is, after all, her national dance.

The performers were arranged in 2 parallel lines at first on the grass, kneeling then stepping & swaying in nearly perfect rhythm, with a touching pathos in their gestures – infinitely fluid, graceful & eloquent movement, especially of the hands. After which, a change in mood & a faster tempo – followed within the hour by the most astounding & energetic feats of motion I have ever seen. Motion is not the right word for it – something essentially, electrically beyond that – a sort of controlled abandon. Wild & yearning, primeval with a suggestion of tremendous violence in it – yet orderly too – and more & more as the hour grew late, seasoned & spiced with laughter.

At first I shivered & doubted – then gave myself up to the pure enchantment of it. The two ranks of dancers finally faced one another & finished with a series of cries, thrusting motions & convolutions of the body that were considered hilarious. Great applause, glee triumphant & the children rolled on the grass, howling with delight! So transported by this time was I, that I might have rolled & howled along with them, had I felt limberer.

They are all so kind & careful with me! They had arranged a sort of litter for me to lie on – with piles of silken cushions, quite like a Rajah & 2 small boys plying fans against mosquitoes whenever they thought of it. The darling Queen had lent me a gown for the occasion – the loose & kindly sort that conceals the worst of Nature's blunders. It's said to be a pattern taken by American missionary wives from their own sensible, flannel nightgowns – so of course, a perfect shape for me – no need for a shawl to hide in, thank God in this heat. So exquisite is Emma's tact & hospitality, I'm under royal command to keep this costume & have it copied in different fabrics. This one is ever so pretty – simple & cool, made of white lawn with lace at the wrists & throat. I'll have one like it made for you, so you may startle all Edinburgh.

But dearest must close now – and I'll tuck in a small cutting from this week's <u>Mercantile Gazette</u>. It's a paper run by Americans, thus filled with scandal and prejudice, but always entertaining – and accurate often enough as to fact so that everyone reads it.

Love now and always from your Julia/F.C.

A Reader's Complaint

Mr. Editor: I was shocked and aggrieved when
walking near the home of Queen Emma last
evening to discover that hula was at the time taking
place on her premises, before a large audience of
natives. Even at its least objectionable, the hula is
a miserable relic of barbarism, not to be tolerated in
the presence of Christian people. But the testimony
of one native with whom I spoke revealed that this was
"the old-fashioned sort – very satisfying!" he said.
According to this person, who had been watching
from the shrubbery, the Dowager Queen was not only
a witness to the outrage, but had herself requested
it, and set it in operation. As an ornament of the
Anglican Church (which professes to be Christian)
surely the lady in question should set a different
example. If she pleads the frailty of a woman
widowed, where may I ask are her spiritual
advisors?

Pilgrym

PS - Darling, can you imagine the mentality – to produce this? After all that beauty! And the kindness, the bliss & the laughter – the happy little children. Oh what glorious stars we had that night! The moon when it came up was enormous – nearly full, not at all the usual pale Diana or Selene – but a great Hawaiian Goddess of a moon – milky & chaste & opulent as a woman about to give birth, a lavish, mothering presence so near & immense – a healing power so radiant – And I watched while she bathed us all in her silver fire that night, till I wondered whether we might arise from it to find ourselves immortal –

F. C.

14

"Fast and pray, Mr. Wilkinson," said the Bishop. "Fast and pray!" But the young man's face, usually so expressive, showed neither appropriate humility, nor gratitude, nor any sort of emotion this morning. *Sulking*, thought Coldwell. *Thinks he is such a fine fellow, he's not even thankful that he is about to be made priest.*

For those who had stayed on at the royal reception, it had been a long night. Toward the end of it, Lord Henry Chatham had invited a dozen or so of the palace guests to come for an early breakfast on his yacht. Coldwell was gratified to be included in their number, but the meal of hard boiled eggs with tinned snails and anchovies, coffee, Belgian chocolates and cognac had put his head into a vise and left his innards in full rebellion. He had arrived home at ten o'clock that morning to face a furious wife, whining children, disobedient or absent servants, and a knock on the door at eleven by his most irritating deacon. When he told David Wilkinson that he would be ordained priest on the following Sunday, the youth said simply "Yes, sir" and then began talking about money again. Some project of his own, some sort of legacy.

The Bishop forced a smile. "Legacy? For the Hawaiian Mission? Well, I suppose that is good news!"

"Yes, your Lordship. As to the terms of the bequest…"

"Don't tell me about it, show it to me."

"Actually, sir, the papers are already in the bank."

"Bank? What bank?"

"It happened, Your Lordship, that I had a conversation at the reception last evening with Mr. Charles Bishop. So I brought the note in question to him at nine o'clock this morning."

"Well, well," said the Bishop. "Gracious me. Charles' bank! That was enterprising of you. How much?"

"£500, sir."

Bishop Coldwell was so astounded that he thought his heart had stopped for a moment. In fact, it was still beating, though erratically. He took a deep breath and held it; that usually nudged it back into normal rhythm. Then he smiled and nodded approval at David, trying to remember whether he had taken his medicine the night before. What night? There had been no night for him – only hours of darkness, boredom, fatigue, anxiety – and not a sign in the end that Chatham would give a farthing to the Church. No, it had been a dreadful night, truly a sample of death – but now the sun was up, and here was resurrection.

"Five hundred pounds sterling, you said?" he asked, and the young man nodded. For the Bishop, such a windfall meant that he would not have to go begging again for months, or perhaps even years, to the hateful, miserly Gospel Society. This was nearly an entire year's salary for him. Mrs. Coldwell might stop her weeping and come with him to Switzerland in September.

"Of course, it will be some months before the funds are available?"

"No sir, I was told that I might have immediate credit."

"Immediate credit, I see. My goodness. And the donor? And the papers? I must have a look at those directly."

"Sir, they are also in the bank. The anonymous donor states that the entire amount is to be spent raising a church at Kealakekua in memory of Captain James Cook."

Now for a moment, the Bishop thought that he might

swoon. "Are you quite all right, sir?" David Wilkinson asked in alarm, but Coldwell recovered quickly, and made a valiant attempt to conceal his emotion. Some day, he promised himself – some day, he would bring this upstart to his knees and make him grovel. He wanted to say, "Wilkinson, I have the power to send you home in disgrace, and if I do, you will be ruined – no one will want you ever again." But he waited until the worst wave of rage had passed, and then gave a dry little laugh, imagining David Wilkinson lying lie face down in front of him on the stone floor of the church during his ordination ceremonies.

"So. Who is it this time?" he asked, when he found his voice. "I have already told you that I have no interest in a memorial for Captain Cook. Who is behind this? Is it Wilberforce? He cannot hurt me! Is it the GSBE? They are fools. Wilkinson, if you are in league with the Low Church party, you are very far out of your depth here, and you will regret it. And do not count on the favor of the new man at Lambeth Palace! Archbishop Archibald Tait is a wolf in sheep's clothing – a Scots Presbyterian through and through. No one will take him seriously. He will not prevail."

"Your Lordship, I am sorry. I don't understand you."

"Of course you understand me. Who is it? Who wants to usurp my authority?"

"No one, sir. The legacy is a simple gift, a personal matter. Quite naturally, people at home – people who care for me – wish to support my mission."

This was too much. The Bishop rose from his chair and shouted, "Your mission! Your mission! Perhaps you will not stop there, Mr. Wilkinson. Perhaps you wish to be in charge here, instead of me. Yes? Is that it? You'd like to be Bishop, would you? A fine thing! I suppose you would like to make the decisions that I must make? Bear the weight, suffer the anguish, deal with the vile Americans, the eternal gossip, all the cruel, lying misrepresentations? And the expense! The expense! Overwhelming. A man would have to be – to be – a Midas, and my wife is not well. Not well at all. And I don't sleep lately.

I was awake all last night. And my children, living like savages in this place."

"Please believe me, sir, I am truly sorry."

After this outburst, Coldwell sank into his chair again and closed his eyes. In another moment, his mouth fell open and his head rolled onto his shoulder. David looked away, and decided to make a close study of a map of Oahu that was framed on the wall. Later, after listening intently to make certain that his prelate was still breathing, he bent to pick up a small piece of newsprint that had fallen to the floor. It was an article torn from a recent issue of the Mercantile Gazette:

Rumor has it that the Anglican Bishop of Honolulu will be departing again soon, this time with family and furniture. A corresponding sigh of relief will be heard in many a pious household in our city! This unfortunate prelate has done no good to the cause of his church, with his lengthy absences from duty, as well as his conduct, while in residence here, which is so injudicious and impious that he has become a laughing-stock.

His outspoken scorn for faithful Christians who abhor his Papist, Romish ways has not endeared him even to members of his own party, or his own congregations, all the while rendering him obnoxious to Honolulu's leaders, and the great numbers of devout American Protestants who grace these shores. Yet do not rejoice too soon, Faithful Readers, for mark our words, soon England will send us a second Coldwell under another name freshly crowned and diademed, yet reeking of the same noxious political perfume. It may be done with a finer glove next time, but beneath the velvet cloth will be the same iron hand of Britain, reaching for a naval station in the Mid-Pacific.

David put the clipping carefully back on the Bishop's desk, and waited. After a few moments Coldwell opened his eyes and said, "Oh, Mr. Partridge, there you are. I must have dozed off."

"Wilkinson here, sir. I fear you are not well, Your Lordship.

Perhaps you ought to lie down and rest a while. Is there anything at all that I can do for you?"

"Get rid of those shoes."

"Yes, sir."

"Before next Sunday. They are a terrible sight. And have your hair cut, both of you. At least, Wilkinson, you generally appear to be clean. Tell the other chap to find a bath, a barber and a laundress. I have rarely seen two less promising candidates for the priesthood."

"Very well, Your Lordship."

Coldwell yawned, and then inspected his fingernails. David expected to be dismissed, but instead, in a low, melancholy voice Coldwell said to him, "Poor lad, you imagine that Hawaii is a delightful place, don't you? A simple place, a healthy and beautiful place, where people may please themselves and everyone can be happy. It is not. It is no such thing. There is evil here, believe me. Evil beyond every tree and every turning in the road. Evil awaits us all, and there are miasmas in the darkness here where Satan dwells. He is very active in these islands. Now you must go away and behave yourself, and I must rest and gather my forces for the morrow. Good day to you, young man. Good day. "

As David turned to leave, there was a sharp jolt under the floor, and a brief tremor shook the house. While the floor heaved and then settled beneath him, David thought,

So this is what an earthquake feels like! The framed map of Oahu rattled against the wall, but did not fall.

"That was an earthquake," said the Bishop. "A small one. You will experience far more violent agitations of the earth when I have sent you to Kealakekua. Volcanic eruptions too, no doubt. There are active volcanos on that island. Best be careful where you put that church."

*

David Wilkinson walked over a mile down the Nu'uanu Valley road with a painful stone in his shoe before becoming aware of it. He stopped at last under a towering breadfruit tree, sat down in the shade, took off his shoes and stockings, and shook them out. Then he stayed there, gazing at his feet that were pale and pinched and altogether unbeautiful, and he laughed from time to time because he was too sad to cry.

Soon a native family appeared, walking up the mountain together all decked with flowers, carrying baskets and calabashes, and obviously in a holiday mood. David had only a few dozen words of Hawaiian by now, and soon exhausted those, but the Hawaiians seemed to be grateful for his efforts; and they made it plain that they were glad to find such an odd duck sitting by the wayside. The sight of his ghastly white feet was of particular interest. Without knowing that they echoed the advice of an Anglican bishop, they urged him to get rid of his shoes, pointing to the bottoms of their own well-calloused Hawaiian feet. He agreed, and tossed his aged English brogues into the air, where one caught itself on a vine, and hung there like a piece of rotten fruit.

The Hawaiians laughed and cheered. Then old Grandpa insisted upon giving David a drink of water from his gourd, and five small brown children watched, entranced, while Granny smeared the sap from a stalk of aloe over his sunburned nose. Two beguiling young maidens devised an impromptu hat for him with a length of vine and a large leaf from the breadfruit tree, and put it on his head. Everyone laughed again. David could do nothing but submit, and to his considerable embarrassment, as they prepared to leave, he suddenly found himself the new owner of a fine water-gourd and a hempen bag filled with oranges. Turning his pockets out, he tried to show them that he had nothing to offer in return – only a Prayer Book, a handkerchief, and his father's watch. They were most interested in the Prayer Book until he made the watch chime for them; then the children clapped their hands and jumped for joy. Soon the smallest of them began climbing into his lap and putting their own garlands around his neck. He thought – *So, these are the terrors and miasmas of Hawaii?*

In the end he persuaded Granny to take his handkerchief,

which as usual was clean and folded, with his embroidered initials on it. Then the little group continued up the hill while he slowly ate the most exquisite orange he had ever tasted. Soon after that his eyes began to close. The heat by now was nearly overpowering. He stretched out under the tree, fell instantly into a deep sleep, and dreamed that he was traveling – a long journey over water that would not hold him up, so that he kept sinking below the surface, in danger of drowning. Then, after an incalculable time of darkness, he dreamed distinctly that he was the prophet Jonah, trapped in the belly of a whale that had bones like flying buttresses, and skin that was curiously made of soft, sea-worn stained glass.

*

"Mr. Wilkinson!" He awoke not knowing where he was, hearing someone calling in a familiar voice, "Is that you, David?" A small cabriolet had stopped in the road beside him. Its liveried driver had already dismounted, and was tending a stamping, blowing team of handsome black horses. From the seat of the little vehicle, which was decorated with a coat-of-arms on its door, a rosy face was leaning out. It was Julia Stuart – or rather, Fiona Cameron, glowing under a crown of pink blossoms, with a nose nearly as sunburnt as his own. Beside her sat Queen Emma, and both ladies were in white, wearing the flowing Hawaiian gowns that resemble an Englishwoman's nightdress. He scrambled to his feet and ran to the carriage without stopping to think of his own appearance, barefoot, bedecked and disheveled as he was.

Fiona greeted him without a hint of surprise or dismay. "This is my friend," she told her companion. "The gentleman who was so kind to me on the ship. Emma dear, may I present the Reverend David Wilkinson?"

"Your Majesty!" said David, as he doffed his leaf and bowed.

Queen Emma, even more beautiful than in her photograph, was inspecting him somewhat curiously, but apparently without disapproval. Then she said with a merry smile, "Yes, of course, Mr. Wilkinson! You were at St. Columba's in Canterbury. I am happy to see that you are making yourself at home in my country."

"Yes Ma'am," said David, feeling like a thorough fool.

"Where are your shoes?" Fiona asked.

"Actually," he replied, "the Bishop told me to get rid of them."

"And you still obey him, of course, in all things?"

"*Deus vult.* But where have you been? I looked for you – for both of you – last evening at the palace."

"I thought it best," said the Queen, "that we stay quietly at home. We are going now to my summer house on the mountain, where it is cooler. Miss Cameron has been recovering from the fatigue of the voyage. Until the trade winds return, I am afraid that the air of Honolulu will not be salubrious."

He wondered how the two had met, and thought how very British the Queen seemed in her own country. In her photograph she had seemed far more foreign and exotic. "Well, I am overcome," he said, still studying the two faces, one dusky, one bright. The pleasure of the encounter was so keen as to be disturbing. Fiona had turned away so that he saw her now only in profile, but the Queen, who faced him, took out a small ivory fan, and began to flutter it under her chin.

"This is something by way of a small miracle," he said at last. "I mean, that you are here just now, both of you. That you have come by this road at this very moment. That is to say," he concluded lamely, "I might not have seen you passing by."

"God is kind," said Queen Emma.

*

The little cabriolet soon continued on its way up the valley, but only after the Queen had invited David to visit her on the Isle of Kauai. "My house there is simple," said Her Majesty. "But it offers peace and repose. Shoes, for example, are not required in that setting. In fact, Mr. Wilkinson, I insist that you come to us. I shall send the Bishop a note about it immediately! You could do so much good for the people of that Island. Many children there have been waiting to be baptized. Will you come?"

"Of course I will, Ma'am," he said.

"If you do," said Fiona, "I shall be pleased."

As soon as they were out of sight, he threw off his foliage and ran on bare feet all the way back to Honolulu. When he arrived at the inn, he found Scott sweating and groaning on his bed like the victim of a beating. He and the Bishop, he said, had seen the dawn from the deck of Lord Henry's yacht *Amaryllis*, where Scotty claimed there was nothing on board for a thirsty man to drink except champagne.

David showed him no pity, but leaned down and shouted directly into his ear, "FAST AND PRAY, MR. PARTRIDGE – FAST AND PRAY!" and then emptied the water-gourd over his head.

Scotty gasped. "Stop it, you idiot!"

"Good news, you clown. On your feet! Look sharp! Next Sunday you are to be made Archbishop!"

"Go away, Wilks. Just vanish, will you please?"

"Archbishop of Polynesia, that is. Providing of course that you have your hair cut beforehand, and find a clean shirt."

*

The Bishop of Hawaii was resplendent, on the day of their ordination, in the most elaborate vestments that had appeared in any Anglican Church since the Reformation. "TRIUMPH OF ROMANISM!" declared the Mercantile Gazette. "PARISHIONERS SCANDALIZED!" And this was true enough, but neither Scott Partridge nor David Wilkinson cared much what the Bishop was wearing that day, so long as he could stand up and read the service. Side by side they lay face down on the floor, perspiring, while a dozen candles blazed at midday and the small, uncertain choir lifted its voice in song.

The little "pro-cathedral" was hot as an oven, and the air was stuporous with the fragrance of ginger, maile, and tuberose. There was a row of empty seats near the front where furious parishioners had departed immediately, outraged to see Bishop Coldwell in a cope and miter that would have been appropriate at the Vatican.

Unprepared as they were, after only a few weeks as deacons, and in a strange land far from home, it was a curiously bitter experience for the two young men. Scott Partridge found himself in tears at the crucial moment when Bishop Coldwell performed the laying-on-of-hands that was supposed to convey the powers of the Holy Spirit. David clenched his teeth when the Bishop touched him, and prayed for a vision. Somewhat to his surprise, he was granted one. Not of any transcendent insight or bliss, to be sure, but of his mother's tenderly smiling face, and then of his father, proudly beaming as he stood, carving knife in hand, before a large leg of mutton.

The two new priests celebrated their ordination Eucharist together and stayed for a brief reception outside the little church. Then they conducted private festivities with a bottle of good Spanish sherry and a long walk on the beach at Waikiki.

A few days after the ordination, Bishop Coldwell announced that he was going to Kauai to visit the Queen. Smiling broadly at David Wilkinson, he said that Her Majesty had implored him to stay with her for a fortnight so that he might baptize a number of local children. Then, before embarking with Lord Henry on the *Amaryllis*, he sent Scott Partridge to take charge of an abandoned mission on the Isle of Maui, and dispatched David to the Big Island of Hawaii's Kona Coast.

15

The only inter-island steamship was under repairs at the time, so that David found he must travel instead in a small, heavily overloaded commercial schooner. For two days and nights they sailed over stormy seas in strong southerly winds, tacking back and forth toward the bay where Captain Cook had landed nearly 100 years earlier. The other passengers appeared at first to be poor working folk, mainly either Hawaiian or Chinese. They all huddled on deck, the men with their tools and saddles, the women with their children, their chickens, their goats, and large, anonymous bundles of household goods. Then, to his great delight, David found William Green, the British Consul, amid the crowd. "But I had heard that you were going to Japan!" said Green.

"Other plans had been made for me."

Green gave him a sympathetic glance and said, "Ah, too bad. But I am sure you are needed here on the Big Island." He was on his way, he said, to make a survey of the famous lake of fire at Kilauea Volcano. Would David Wilkinson care to join his scientific party? David was grateful for the invitation, for he was curious about that "devilish big hole in the ground," and would have enjoyed helping with measurements. However, he was bound by duty to find a site for a mission.

The Consul was a faithful Anglican, who soon told David that he would gladly give a piece of his Kona land for the cause. "How much will you need?" he asked. David said that he thought an acre would do. "In that case, I'll give you two," said Green. "Have a look round while you are there and let me know which two you'd like." He was a delightful companion, and the two men talked freely together as if they were old friends. David soon learned from Green, among other things, that he had been pronouncing *Kealakekua* wrong all his life. This was a word, the consul explained, among many in the Hawaiian lexicon that must be coaxed gently out of its formidable appearance. "The language of the Islands," he said, "is like a woman, divinely mysterious. In its written form it threatens to lash and sting, but rightly spoken, its sounds are gentle and rhythmical as a ship in halcyon seas!"

As if in obedience to that description, the winds were suddenly stilled on the third night of their voyage. An old moon sank slowly in the west like a shard of ivory, as they drifted in perfect silence over the deeps. Without a breaking wave to be seen, the water was black and smooth as a lake of polished marble; only their wake disturbed its surface, sliding and whispering along behind them as it tossed its lacy froth into the dark. With the sea finally at peace, people and animals lay on deck in the postures of exhaustion, while the captain stood by the bowsprit, peering into the night. It was near morning when he sent a sailor swinging aloft with a spyglass. For many hours already David had kept his eyes on the distance, imagining from time to time that he saw a light ahead that was not dawn.

"Look! There she is!" cried William Green at last, and the two made their way to the rail together, staring at the surge of brilliance that had suddenly appeared. A scarlet glow touched the dark waters, while clouds of fiery vapor emerged into the sky above a vast mountain that lay directly ahead. "Huzzah!" cried Green. "We are fortunate, my friend! She is active tonight! There she is, Pele, the goddess of the volcano, stirring up a witch's brew for us!"

"Goddess! Witches brew!" David was astonished, and chided him, "I never thought I would hear a scientist speak so!"

Green laughed, and said lightly, "Manner of speech, Wilkinson. This is Hawaii, after all. When in Rome, do as the Romans do!"

"No, said David. "I shall do no such thing, neither here nor in Rome either.

Please, sir, when molten rock and gasses rise from natural causes, don't claim it as the work of a pagan goddess! Say rather that it is an act of God."

His new friend turned and asked rather solemnly, "You find no conflict then between the scientific and the religious views?"

"No indeed," said David calmly, forgetting for the moment how keen his distress had been over Darwin's findings. "God does what he likes, after all. If he chooses the realm of science in which to display his handiwork, should we object? Let us rather rejoice and sing praises! As for the argument with Darwin, why is one necessary?"

"How then do you reconcile the Book of Genesis with evolution?" Green asked.

"I don't," said David.

"Come now, what do you mean?" Green was both amused and surprised. But David said only, "People standing in different places at different times see things differently."

After a silence between them, Green remarked, "Pele as Goddess was perhaps not entirely correct. Ancestral spirit might have been closer to it. But David, be warned. You cannot take Pele away from the Hawaiian people. They won't stand for it." All around them now, passengers were stirring, gazing at the mountain ahead with awe and adoration. It was plain that they worshipped Madame Pele and all her works; David felt puzzled and increasingly saddened as he heard the name of the goddess on every side.

"They are saying in Honolulu," the Consul told him, "that you are a sensible fellow. A man of faith who also has an open, inquiring mind."

"Who is saying? Why should anyone speak of me?"

"Coconut telegraph," said Green. "In these parts, it is never still. Quite a puzzle, I grant you, but it is remarkably useful and efficient. You'll find that knowledge of you has arrived on this island long before you set foot on it. You dined out in Honolulu a few times, met some people, and preached two first-rate sermons. Therefore you are now famous throughout the archipelago!"

"Famous? No!"

"Oh yes indeed. Church folk and their neighbors over yonder in Kona will be saying tonight, "We hear this Wilkinson is a good chap, and now he's on his way over – be here any day. A man of the cloth with some plain horse-sense for a change.""

"Is that true? Are you serious?"

"I am. There are no secrets in these islands. And you're exactly what is wanted here: a Broad Churchman with a mind of his own. There has been far too much cold Puritan fanaticism from the American Protestants here, and far too much High Church, Anglo-Catholic lah-de-dah in our own, Anglican presence. The C. of E. is supposed to be Protestant, isn't it? I mean, wasn't that settled under good Queen Elizabeth quite some time ago? But for decades here in Hawaii there has been no end of political humbug on both sides. Politics should be left to sinners like me. Clergy should tend to religion!"

"Well, of course I thank you for your kind words. I am glad to be thought open-minded. But I must insist that my mind is not open to any flotsam and jetsam that may wash up on the tide." David might have said more, but was interrupted here by the sound of drums nearby on the ship. Beginning softly, they quickly built to a tumult. Then came an unearthly shriek, in a woman's high, thrilling voice. The drums stopped abruptly at the sound of it; then from the shadows came an outpouring of chanted, wailing, keening syllables in the same uncanny tones as the earlier cry. David searched the crowded dark for its source, unsuccessfully. Yet its wild, passionate quality of command was such that no one moved or spoke, and even the drums were silent while it lasted.

William Green whispered to him that this was a *mele*: a chant that had been treasured by generations of Hawaiians. Indeed, David thought, it was wondrously beautiful and strange, but when he later saw the words translated, he understood that this was an epic poem, much like those that were composed in Europe and Britain at the dawn of his own history. It was about the goddess Pele, and it began:

> *MaiKahiki ka wahine, o Pele,*
> *Mai ka aina i Pola-pola,*
> *Mai Kai punohu ula a Kane,*
> *Mai ke ao lalapa i ka lani,*
> *Mai ka opua lapa i Kahiki…*

> The meaning of which in English is:
> *From Tahiti came the woman, Pele,*
> *From the land of Bora Bora,*
> *From the red cloud of Kane,*
> *Cloud blazing in the heavens,*
> *Fiery cloud-pile in Tahiti…&c*

This *mele,* said Green, relates an essential story about the goddess, or ancestral spirit, fleeing from her birthplace in Tahiti, and coming after many strange adventures to her present home in the "lake of fire" of Kilauea Volcano. Here, on the Big Island, she lives in especially intimate relation to the Hawaiian people. Pele is understood to be both Destroyer and Creator; therefore she is both dreaded and adored. When she is angry or troubled, tradition says, Pele shakes the earth, sending forth blazing lava-flows that destroy forests and meadows, and people, their homes, and entire villages. Later, however, after the lava cools, it softens and crumbles under the annealing influence of sun and rain, and is transformed into new land. And land – *aina* – is the heart's blood of the Hawaiian people.

In later years David Wilkinson heard many of the Hawaiians' songs and legends, and he often witnessed their drumming, their chanting and their dancing, both sacred and profane. But never again after that night at sea was he so wholly captivated by the passion of the Hawaiian soul. On that dark night the very flame of the mountain seemed to cry out to him like a living creature, flinging its echoes down to the ocean and up into the turbulent sky. The human voice that continued unabated seemed to him a force of Nature, both tragic and triumphant in its beauty.

"Thank God for art!" he said as the song ended. "Whatever the words may be, I know a Psalm of Praise when I hear one!"

"Actually," Green replied, "in this Pele myth of theirs they may be onto something perfectly scientific. The origin of their people in the South Seas, for example – and the source of their land in volcanic activity."

"WOMAN, BE STILL!" The hoarse cry came from a place near the center of the ship, where a tall figure stood wrapped in a cape with a cowl, so that his features were indistinguishable. The chanter of the mele looked up at him but did not move. By the light of the lantern beside her, it could be seen that she was elderly and very large, with a flowing mane of silver hair. When she rose to her feet, it was only with considerable help from her companions. Once upright, she glanced at the hooded figure with contempt, and then leaned forward and deliberately spat on the deck at his feet.

"JEZEBEL!" he howled at her. The woman gave a great whooping laugh, and moved slowly away while the man shouted, "WOMAN BE CURSED! THE LORD GOD OF HOST sees your wickedness! BOW DOWN, AND HEAR THE WORDS OF HIS GREATEST PROPHET!"

"Oh dear," said William Green.

"Who is this? David asked him. "Where did he come from?"

"Don't know," said Green. "But I have seen him before. His name is something outlandish that I have forgotten." The hooded man had launched a feverish harangue by now, a patchwork of Hawaiian legends forcibly wedded to the Book of Revelation. Green whispered, "The Mad Prophet, they call him. Has something of a following in the outer islands, I'm sorry to say." Suddenly a brilliant fork of lightning pierced the dark, and the crowd on deck uttered groans of dismay. Cries of terror accompanied a second strike so powerful that it lit up the entire night sky, revealing the ship's position. They were nearing their destination now, having entered a dark bay with steep cliffs to one side of it, and white-crested waves on the other, dashing toward shore. The captain shouted commands, and the thunder that followed those terrible strokes of lightning was mingled, first with the pounding of footsteps on deck, and then with the grim rattle and clang of the anchor chain as it descended into Kealakekua Bay.

They had arrived at last in the place of David's boyhood dreams, but he could not reflect on that happy fact, for the hooded man was shrieking about hell and damnation, and little children were beginning to cry. A heavy rain came suddenly pelting down, followed by a gust of cold wind that swirled about the ship, lifting the mainsail that had already been lowered and partially furled.

"All hail!" cried the furious voice again. "All hail to the Lord God of Hosts! Death to Pele and all of her followers! The end of the world is near! You foolish people, Armageddon is upon you! Listen! Very soon you shall know who I am, and you shall submit your bodies and souls to me when fire falls from the sky and the mountains are thrown down into the sea! Madame Pele is the goddess of sinners! Leave her tonight, come to me and be saved. I tell you, very soon seven trumpets will sound, and all who do not follow me then and walk on the water beside me will be tormented for a thousand years. I am the greatest of all Prophets! Submit! Submit to me and be saved!"

"What's all this in aid of?" asked Green.

"Insanity," said David.

"He's quoting Scripture, isn't he?"

"Garbled, yes. Dismembered. The man is vicious." To his surprise, David was suddenly very angry. Pele or no Pele, this madman had no right to spew poison over his fellow human beings, especially in a place so hallowed by cherished memory. Impulsively, he picked up a nearby lantern, climbed up on a bench and shouted, "No! No!! Do not listen to him! Let me speak!"

The hooded man fell silent. Men, women and children turned toward David, to hear what he would say. He had no idea at the moment what that might be. He drew a deep, anxious breath, and then his eyes fastened on the figure of a small, pigtailed Chinaman who sat nearby, apparently quite unafraid, and gazing at him with perfect serenity. David continued to watch the Chinese man as he spoke.

"Listen, good people!" he said. "Peace! Peace be with you! We are safe now. Do not be afraid! We have come to our destination, we are safely at anchor. Our God is with us, now and always! Do not listen to this foolish man who says he is a great prophet. He is not. The servants of our God come to help us, not to frighten and torment. Be of good courage, be of good faith! Comfort one another, comfort the little children. The worst of the storm has passed, and morning will come, and the sun will rise again, so that we may see once more the beautiful world He has given us to live in. In the name of the Father, and the Son and the Holy Ghost, Amen."

The people were quieted by his words, and the Chinese man's face wore a wide smile of appreciation as David climbed down from his bench. Meantime the "prophet" stood with his arms folded, gazing intently at the shore. A little later, just before dawn, William Green saw him signaling someone on shore with a light, and soon after that he slipped away from the ship in a silent canoe.

"Well done!" said Green, when the people had responded to David and the storm had passed out to sea. "After that little episode, the rest of your ministry here should be easy!"

"I doubt it," David replied. "In fact, I begin to suspect that I may have more trouble here than I have ever imagined." He felt strangely shocked by the bizarre experience. It was unlike him to put himself forward in such a commanding way, and he refused to believe that the miserable Bishop's laying-on-of-hands had given him some mysterious new power. Yet it was clear to him that the warm smiles and approving nods of the unknown Chinese traveler had encouraged him to speak so boldly. It was more than a year later when he discovered that Chin Wong Lo had not understood a word that he said.

16

3 May - Mauna Kilohana, Kauai

Dearest Beth –

I could not believe the post, only 7 weeks to Honolulu from Edinburgh! Your letter flew to my hands like a celebration of the silver thread between us, that knows naught of distance or time. Thank you 1,000 times for your news, all good thank heaven. Now for mine, though I really must learn somehow to write as small & neat as you. We've come to this nearby isle called Kauai for a restful fortnight & I've been wanting to tell you of a rather strange evening – just before leaving Honolulu – with the young man from the ship, David Wilkinson.

But first to your questions. The population of Honolulu is about 13,500 – some 10,500 being native Hawaiians & several hundreds more "half caste". There are 300+ Chinese men here (& only a dozen women from that country, which must be trying) and the rest are generally lumped together as "foreigners" – Europeans, Americans etc. of every sort & condition – approx. 3 males to every 1 female in this lot. The native population – yes – is still dying out in these Islands but the reasons why are somewhat mysterious. The obvious being – as you say – loathsome diseases brought in by whalers, traders etc. to an innocent people. However, there are also some unhealthy habits of the Hawaiians themselves, and underlying all, a pitiable woundedness of the soul or spirit – a melancholy *tending to sicken the strongest – as we know only too well, for we saw it among our own Highlanders, after the wars & the cursed "Clearances."*

Yet I've also heard some natives say that life was even harder before white men came. Constant wars among their clans – the Hwn. peasants had no rights – no freedom – were used by the "ali'i" (chiefs & nobles) as slave labor, brutally slain at the least whim or transgression. Many were sacrificed to idols. A large class of outcasts, literally untouchable – in a caste system so rigid that the ordinary British snob – by comparison – would seem a radical democrat. Then too, thousands of these poor souls perished recently when sent by their chiefs to the frigid mountains – without warm clothing – to bring down sandalwood for the China trade. Tremendous profit for the ali'i of course – but the workers suffered terribly & now there is almost no sandalwood left in the Islands.

Also, the <u>kapu</u> (same as taboo) such as: if you failed to prostrate yourself – face down on the ground whenever a chief came near – you had your brains bashed out on the spot! And many kapus especially demeaning to women. For ex., making them eat separately, denied the best foods – bananas, cocoa nuts, pork, etc. One might think it nice that men did all the cooking – but this, too, used as a means of control. Plus ça change, darling, plus c'est la même chose. So much for the Noble Savage! It's clear to me that he was no better than our own ancestors in the Dark Ages – or the English quite a bit more recently.

The book you gave me – on Hawaii, by Manley Hopkins – no, I'm sorry, I couldn't finish it. Tried my best, but these bloody Englishmen do irk me so with their swollen opinions about places they have never seen – yet obviously long to gobble up for their blasted Empire. I'm told that Hopkins heads a business firm in London, as well as being Chargé d'Affaires for Hawaii – so cannot be a total idiot, but I do darkly suspect him of being a villain. His brother Charles was in the Isles for a time noodling around – was admired for his charm, but not for his character. Joined the gov't for a time – as does everyone, it seems, out here who can read or write. Then escorted Queen Emma to London & made a terrible ass of himself. Of course, she would never say such a thing – she is much too kind – but others did & word came back – as it always does, in these islands..

As for David Wilkinson, why such a man has come out here as a missionary I can't fathom. I think I told you – he was the youth who tapped at my door each morning and evening during that storm at sea – to be certain I was still among the living. And did in a quiet way so many other kindnesses, to me and others. He is said to have preached a marvelous sermon (which surely the Bsp. should have done) upon his ordination – I was sorry to miss it, was feeling "dreſful poorly"that day. Emma thinks highly of D and what is more surprising, becomes quite girlishly gay – even rather flirtatious – in his presence. That startled me at first – it's so unlike her. But such, I suppose, is the privilege of age and station.

She told me in some excitement before he arrived that we were dining "tête à tête" – though knowing her habits I thought that meant about a dozen! This time only four of us, seated on the verandah at a small round table– the Queen and myself, Mr. Wilkinson & his friend Partridge, also a priest newly ordained – those two on their way to the Outer Islands, not to say Outer Darkness. (Both of them, I'm told, out of favor with this dreadful Bishop.)

The menu was European this time: consommé, tongue en croute w. various savories – breast of chicken, tiny, fresh garden peas & carrots in a mint sauce – green salad with herbs– raspberry sorbet &. petit fours – chilled slices of "mountain apples" deliciously served with cheese & biscuits, then demi-tasses. I give you the whole bank & solicitor 'counting of it, darling – so you'll see I am in no danger of starving, out here among the pirates and the cannibals. Actually, I am in danger of getting fat.

"I am dazzled," said David – I thought he meant the glory of provender. But no, he was looking at the Queen – and indeed she was looking lovely. Then he turned to me and – courteously enough, said the same thing, after which the following:

David: I am glad to see you, but sorry not to have seen you in church.

Myself: I am sorry, but church is not one of my habits.

Q.E.: Gentlemen, we shall redress that, I trust.

Partridge: David, shall I tell the story about the beautiful nun who lost all her habits?

David: No, Mr. Partridge, you shall not.

Q.E.: But it sounds amusing, David. If it is not a _very_ naughty story I should like to hear it.

Partridge: It's a delightful story, Ma'am – but in the presence of a man like

Bishop Wilkinson here, memory fails me. (Laughter)

Now Bethy, you and I might smile a little – but laugh aloud at such nonsense? Never. Yet this was the sort of thing we laughed at uproariously – until I began to wonder if the miserable "Pilgrim" might be lurking, to see if we were having another hula! It was a hula sort of mood, I suppose – exuberant to the point of being giddy. All this, mind you, on lemonade, water and a single glass of champagne – Q. Emma is quite abstemious.

Then much talk of the Islands – David on his way to Kona to build a new church – Scott Partridge to Lahaina, to take on a ruined mission that sounded ghastly. At first I behaved myself beautifully – truly, I did – stayed quiet as a mouse while the other three spoke of their "purer" religion, which must be pressed upon all the foreigners here, evidently, as well as the natives.

By this time the mood had shifted – little gaps in the conversation, filled by the "chuck-chuck" of tiny lizards running up and down the white walls beside us.

They are my friends & allies – they eat mosquitoes. Finally I asked David Wilkinson what it was – truly, honestly, precisely – that had brought him all the way from Yorkshire to the mid-Pacific. He hesitated for quite a time before responding. I turned away thinking I heard a footfall in the garden – but it was nothing – and turned back after a full quarter of a minute, only to see the silent Mr. Wilkinson still struggling. A strange thing happened then, Bethy – I began to hear his thought as clearly as if he was speaking it – exactly as I do so often with you. "I want to make a stand against the world's evil" was what I heard, and thought – oh my! This man will soon be in serious trouble!

His appearance is a part of the mystery I suppose, because there is nothing modern about his features. He has the long, oval face of the old Norman effigies – you know the ones – lying in cold stone under their shields in cathedrals. But in his case the lines of the nose & jaw are so perfectly chiseled as to be somehow annoying. I suppose one wonders how fragile he is – what would happen, for ex. if a horse stepped on that face. As you see, I am still rude as ever, at least in my thoughts.

But such a man would be hateful if he flaunted his beauty – while D. is saved by the fact that he obviously has no interest in his appearance at all – & no idea how extraordinary it is. When he finally spoke, he said "Perhaps it is connected with a family tradition, but I have always wanted *to be of service. There is, I think, a work to be done in Hawaii. A quiet work — a modest work — a work that may be simple, even tedious. Nevertheless it partakes of eternity, for it is the effort of a mere mortal to bring soul out of self — truth out of falsehood — good out of evil — and all by way of spending and being spent for Christ."*

I felt tears springing to my eyes — wanted to speak but could not find voice. The Queen was smiling her fond approval — tapped his wrist with her little fan & said, "But there is more to this story. Mr. Wilkinson has come to us because of the English explorer, Captain Cook. Am I right, David? Not for us, for Cook! And now he will abandon us — leave us comfortless here — while he goes off to the Big Island to build a monument for his hero. Is that not the truth?"

D: Your Majesty, that is a part of it, yes.

Scott: Admit it, David. Your desire to build that church has been an obsession.

D: An obsession? No, although it is a fact that we all do what we must. However, Cook was a great man and a devout Christian. His wretched end in these islands has haunted me for years.

Q,E: We all do what we must? I suppose so. It is true that we did kill your Captain Cook. But despite the rumors abroad, we did not eat him.

After this curious remark, we all fell silent. There were moths at the candles & in the air around us the fiercely sweet — almost hypnotic — odor of night-blooming jasmine. Of most flowers you may say there is a fragrance, but for this one, the word is not strong enough. It came to me that this was the first time I had heard the Queen speak of herself simply as Hawaiian — "We killed your Captain Cook" — and not as part English, which of course she is. Depths beyond depths of her character were suddenly revealed & I saw an enigma spread before me, with vast darkened landscapes — unfamiliar colors bleeding & melting into one another — like the twilight reflections in a moat.

David Wilkinson was gravely studying her, as if she had suddenly become ill, or else hurt somehow. Then he smiled, and asked if he might go with her to thank the chef who had provided us with such a splendid dinner. Off they went together to the kitchen — in another separate building — while Scott Partridge entertained me. Or rather, while we scratched at one another, but only lightly. He is a charmer and a rascal —

insisted that he did not remember the story about the nun. Liar! So I was given another joke instead – which of course I forgot right away – & then he spoke of his devotion to his father, and his unbounded love & admiration for David Wilkinson. "David is a far stronger character than I," said Scott. "He is all that I am not. Valiant – conscientious – works like a fiend. One day he will make bishop."

"God forbid," said I, "a fiendish bishop!"

"It does happen," said he.

"But why should David Wilkinson want any such thing?"

Scott was surprised & said rather huffily – Bishops did whatever they liked & had to be obeyed. They had far less work to do & were paid monstrous amounts of money. Also, plenty of them got to sit in the House of Lords even if they were not gentlemen! Albert Coldwell, who definitely was not, had a jolly old time of it dashing about with the yachting crowd – but did I understand that he & David were likely to starve, here in Hawaii? The Church here, he said was frightfully poor – close to collapse.

I told him I'd always thought poverty came into priestly vows somewhere. What, no mention of it? Only chastity & obedience?

"Not those either," he said. "Just a general promise of purity. Nothing a gentleman wouldn't do –"

"Hah!" said I & burst into rude laughter – he pretended not to see what was funny. Then I told him I seemed to remember – that once long ago they had to kidnap a man of the cloth and torture him a bit before he'd agree to become a bishop? Scott was doubtful. "I've heard it. An old story, who knows whether it is true? Perhaps one of the Desert Fathers – second century or so. People were different then." Still, he said, I had a point. He never knew what Wilks was going to do. "He might just find some highly principled objection – & if it came to that, he'd stand up to torture very well. I should give in immediately."

"But what about Captain Cook? Did the natives devour him or not?"

"Haven't the foggiest," he said. "Does it matter?"

That roused my wrath & I told him everything matters. People remember – yes, they do – even things they think they have forgotten. And I told him the old motto from our Breton line – <u>What blood has forgot, bone remembers</u>. His eyes grew large & he muttered about uncanny Celts as he poured the last of the champagne into our two glasses. I was suddenly exhausted. He took a little silver flask from his pocket. "Even nicer with a nip of brandy in it," he said. "Will you have some?" I told him to finish the wine himself and give me some brandy – if he could bear to part with it!

LATER: You see, Bethy, the truth about Capt. Cook seems to be that he was not at his best & probably quite ill toward the end – so his judgment was off & he got into a fracas with the natives that turned out badly. Thus his ignominious end – beaten & stabbed to death on the shore. Earlier he had been welcomed as a chief – something near deity. Some say they thought at first that he was their god Lono, others that they welcomed him because it was a season sacred to hospitality. Maybe both? Then he came back again at a different time, when they were not so glad to see him – all so perplexing because there are different accounts that don't tally.

For ex., what happened to his body? The English didn't dare go back to shore & collect it right away – so the natives began their own procedures. Quite naturally those were not in line with British ideas on how to do a proper funeral.

Ordinary people here it seems were tied in a sort of bundle with knees drawn up – after having been gutted & packed w. salt and/or some woolly stuff that grows at the base of ferns. Then they were stashed away in caves most secretly – darling, I trust all this doesn't upset you – I confess that I am fascinated. But you see the homage necessary for a great warrior or a noble required a certain amount of cooking, for flesh to be parted from bones – it was the bones they were after. The sailors watching from Cook's ship didn't know that & got alarmed – assuming they were roasting the poor man up for a feast.

The ultimate problem in Cook's case being that everyone ashore wanted a piece of him, literally – so he ended up in scraps, rather distressingly spread about the landscape. When the English cried halt, quite a few morsels were returned – & the sailors gave those a ceremonial burial in the bay. Not all of him by any means – but they did get the skull – part of one thigh, a recognizable hand, etcetera.. I imagine the English did not like to think about it too much & left as soon as possible. Here in the Islands, though, there are rumors – 80 plus- year-old items of gossip – on the whereabouts of the rest.

A wicker basket covered with red feathers, for ex. was seen by an early missionary – with parts & particles of the great man said to be inside. This object was supposedly carried about by the Hawaiians in solemn processions for years afterwards – rather as I suppose the Italians like to parade with the thighbone, the wrist or whatnot of some medieval saint. In time the natives themselves banned this sort of thing as idolatry – even before the missionaries came. Which is why the Americans had so little trouble introducing a new religion – the H'waians by that time were through with their old one. But this must end, and now I must sleep.

LATER AGAIN: Still haven't found a reliable messenger. Oh, how I wish I could paint! My usual little drawings are so inadequate to what I am seeing here. Truly, Kauai is like a waking dream. I accomplish nothing! Emma by contrast is forever busy – now overseeing the planting of a rocky cliff nearby, all to be adorned in magenta blooms – of a sort named for the French explorer, Captain Bougainville. This plant is a wayward, thorny little creature with more limbs than an octopus – all sending out fireworks & fountaining bursts of brilliant color – like glass aflame, or the burning bush seen by Moses.

Here at Lawai – oh, it is a bit of heaven – we are only steps away from the purest, softest white beach sand – from which description you may guess that I've had my feet in it & you will be right! Also, my self entire has been surrendered to the salt sea water here, which is sheer azure bliss – warm enough to be comforting – cool enough to startle and refresh – rather like a tonic or magic potion part amniotic, part aquavit.

A pu'ukiloia (fish-spotter's rock) stands by the shore where a fresh-water stream emerges - after meandering through a ferny dale sumptuous with palms, pandanus, kukui trees & breadfruit – while farther inland I'm told there are many springs, once-planted gardens & ruins of ancient dwellings. There is also a rumor of ghosts & burial caves – no one will go near them – it would be dangerous as well as sacrilegious. An elderly gardener here – though he says he is Christian – insists that a spiritual power or mana emanates from these caves, strong enough to knock a man down. In fact, he says it felled him one day when he came too close – and I think I believe him.

I'll enclose a clipping from the <u>Mercantile Gazette</u> – a more bizarre event than ever. Bsp. Coldwell came here to Lawai for 3 days with a sad *old priest & a pair of bewildered new deacons (Truckle & White, both from the <u>Hermes</u>) trailing after him. He baptized a few children, confirmed one & then left again – seized by a sudden desire, he said, to sail the ocean blue & visit Maui. Emma was perfect in formal courtesy to the Bsp, though very cool indeed & he took no notice of that. I believe there is something seriously lacking in this man's noticing powers. How could anyone with eyes in head not realize – on a small sailing yacht – that contraband is aboard in the form of an alluring young woman? Coldwell says it was all news to him.*

So the girl was delivered to Emma – poor foolish Lily Pae'aina, all penitent with hair in a tangle & her pretty red dress stained & disheveled. The Queen wept when she saw her – the Bsp. did not notice that, either. Said there had been some sort of fuss outside the harbor, caused by a misunderstanding! "It seems there was a promised bridegroom – a native youth with a horrid temper!"

Must stop now – messenger here – Love, love and love – Ever Your F.C.

LORD HENRY CHATHAM & FRIENDS

Only last week in this space we informed our readers that the English Bishop had been soliciting a yacht to go with his pretty new flag - and lo and behold, it appears he has got one. The obliging Lord Henry Chatham invited Bishop Coldwell on a sailing trip to Kauai in his yacht *Amaryllis*. With great fanfare and all flags flying (the striking, red and blue banner of the Anglican Church at the mainmast) the party set sail last Friday with an interesting cast of characters aboard. We have it on the best authority that their larder was provisioned for an extended excursion, with dozens of cases of wine and spirits, and a new Chinese cook. Some of our readers may have noticed, shortly before noon on Friday, an unusual disturbance taking place in the waters just off Diamond Head. A government boat had set off in hot pursuit of the *Amaryllis*. According to the officer in charge of the second vessel, several shots were fired during the course of the "difference of opinion" that followed; the view of Lord Henry being that an innocent voyage was under way; the view of the government officer that an abduction was taking place. Having demanded the return of a certain female passenger, the officer says he was met with defiance by the principals in the affair, one of whom told him "You must not take this woman off, it would damage the cause of our Church" – presumably referring to the Church whose banner was at the main. But half the population of the city knew already that this girl was aboard with Chatham. Shame! And fie on the hypocrisy of this "Bishop" and this "Lord" and all of their ilk!

17

The storm had passed, and dawn at Kealakekua Bay brought clear skies, calm seas, and a rising sun that adorned the heights above the bay with spangled fire. Clusters of grass-roofed huts stood about the shore amid tall groves of coconut palms. Even at this hour, native swimmers were frolicking near the shore, and their swift canoes darted about in the sparkling waters. David Wilkinson stood barefoot on the very shelf of lava where the hero of his boyhood had fallen, while minnows played in the shallows around him, and small transparent waves washed over his feet.

Consul Green came to stand beside him and said, "Imagine it! Ten thousand Hawaiians greeted the *Resolution* when Cook anchored here. Today we see only a few hundred. Alas, we know why – or at least, what is the most disgraceful reason."

"True," said David, "but that must not be blamed on Cook. I am convinced that he himself never touched a native woman. And I know that he went to extraordinary lengths to protect the Hawaiian people from infection by his men."

"An all but impossible task," Green admitted.

"Yes, they were young and they were lonely."

"Indeed. And the young women of these islands are very beautiful. As you may   possibly have noticed." There was amusement in his tone.

David did not reply.

"Well, Mr. Wilkinson, you must behave yourself, I suppose."

"And I suppose, Mr. Green, that you had better do the same."

They put on their boots, took up their knapsacks and began walking inland together, for Green wanted David to see a small memorial to Cook that had been placed there some years ago. On the way, David noticed a white spire above trees on the southern coast of the bay. "Is that a church?" he asked, and learned to his deep disappointment that it was an American mission. No one had warned him of this! He felt the dreams of a lifetime suddenly slipping away from him. On rising ground farther inland he suffered another keen disappointment. The memorial plaque for Cook was no more than a soiled scrap of copper nailed to the stump of a dead coconut tree, and pierced with the crudest of markings. David began to wonder what sort of Englishmen he would find on this island.

"You must visit Captain Hawkins," the Consul was saying. "He is here from Devon, twenty years or more. He's the area's leading citizen. Knows everyone, and has always promised support to the Church. Soper Hawkins has a large plantation south of here: cattle, coffee, and so on. My own much smaller piece adjoins. "

"Not very nice is it?" said a sympathetic voice, as they stood looking at the hideous plaque. They looked up and saw a portly figure with wide blue eyes and a beaming face; this was David's first glimpse of Richard Cornwall. He was wearing a faded cotton shirt over his trousers, and he carried with him the fragrance of horses and hard labor in tropical heat.

"We thought we saw you coming in last night." Cornwall continued cheerfully." I told the Missus, that'll be the new Reverend. Better go down and bid him welcome. Aloha, Mr. Wilkinson – how d'ye do? This is a great day for us all, and a long time coming. Mr. Green, sir, how did you like that tempest? Bit of a blow, wasn't it? Will you be stopping with us, or are you on your way to the volcano?"

"To the volcano, thank you," said Green. He bade farewell to David, assuring him that he was in good hands, for Cornwall knew the territory and kept in his shop any odd bit of gear that David might need. "But by all means, stop at the Hawkins ranch. There's a sign – you'll see it, *Kihapai O'Ekena* – on the main trail about thirty miles south of here. You'll find a pack of youngsters on the place needing to be baptized. Most of 'em are Hawkins' – one way or t'other. Isn't that right, Cornwall?"

"Sir?" But Green had already left, with a wink and a grin. Cornwall turned to David, embarrassed. "Please Mr. Wilkinson, don't think... But then you know how it is, I'm sure, here in the Islands. Never mind, you'll find the Captain a substantial citizen. He'll be a great help to you."

"We shall see." By now David Wilkinson was in a somewhat cross and contrary frame of mind. As soon as he had climbed the steep cliff that lay ahead, and found a horse to hire, and bought a few oddments from Cornwall, and settled his gear behind the saddle, he began to follow the first trail he found going due north. After all, he thought, why must I go the recommended direction? All islands are in some sense round; therefore I shall find what I want in due time, by going the wrong way.

It was a narrow, but well-defined path that brought him parallel to the coast at heights of 1,000 to 1,500 feet above the sea. After passing by a number of humble dwellings above Kealakekua Bay, he plunged into primeval forest. Beneath his horse's hooves the ground was deep and soft, embellished like a Persian carpet with countless varieties of ferns and mosses. Above him, an over-arching canopy of vines and leafy branches shielded him from the sun and shook down crystal drops of moisture as he passed. Flashes of light, green and gold, darted from tree to tree – tiny Hawaiian songbirds greeting the day with joyous pips and cheeps. Another bird, invisible to the eye, tapped out a message like that of an English woodpecker's. A good many busy spiders had been out before him, putting their gossamer architectures into place, but of tigers, wolves and bears he knew there were none in these Islands, and no snakes either. *Praise the Lord, O my soul: and all that is within me, praise his holy name!*

He began to sing aloud as he made his way through dense forest that was pierced only by an occasional shaft of sunlight. Not many flowers showed themselves here, but now and then he stopped to pick wild fruits, for delicious bananas grew in some of the sunny spots, and in the shade he found miniature apples and succulent, thornless raspberries. He fed a few of these delicacies to his horse, who appeared to be grateful for the offerings, and sang to him, *Praise the Lord: Who satisfieth thy mouth with good things: making thee young and lusty as an eagle...* The horse, in fact, was no longer young, but he was a sturdy, amiable fellow. He was large, broad-beamed and a mottled gray, a creature indifferent as to appearance, and as to pace, rather loose and shambling. However, in such a setting, and on such a day as this, David found nothing about him to regret.

The kind storekeeper had put several coconuts into his saddlebags, and he knew by now that their milk was delicious. However, David planned to save them for supper; thus by early afternoon he was happy to hear the sound of running water nearby. A short distance from the main trail he discovered a hidden dell, a lush green bower dappled with sunlight. At the center of it was a waterfall that fell to a dark, clear pool fringed with ferns. Both horse and rider drank deeply there, and David refilled his water flask. He was tempted to strip off his clothing and take a refreshing plunge into the pool. In fact, he was tempted to stop in that idyllic place, and build himself a little hut, and stay there for the rest of his life.

However, his solemn task at present was to explore the island so as to identify the most promising place for an Anglican mission. In a lunatic moment at Honolulu he had imagined that he was free to indulge in a wild Asian adventure; but that was clearly impossible for a man bound as he was to his family, his country and his Church. He must humble himself instead and serve where fate had cast him, however miserable the rest of his days might be. *The days of man are but as grass: for he flourisheth as a flower of the field. For as soon as the wind goeth over it, it is gone: and the place thereof shall know it no more.* Before such a gust of wind that morning, his memorial church for Captain Cook at Kealakekua had vanished. With American missionaries already there, the presence of an English rival would be most unwelcome. Bishop Coldwell had not warned him of this, and he wondered why. Russell and Riggs had said only to beware of the Roman Catholics in Ka'u.

Heavy of heart, he loosened the reins after a time and watched in an absent-minded way while his shambling mount entertained himself at the side of the trail, nosing and browsing. Here a vine, there a shrub attracted his attention; he was equally interested in berries and beetles, flies and fallen leaves. Even a small spot of moving sunlight aroused his curiosity. What a fine, intelligent beast!

David dismounted and allowed the good gray horse to wander at will in the woods while he followed, doing approximately the same. Twenty minutes later, as he stood looking up at a graceful tree-fern that arched above his head, David suddenly saw in his mind's eye the church that he should build. It would not be a formal monument in stone and glass, after all. Instead, it would be a modest place of shelter, born of the forest, and made of wood, with its roof and walls painted green. He would try to make it look as if it had always been here, a part of the landscape. In traditional Hawaiian style, it would have broad eaves, and wide, welcoming steps leading up to it. He saw it situated on a seaward slope with a waterfall and a deep, clear pool nearby. And a bell to ring – yes, he must have a bell. He summoned his horse and rode north on the trail once again. He was imagining happily that the church was already built, and the bell ringing on a Sunday morning, and families coming to worship, when a sudden shot rang out.

Gunshot! And from the sound of it, quite nearby. It was followed by another sharp report, and then three or four more in a volley, a short distance ahead of him on the trail. Moments later he heard hoofbeats approaching at a gallop. Several riders came into view, with a tall white man in the lead. He was carrying a whip, and wearing a leather hat above long, pale moustaches. Three darker men with kerchiefs knotted around their heads came shouting and scrambling after him on smaller mounts, with rifles in their hands. When they saw David they all drew up hastily, and stopped a few feet away from him on the path.

"Pig!" shouted the white man. "Damn big one up *mauka*."

"Oh," said David. "I see. Pig. Are they troublesome?"

"Missed the son of a bitch," the man said, still breathing hard.

"I am sorry to hear it."

"Troublesome? Where the hell are you from?"

"Yorkshire. Church of England. My name is Wilkinson."

The man's horse danced around David's as he offered his hand. "Sorry about that. Hawkins here, Captain Soper Hawkins. Avast, boys! Well, you had me foxed. You don't look like a clergyman. Welcome to my island!"

"Thank you."

"So, the ship's in?"

"Yes, last night."

"Quite a little storm that was. You're going in the wrong direction. We're expecting you at my place."

David explained that he needed to explore the island first.

"Well, keep to the trail. Don't want to lose you, now you're here. Next week, then? Plenty of space, nothing fancy, but you won't starve. Know where to find us?"

"I believe so. I was given directions. Thank you very much."

"Good. Well then, steady on and keep your eyes open! Ship's in, boys," he said to his companions. "Better get to the bay. They're bringing me a load of feed and a Chinaman." He swung a hasty salute in David's direction and charged away. As his men filed past David on the path, one laughed and said "Plenty big one, Mister. Better watch out, he stick you good!"

David Wilkinson did not carry a weapon, but he knew that a feral boar was not a creature to trifle with. There had been talk in Honolulu about the goats, cattle and pigs that had gone wild on the Big Island, many brought as gifts by foreigners. Vancouver had given a fine breed of horned cattle to King Kamehameha I in the 1790s, and the King had placed a 10-year *kapu* on them. The result was that they had multiplied into a menace. William Hillebrand had spoken of it to David with strong emotion, for these animals trampled and devoured the native plants, preferring the tender young shoots that might have replenished Nature's store. Even the magnificent stands of virgin timber high in the mountains were threatened with destruction by that year of 1867.

Vowing to keep a sharper watch in the future, David proceeded with caution for another hundred yards or so before the good gray horse stopped suddenly in the trail and then moved several paces backward. The rolling of his eyes and the set of his haunches told David that he was unwilling to go on. The voices of the songbirds were still; in fact, there was no sound at all except the whispering of the wind in the high branches and a delicate rustling, shifting and stirring below, as if the forest were a live creature, breathing and aware.

A louder noise quite nearby suddenly startled him: surely the sound of a weighty footfall. Its location was just behind a tree that lay by the trail in a tangle with its broken branches. Now a great head with blazing eyes lifted itself from that spot, approximately twelve feet away. Its dark visage was grizzled and scarred, massively crowned with sharp, curving antlers of horn. The immense creature regarding David was not a boar, but a wild bullock.

He considered the wisdom of beating a hasty retreat, but all in all, it seemed best to remain where he was. Man and bull looked at one another for the space of a dozen heartbeats: the tame and the wild, the all-too-conscious and the majestically unconcerned. David was proud of his horse. On a firm rein, with a calming hand at his withers, the noble fellow stood his ground like a hero.

A fly crept slowly across the bullock's forehead and settled on one of his eyelids. A rank, carnal scent wafted from his exceptionally rough and grimy coat. However, the fearsome horns were all the garb and regalia he needed to show who was monarch here.

"A man may look at a king," David ventured softly. At this, the creature regarded him with as much interest as if he had been a talking shrub, not to a bull's taste in edibles. Then his eyelids drooped, his nose lifted and he actually sneered, with his lip curled as if in utmost contempt of the man, the horse, and all of their pedigree. Obviously, they were dismissed from the royal presence. When they still did not move, the immense creature turned his back and lumbered away.

"You are a champion," said David to his horse. "Only take me a little farther today, and I will let you rest." Soon after this, they emerged from the forest into a high, open landscape with grassland spread before them, a vast, dry savannah the shade of a lion's hide, with hot winds racing. A gleam of snow was visible high on the crest of a pale blue mountain range to the east. Cloud-shadows of darkest indigo lay across the long trail ahead. Here David once more discovered the wisdom of his mount, for he wanted to canter across the grassy slopes, but the horse refused. David dismounted to look him in the eye and ask what was the matter; but as soon as his foot touched the ground, he found himself down on his knees with bloodied hands and a twisted ankle. What he had seen as a pleasant meadow was actually an old lava field, with sharp rocks hidden under its plumy grasses. This was the variety of lava called *a'a,* perhaps from the sounds uttered by the first unhappy man who fell on it.

He had imagined earlier that they might reach the northerly village of Waimea by nightfall. After another thirty minutes in this terrain, he saw his error. The shadows on the trail ahead were not made by clouds; they were all substantial, consisting of cascades of lava. It was a slow, dangerous business to cross these ruined miles, rather like making his way through a stormy ocean that had turned to stone. Much of it was the kind of lava called in Hawaiian *pahoehoe* – raven dark and glistening, in swirls like petrified treacle. The *a'a'* sort, he soon realized, is ashen, russet or elephant-color, all jumbled together in dismembered chunks and clinkers.

Like most Hawaiian horses in those days, David's was unshod; yet he picked his way nimbly along the narrow trail that was sometimes invisible to his rider. Then, suddenly, it was dark, and David spent the first night of his journey around the island on a lava bed beside the splintered remains of an *ohia* tree. Both man and horse had an uneasy time of it, although David, after quite a struggle, finally managed to open a coconut. He had seen an old Hawaiian man do it by holding the slippery object between his bare feet, then giving it a violent blow with a heavy blade. However, he decided not to try that.

18

D*avid Wilkinson, Journal: 28 May 1867:*

Kona Coffee 5 pence per pound
25 oranges per 1 shilling
Lorenzo Scuppers = "Mad Prophet"

On to village of Waimea early, met an old man leaning on a cane. Ezekiel Calhoun! Same man, older, grimmer than ever. Said he, "Don't come preaching your heresy around here!" Still scowling, he watered my good gray horse & set him grazing. Then wife Matilda with never a smile or pleasant word fed me bananas, eggs, bacon, fried potatoes, buttermilk biscuits, butter, guava jam, Kona coffee & sugar& cream, plus ½ of a rhubarb pie. Afterward wrapped rest of pie in paper, ordered me crossly to put it into my saddlebag.

He was ashamed, for it was obvious that the Calhouns were not rich. Their house was shabby and plain, with furniture largely consisting of old packing cases. Forty years' work for their God had not brought wealth to this couple. Far from it, despite the remarks David had heard in Honolulu. According to his Bishop's disdainful wife, the American missionaries had all made fortunes in Hawaii by fraud and chicanery. He had doubted it then, and he knew now that he would never believe it.

30 May, Waimea: Cool rain & mist. Settlers from North of England & Scotland find a more congenial climate here. Kindness of the Spencer family. Two services, 11 baptisms, 19 communicants. The old one-armed mariner who wept. Wondering faces of children, squalling of infants, rainbows arching over the high green hills.

He had never seen such luminous rainbows before, glimmering, vanishing, then reappearing. He stayed two nights with an English family named Spencer, and wondered whether this ought to be the site of the new Anglican mission. Preaching twice from their verandah, he searched the faces of his little congregations as they stood to hear him, or squatted on the ground. These were sturdy ranchers and farmers for the most part, many with native wives and black-haired, barefoot children. He would always remember the villainous-looking old sailor from Portsmouth, one-armed and bent with rheumatism, whose face was awash with tears of joy when he heard the old familiar hymns. And then, there was the splendid little Hawaiian girl named Pua, no more than five years old, with the eyes of an angel, who died of a fever only a few weeks after he had baptized her.

The parents of the district were overjoyed by his arrival, since the American missionaries refused to baptize little ones, thinking them unready or unable, David supposed, to understand their morbid teachings. Everywhere he stopped on this journey there was terror lest children be snatched away by death and sent to Hell before being safely marked for Christ. David Wilkinson told the grieving parents not to fear. "Read the Gospels!" he told them. "They show us that Jesus would never turn a little child away."

3 June, Hamakua Coast: Mud, rocks gales+ rushing waters — 79 gulches each 200-300 ft. deep, slopes nearly perpendicular. Brave horse — heroic performance, nearly up to his belly at times in mud. Endless rain in torrents, racing streams to be forded among more rocks. Small earthquake 2nd day, 4:07 p.m. At last at sea-level, the little town of Hilo steaming in the sun.

This page of the journal was permanently streaked and puckered by the rain and damp. As some visitors have observed, the mountains on the northeast side of this Island fall to the sea in fluted pleats and folds like the drapery in an ancient Flemish painting. Well may they rhapsodize over the beauty of the scene while reclining in deck-chairs on a passing steamer, but traveling the same landscape on foot or on horseback was never a holiday. David Wilkinson had the advantage of an oilskin coat, so that only about half of the rain that fell during those two unhappy days went directly down his neck. Still, the patience of his horse was the greatest wonder. Mile after mile the agreeable beast plodded on without complaint, climbing almost straight up or else (which was worse) straight down again. At the bottom of each gully they plunged together into storm-fed streams that rushed headlong into the sea.

On the second day of this misery, partway up a steep incline, there came an earthquake – not a violent one, but a sharp little shock followed by a shudder of the earth that brought some large pebbles down upon them. By this time David had named his faithful companion "Mr. Gray," and when the horse failed to panic even at this event, he promised Mr. Gray that he would buy him a hat and make him a Perpetual Curate. This was a private joke of sorts, for in those days it was often a threadbare Anglican curate who did most of the work for a lazy or absent parish priest.

6 June: On the mt. above Hilo: Heavy fog, trail obscure, ground frozen in places. Three days in Hilo, only one fair – others hot, dark & wet. Left town hastily, without recommended guide. This territory not for foreigner's traveling sole. Hilo a handsome town with good beach for swimming – but not altogether pleasant experience, thanks to the Rev. Mr. Coan & his posse of fanatics. Still, God willing, we shall persevere.

He had thought that he might do well to establish his mission in the busy seaport of Hilo, but soon changed his mind. A certain Mr. Coan was the American missionary there, and upon learning that David was in town, he immediately lost his temper. David came to the man's house to pay his respects and knocked at the front door, but the American pastor would not speak to him, and in fact, slammed the door shut in his face. David Wilkinson responded to this insult by walking to the nearby beach, stripping his clothes off, and plunging into the waters of Hilo Bay. Thirty minutes of refreshing exercise there washed away his resentment and left him cheerful once again.

When he returned to shore, however, there was a committee waiting for him. Five men – one Hawaiian and four American – stood scowling furiously on the strand, and two of the Americans were carrying shotguns. They made it known to him that he had committed a public outrage that endangered the morals of the natives. His action, they said, threatened to undo all the progress in decency and morality that had been made by American missionaries in the past 47 years, all because he had not worn a "suit" for bathing!

David Wilkinson told them that he owned no such costume, that in England, gentlemen did not wear suits, or anything else at such times. He explained that they merely took care not to intrude on one another's privacy. That the beach had been quite deserted when he came there. That he could not possibly have harmed anyone's morals. That he reckoned his own morals were at least as refined as theirs, if not more so, for he was growing angry again, and feeling at a certain disadvantage without his trousers.

They paid no attention, and in fact he did not regain possession of his garments, or permission to leave town, until after he mentioned by chance that he had been sea-bathing recently with the King. He had intended to say something about the use of a *malo*, a traditional Hawaiian loincloth that the King had given him that day, since the water was rough and they were riding the waves on boards. Only a fool would go naked in such a situation. But the men of the posse were not interested in rational discourse; they were gaping in awe because David Wilkinson was the friend of a monarch! This reaction by Americans was perplexing to an Englishman. They were the sons and grandsons of rebels, after all – citizens of a democratic republic. But there it was, and so, thanks to the hospitality of King Kamehameha, David was given back his freedom and his dignity.

After this he bade a quick farewell to Hilo town without stopping to hire a guide as he should have done, for the mountain passage ahead was extremely dangerous. A foreign visitor had attempted the journey recently, and had never been seen or heard of since.

June: On the mountain. Fiery glow of Kilauea in the distance- frigid air after dark. Eternal mystery of the night. Thanks be to God for stars, for sky, for wind, for man's imagination, for the kind shepherd boy. Ate with him that eve, God knows what. Next morning learned to make a straw hat, but Mr. G did not like it. Later found haven with fine old German fellow Lindt – baptized, never confirmed. Needs more visits, medicines, etc. Lord, keep him under the shadow of your wings. Sheep in town said to cost 8 shillings.

It was difficult riding on the mountain, demanding the utmost in attention, for there were dozens of wild cattle tracks on every side, and only a single track for horses. The cold was very great so far above sea level and the entire area was often shrouded in a thick fog or mist that erased all sense of direction. This was particularly true at night, when at times David could only guess his position by the glow from Mount Kilauea's lake of fire.

On the night of June 8th he huddled on the frosty ground waiting for morning, but after a time his nose roused him and led him to the hut of a young Hawaiian shepherd who was just cooking his dinner. He welcomed David and filled his plate with a steaming, savory stew, for which he would not allow his visitor to pay him anything. After that, David had the choice either of freezing outdoors or of providing a feast for the fleas inside, and he gratefully chose the latter. This friendly lad told him that a good fat lamb cost 8 shillings these days in Hilo – a scandal! He himself, he said, preferred roast dog, and so David did not ask what had been in the stew. In the morning, the shepherd taught his visitor several new words in Hawaiian, and showed him how to weave a straw hat, a technique he managed for the moment with considerable help, and then immediately forgot.

His second and third nights on the mountain were spent with a delightful old German chap who had wandered there one day some 40 years earlier, and stayed. Herr Lindt was lonely and frail, but he could not bear to leave the quaint little cottage he had built with his own hands. Since the death of his wife some years earlier he had counted upon his Bible, his old violin and the occasional wayfarer for company. David Wilkinson gave him some medicine for his cough and then mended a corner of his roof for him while Lindt sat on the doorstep, playing the country airs of Bavaria.

After this, the priest and his curate managed to lose themselves quite completely on Mauna Loa for two days, but they rambled around here and there in a hopeful frame of mind. Fortunately, the weather was clear and dry, rather like a perfect winter day in Yorkshire, with the blue Pacific shimmering in the far distance. Finally they heard voices, and the whinnying of horses, and following those, discovered a rough camp on the southeastern slopes of the mountain. There David preached to a few hardy souls, celebrated the Eucharist, and baptized two infants before moving on, certain that this was not the most promising place on the island for a mission.

11th - 14th June: Ka'u to South Pt: Painting angels w. Pierre Armand. Chocolate in blue paper from Marseilles. Kihapai O'Ekena ("Garden of Eden") – not entirely what one might expect. Pillars of the Church both Green and Hawkins – 2 very different men, yet their land side by side. How to manage? Problematic. O God you will keep in perfect

151

peace those whose minds are fixed on you: in quietness and trust shall be our strength. Amen.

He began on the 11th of June to ride south through the district of Ka'u. This part of the journey was made in some trepidation, since Ka'u at the time was a stronghold of Roman Catholicism, with several of their missions up and down the coast. Russell and Riggs had told David to avoid the place, for any Catholic missionary he might meet there would breathe fire upon him and order him to leave. Even so, he was captivated by the beauty around him as he rode. A well-marked trail led across miles of tawny grasslands that swept to the edge of the island and then plunged steeply into the sea. The trade winds here were in full force, whipping the dark blue water into a silver froth as it dashed against the shore. It was an exhilarating ride, and David was in high spirits all day. He saw a number of small Catholic missions on the wayside without feeling obliged to stop and explain his presence, and began to wonder whether he would be sleeping on the ground again that night. Then, very late in the afternoon he spied a small building overlooking the sea, and drawing near, found that it, too, was a Roman Catholic mission. The valiant Mr. Gray was near exhaustion by now, and David was hungry enough to stop and knock somewhat hesitantly at the door.

It was opened immediately by a wiry, dark-skinned little Frenchman in a paint-spattered artist's smock. When David explained himself and his purpose, Fr. Pierre Armand seemed not at all troubled, but embraced him warmly and invited him to come in. Homesick for the metropolitan beauties he had left behind, Father Armand was decorating the walls of his tiny chapel with murals to make it look as much as possible like a miniature European cathedral, while he himself lived in a hut a few steps away. Mr. Gray was soon fed and watered, then covered with David's own blanket and led to a small corral that was home to Fr. Armand's mule. The two animals evidently found nothing to quarrel about, and the two men fell easily into agreeable conversation. Their supper was a slice of good bread with goat cheese and herbs, then a delicious broth made from vegetables that Armand had grown himself. Afterward he produced a piece of bittersweet chocolate from Marseilles that was obviously his treasure, and insisted that David take the larger share of it. At the evening's end, he insisted that the honored visitor should sleep in his bed, while he himself slept on a narrow pew before the altar. They knelt side by side, each at his own devotions before retiring, and said the Lord's Prayer together in Latin.

In the morning, after some earnest negotiations, David was given permission to spend the next two days on a ladder, painting angels on the ceiling of the little church. The Frenchman had drawn the outlines of his design, but he had to stop there because he was terrified by heights. David put golden (which is to say, yellow) wings on the angels, and gave them brilliant gowns of red, blue and purple, so as to make them look as Catholic as possible. Then, thoroughly enjoying himself, he went on to paint golden moons and stars on the ceiling that would surely please a Hindu, a Buddhist, a Muslim or a Jew, as well as any footsore Christian or pagan who might happen by. Pierre Armand was ecstatic over the result, and the two priests pledged enduring friendship before David Wilkinson saddled his horse once again and rode away

Thanks to the pleasure of this visit and the beauty of the landscape, David was in a contented frame of mind when he rounded the southern tip of the Island and began to look west and north for the Hawkins ranch. His future course lay clear before him now: he ought to place his mission church either on the Hawkins property or on the plot nearby offered to him by Consul Green. Both places would offer service to emigrant Anglicans, and either would be within a half day's ride from Kealakekua Bay. He was happy to see several apparently inhabited ranches in the neighborhood as he headed north again. When in the early afternoon he saw a hand-lettered sign reading *Kihapai O'Ekena*, he turned into a long driveway of beaten earth that meandered upward, with ferns growing on either side amid fragrant stands of ginger.

As they started up the driveway, the faithful Curate seemed to sense that his nose might soon be deep into something agreeable, and he quickened his pace accordingly. Barking dogs greeted them at the top of the hill. The ranch house was large and rambling, made of wood that had been painted white some seasons ago, with half a dozen pillars at the front and an ill-trimmed but expansive lawn. The master was not at home, but a silent Hawaiian lad met him at the door and escorted him to the stables. There Mr. Gray was fed, watered, cleaned and curried without a word by the same boy, and then David was shown to his room by an equally silent woman, dark of skin and hair. She, evidently, was the boy's mother.

Hawkins did not return until late in the day. "So there you are, Wilson," he remarked when he saw his guest.

"Wilkinson," said David.

"Wilkinson? Supposed to be Wilson. Well then, they got it wrong as usual. That's Hawaii for you! Have a seat. Sherry? Whisky? We're dining alone tonight."

They sat at one end of a long, narrow dining table made of highly polished koa wood. The food, which was uninviting but plentiful, was served by an Asian waiter on silent feet: baked fish, roasted beef, potatoes, onions, great heavy biscuits crowned with greasy pan drippings, and finally a pudding whose taste was remarkably sweet, though unfamiliar. Elaborate silver candelabra decked the table, and two large hunting dogs crunched on bones beneath.

Captain Hawkins was a muscular and heavy, though not corpulent, Englishman in his late fifties, with thinning gray hair that had once been blond, and long, drooping moustaches. He tipped his head back when he spoke, and gazed either to one side or another of the person he was addressing, or else at the far distance. This curious habit suggested that he spoke for the benefit of someone invisible, and the impression was increased by the fact that he often spoke quite a bit more loudly than necessary.

Hawkins pronounced immediately that the Rev. David Wilkinson would be one of his dependents, since the clergyman's living, or benefice in this domain, was his to provide. He told Wilkinson that he owned a tremendous amount of land, running from the crest of the mountain all the way down to the sea, in a pie-shaped section that was narrow at the top, but many miles wide at its lowest point. Most of this, he said, he had got either by grant or purchase from the former monarchy, after the division of lands known as the Great Mahele. He was farming part of his property and raising cattle, sheep, pigs, dogs and children (as he put it) on the rest. The work of such a plantation was never done. He was up before dawn each day and often on horseback long into the night. He had no time for the niceties. He was a simple, seagoing man, he said, who had found in Hawaii a harbor that suited him. He was content with what he had achieved, but he wanted his sons to be gentlemen. That, he said, would be David Wilkinson's project.

After this he named his terms. David would be allowed to build a church and a parsonage on his property, and he would lend some plantation labor for that. Of course, it would cost David dearly, since these men would not work for less than 10 shillings per day. But those were the facts. David might stay on in this house as a guest until he had his own dwelling built, but he must do that first, and live there while he built his church. Hawkins would like to see something dignified in a Gothic style, made of stone, with stained glass windows. In return for allowing David Wilkinson to work on his property, he would be invited to the Hawkins table once each week for "a good feed" after Sunday services. He would also provide David an allowance of 10 pounds sterling per year, plus the use of one milk cow. In return, David was to serve the Hawkins family, their neighbors and visitors on a regular basis, and teach the Hawkins boys to read, write and speak proper English.

David said little during all this, but when his host had finished speaking, he indicated in a mannerly way that he had a different plan. He made his immediate response in the form of several questions: First, were members of the Hawkins family in any way religious? Did they consider themselves Christians?

Were they baptized? Was there a Bible in the house? What spiritual guidance had the children received thus far? Who was their mother, what was her place of origin and what were her beliefs? Why did the children not read, speak or write English? Did he have daughters as well as sons, and if so, did he intend to educate them?

Hawkins expressed contempt for all these questions, and began shouting about the difficulty of getting inexpensive labor. Then, in an apparent non-sequitur, he said suddenly, "I was there, you know, when that bloke shot Lincoln."

"You were there? In the theater in Washington?"

"In the city. I was there on business at the time. Oh yes. Bad luck about Mister Abraham! But I won't say it surprised me."

"I understand, from all I know about him, that President Lincoln was an excellent man,"

"You wouldn't think he was so excellent, "said Hawkins, "if you had 1,000 acres of cotton planted in Georgia. My brother Arthur did. All wrecked now. Ruined, after the slaves ran off. You can't treat crops like that and get away with it." He turned from the table then in a sudden rage, shouting, "Chun! Hey, Lo! Come here Ching Chung – whatever the hell your name is!"

The Chinese servant appeared, bowing, obviously alarmed, and his glance met David's for a moment.

"What are you trying to do, you heathen, POISON us?" Hawkins roared. "Look, you brought the wrong damn bottle! We drink port after dinner, not sherry. BRING US THE PORT, you idiot." The servant bowed again, and scurried away with his pigtail flying.

"I have seen this man before," said David slowly. "He was on the ship, when I came over from Honolulu."

"They're all the same," said Hawkins. "Alligator bait!" He slapped his knee and laughed uproariously. "Alligator bait, that's what my brother calls 'em. Only difference, his were black."

19

He rode out to look at William Green's land the following morning on a borrowed horse, since the Curate had earned a rest. Keoki, the dark-skinned stable boy who served as his guide, spoke the slaughtered version of English known as "pidgin" although David suspected that his family name might actually be Hawkins. They struggled to communicate with one another as they rode, and David managed to learn that the woman who had welcomed him was named Maria. Indeed she was the boy's mother, but they lived at the back of the house, and always ate in the kitchen. By now, David had noticed a number of other children at *Kihapai O'Ekena*, all of them too shy to talk with him.

Close below and beyond the Hawkins property he found a relatively open landscape that particularly pleased him, sweeping down toward the sea with golden grasses, wind-torn guava shrubs, a few handsome trees, and a wide view of the sparkling ocean. It appeared that no sugar cane or other crop had ever been planted here, although there were signs that a rough path had been made from time to time by human traffic. Best of all, there was no sound to be heard except birdsong and the rush and splash of waves below. He imagined himself living happily alone in a tent on such a hillside, lulled to sleep by the sounds of the ocean, waking to watch the moon go down and the sun come up. Birds would eat crumbs from his hands in such a place of peace and beauty; here he would become an entirely good person, never again to be tormented by anger, scorn, impatience or illicit desire. He imagined himself meeting a ship filled with lumber at the shore below, and loading it up the hill, either upon his own back or on mules. It would be a terrible labor, and yet, somehow he would manage it, for he felt with almost magical certainty that this was where his mission belonged.

He told Captain Hawkins of his decision that evening, half expecting to be sent from the house without dinner, but Hawkins simply looked at him with vague curiosity, as if he had forgotten who David Wilkinson was, and what he was there for. Then, in the same bland manner, he announced that a small gathering would take place in his parlor that evening, to introduce the new clergyman to some of his future parishioners.

The neighbors who came to the door at sunset were all white men, though darkened or reddened in various degrees by the circumstances of their labor. But for two Americans, they were all English farmers and ranchers with the names of the yeoman of antiquity: Smith, Carpenter, Cooper, Brewster, and so on. It was clear from the first that Hawkins was in some sense their leader. Drinks were handed round and eagerly accepted, while the men studied David Wilkinson as cautiously as buyers at a market fair. When it was time for him to speak about the Church they listened politely enough, but their eyes were soon glazed over, and their heads began to nod; it was plain that they were, to a man, exhausted. Hawkins sat in a large wing chair by the fireplace, with his legs crossed and one foot bobbing impatiently as David spoke.

"Let us pray," David said, sooner than he had planned. The liquor was quickly put aside, weary heads were bowed, and calloused hands were humbly folded. Beside him as he bowed his own head he could see cuffs of dirt-stained trousers, and the string of a worn boot that had been broken twice, and then knotted. He prayed in silence that he would be a worthy minister to these men, and then aloud, for all of them, for their families, and for the Kona Coast, that the drought would soon end and rains would come, and last of all, for the future of the first Anglican mission on the island.

*

The weeks that followed were laborious, but they were also some of the happiest that David had ever known. As he toiled for long hours in the blazing sun, he was astonished by his own strength and capability. Neither the bank nor the missionary college had demanded much physical work, and he soon found an unexpected joy in it. Lumber arrived with little help in storing or sorting it, and as he struggled to build the little hut that would serve as his own dwelling, he wondered daily at the beauty he found all around him. Sunlight and starlight alike were entrancing in this place; dawn and sunset were his favorite hours of all, for then the light came down like a blessing, and the owl called softly from the young *kukui* tree; and the wind was stilled, and the waves of the sea were small and quiet on the shore below.

It turned out that he had chosen his site better than he knew, for the dim trail he had noted served to connect several outlying farms and ranches. His new neighbors stopped by at times to watch him work, and to tell him how he should be doing things differently. This in turn often led to discussions of theology, although the farmers did not know it by that name. Bishop Coldwell had told him not to bother with the natives, but to search out the wealthy foreign landowners instead. This advice had keenly annoyed David, but now he realized the extent of Coldwell's ignorance more than ever; for no one on this coast, either native or foreign, had money in those days. What they had was land and livestock, courage, hard work and hope for the future.

After the night of the boat that had come ashore with its terrible cargo, David returned frequently to the native village by the sea, walking across the fields and clambering down the seaside cliff. There he spent happy hours swimming in the ocean, talking with the children, fishing with Harold Lopaka, and taking instruction from Mailelani on Hawaiian lore and medicinal herbs. Maile always seized him in a crushing embrace when he arrived, and treated him as if he were a rather foolish child, unaccountably slow and stupid, yet beloved.

"You got too much *haole* talk, Pelekane," she said. "Too much *haole* religion. What you going do when Pele come down one day burn your church?"

"I suppose, build another one."

"Maybe she no like that," she said, laughing. "Moah bettah you run 'way, come stay here my place with me!"

As for Captain Hawkins, David suggested one day while the church was being built that he might like to take an interest in Christianity, and Hawkins retorted angrily that he had already been baptized and confirmed – what more? David told him those facts recommended his parents more than himself, and mentioned some elementary Christian moral principles. Hawkins took no interest in these, and so one day, David offered him a sterner challenge. The Captain's domestic arrangements were troubling, David told him. For example, he had not met Mrs. Hawkins, nor had he been introduced to Maria, the cook and housekeeper. Were they one and the same? If the two were a married couple, why not live as such? He had never seen Maria in the parlor or at his table. Furthermore, which of the children were servants, and which were his own? To this he added that even more troubling to him was a certain lack of Christian charity and forbearance that he had noticed in the Captain's treatment of his Chinese servant, Chin Wong Lo.

Hawkins was astonished and furious. In violent language he demanded an immediate apology, which David refused to give him. Instead, he told the Captain that he would not be silenced, for he was his own man, and he would have no master but Christ. David went to bed in his parsonage that night believing that he had lost the battle; yet, in time, he baptized all nine of Soper Hawkins' children and taught most of them to read, write and speak something more or less closely resembling English. He also managed to marry Soper

Hawkins to Maria, for the Captain had neglected that little chore since the death of his first wife many years earlier. But Soper's domestic life was never blameless, and so his offspring were a mixed lot.

On a exceedingly hot day that August, while David was painfully hauling lumber for the church on his back, a ship came in from Honolulu bringing several letters, the first of which was written in a hasty, partly illegible scrawl by Bishop Albert Coldwell:

Wilkinson ~   (undated)

*I cannot say that I am surprised, but cruelly
disappointed as I have been tending my faithful
flock in Kauai & then come back to find you
have <u>disgraced</u> yourself and the Church.
[illegible] my back is turned. In fact you have
shown your ungovernable pride and
<u>insolence</u> once again in giving <u>offense</u> to Capt.
Hawkins who was expected [illegible] our
Chief support. Now he [illegible] that you are an
arrogant pup who will have no master but yourself.
I expect your apology to the Captain. When it is
done, let me see your affidavit. I know whereof
he speaks, and you shall taste <u>discipline</u>. This
is not a democracy, Wilkinson ~ this is the
Church of England !!*

*Play the traitor if you will ~ <u>Resign!</u> I shall
be only too glad to sign your papers! My wife
and I leave next steamer & I shall send
someone to take the cathedral. Until further
notice Russell is in charge. If he is [illegible]
then Riggs, not you. Not Partridge; he is of no
use to me. Maui tells me he is proud, ill-
tempered and indiscreet ~ I have made it plain*

to your headmaster that I want no more of your
kind from his College.

† *Albert Honolulu*

*

St. Columba's Missionary College   16 July 1867
Canterbury

My Dear David,

I have just received a most distressing letter from the Bishop of Hawaii, who tells me that you have fallen from his favour. While I might be expected to rebuke you for whatever you have done to deserve this, I shall refrain, since the Bishop did not disclose his reasons. He expressed only anger, and hinted at serious transgressions. This is a painful business, indeed! I remember you well as one of our finest students, one whose frank and manly deportment was ever a credit to his Family, his Church, and his School.

I can only suppose that the idleness and laxity of the Islands, together with the weakening effects of a tropical climate, may have influenced you unduly. There was mention in the Bishop's report of "intemperance." More precisely, the Bishop did not state. I scarcely know what else to say just now. Please remember that we are all your friends here, and that we shall be praying daily for your improvement.

Yours Very Truly,
Hilary P. Egglestone † Headmaster

*

Mauna Kilohana   *(undated)*
Kauai

My Dear Mr. Wilkinson – I think of you in this blessed place where thanks to the Queen, I aestivate most gratefully. But I do wonder how you are, for life goes on apace and now I hear that you are fast abuilding a little church in the wilderness. How absolutely splendid! I wish you the best of luck with every beam and board of it. Perhaps I may see it finished one day – I hope so – but don't expect me to change my heathen habits. The bit of news print here enclosed is for your amusement, merely – the usual rubbish – usual source. What sort of person is "Pilgrym," do you think? Do you suppose he never – ever – smiles? The Queen sends good wishes and asks me to say that she is determined to visit you and see your church early next year when she comes to the Big Island.

With much aloha,
F. Cameron

A SPIRITUOUS COMPLAINT

To the Editor:

The new Anglican priest, Mr. David Wilkinson, has lost no time in showing his true character. Some on this coast had expected better of him. But at his first appearance on the Big Island, at Captain Hawkins' ranch, Mr. Wilkinson preached quite a *spirited* sermon; after which members of his party indulged in such a quantity of *spirits* that several were seen to fall from their horses on the way home. How long, Jehovah, must we suffer these blasphemers in our midst?

Pilgrym

*

From Scott Partridge, in the same bundle, came a copy of

an inflammatory public statement recently issued by Bishop Coldwell, to the effect that every church in Hawaii except his own was made up of Traitors, Dissenters, Imposters, Pretenders, and Frauds. All Honolulu, Scotty wrote, was in an uproar over it, and vibrations of the fury were even now reaching Maui. A large contingent of Anglicans, as well as Americans, called openly for the Bishop's resignation. *It is easy enough*, wrote Scott, *to guess why the Coldwells have suddenly decided to pack up and go abroad again.*

David felt almost entirely separated by now from the regime that had sent him to the Kona Coast. By the first of November, after two weeks of help from a local workman, his church was as finished as he could make it, and a modest *prie dieu* beside the front steps had been set aside for the memory of Captain Cook. The immense and smiling Hawaiian man who helped him at the end was so powerful that he could actually hold up the roof of the little building while David attached it to the walls.

In the absence of any orders to the contrary, he had chosen its name himself: this would be forever afterward known as Grace Memorial Church. It came to him one evening as he watched a sunset over the sea, when his rough little buildings were suddenly filled like enchanted honeycombs from floor to ceiling with radiant golden light.

By the end of the month, he found himself ministering to about a dozen souls, some of whom rode 15 miles or more for Sunday worship. Thus he saw the beginnings of a good little parish, with people meeting for prayer, caring for one another, and bringing the fruits of their orchards and gardens to share. On weekdays he read Morning Prayer, mainly for himself and a few curious birds and lizards, though the Cornwalls sometimes came to join him then with their rather frail infant son. He was disappointed that the Hawaiian population did not appear for services, but their children, he thought, might lead the way in time, since both English and Hawaiian youngsters attended his schoolroom classes.

The little green building with its broad eaves and covered

porches was as close to his dreams as he could make it, and it also made a delightful schoolhouse in all weathers. His pupils were excited to see – some for the first time – books written in English. The American missionaries had taught the native people only in Hawaiian, and this, David felt, left them at a practical disadvantage.

As for Soper Hawkins, David made no apology, nor did he send any response to the Bishop's letter, which seemed to him so rash and intemperate as to be a thing Coldwell might prefer to forget. To his surprise, Captain Hawkins came to church now and then, and even put a few small coins at times into the plate. Relations between the two men might have become more cordial now, had David not insisted that the Hawkins daughters, as well as his sons should be educated. Hawkins disagreed, and then, in an unfortunate turn of events, the eldest daughter developed an awkward attachment to David Wilkinson.

This was particularly vexing because Melissa Hawkins was already less a child than a young woman. With a comely little figure and masses of yellow hair, she took to gazing at David with dark, devouring eyes while he tried to give her the simplest of instructions: how to tell letters from numbers, and how to pronounce the words of her own language correctly. None of these matters, evidently, came to her attention at home. He sensed danger, and made certain that the two of them were never alone. Still, something must have been said, for one day Chin Wong Lo appeared at the parsonage to warn him, "Pelekane, you bettah get you wife!" David replied that he was far too poor and far too busy to think of marriage.

"No woman, no good!" he said. "I hear they talk."

"Who talks?"

"Boss he say something at table 'bout Lissy girl. Maybe you make one damn big *pilikia*."

David was amazed. *Pilikia* in Hawaiian meant *trouble*. Then he noticed that Chin Wong Lo was looking poorly; he was stooped and trembling, and the whites of his eyes had an unhealthy tinge. David took his hand and asked, "Lo, are you all right?" Lo nodded and looked away. "As for myself," David told him, "No *pilikia* here. My church says no wife for me, you see. Not now! I signed a paper. Not for quite some time, while I do this work. Do you understand?"

Lo gave a deep sigh, and nodded again. "Same damn thing Chinaman! Make name on paper, come this crazy place. All work, no woman, no good!"

*

His parents had promised to send David the harmonium from the parlor at Green Gardens, and one day it arrived in a large packing case. This instrument is somewhat difficult to play; you must not only press the keys, as with a piano, but also work a pedal with your feet. The resulting sounds, with David at the keyboard, were not always delightful, but he hoped to find a better artist among his congregation. Quite unexpectedly then a second crate arrived, about half the size of the first one, and upon opening it, he found that he was the owner of an amazing modern device called a "Noiseless Family Sewing Machine."

"Exactly what I have been needing," he told his chattering students as they gathered round. "A Noiseless Family! Why has no one thought of such a thing before?" Classwork had ended abruptly, and the children began to argue about which of them should try the new machine first.

"Pelekane!" said little Noni. "You are joking us! This is for make sewing!"

"A machine for sewing! Why, of course. Good for you, Noni. How did you know that?"

"Because it says," said Melissa at her haughtiest. "Just look, there on the cover. S-E-W-I-N-G M-A-C-H-I-N-E. *Machine for make sewing!*"

"But how does it work?" he asked. "Does anyone here know how to start it?"

"No! This is one woman thing," said Kimo. "Why you get this kine?"

Noni was on hands and knees, looking at the strange new object. "This kine like making music!" she cried. "Look, a pusher for the feet. Make it go *wiki-wiki*, then it sew."

She was right, of course. "We'll go back to our lessons now," said David. "Tomorrow we'll work together on the new machine, and see if we can make something useful.."

"Never!" said Kimo, sneering. "I never do that stupid thing."

*

By now David had raised a small shelter like the wing of a bird on one side of the little parsonage, calling it rather grandly his "pavilion." Here lived various objects that would not fit inside the hut, and here he also liked to sit and smoke his pipe at the end of the day. He carried the machine to that spot, and as he read over its puzzling directions, thought of Chin Wong Lo saying, "No woman, no good!" That indeed was his own situation. A picture rose before his eyes of a female person without a face or a name, seated at this device. What wonders she might perform! Hours of laborious handwork might be saved, and David might soon have some surplices for his tiny choir as well as curtains for the parsonage window. He had felt the need of a covering there, since people were curious about him, and he never knew who might be looking in.

And yet, no woman for sewing. There was Nancy Cornwall, who was always obliging, but she had more than enough on her plate already with a homestead to care for and an infant in delicate health. There were very few *haole* women in the district at the time, since most of the foreign settlers had married natives who rarely came to church. He did not expect Hawaiian volunteers, and most certainly, he would not ask Melissa Hawkins to help!

Therefore, Q.E.D., he would have to learn the management of the thing himself. One morning soon after this decision he was sitting in his pavilion with the pipe between his teeth, trying to introduce a thread for the first time into the machine's private places. The sun was only a hand's width above the horizon, and its light streamed brilliantly into the little shelter. At the sound of approaching hoof beats, he looked up half-blinded, wondering impatiently who this could be, for he did not want to be disturbed in the midst of such a delicate operation.

When the rider came into view, he saw that it was a heroic figure on a great white horse so handsome that it must have cost him a fortune. Caught by surprise, David felt a keen pang of envy. Against the sunset he could only see the outline of a form, which was tall and slender. A hat was placed squarely on his head and low across the brow, in the Hawaiian manner, with a floral wreath on the brim. Behind him was the silhouette of a bedroll and a pair of bulging saddlebags. The youth stopped beside the parsonage, and after a moment of regarding David, wondering perhaps at his curious occupation, swung himself easily from his horse and approached with a light, swift stride, saying, "Is that you, Mr. Wilkinson?"

The voice, he thought, was oddly familiar. Who could this be? The lad took off his hat and ran his fingers through short-cropped, curling hair. "Whew! I am hot! What a furnace of a day! Murderous! How are you, David? What on earth are you doing? Don't you know me? Well then, may a poor thirsty traveler trouble you for something cool to drink?" His visitor said all of this in the same familiar voice, while David Wilkinson stared. And stared and stared, for this was not a relative, or a younger brother, or a son of Julia Stuart's. It was Julia, which is to say, it was Fiona Cameron herself.

20

"But my dear, I know nothing whatever about sewing!" Fiona was squatting like a native on the ground, with her arms wrapped around her knees. "I can put on a button in emergency, no more. As for machines –" She left that thought unfinished.

He realized that he was still staring at her and looked away, though not for long. Only the voice was the same; she was strangely different in shape and color. Her waist was slender, her skin was darkened and flushed, her hair was shorn, with small, moist curls clinging to the nape of her neck. She was wearing a sort of garment he had never seen before, something made of plaid, neither a man's trousers quite, nor a woman's riding skirt.

"Are you cooking for yourself as well?" she asked. "I know how to make tea, and I can boil an egg very nicely if you like." She scrambled to her feet and stretched her arms over her head. "What a fine wee house you have! May I see it inside? And is that your church? Did you build that, too? What an odd, interesting structure! I've never seen anything like it."

"Of course. Please excuse me for being a poor host."

"You are surprised to see me."

"Yes."

"Surprised, but delighted. You've been wondering all this time when I might turn up?" Her dark eyes were sparkling with mischief.

"Actually…"

She laughed. "Actually, not. But the sight of me, I hope, does not make you actively unhappy."

"The sight of you is – well, astonishing. Wonderful beyond words. But Miss Stuart – Miss Cameron, rather, I must remark that you are changed."

"Fiona, please. You've changed too. You look marvelous. Absolutely glowing with health! Bravo! I'm going across the island by way of the volcano. Have you yet seen the famous Lake of Fire?? No? Well, I long to go there, but I thought on the way I'd stop for a bit with you. That is, if I may."

"You may indeed. In fact, you are most welcome. If I seem at all bothered, it's just that I didn't recognize you at first."

"Yes, well I suppose I did cut off most of my hair. I didn't expect it to be quite so short, but these things happen. Must I apologize? Are you shocked?"

"Of course not. Come, I'll show you the church."

They crossed the few intervening yards together to the little wooden building. Her eyes grew wide with pleasure as they approached. She walked now in a light and fluid, careless gait, almost as if she had cast her body aside and forgotten it. Inside the church it was dim and quiet, filled with the fragrance of new wood and the heady musk of beeswax candles from Yorkshire. He had not yet made the window that he would cut later, high on the eastern wall to capture the sunrise. He had built a dozen pews, and the interior space was otherwise empty and unadorned except for the harmonium, and a small cabinet covered with a green cloth, serving as altar. A pewter candlestick stood at either side of the altar, and on the eastern wall behind it there was a simple cross made from two sticks.

"It's beautiful!" she said. "I have never, ever seen anything like it."

"It's a beginning," said David "Just the essentials, as you see."

She moved about from place to place, looking and touching as if enchanted. Then she sat down on the last pew and closed her eyes for so long that David wondered whether she might be praying.

"I wouldn't be afraid here," she said quietly, after a time.

"Afraid?"

"To think about things. Death. Life. Pain, suffering, all of it. In such a place one might even manage to think good sense about God." She opened her eyes and smiled at him. "Well, you are in your element, I can see that!"

"And you in yours, I rather think. You seem so well!"

"That remains to be seen. But in the meantime, I am here and glad of it."

*

They had scraps for dinner, and then, after a certain amount of discussion, Fiona agreed to sleep in his bed. The floor of the pavilion with a *lau hala* mat, he insisted, was more than adequate for him. Still, he did not close his eyes until after midnight, but lay awake in a troubled frame of mind, caught between the keen pleasure of seeing her again and the annoying sense of having his privacy invaded. When he awakened somewhat later than usual, he found that his visitor had left. The bed was neatly arranged, and her horse and her belongings were nowhere to be seen. A heavy dew had fallen and the morning air was crisp. He went on bare feet to the church, where he stopped on an impulse at the steps and read Morning Prayer to the world at large, by way of a cheeping, scampering, scuttling congregation. Back at the parsonage, just as the sun appeared above the mountain, he discovered a message that he had failed to notice earlier. It was on a sheet of pale blue notepaper, curled into the spout of his teakettle.

I took an apple – thank you! Have gone exploring – back by teatime. F.C.

Teatime! He had forgotten its existence. It was his habit by now to drink the local Kona coffee at all odd hours, whether hot, cold or tepid made little difference, since he did not care for coffee in any case. He did have a tea pot, with a family of

171

spiders living in it. There was honey in the larder, but nothing by way of biscuits. The nearest crumpet was probably 250 miles away. She had sweetly volunteered to manage the boiling of an egg; however, he did not keep chickens. No chickens, no ducks, no eggs, no bread, no cake, no jam! He knew what he should do: Fiona should be escorted as soon as possible to the Hawkins homestead, where she would be far more comfortable. He thought about that for less than half a minute before realizing that he was not willing to do it.

All through the day he felt uneasy, while coping as usual with the children's lessons and trying to master the arcane mysteries of the sewing machine. Was it selfishness on his part, wanting to keep Fiona Cameron with him? Or was it an honest effort to protect her from something unhappy, something perhaps truly menacing, that he sensed in that house? Hawkins' eldest daughter Melissa lingered as usual after school. Then she asked softly, "Tell me something, Pelekane –"

"Yes?"

"Who was that in your bed last night?"

"In my what?" He was furious. "Who has been peering into my window? You? Have you any idea what that tells me about your character?"

She had never seen him lose his temper before, and she was fascinated. He went on to preach a fiery sermon on the sanctity of the home, on every man's right to privacy, on the duty of a host to protect his guest from every form of injury, assault or intrusion, and on the wickedness of spying and prying in general. By the time he finished, he knew that he sounded like one of the angry American Calvinists, and Melissa was making it plain that she was quite bored. He had the impression that she would have no respect for him, or for anything he said, unless he should take up a stick and beat her. Was that what happened at home? Was it what they taught her on the hilltop while he struggled here below to teach Christian kindness? "Melissa Hawkins!" he said. "Where is your sense of decency?"

She shrugged. "It was Pa. He wanted to know."

"Wanted to know what?"

"If it was a boy or a girl. Maybe one *paniolo* looked in and saw. I never spy in your window." Her voice was low, and she closely examined her fingers one by one.

"In that case, Miss Hawkins, I owe you an apology. I am sorry to have spoken so sharply, and now we shall say no more about it." And he turned away in disgust, for he was wholly unable to believe her.

*

Fiona arrived late in the afternoon, rosy and joyful, with a package that was elegantly done up in a banana leaf and tied with braided stems. "Tea!" she cried triumphantly. "Or supper, if you prefer." She had been down at the seaside village, she said, and had met everyone there. Such splendid people! They had all spoken so well of David, and were delighted to hear where she was staying. There had been a gigantic person named Maile, a brilliant woman, who had given her something called a *lomi lomi*, even better than the ones at Emma's, she said. David made a mental note to find out what a *lomi lomi* was.

After that she had been bathing in the sea and playing for hours in the tide pools with the children. Glorious fun! Her bathing garment must be hung out to dry – it was a *muu muu* in the Island style, a fine costume for such adventures, she said - though so tattered by now that she must have a new one made. Finally, she had met a kind old man called *Kupuna*, who had approached her with a great glistening, tremendous silver fish just pulled from the ocean. He had given her a fine fat slice of it, and said, "Take! Eat! This is good eating kind."

"I believe that *Kupuna* is an honorific – a title – rather than a name," said David.

"Oh I see. Well, he was indeed a most patrician being. A beautiful man with dark mahogany skin that looked actually polished, and the cleanest, whitest hair, and the most brilliant black eyes. He called you "Pelican" and said he was your friend. Do you know the one I mean? He told me that all the people there love you. Are you aware of that? He is sorry he does not come to your church services. Perhaps he will come one day, he said. Well, you see, this splendid chunk of fish was his gift – from the heart, I could see – so how could I refuse it? I was terribly ashamed that I had nothing to give in return. Money, I thought, would not be appropriate, so I gave him one of the best shells I had found, and he seemed pleased. To Maile who had done so much for me, I had already given my little traveling mirror, the folding kind, in a rather nice leather case. Was that right, do you think? She opened it and laughed when she saw her face."

Chattering on in this lively fashion, Fiona was sitting cross-legged in the pavilion while David cleaned the fish. He had already prepared his *imu* – a Hawaiian version of an oven in the ground – and island grown sweet potatoes were roasting there, covered in banana leaves. He had picked the first of his ripening mangoes, and was slicing it when she gave a great yawn and said, "I am talking far too much, and you are doing all the work. What may I do to help? Nothing? Are you sure? Then tell me, at least, did you have a good day?"

"Much as usual. Not nearly so interesting as yours."

"Will you need a fire for the fish? That's something, at least, that I can do." She scavenged twigs and knelt at his stove that consisted of a circle of lava rocks among weeds; then purposefully, without a waste motion, kindled an excellent little blaze.

"Very nice!" he said. "And you have done some fine missionary work today."

"Ha!" said she. "I never said a word about religion."

"Of course not. You offered your friendship. When I taught children from the Yorkshire mills, I am sure that my soup showed them more of God's love than my sermons. Looking back, I suppose I was quite a bleak, unhappy person in those days."

"You made soup for them?"

"Well, yes."

"How ever in the world did you learn to do that? But I fed

no one today. In fact, I allowed them to give me this splendid fish, which I certainly didn't deserve."

"It's called Grace," he said lightly. "Giving and receiving – you'll see a lot of it here in these islands. But enough talk. Our meal is ready. Shall we go in?"

"Oh no. Please! Couldn't we just stay here by the fire?

"Well, why not? Yes, of course. Blessed, praised and adored be Christ our Lord, who gives us this good food and this welcome visitor – in the name of the Father, the Son and the Holy Ghost, Amen."

"Amen, amen!" she cried. "I'm starving!"

At this, David smiled a secret smile to himself, remembering the moment when this impetuous Scottish lady had suddenly thrown her bonnet overboard, and then had burst into tears; and now he remembered that she had never given him back his handkerchief.

"Actually," she said, "I am indeed most thankful. What a beautiful meal! And how very civilized of you to have nice china plates, here in the wilderness. Do tell me what kind of fish this is, and where it has been living."

"This is *ono*," he told her, "a particularly sweet, succulent sort of white fish that dwells in the deeper ocean nearby. I have cooked it only a little, quite gently, with garden herbs, and have dressed it in tender young taro leaves that were steamed over the same pot. After this we shall have roasted sweet potatoes with a bit of butter, and roasted taro root as well, if you care for it. Next, a modest salad of greens from my garden."

"Amazing! And what, pray, for dessert?"

"Surprise," he said. "Wait and see." The mango had been picked too soon, but he was soaking it in sherry. Actually, the fruit was an unexpected gift for him; he had not known what kind of tree it was when he placed his hut beside it. Then quite suddenly it had nearly doubled in size, growing visibly from day to day, and fruiting with a speed that astonished him. Only later had he learned that a mango tree beside a dwelling was considered by local folk to be a lucky omen.

So it was that the two dined that night in the warm, soft air under a starlit canopy of darkness, rarely speaking at first because they were both so hungry. Later in the meal they fell into conversation that was random, spare, and contented as if they had been the oldest of friends and comrades. Reluctant to let the evening end, David dug out from his larder a wedge of Holland cheese, while Fiona fetched a pair of biscuits from her saddlebags. They had made a mutual decision against either tea or coffee, but their wine was the rarest, most extravagant part of the menu: it was pure Kona rain-water, vintage 1867, collected by Richard Cornwall, and kept like the precious substance it was, in glass bottles topped with cork. At last they were both replete, and there was a long, tranquil silence. "Bliss!" said Fiona.

"Paradise" he replied. "Yes indeed."

She closed her eyes and shook her head, as if in unbelief. He lit his pipe and leaned back to gaze at the stars. The Southern Cross glittered on the seaward horizon, while Cygnus the Swan flew down the Milky Way, and noble Arcturus blazed overhead. He explained to her that Arcturus was known to Hawaiians as the Star of Gladness – *Hokulea*. Gladness indeed! He was nearly overcome with it. She said that she was overcome entirely, then stretched like a cat, yawned and took herself off to the pavilion. She had murmured something earlier about washing up, but soon afterward he found her fast asleep, curled on the *lau hala* mat. He did not want to wake her, and so found her own woolen blanket, covered her with it, and made his way into the house.

Before retiring, he wrote a single word in his diary for the day: EDEN. Then he fell asleep and slept more deeply than he had at any time since leaving home. Late in the night something changed, and he began fearing that he was lost, or that he had lost some part of his powers, so that he would soon find himself in *pilikia*. Then toward morning he dreamed of the fruit that was forbidden, for his narrow bed was changed now that her head had rested for a night on his pillow, and his blanket carried her scent.

21

"Ho there, anyone home? Ho, Mr. Wilkinson?" It was morning, and the sun was already over the mountain. He dredged himself from Stygean depths, pulled trousers on over his nightshirt, and staggered to the door. There were four horsemen: Captain Hawkins on his stallion, whip in hand, and three paniolos behind him grinning while their ponies kicked up dust.

"Where's my Chinaman?" Hawkins shouted to the air above David's head. "Have you got him here?"

"Good morning. No, sir. I have no idea."

"He's run away. Hiding somewhere. A little fella, he don't speak English so good. You know the one."

"He is not here," said David.

"I have reason to believe he's come to you! We're going to look around."

"That is not the case, sir, I assure you. And I regret that I cannot give you permission…"

"Cannot give…? Just a minute! This man is a criminal! He has stolen food from me, food and wine, and he's taken a blanket. Whose horse is that?"

"Captain Hawkins, I have told you that your servant is not here. Now, if you'll excuse me…"

"Whose horse is that over there, the white one?" he shouted.

"It is mine." Fiona Cameron had emerged from the pavilion wrapped in her blanket, dazed with sleep and blinking against the sunlight.

"What's that you say? Who are you?" snapped Hawkins.

"The horse is mine," she repeated.

"Who are you?" he shouted again.

She laughed. "And who, may I ask, are you?" Hawkins looked from Fiona to David and back again.

"Lady Fiona Cameron," David said, with a bow, "May I present Captain Soper Hawkins, owner of the ranch nearby, and a member of my Church."

She thought it over. "No, you may not," she said coolly. "I do not wish to know this person. Especially, not before breakfast," She turned with the look of a swan drifting on a lake, and floated off toward the tree where her horse was tethered.

"What in the hell…" Hawkins began, with a curious light in his eyes. "Who is that?"

"That is a lady, sir. My guest."

"Staying with you? Alone?"

David Wilkinson did not answer him.

"No family? No servants? Where did she come from?"

Again, David said nothing.

"Well, boys," he told his paniolos, "You've seen it all now. You can put your eyes back in your heads. Vicar says Chinaman's not here, and that's good enough for me. Manuel! Give him the message." Manuel handed David a crumpled piece of paper.

"Never a dull moment, eh?" Hawkins said to David with a sneer. Then he applied his spurs so that his mount leapt forward, and the four men hastily departed.

David looked at the message. It was from poor old Herr Lindt, 75 miles away on the mountain. He begged David to come quickly, for he was on his deathbed, and it had been written nearly a week ago.

*

Two days later, very nearly too late, David reached the mountain cottage. His good gray Curate had been unavailable, and so he was forced to hire an inferior horse, a lazy, quarrelsome creature. The curse of the journey was lifted, however, because Fiona Cameron was with him. She said that she had already planned to ride in that direction, and also that she might be of help with old Lindt, since she had some experience of nursing.

Little was said between them on the way, for they were in a constant hurry, tending only to distance and weather, the compass and the map, the water they had with them, the food and the medicines. By now David understood better the way she had chosen to dress, for the plaid that covered Fiona from waist to ankles was cleverly designed as a pair of loose, flaring trousers, so that she could ride as the Hawaiian women did, modestly astride. She was an excellent rider although, he thought, far bolder than was wise. He asked himself why a woman, after having been seriously ill, or perhaps gravely injured, would be riding now with such verve and abandon. Had the new name brought about a mysterious change in her character? He thought of the Hawaiian custom of changing a sick child's name in order to effect a cure. Mailelani had been surprised to hear that this was not a regular part of British medicine; she claimed that it always worked.

Poor Lindt, when they found him, was breathing in gasps and nearly consumed with fever. The odor of the sickroom was a terrible thing. David threw windows open and started a fire while Fiona knelt beside the old man, bathing his face and hands with cool water, and trying to help him drink. When he could not do it, she wiped his mouth out gently with a bit of gauze, and gave him a clean wet cloth to suck on.

"How do you say baby in German?" she asked.

"Don't know. Sorry."

"Never mind, he understands. There, Liebschen, that will give you a little comfort." They boiled water, scrubbed sheets, and hung them out on a line together, using curiously carved clothespins that Lindt must have made himself. Then Fiona bathed the old man with great tenderness, preserving his modesty as well as possible, and calling him her Liebschen all the while.

"He will fall in love with you," David told her.

"It's the only German word I know."

"He speaks English, or used to. Herr Lindt? Do you hear me? It's David Wilkinson. You are quite safe now. We are here, and we will stay as long as you need us. I will say some prayers now, and anoint you with holy oil. Do you understand?"

"Take his hand," she said, "Like this. Ask him to press you hand, to say yes."

The hand of the invalid was so frail and light that it was almost like holding a leaf. Yet when it stirred, its meaning was clear. When, very gently, David placed the mark of Christ upon the old man's forehead, Lindt's eyes rolled so far back into his skull that he thought the end had come. But it had not, and in a short time he emerged from his deathlike swoon, muttering something unintelligible.

"What was that?" David asked. "Herr Lindt? What did you say?"

"Zuckerdo..."

"Zucker - ? What's that again? "

"Dich…deine…Zuckerdose."

"Fiona, something about sugar?"

"I think so," she said. "It's something for you – it's deine – thine. David, there's something he says is yours. It's important to him and he wants you to have it. A zuckerdose. A dose of sugar? No. A *something* of sugar. A loaf? A lump? A spoonful? A cup? A tin? A sack? A sugar bowl?"

With surprising strength, Lindt pressed David's hand.

"Bowl. I'll look for it," she said, and found it rather quickly, on the highest shelf of a kitchen cupboard. It was a beautiful old piece of china made in Dresden, with painted garlands of blue and yellow flowers all around. The top of its lid was fashioned like a beehive, with tiny china bees going in and out.

Such a valuable object was seldom found in any home so rough and simple as this; in fact, it may have been the dying man's chief treasure. She put her finger inside and tasted. "Yes, of course. Sugar."

"I am honored, Herr Lindt," David told him. "Thank you for such a splendid gift. I shall keep it always, in your memory. And now my dear sir, it is time for you to put your burdens down and allow yourself to rest. Never fear, the lady Fiona – the nurse – and I will take care of everything, and if you go to sleep, we will still be here, watching over you."

The poor soul had been alone for so long, and under such frightening conditions, that David felt it best to stay close for some time, holding the old man's hand. Fiona crouched at the other side of the bed, holding Lindt's other hand, and after a while began to sing very softly, as if to soothe a fretful infant. It was a sentimental tune quite familiar to David – a bit of age-old nonsense from the nursery, about a tired little shepherd boy, and his horn, and sheep in the meadow, and cows in the corn.

Lindt closed his eyes and did not speak or move again, except for the occasional fluttering of his eyelids. A little more than an hour later, just as David thought of speaking to him again, he drew a shallow breath with a catch in it, and then another of the same, and then he was gone. To David's amazement, Fiona fled as soon as she saw what had happened. He found her standing outside with her arms folded, perfectly silent, but with a flood of tears pouring down her face.

"Don't! Oh my dear, you have been so brave. He is safe now. Nothing can hurt or frighten him ever again. And he was a very old man, who told me plainly quite some time ago that he was ready to go."

"I am no one's dear!" she said, and began to sob. He fought a powerful urge to take her in his arms, and then simply stood still, looking at her, wondering what to do. But she quickly regained her composure and began wiping her eyes, like an angry child, on the back of her hand. Relieved, he gave her his handkerchief.

"Thank you," she said absently, and thrust it into her pocket. "So, what happens now?"

"I'll bury him here beside his wife. We had talked about it. Then I'll notify Kevin Kildare, the sheriff. He is a good man; he'll manage the rest."

"He will need a cairn!" she said. "Yes, we must build a cairn for him. But I am suddenly so terribly hungry. Ravenous, in fact. Wicked of me at such a time I know, but I can't help it."

He looked at his watch. "Nearly four in the morning. Time for tea."

*

She did not weep again, but insisted upon washing the body herself and helping him to dress it in the only suit they could find. They buried him at noon, and managed to build together a rather large cairn of lava rocks above the grave. Fiona said that she must go on to the volcano the following day; he thought it unwise, but nothing that he said would sway her. After a long, somewhat heated discussion, they came to an agreement: she would stop at the shepherd's station for the first night, and ask there for a guide to the summit.

"I am not afraid," she said stubbornly, "because there is nothing to be afraid of here in Hawaii. Nothing evil in all these lovely islands."

"On the contrary! You are far too trusting! And you might have an accident."

"No more likely than at home. As a child I was always roaming the hills. And here, the climate is so much kinder."

"It can be extremely cold in these mountains. You may wake up some morning covered with snow."

"I have my blanket, my bedroll, a good long cape lined in oiled cloth. I have dried beef with me, and oranges. I have biscuits in a tin, and plenty of water. All that I could possibly need. And, I always carry a knife. So…" She stretched her arms upward, arching her back. "I could hardly bear the heat in Honolulu. This mountain air is so much better. So I shall go out yonder and sleep under the moon tonight."

"Very well," said David, finding himself quite annoyed with her. "But there will be no moon." And then, cruelly, "What would your uncle have said about all this rambling about on your own?"

"Hah!" was her answer. "<u>That</u> one!"

But he persisted. "Well then, your parents?"

"I am not a child, Mr. Wilkinson! In any case, they are all dead. Surely I told you that both of my parents died long ago, and that was why I had to live with Uncle."

"The chess player."

"Yes." She turned and left him then, without saying so much as goodnight. He walked about in the house for a while, wondering what would become of Lindt's possessions. He plucked a string of the old violin, but did not know how to play it. He picked up Lindt's Bible only to find that it was in German, so he could not read it. He searched shelves and cupboards, but the Bible was the only book in the house. They had buried him in a relatively new pair of shoes, but his old boots were still there on the floor, wearing in their folds and wrinkles the memory of his flesh.

He walked around the bed without touching it, and decided that it would be best to burn the mattress and all of Lindt's linens in the morning. He washed his hands with soap several times and ate an apple, wishing for a piece of cheese and a bit of bread to go with it. Then, determined to rest even if he could not sleep, he lay down on the parlor floor and drew a *lau hala* mat over him. The night was very silent, and very dark.

Several times during the following hour, David started up and looked all around him, imagining that he had heard a sound, or that he had seen the flicker of a movement at the edge of his vision. It occurred to him repeatedly that something in the night air was alive, awake and stirring. Christian though he was, and a priest at that, he had been led by some primitive impulse to leave all the windows open, and to keep a lamp burning on the floor. Perhaps he imagined that the power of ghosts was not yet fully banished in this alien land; or that the spiritual presence of the dead man might not depart willingly from the house; or even that other, more dangerous phantoms might be abroad.

At long last he fell into a sleep so deep that he was bewildered when he awakened. Consciousness came suddenly then, with a strong sense of alarm. He looked first at the lamp beside him, which was very low, though still burning. Then he realized that the cottage door had blown open. A tall figure stood there motionless. The night was black beyond, and heavy with mist, but there was no wind.

"Who's there?" he cried. Without taking his eyes from the intruder, he rose slowly to his feet with the lamp in his hand, and took a step forward. Then another, and another, until he could see before him the body of a woman with bare feet, and in fact, wholly naked below the waist. Wide-eyed and staring, Fiona Cameron was standing there still and cold as a statue, with her hands thrust forward as if to push someone or something away. Holding the lamp to her face, David saw that she was in a trance, with her mind utterly lost in darkness.

"Fiona! What is the matter? What are you doing?"

She answered at once, without any show of emotion, "Kindly ignore me, Uncle, I am just passing through."

He put the lamp down, and took both of her cold hands in his. "Wake up, Fiona! You are dreaming!" Her skin was like marble, and he could not find a pulse at her wrist. "Come, I will cover you! Fiona, I must make you warm, or you may be ill. Come, sit down here, it is perfectly safe. I will not let anything hurt you! Fiona!"

Still, she did not move. She seemed scarcely to be breathing. On a sudden impulse, he shouted close to her ear, "Miss Stewart! Lady Julia! It is time for you to wake up!" At this, she moaned a little, and allowed him to bring her down gently to a crouching position, where he quickly covered her with his own blanket, and held her fast. She gave one great sob, and then began to rock gently back and forth, back and forth with a low whimpering or keening sound that was like that of a small, hurt animal. It was also – as he recalled from the dim, distant past – like the moan of a woman approaching the peak of her ecstasy. "Oh, it is you! It is really you! Love me, love me!" she said in tranced, uncanny tones; and then, with a little cry, drew the coverings away from her nudity, and pressed her body close to his. Alas for David Wilkinson and all his tribe, whatever their suffering, there are some things a gentleman does not do. Therefore he covered her again, and hushed her, and told her that she was his own sweet dear, and stroked her head, and rocked her in his arms until she slipped away at last into a tranquil sleep. For the rest of the night they lay together, and she slept on his shoulder with her soft breath stirring against his throat. *God help me, what is the meaning of this?* David thought. *Surely she does not know what she has done – what she has said just now! For she must be still a maiden – yes, as surely as she is a lady, gently bred. But her secret thoughts are wild, for life has somehow injured her, and left a touch of madness, or a moral scar.*

Her skin was like silk, and the fullness of her soft flesh at bosom and thigh was something he could not have guessed, or dreamed of, seeing her clothed. For the longest night in his memory he made a valiant effort not to move or stir in any way that might disturb her, trying not to touch, or even to think about the nearness of her body's private places, all surrendered to him in such childlike trust. Above all, he knew that he must not fall asleep even for a moment, for fear of what might happen next.

22

S hortly after dawn she turned her head and stared at him, horror-struck. Without a word she leapt away, snatched the blanket around her, and fled out of doors. When David followed, she turned on him in a fury and cried, "God in heaven! What has happened? What have you done? My God, how dare you!"

"Done? What have I done? Nothing, by the grace of God. Nothing at all. What have you done to me?"

"What? What are you saying?"

"You tempted me, woman! All night long, you tempted me!"

"I what?"

"Tempted me to abandon every principle – every solemn vow! Made my night a hell, hour after hour! And now you run away and try to blame me for nothing at all!"

"Do you mean, nothing happened?" She was incredulous.

"I have said it."

"I came to you like this, and…"

"Nothing happened."

"And we lay together, and…"

"Nothing. Fiona, you were not yourself. You were deeply asleep, in a trance, unconscious. Don't you understand? And you were unhappy, you were grieving!" *Hellfire*, he thought, *this woman is impossible! Now she has me apologizing because I didn't violate her.*

"Grieving?" Suddenly she was quite calm. "Oh I see, I see. I must have been walking in my sleep again. But I haven't done that for ages."

"Whatever you were doing, Fiona, the point is that I did not take advantage of you. I hope that proves, at least, that I am worthy of your trust."

"It started when my parents died," she said. "I used to wander about in the garden at night – sound asleep, and looking for something, I never knew what. But I didn't scream this time, did I?"

"No, nothing like that, but at first you were weeping."

"I used to scream terribly, and that upset the household, So Uncle tied me to the bed, and sometimes he would throw cold water on me."

"Fiona, listen to me, please. I want you to understand that I am a civilized being, with a rather keen sense of responsibility."

"But why now, do you suppose? And why undressed? I'm certain that I have never, ever gone roaming in such a state before."

"Never mind, Fiona, all is forgiven, and no one shall ever hear of this from me. But above all, I want you to understand that you can trust me. And I want help you, truly I do. Some day, I hope – that is to say, young and penniless as I am, and otherwise no doubt unworthy, I dare dream even now that one day you and I –"

"Oh damn!" she cried. "It's coming back to me now. What did I do? Did I say anything?"

"Never mind. I am not going to tell you."

"Why on earth not?"

"Because I don't care to, that's why. Because you won't listen."

"I believe," she said with her chin in the air, "that I have entirely disgraced myself."

"What difference does that make, if you trust me? That is

the point. If you have any regard for me at all, why then… Look here, either you respect me or you don't, Fiona. Either you trust me or you do not. Now, make up your mind, which will it be?"

"At this hour of the morning?" she said. "You can't be serious. I'm scarcely awake enough to remember who you are!"

David was outraged. "That does it!" he shouted. "Take care of yourself, then! I want nothing further to do with you. In fact, I shall never speak to you again!" He strode toward the house in a fury, and as he reached the door, a rather large chunk of lava sailed past his ear and smashed into the lintel. He looked back at Fiona in astonishment, and called to her, "See here, what do you think you are doing?" She was panting and scowling in the cruel morning light, with her hair in a tangle and one hand flailing. He had never known a woman who could look so alluring at one moment, and then at the next, so ugly and mean.

"You vermin!" she shrieked. "Someone should beat you black and blue!"

"Just you try it!" was his answer. "Just try it and see what happens." For a few moments she seemed to give the thought some serious consideration. Then she sank to the ground with the blanket largely ignored, and put her hands over her face. Much as she had done the night before, she began to rock back and forth, and he was afraid that she would begin again with her pitiful keening. He could not bear to see a woman weep, and yet he knew that if he approached, she might claw his eyes out.

Then it came to him that she was not grieving. She was laughing, rocking back and forth in violent seizures of merriment. Against his better judgment, he could not help chuckling along with her, and when she saw his response, she began to howl with glee. Moments later, both of them were well on their way toward hysteria. "Oh stop it!" she cried. "Oh we mustn't! Oh this is so wicked, we must stop."

He could not speak for laughter.

Fiona shrieked, "To go on like this when the poor man is

dead, right here beside us. Oh God, I hope he can't hear. This is terrible! We must stop."

"But Fiona, the sight of you dodging about, and the look on your face!" He dried his eyes on his sleeve. "Actually, I have no idea why this is all so funny. But it is."

"Oh dear, oh dear," she said, and then again, "Oh dear."

"Look here, you thief," he said. "Don't you ever give a man's handkerchief back to him? You must have half a dozen of mine by now."

"Liar," she said. "Go away and allow me to dress."

*

A short time later she came quietly into the cottage, wearing her usual riding costume with a fresh white silk scarf. She looked beautiful again, in her curiously shorn way, but very tired. They sat down together at the kitchen table, he with his coffee, she with her tea. He had developed a plan of Euclidian clarity and simplicity. He would say (1) that they had shared some unusual experiences in the past few days, (2) that nothing of the sort must happen again, (3) that he could not consider the prospect of marriage in the near future, on account of his pledge to the Church, and (4) that they ought to shake hands as friends and part amicably.

"I have been thinking," he remarked. All in all, not a strong beginning.

"Well yes," she said, "one does." Her expression was quizzical, lacking something of respect.

He soldiered on. "A few days ago we were, quite honestly, in Paradise. You said so yourself. Then everything changed."

"That idiot from your Church came shouting round —"

"Yes, but I mean to say —"

"— and ruined a perfectly lovely morning."

"Ruined more than that. But the trouble began earlier, by my own fault. The fact is that I was proud and greedy enough to want more than we – ah —"

"More of what?" She regarded him without a quiver of

189

embarrassment. He rose from his chair, went outside for the coffee pot, brought it in from the fire, and filled his cup. "Will you be wanting more tea?"

"No," she said. "But I understand the situation better now. I came to stay with you in all innocence, in all ignorance I should say, and selfishly, stupidly trusting on the basis of brief acquaintanceship. And I have made you unhappy, and also I very much fear that I may have damaged your reputation. If that is true, then I am extremely sorry. How can it be mended? I must leave you now, immediately, and your next guest, I think, must be a respectable gentleman, preferably a fellow clergyman. Scott Partridge, perhaps?"

"I am sure you imagined, Fiona, that I must have a manse, and servants, and so on, like the vicars at home. Instead, you found yourself alone with a pauper in a wilderness."

"In an Eden!" she said with a beautiful smile. "In Paradise! Yes! And so I suppose we might have behaved accordingly. But I am truly sorry that I tempted you." She stood up and offered him her hand. "And now I must go."

"It's the human condition," he said, standing up but refusing the hand. "It's a ruinous thing that has happened again and again ever since Genesis, and I suppose it will happen again forever."

"<u>Genesis</u>!" She was instantly angry again. "Oh my God, what are you saying? That everything bad in this world is the fault of Eve? Of her sinfulness? Eve and the snake? Is that what you mean?" But David was no woman-hater. He had an answer that he was proud of, having used it in several very well-received sermons. "Eve has been much despised throughout the ages," he said, "but God made her, and Adam loved her! Let us never forget that."

The ladies generally dabbed at their eyes after this, and sighed contentedly. Not Fiona. She grinned in a nasty way, showing two rows of perfectly even little white teeth. "Love? She asked. "Love, indeed! Are you certain? *Bone of my bone, Flesh of my flesh,* Adam said. That tells me he was extremely fond of himself. And they obeyed, yes, the two of them did – they were fruitful and multiplied. That's easy! A fly or a flea can do that. But if a world full of little human babies was the object, God might have grown them on trees."

"That is − so − that is the most −" he began, but could not finish. It had come to him in a flash that he might easily seize this woman, throw her to the floor and violate her. She was near to his own height, but he was heavier, stronger and much angrier, suffering simultaneously from fatigue, confusion, embarrassment, disappointment, and an excess of sexual irritation that left him almost unable to think. What a fool she was! Alone here with him on the mountain! Was he not a man, after all? Was he not human?

All this time she was gazing at him with a look so pure, level and strong that a troop of angels might have walked upon it safely. Her eyes, he now realized, were not black after all, but extremely dark brown, with unusual depth and brilliance. In her pupils, as in a camera obscura, he could see his own image: a tiny homunculus captured in light.

He must have lost more than half of his wits during that long glance, for he touched her face then, and said, "Dear heart, you need looking after. Stay with me for a while."

"No David, I don't want looking after. And surely you don't want a woman who throws rocks."

"But I do. So long as it is you."

There were suddenly tears in her eyes.

"Please don't cry."

"Remember the zuckerdose! Wrap it carefully in something soft so it won't break."

"Yes, I will."

"Well, then −"

"Yes? Anything. Say it."

"We two are so very different," she said sadly. "I've been wondering why it is that there is this strange knowledge − or mental connection − between us. At times, I promise you that I can actually hear what you are thinking."

"Madam, I sincerely hope not."

"But yes. And I know that you are such a good man that

you often suffer for it. Then last night, you understood me perfectly. You didn't scorn me, or scold, or decide that I was insane."

Simple, he thought. *Love understands*. But she was sitting firm in the saddle now, with her hat tucked down at a rakish, defiant angle. So he said, "Oh, that roaming about in the night, you mean? Think nothing of it. When we were at school, Scotty used to walk in his sleep all the time."

"Didn't climb naked into your bed, I trust."

He laughed. "No, none of that. What Scott wanted was always in the kitchen. He used to wake in the morning at St. Columba's and find that he'd stolen half a dozen crumpets and a pie."

"He didn't devour them while he was unconscious?"

"Well no," said David. "That wouldn't have given him any satisfaction, now would it? Sound asleep? You should know!"

"I should?"

"Why yes. Scotty wasn't stupid. He saved up the lot until he was wide awake. Then he feasted."

"No! Shameless creature! Oh! Goodbye, goodbye!" She was laughing again now, and perhaps even blushing a little. Yes, definitely, she was looking quite rosy.

"Well then, off with you, girl! Be careful! God bless!" He slapped her horse's rump and she rode away from him, still laughing. He watched her until she was out of sight, and after that, stood in the same spot for quite a long time, kicking at pebbles and grinding his teeth.

BOOK THREE: WILDERNESS

23

The obstreperous horse gave David a taste of hellfire on the way home. After trying to scrape off his rider with the aid of various low-hanging tree limbs, he repeatedly bolted away at full gallop downhill. Finally, when David dismounted to check the harness and have a soothing talk with him, the villainous beast kicked him in the face.

Fortunately, David had moved quickly enough so that it was a glancing blow. Without stopping to assess the damage, he remounted and drove the creature mercilessly, pushing him to the point of shuddering exhaustion over the last ten miles; in fact, the old Mauna Loa trail may never have been covered faster. Back at the stables, he threw the reins at the liveryman without a word, and walked home in a miserable state, for of all things he loathed in fellow human beings, it was cruelty – either to people or animals.

While he hung up his saddlebags in the pavilion, blood continued to flow from his jaw, and so he reached for his handkerchief, only to recall that Fiona had it. At this, he turned with a great, unseemly roar and kicked the innocent sewing machine. Then he stripped off his bloodstained shirt, mopped his throat with it, and hurled it furiously to the floor. At the same time, something new crept into his consciousness: the sense that there was someone watching him, quite nearby.

"Hell and damnation!" he cried, without stopping to think who his audience might be. "Is there no privacy on this island?"

Cross-legged in a corner of the pavilion, Chin Wong Lo sat smiling as blissfully as a small contemplative Buddha. "Oh-ho!" he said, "Velly bad face. Lady make you that?"

"Of course not. A horse kicked me. And by the way, friend, you are in trouble. The Captain was here looking for you."

"Damn good lady! I see her talk to Boss." His shoulders shook with mirth.

"Don't say damn unless you mean it. So you've been here all along, have you? In hiding, I suppose. But where?"

"No *pilikia*! Undah house. Only sleep, no take thing. Lookee, Mistah Pelekane, you pay dollah for this *Pake*" – using the local word for Chinese – "then I blong you."

"What are you saying? I don't buy people."

"You good man sure. Captain no good. You make paper, I work for you, more bettah."

"I can't do that, Lo. But look here, Captain Hawkins doesn't own you! He is only your boss, your employer. You are being paid?"

"Boss say, work now, pay later. *Auwe!* Too much hard. Too much all wore out."

"Same thing my line of work," said David. "But we must both keep to our agreements." He reminded Lo that he had signed a contract for five years of labor. How much of it was already past? Nearly a year, said Lo, since he had already spent some months cooking on a "*haole* ship" before being turned over to Soper Hawkins. The name of the yacht, curiously enough, was the *Amaryllis*. David had him repeat it so that he could be sure, and made a mental note to ask Lo later about that interesting part of his servitude.

"Well, I understand your point a little better now," he told the Chinese servant. "Your contract has already been turned over once to a new owner. Were you given any choice in the matter? No? I am sorry. I wish I could help you out, but even if it could be arranged with the Captain, I have no money to pay you."

"You got three English undah bed!" David let out another roar, for all in all, this was not one of his better days.

"Entertaining yourself, were you, while I was away, going through my belongings?"

"No, no Mistah. No *pilikia*. See, I make nice." His face glowing with pride, he showed the priest into his little house, which was now immaculate. Every object he owned had been scrubbed and polished. The very walls had been washed down, and the eight panes of glass in his windows were shining. All was in place, including the three English pound notes that David had hidden under his mattress. He felt like a trespasser himself, filthy, reeling and bedraggled. He thanked Lo heartily as his knees began to tremble and his head to spin.

"You got bad face, Boss," said Lo. "Too much bloody. Sit, sit! Take easy! I bling water, *wiki-wiki*, I bling tea!"

David Wilkinson groaned as he lowered himself to the bed. How nice it was, after all, to have a servant! If only he could afford it, he could very much enjoy such a life. Lo soon brought him a bowl with a steaming cloth that he applied to his jaw.

"Coffee, please, Lo. I don't think you'll find any tea in the larder. On the other hand, what time is it? Nearly six in the afternoon. Must I assume that you have already finished up my sherry?"

"No, no Boss. Never touch. I got whiskey, Captain place."

"He told me it was wine you stole from him."

"Oh-oh! Big lie. One bottah whiskey, no more. Velly bad man, him Captain, him no tell troof."

"Tomorrow morning," said David, "You and I shall have a serious discussion of the Eighth Commandment. It is on the subject of stealing, which is something we are not supposed to do. After that, we'll go back to the Hawkins place together. Don't be afraid, I'll ask him not to punish you. Just now, for a moment or two, I think that I must close my eyes."

"Sleep," said his visitor. "I wait for you." And almost without moving, David slept for the next fourteen hours.

When he brought Chin Wong Lo back to the ranch the following day, Hawkins was not at home. A ship's surgeon, visiting from an English vessel at Kealakekua Bay, had a look

195

at his wound, clucked over it, cleaned it up and bandaged it for him. He would also have done some sewing on it if David had agreed, but he did not care for the smell of the surgeon's breath nor the look of his needles either, so he declined. Since he had never been seriously ill, David paid little attention to the man's warnings about "inflammation of the blood" and only felt surprised to see himself in a looking glass as he departed, with one side of his face a good deal larger than the other. Before quitting the house, he left a note for Captain Hawkins on the front hall table, asking him to treat his Chinese servant with kindness and mercy.

*

Three days later, David realized that he was in serious trouble. Despite a rising fever, he had held services and taught classes in the meantime, wondering why so many of the children were missing. A coffee crop had just come in, and he knew that the Hawkins brood, along with the Coopers and the Brewsters, must be in the fields collecting the ripe red berries. But where were Noni, Kualani and the other Hawaiian youngsters? He decided on the following Saturday that he must investigate.

Down the pali he went, under a brilliant sun, with every bone aching. The village was nearly deserted; he had never seen it so lifeless. In time he found Harold Lopaka mending his fishing nets under a coconut tree. They exchanged a few pleasantries while David explained the bandage on his jaw, then gave him some ripe mangos, and thanked him for the fish he had sent by way of the recent visitor. In Hawaii, one must not go directly to the business at hand, for that is considered unmannerly. When David finally asked him "Where is everyone?" Lopaka looked troubled and did not reply at once. Gradually, then, the following tale emerged.

It seemed that a man calling himself a prophet had set up camp several miles north of the village. This person was simply an outlaw, Harold said, who tried to make himself respectable by quoting the Bible incessantly. He claimed that it had been revealed to him and to him alone, that the world would end in four months: in fact, on the 11th of February. The Day of Judgment would soon follow, and none could be saved from eternal torment unless they obeyed him.

Native people had been gathering, bringing their families, food and possessions to the camp, where they worked no more, either at fishing or farming, but put on white garments and prayed, and sang hymns, and listened to the "Great Prophet." The man preached nonsense, Harold Lopaka said, all about darkness, evil, fear and death.

"What is his name?" David asked. "Lorenzo Scuppers? Or perhaps, Billy Smith?" Lopaka did not know, but said, "He is no man of God; that is easy to see. And yet people believe him, and now my son Kimo has gone to him!"

"I am very sorry to hear that," said David. "I have failed to reach your son's heart, and I am ashamed that I could not do better. Tell me, Harold, how is it that you understand all this so well?"

Lopaka looked with deep sadness out to sea. "I am an old man, Pelekane," he said. "I see many things before missionaries come here to Hawaii Nei. Listen, I tell you, I love your Jesus long time before I hear his name. I know this Holy Spirit all my life. I try to do what is good always for love of that Spirit that lives in my heart. So it may be I am saved when I go before the Throne. But many, many of my people are lost now, and in all my years, I do not know why."

Even in the heat of the day, with his head aflame, David was shivering now as if with ague. He began to understand that the recent wound had poisoned him, or else, perhaps, that he had caught the wasting lung disease of old Herr Lindt. If either, or both, were true, he knew that he might be not long for this world. Lopaka had fallen silent, and the weight of his friend's melancholy pressed upon David so that his own throat and chest began to feel crushed, and it was becoming hard for him to breathe.

"Listen to me, Harold," he said. "He is not my Jesus. He

belongs to you as well. And do not fear Judgment Day. He knows us already, better than we know ourselves. Truly, he may ask us only one question then – *Did you love me?*"

"John 21:15!" said Lopaka.

"Yes," said David. "Those are the numbers – but don't forget the words." He followed the old man's gaze out to the dazzling blaze of the ocean, and black spots began to dance before his eyes, while the air around him quivered with vibration. He heard himself asking then, as if from a vast distance, "Where is Mailelani?" The old man replied that she was at home, desperately ill. Then he went on to say quite calmly that it was a clear case of sorcery. Maile's way of life had been condemned by the "Prophet." He had cast an evil spell upon her, and so she would soon die.

"No! Don't believe it! I must go to her!"

"Nothing to do," said Lopaka. "Now he go pray Maile to death, the old Kanaka way. This one has Kanaka blood, Kanaka power, very old, very strong. He carry the head of a sacred bird with him, and he keep this thing in a calabash near him always. So now he make evil spirits come in the night, fly to Maile's house."

"What are you saying, Harold? What do you mean?"

"Pelekane, I tell you, I know – I see, I hear them. They are balls of fire flying in the air, with a terrible noise. Everyone hear them, not just Maile. And we all hear the drumming, and we see the people of darkness in the night. Then in the morning we find the footprints of the dead."

"But Harold, this is madness!"

Lopaka leaned over and patted David Wilkinson's hand to quiet him. "Now I tell you something," he continued. "One day your haole lady give Maile a special glass for looking in. Do you know this? And now when Maile look there, she see all that will happen. She see she is lying dead by the water, and birds come dig out her eyes. So now she will die soon, and then birds will come. One week now she touch no food or drink. I tell you truly, Pelekane, nothing we can do."

David could scarcely believe what he was hearing, after the

same intelligent elder had just finished confessing a sincere Christian faith. "Harold, surely you cannot believe this rubbish! You know that this man is no prophet, you know that he is a villain, an outlaw! You have said this yourself. And you know that is true because he brings fear, not joy – illness, not health – hatred, not love. Any man who brings death of the body and death of the soul, Harold – death of the soul, instead of life eternal! Death instead of everlasting life –" but he could not finish, and when he stood up suddenly with the last of his strength, David saw a great pit yawning before him, and fell into it, senseless.

*

An entry in his journal records subsequent events as follows:

South Kona 2 October, 1867.

Believing as I do that, by God's great mercy, I am once again in my right mind, I shall make here a record of recent events that may be of interest to future scholars and explorers of these Islands. In obedience to the demands of Truth I shall describe my experience here as accurately as I can, adding only what I have been told by reliable witnesses.

It seems that I was extremely ill, and in fact close to death, one day last month, after having been injured by an unruly horse. I was speaking to one of the natives when I swooned and fell unconscious at the village that lies on the shore of South Kona below Grace Church. Memory has preserved for me very little about the time immediately afterward, tho' I do recall a sense of being entirely null and void, amidst a great pall of Blackness. Yet rather soon I became somewhat aware again, and to a degree anxious and striving, as a babe soon to be born may be in the dark confines of the womb. It was then that I began to feel certain once more that I actually existed, and that I had a brain to think with. Yet, removed so far was I from my usual state that I could not know myself in any personal way, but only as an anonymous mote or spark of human consciousness.

After this, still without words, concepts or any form of history to guide me, I began to feel that I might serve as a witness – an idle witness, to be sure, with neither power nor responsibility toward the outcome – to a mighty struggle between cataclysmic forces in the universe. This conflict appeared to me as a tremendous battle between opposing elements: Darkness and Light, Order and Chaos, Grandeur and Baseness, Love and Hate, Agony and Bliss. In my altered state I saw all this as a reflection, or subsidiary expression, of an even greater struggle taking place beyond it – and of yet another beyond that, and then of another greater still, ad infinitum. And all this came to me as a musical note may echo in human memory, or as a faceted crystal may reflect a myriad of rainbows, none of them less than astonishing.

Regarding this vision, if such it was, the first fully human emotion that I recall was a melancholy Sadness, even while I knew at the same time that I ought to be Thankful, for I saw that the gift of Life itself could not exist without these oppositions. And I also saw that God was in the midst of the struggle, making it happen, and in fact, causing it to Happen to Himself. Putting it differently, I saw our Creator God in an eternal act of holy Sacrifice, struggling to produce all of the Being that exists – all thoughts, all creatures, all worlds, all universes – like a woman eternally laboring in the agony of Birth.

After this, in utmost solemn awe, I saw this Terrible Vision transform itself into something of overwhelming Light and Beauty. Even as I watched, the warring opposites became fluid, visible forces flaring up, then folding down upon one another like the petals of a flower, or flames in the wind, or a soaring, fountain filled with stars, and within this fountain I saw the Sign of a great Reconciliation, in which negative forces were continually embraced, persuaded, subdued and incorporated into the living substance of all that was higher, better and more beautiful. After this I was swept away to a far realm of Peace and Harmony that I scarcely remember, except that it lasted for aeons and finally I heard a woman's voice saying that all would be well and all manner of things would be well. After that I walked on the wind between planets and stars, listening with the greatest of Joy and Pleasure to their music even while beginning to hear with vague dismay some human cries that were, in all probability, my own. So, imagining then that I was returning to a life of peril and suffering, I looked down from a great height at the native village; and saw my body lying there helpless, I rose up from the mat where the people had placed me, and tried to fight with them all. There were seven natives caring for me, four men and three women, and they told me later that this actually happened. Fortunately, I was far too weak to hurt them, and then as I continued my descent into the low and Narrow realm of human consciousness, I thought I was sitting on the shore with the native called Harold when a great bird of prey came out of the sky to devour us both. It was an eagle, with huge wings and a foul, suffocating odor in its feathers. I felt that savage beak beginning to wrench and tear my heart out, so I thought that all was lost, and I cried out to Jesus. They told me later that this, too, happened. Harold Lopaka and the others who had stayed with me said that in the extremity of my distress I had indeed called out to my Lord and then cried, "Help me!" and made the sign of the Cross on my breast. This, they said, was the turning point of my illness. A short time afterward I broke into a violent sweat; the moisture poured from my body in rivers, and then, I opened my eyes and smiled, and asked for ono. They greeted me joyfully, as one returned from the dead, and sent one of their number out in a canoe to catch some ono — those good souls! I will never confess to them that it was not "the ono" I wanted, but "Fiona."

Until this moment, my valiant native nurses had nearly despaired of me. Every one of them believed that I, too, was under a spell cast by the "Great Prophet." Hastily, they had prepared an umu loa ("long oven") for me, since this was one of their most powerful weapons against sorcery. But in my crazed state I imagined that they were going to roast me alive in that oven and then devour me. I was mistaken of course. In the first place, the Hawaiians are not cannibals; in fact, the only cannibal I have met in these islands was a white man. In the second, I would not flatter myself that they had nothing better to eat that day than a diseased Anglican missionary. It was an old custom, as they later explained, to heat certain healing plants in the umu to make a sort of matting on which the victim must lie, to counter-act the spell of the magician. But, as it turned out, Deo Gratias, that was not necessary after all.

*Written on the 2nd and 3rd days of October, 1867
in Kona, Hawaii by the Rev. David C. P. Wilkinson.*

*

How, then, was David Wilkinson healed? For many years afterward, he was remembered among natives in Kona as the *haole* priest who had managed to survive a powerful work of sorcery by the magic of calling on Christ. Indeed, his healing may have been a miracle. But it is also true that he was fortunate not to have been mortally ill in a civilized metropolis in 1867. Thus he was spared the cures that might well have killed him – the bleeding and the starving, the leech and the cupping-glass, the airless, overheated sickroom, the filthy surgeon and his contaminated knife.

By contrast, in the Hawaiian village he lay comfortably in the shade, fanned by soft breezes, cleansed with pure sea-water, and his wound was dressed in time-honored medicinal herbs. He was given cool spring water to drink, and a small cup of salt water from time to time, to balance the contents of his blood. For his pain and misery, he received regular doses of a mildly narcotic tea made from the *awa* plant (*Piper methysticum*). Fortunately, he was not subjected to the violent purges that were a less appealing aspect of Hawaiian medicine at the time; perhaps the villagers doubted his ability, as a foreigner, to survive them. Quite sensibly, they burned all of his clothing, preserving only his watch, his shoes, his diary and his Prayer Book, all of which were well-aired and purified by the sun. The patient himself was dressed only in a clean *malo*, and lightly covered with a length of *tapa* cloth.

They told him afterward that his body had been stroked many times with leaves of the *ti* plant, to draw out the power of the sorcery. Also, that they had voided their urine in a circular path around the mat where he lay, so as to keep evil spirits out. David Wilkinson found the latter technique particularly interesting, for he and his father had done the same thing around the borders of their kitchen-garden at Green Gardens. That was their regimen for keeping four-legged thieves away from the vegetables. To Mama's amusement, it worked very well indeed. In fact, she once remarked that she might have done it herself, if she had more convenient equipment.

24

D earest Beth —

    I've put off telling you — not quite daring to — that I am strong again & actually able to ride!!! So rejoice with me darling as I frolick about the landscape, leaping like a goat from crag to crag — also managing in a somewhat goatish fashion to disgrace myself, from time to time. But never mind, it's the sheer joy of freedom, & people here are kind.

    As for the vile brace, I've left it with the Queen, who said from the beginning that it was witchcraft and threatened to destroy it. She's also keeping most of my other kit, while I explore this amazing Isle. Since uncaged I am so much smaller, I've had to order a new costume — a practical one for riding, made from one of my plaids. The ancestral emerald, by the way, is now in a locked box, under the personal care of Charles Bishop Esq at his Bank in Honolulu. I've left a note with it — they are to send it to you directly, if I should be so careless as to disappear.

    But I won't. And to answer your next 10 questions, the damned Tormenter is banished because I shed it one day on a whim and suddenly felt ever so much better. It was simply too hot & there seemed no great risk at Kauai, for I only had to lie for hours in a hammock — or else loll about in a weightless condition in the lovely, soothing and healing, sea. Also, Emma finally persuaded me to try a helpful Hawaiian regimen — a massage called lomi-lomi – at first, both embarrassing & ticklish, so of course I thought I could not bear it, but they were marvelously patient with me. Time is as naught in these Islands! So slowly, slowly I grew better – and I'm sure that part of the cure has been allowing myself to exist here in a mode so unguarded – in a place so gentle – & safely, of course, among women. You will be glad for me, won't you darling? You see, something has called to me here in Hawaii & my foolish bones have answered, being so lavished & doted upon. Thus like a well-loved child, this back of mine has found its own best manner of being – and if the spine is still crooked, I fail to notice it – or to fear the consequences.

So don't fret & don't think you must send the gendarmes after me, or even the Consul – who happens, in any case, to be traveling with me at this moment. He is a civilized companion – I joined his scientific party a few days ago, on the slopes of Kilauea mountain. His name is Wm. Green – he's writing a book about rocks & what is under them.

The scenery & manner of life are far more primitive here than in Honolulu – which suits me well, & here again I differ from the English Bishop who announced recently – while traveling about the Isles – that he likes Hawaii "because it is like Switzerland, only with servants." You may imagine the local reaction to this! Which reminds me of Mr. Wilkinson, who has the misfortune to be an earnest missionary toiling away under the rule of the selfsame ghastly prelate. When I first came to this island, I forgot my manners long enough to stay – alone!! unchaperoned!! scandal!! – for a day or two at Mr. W's vicarage, which is a tiny wee place like a herder's hut, with guavas and mangoes all around. Actually, I prefer Q. Emma's spelling of the above, for in her letters she always calls it "scandle" which somehow looks cozier and more manageable.

But David Wilkinson is a most interesting person. Your Wm. would undoubtedly like him, for I suspect D. is more of a man's man than a woman's. That is to say, forever logical, with all that implies – & he does not flirt or gossip, but speaks to a woman exactly as if she were a man, which can be tiresome. Or worse, as if she were a lesser sort of man – deficient, perhaps in intelligence – which of course leaves one grinding one's teeth. However, enough about him. He was most kind and chivalrous during my visit – and I am, not unnaturally, grateful.

It was Wm. Green who told me of the Bishop's latest faux pas, about

Switz & servants, which has made the rounds of Honolulu, causing no end of glee. His Toadship is a great embarrassment to the English – and by the Americans, is so despised that I blush for the poor devil. He's off to England and the Continent again now, and Emma – who never says a bad thing about anyone – is quietly stunned by his latest whim. He has put an advertisement into the London newspapers – a public advert, can you imagine? seeking a priest to take charge of his Honolulu Mission – so little, evidently, does he care.

This morning – the middle of October, or thereabouts – is damp and densely, catastrophically hot. During the autumn months this little seaside town, I'm told, can be a real hell's kitchen. At 7 in the morning now, with everything stewing and steaming, I am already wiping my brow – as I see now, with a handkerchief not my own. I really must improve my manners.

But there's a ship in the harbor readying for departure, and so quickly, a few impressions: a handsome seaport, this, on a perfect curve of bay, but all too thoroughly missionized by the Americans. The population here scrubbed quite raw by their passionate Puritanism – esp. the women forever busy a-sewing & a-sweeping & a-praying & a-baking & a-visiting & a praying more. They all apparently spend their spare time making ghastly things like pen-wipers & antimacassars – they press & preserve blossoms & ferns by the thousands, their parlors are crammed with them. They are voraciously hospitable – all very kind, to be sure, but I flee – their voices drive me mad, like scraping on tin.

There are many rather depressed Hawaiians here – a few sad, dignified Chinese – & the usual flotsam of classless, stateless waterfront folk, who lie about drinking all day & are said – at night – to smoke opium. I've taken proper rooms with my own small parlor where I read and draw – some tiny pictures, pen & ink illustrations for the book I am NOT going to write about Hawaii.

The scientists have all departed now for Honolulu – so in the cool of the evening I roam the town – speaking only to dogs & horses, with my hair tucked under my hat, so as to be as nearly as I can, invisible. The dogs here are mongrels, the horses mostly a sad lot too. The Americans at nightfall plod dutifully about – visiting people they have already seen that day, but now it is "company for dinner." So they carry covered dishes to one another – filled with the most disgusting food you can imagine – all swimming in grease. They give this mess to their neighbors, who surely have more of the same in their own larders — but for some reason, no one is insulted. Instead, they all sit down and eat.

I am fascinated by this & only now — after much thought — do I conclude that it's a religious matter — a sort of ritual. That is, what they are sharing is not Food at all, but an unacknowledged, inarticulate Sign of Love. One night as I was half asleep I distinctly heard the voice of Grandfather Stuart say, in his dear old Highland brogue, "Well now, child, these poor benighted Protestants have deprived themselves of the glory of the Mass — & they can't live without it — so behold, the Covered Dish!"

Which reminds me, to my amazement I've been accosted twice, on my evening rambles through this pious town, by members of the male sex with extraordinarily indecent proposals! Once it was a rather distinguished-looking Frenchman who thought I was a boy. Last night it was an American who suspected otherwise, but was too drunk to care one way or another. By contrast, I can go alone among the natives here in perfect safety — they would never, never bother me in that way. Indeed, why should they, when here in Paradise, love hangs from every tree? Still, as usual — I always carry my knife.

Later: Ship delayed another day or two with mechanical problems… So there's time now to tell you a special bit that I was going to save, about the great volcano at Kilauea. It has been quite active lately, though visitors are assured that it is not really dangerous. So of course I went up to view it — everyone must, who comes here. But most visitors climb straight up from Hilo — a hard ride of many hours with frequent downpours & the chill of the heights ever more trying as the summit is neared. They rival one another in saying how dreadful the trip was — and then I become very quiet, for I avoided all that. Never one — I suppose — to do a thing the proper way when there's an alternative, I came to the caldera, the central part of it — from another direction. The last morning was the most beautiful! I shall never forget jogging along with softly lifting mists all about me, and snow-capped peaks to the North, rosy & radiant in the dawn — and the air as ever in these mountains so keen & pure & brilliant — Hebridean, like a tonic. Oh, words won't do it, Becky — I must learn to paint!

Then, after a long, rather barren, desert sort of place I came to a wetter region w. huge tree-ferns – shy little birds like quail in the shrubbery – & ripe red berries near the ground. I'd been told by people both native & foreign not to touch those delicious looking fruits – that Hawaiians believe they are sacred to the Goddess Pele, who is jealous & fanciful. They say that she lives at the volcano, & goes secretly about the island in all sorts of disguises – that if she is angry or does not get her way, she can be cruel & dangerous.

Soon now I began to see steaming fissures in the earth – some very deep & wide – so I dismounted & led my pretty white mare cautiously forward. I've named her Missy – she's part equine saint, I think & part rocking-horse. Soon we came to a clear space & looked ahead – & saw black smoke rising from the earth in a desultory fashion. Well my dear, to be quite honest, I was not impressed. Coming to see a famous, active volcano, I suppose I expected flames & visions, or at least, an interesting display. So I walked on a little farther and looked down at sloping, shelving sides of gray/black rock that descended toward a distant floor. There was glutinous red stuff rolling around down there plus nasty smell & that was all. And I'm not ashamed to admit that I was neither awestruck – nor enthralled. Then I noticed on the caldera's rim, far across from me, some tiny men scampering around like ants – and thought, this must be a very large bowl or pit indeed, to make people on the other side of it look so small. Actually, I know now that the caldera has a 3-mile diameter! But at the time I stood there yawning rudely – staring at the ugly abyss & thinking how I longed to be somewhere, almost anywhere else – and how I wished that someone would bring me a biscuit and a cup of tea.

I was standing there in this disgruntled state when suddenly I heard a soft, musical voice quite nearby – a woman speaking, saying something both familiar & incomprehensible – perhaps in Hawaiian? Turning, I saw that she was already close beside me – less than a yard away. She was a native about my age or younger – barefooted, bareheaded, wearing a skirt of tapa cloth & nothing more. Rarely indeed had I seen such nonchalance of dress in the Islands. Yet she was so finely formed – & had such an air of dignity about her – that I imagine even stodgy Q. Victoria would not have been shocked. She was as tall as I am – with long curling hair of dark, reddish brown, generous enough to serve almost as a garment

– & she wore a garland of red ohia blossoms that fell to her waist. Since I could not speak her language, I put my hands together palm to palm - & made a little bow, by way of respectful greeting.

She seemed charmed by this & gazed at me from her great, dark eyes – with heavy, beautifully full & curving eyelids of the sort one sees in ancient paintings of the Madonna. I don't know quite what I said – except to tell her my name and ask for hers – all this, of course, in English. She shook her head, looking quite serious – then took a covered basket from her arm & lifted the lid to show me what was inside.

Ohelo berries! I thanked her – but said no, I would not have any, since they are sacred to the Goddess. Then she said, in perfect English – "Yes, yes my dear, I know. But these are for you, so take them!"

Well, Beth I was touched of course – and after I saw her eat one of the berries herself, as if to show me that the ban was lifted, I thought – she must know. So I took three or four & ate them most gratefully. They are delicious, somewhat like strawberries, but with a lingering tang of oddity. I thanked her and bowed again – at which, to my astonishment, she kissed me in a grave, ceremonial manner, first on one cheek, then on the other. I felt rather as if I were being knighted. Tears came to my eyes – and I wondered if I ought to kneel.

"But who are you, please?" I asked her again, "And what is the meaning of this?" Again she did not answer, but put her basket onto my arm. Then taking my two cold hands into her warm ones, she said softly, "This is my gift. Take it, for you will be needing it soon."

Just then, Missy began stamping and shaking her head about in a restless manner – a strange white dog had appeared, was frisking around – and that had alarmed her. I was momentarily distracted – and when I looked back the mysterious woman had vanished, as if she had never been there at all. I ran a few steps after her, uncertain which way to go – turned my ankle on a rolling bit of lava rock – then lost my footing entirely, began sliding downhill, and slid quite helplessly into the volcano.

Mind you, darling, I am still alive and writing this – so you know that I did not fall very far. Barring a few bruises – I tell you truly – was not in the least injured. But I had tumbled & slithered a distance down of perhaps 35-40 feet & was neatly caught on a rocky ledge with shrubs growing on it & some small ohias. The problem was – of course – that I could not get back up again.

I shouted at first, hoping in vain that someone might hear me. Then I decided not to struggle, lest I make my situation worse. So I settled in — for it was quickly growing dark — to spend the night as comfortably as possible on my ledge. It was wide enough to be safe if I did not go roaming. As luck would have it, I had the essentials with me — the warm cape I was wearing — the basket of berries still on my arm — & an aged pair of Mother's opera glasses, that I often wear hanging about my neck. So I thought, what a fine adventure this will be! With my cape for a blanket I'll lie here happily waiting for signs, either of rescue or eruption — while watching through glasses that have hunted grouse and seen the operas of Mozart in their day! I'll not go hungry or thirsty in the least, for I shall be eating berries that are sacred to a goddess. Missy will manage — & someone will find me, or else I'll be able to climb up this troublesome cliff in the morning.

Strangely enough, I was not much frightened. All was profoundly quiet and peaceful at first — no sound of man nor beast, and no sign of disturbance in the chasm below. A gentle breeze wafted the fumes away & brought me fresh, cool air. I slept for a while — woke up with rain on my face — then imagined that I heard the sea very far away — a hushing, soothing, throbbing sort of sound that grew gradually louder. But it was not the sea — could not be the sea, from so many miles away. And still the sound grew louder, nearer — what was it? And nearer yet, until, like an apparition from the Underworld, a cloud of vapor appeared, the color of amber — steaming & roiling over the farthest part of the caldera. As it continued to swell and rise higher, it arrayed itself in a myriad of different hues — royal purples, violets & blues — and then gold, then bronze, and then scarlet and vermilion. Meantime I thought I saw flickering lights there at play, as if ghosts or demons walked in that deep part of the cave, with the striking of their flints like lightning, and all of them carrying enormous blazing torches. Along with this came louder and louder crashing sounds, like huge rocks falling great distances, and at the same time, sheets of metal being struck with great iron hammers. By now the earth itself was shaking, shuddering — my rocky ledge began to tremble — I had not counted on that! So I braced myself as well as possible, with my arms round the trunk of a young ohia tree.

Then all at once, in a great exuberant, exultant rush, there rose a fountain of fire before my eyes — a tremendous, roaring jet of starry flame —

that was forced upward hundreds of feet in the air, to a height far greater than that of the ledge where I clung & trembled. Though it must have been a mile or two away, the heat and the noise were shattering – indescribable. I'd forgotten glasses by now & watched with my own aching eyes while the immense column of fire soared, plumed, crested & cascaded, all coruscating & bejeweled, simultaneously falling into darkness as a similar column even more powerful arose. It was a scene of terrifying power, coupled at the same time with a soft, spumy glitter and iridescence that was exquisitely lovely – a tossing, shaking & showering down of such rare beauty as humans rarely see, even on this magical island.

The sulphurous fumes, thank God, were being blown away from me or I suppose I might have perished – even though at the time I did not much care. And still the fountain continued, ever more beautiful, rising, sinking, changing its shapes and sizes, changing its colors – flowering now & again into spurting, bubbling red clusters, as if the blood of all the earth were pouring forth. And in all that time, I promise you, I had not one single coherent thought until finally I asked myself, was this the Pillar of Fire seen by the wandering Israelites? For I did sense surpassing might and majesty there, and yet I thought I saw something else as well – something supremely intimate, like a birth happening in blood and fire – something alive, beautiful – unimaginably so – something in progress, still happening, not yet finished. It was like watching while life itself was torn out of a great dark emptiness, and not without anguish – as if the earth had feelings of its own, as if it were alive – something so creaturely as to be nearly animal, or even human.

During the last few hours before dawn, the single glorious fountain divided itself into two leaping & sinking jets – overlapping, intertwining. As if in ecstasy they spiraled about one another – drawing nearer at their molten tips, lapsing away – meeting again – rising & melting into one another – shimmering, showering down.

All the time the pulsing roar continued & I watched until daybreak, when the partners in this exotic dance, as if in sudden modesty, wrapped themselves in smoke & mist so dense that I could see no more. Raindrops descended – hissing against the rocks below & then shining strands of "Pele's hair" drifted over me as I lay there on my ledge – cold, wet, exalted, exhausted & weeping – not from any sadness or fear, but unendurable joy.

Pele's hair is the Hawaiian name for glassy strands & filaments of crystal that scientist friend Green explains as a chemical reaction, born in the heat of the volcano. In the sunlight they are very beautiful – pale & translucent, amber, gold or darker, they float down to adorn a landscape with the most enchanting glitter. But they are exceedingly sharp & fragile – touch them and they break. I tried to save some, thinking of you and the bairns, but bleeding hands soon taught me that it was not meant to be.

By the way, I have not tried to tell anyone about the experience just described. As always, dear sister mine, you alone are my journal, my diary. Green & his party are forever busy with their mathematical calculations – & as for the local people I've met – I wouldn't dare. I'm afraid they might ask, did I see God on the mountain – and if so, was he definitely Protestant?

But you'll want to know how I escaped from my little ledge of safety. Well, of course there was no going down, so I tried to climb up at daybreak, but soon found it too difficult and dangerous. Thought it over for a time, decided that I'd rather die where I was, in one piece. Thought about death for a while, wondered how long it would take – how much it would hurt, what happens afterward, etc.

Then a little after noon I heard shouts, and four brown heads appeared over the brink of the caldera, looking down at me – Hawaiians. One huge, smiling man came down on a rope – picked me up like a sheep for shearing – tied me firmly – shouted to the others & they pulled. So I reached the top – quite without ceremony, I assure you! – in about three minutes & greeted the patient Missy.

"How did you know I was here?" I asked the men, after thanking them – I could have kissed their feet – & offered them gifts of course, such as I had – & money, which they adamantly refused. They seemed to think it was all tremendous fun! Hearing them laugh, you'd have thought I provided the best entertainment in years. They had some very bad wine with them – though it's illegal for Hawaiians to buy alcohol – but I said I'd join them in a wee dram because suddenly I was shaking so badly, I had to sit down.

"How on earth did you find me?" I asked again. The laughter stopped – they looked solemnly at one another – then out at the volcano, where the mist had cleared and the great fire-fountains were no more. Gabriel, the man who had come down for me, went to the cliff's edge –

took the wreath from his hat – said something I did not understand &
then tossed the flowers gracefully into the caldera. This, I now understand,
was a tribute to the Goddess. Then he came back and said in a low voice,
"One old wahine come in camp last night. One small kine lady, bent
over cripple – maybe your Mama, look for you?"

"No – my mother is not – not here in Hawaii."

The four men looked at one another again, with fear in their eyes.

"Phew!" Gabriel rubbed his face with a large brown hand, thought for
a moment, and then the words came tumbling out: "This thing – I don't
know – you got some friend! She wake me up! I sleep, this old wahine
come – she shake me, push me, kick me round the place. She yell like
crazy! She say, you no-good, you wake up – go get my child! She say that
girl of mine no akamai – she too much haole, she go fall down die! You
bring the men – you find – go now, or I fix you good! I come back here
throw you down the fire, I break your bones!"

"My goodness," I said – or something to that effect. "But how did you
know where to look?" He glanced nervously over his shoulder – this huge,
powerful man who could have easily broken me over his knee. Then he
confided, nearly in a whisper, "She say follow my dog! Go round that way
– then look one big white horse, you find."

"This actually happened? You are sure? Could it be, perhaps, that
you dreamed – or imagined it?" He said nothing, but his look told me
that it was a hopelessly stupid question.

Then I asked, "Could you tell me please – what does akamai mean?
The old lady told you I was not akamai."

"Akamai!" He laughed. "Akamai is akamai! You fall down one
volcano, you no akamai." He laughed uproariously. I hung my head &
said humbly, "I am no akamai." Then I thought more and said,
"Gabriel, you told me it was an old lady who came to you last night – not
a young one. Are you certain of that? Not a beautiful young girl, barefoot,
with long reddish-brown hair?"

He have me the same look again – I was not akamai – so I said no
more. After that we all mounted our horses and I followed the men around
the caldera to their place of work – which was, of course, the scientific
camp of William Green.

That's all for now. Dearest love to you, Wm. and the bairns –

Yours ever,
Fiona

25

As soon as he could walk again, David made his way to Mailelani's dwelling, and discovered his beloved friend sitting inside alone, unadorned, frail and shrunken pitifully. He called her name and tried to embrace her, but there was no response; her rheumy eyes stared out at him with no sign of recognition. "Do you remember me, Maile?" he cried, "Do you know that I am here beside you? Oh my dear, I want so much to help you. Tell me – tell me what I can do!"

Nothing.

He took her hands in his and spoke to her then as well as he could in Hawaiian, telling her that she was safe from all harm – safe from all spells and every form of sorcery. All of that was rubbish, not to be believed. She must not let herself be hurt by it! She must remember that she was a child of God, that he had power to help her, had he not?

Her eyes said: not.

Now he was angry, and lapsed into English. "Mailelani, you must listen! You must try to be well – take some food and drink, come back to us. You are needed here. Your knowledge – your work, your teachings have saved many people, may have saved my own life as well. You must not give up – you have no right to do this, do you hear? Maile, Maile, do you know how many people count on you – how much you are loved?"

Slowly she raised a hand to touch her hair, as if in ghostly remembrance of her old coquettish ways. Her hair had gone nearly white, and the skin of her forearm hung, emptied of substance, from the bone. It was clear to him then that Mailelani was dying, not from witchcraft, but because she was deeply wounded in heart and soul. The Puritan preacher from New England had begun the assault, and the false "prophet" who had placed a curse upon her was that man's illegitimate spiritual offspring.

Maile slipped away one night before David left the village. Birds did not pluck at her eyes; the villagers saw to that. They buried her like royalty, in a secret cliffside cave, and David learned then that her full name had been Jeremiah Mailelani Jones. What irony that was! First, the Old Testament name marking her baptism into a harsh, unloving version of the white man's religion; then a second given name invoking the sweetest plant in all the Islands (*yxia olivaeformis*), one whose subtle fragrance is a breath of heaven. And Lani, in Hawaiian, of course is heaven itself. As for her foreign sire, it was recalled that he had been a British sailor: a brawling, drunken deserter from a merchant ship out of Madagascar, bound for Torquay. Mallory Jones had stayed in the Islands long enough to leave his seed in the care of several obliging Hawaiian maidens; then he had vanished into the silence of history.

*

Richard Cornwall had wondered and worried for more than a week before he found his wounded vicar idling in the seaside village. Horrified to see him untidy and unshaven, dressed only in a *malo* and a garland of green leaves, he rode at once to the vicarage and fetched David's second suit of clothes. "Thank you, my friend," said the priest when he returned, "But did it ever strike you that these garments are unscientifically designed for human usage? These narrow tubes of serge, these constricting collars!"

"You're not going native on us, now, are you sir?" Cornwall's honest face was puckered with dismay. David laughed, and said, "Not likely." Without further complaint he dressed himself in the clothing Cornwall had brought, and then once again they climbed the *pali* together, with David on Richard's horse, and his faithful friend walking alongside. Several letters had arrived at the parsonage in his absence, but there was no sign of the pale blue stationery David wanted most to see. A small note on a scrap of butcher's paper had come from Scott in Maui, asking to borrow a large sum of money, without naming a reason. Another, on creamy vellum, announced that the Honorable Judge and Mrs. Von X requested the honor of his presence at a Honolulu reception, including dinner followed by dancing. The avowed purpose of this enterprise was to introduce their daughter Wilhelmina to society. He searched his memory, but could not recall anyone by that name.

The Mercantile Gazette brought more interesting news: that the new Archbishop of Canterbury was indeed a Scotsman named Archibald Campbell Tait, said to be a Broad Churchman with a reputation for wisdom, kindness and integrity. The article said that he had put a stop to the behavior of an Anglican priest who persisted in hearing Confessions in imitation of Roman Catholic tradition, and David wondered what the archbishop might say to Albert Coldwell, if he found out what was happening in Honolulu.

The same issue of the paper also told him that the American warship Lakawanna was back in port, having captured the Island of Midway; that there had been another gala evening reception at the Palace; that a Reciprocity Treaty with America had been signed in Honolulu. Meantime, a man had been attacked in a Fort Street saloon by a sailor with a knife; the sailor was now in the hands of the law, and said to be penitent. He learned also in the same pages that Dr. William Hillebrand would not be going to Japan after all; that Upham's Toothache Cure was available at C. Fred Pfluger's; that a bill to allow women to vote had been defeated in England; that Brewer & Co. was now able to offer clocks, cement, agricultural tools, and a wide selection of Meerschaum pipes.

Weary beyond words, he lay down on his narrow bed, closed his eyes, and traveled immediately to the idyllic forest glade he had discovered on his first trip around the island. The waterfall and the clear, dark pool were still there, silently reflecting green of leaf and blue of sky. In such a place, he thought, a man might be cleansed and relieved of his mental agony. Prayer, he thought. I must pray – and sent up a bitter complaint to the Almighty about his fatigue and sadness and his miserable poverty. The answer came directly: *You got three English undah bed!* Exasperated, he sat up and said aloud, "Come now, you know that a good horse costs more than that! The horse I want and need is Mr. Gray, but I can't afford him. You also know that children are in danger at the 'prophet's' camp, and if I can't get there, how can I help them? Scotty is obviously in some trouble too, needing a great deal of money. How can I help him if I have none? And what, may I ask, do you intend to do about any of this? Nothing, I suppose." But to all of this whining and complaint, there was no reply. Therefore he took out his diary, dipped his pen, and drew up two columns as if he were God's banker for the Kona Coast:

ASSETS	*LIABILITIES*
Burials – 3	*Some gone to "Prophet"*
Marriages – 2	
Baptisms – 14	
Church, pews, etc.	
Vicarage of sorts	
Sunday services & lessons	
Morning Prayer, Compline	
School w. 31 students (sometimes)	
Harmonium, candles etc.	
Bibles (10) & prayer books (18)	
$ 2.73 left from plate	

"At first glance" he said aloud, "I admit that this looks like a favorable balance. On the other hand, what is the worth of a human soul?" All of the items in the left-hand column failed to match the terrible weight on the right – the one liability that was perhaps irretrievable. After studying the page a second, and then a third time, he had no further suggestions as to how God ought to be running the universe.

To sweeten his mood, he decided to have some coffee with sugar in it. There was the Dresden bowl: a lovely thing, and valuable too, but he had already decided that he must not sell it, and had made a deathbed promise to old Herr Lindt. He took the bowl carefully down from its shelf and removed the lid, only to find that he had an unexpected visitor. Its name was Orthopteran: *Dictyopera blatteria* – a monster of a cockroach, lying in its own offal, its long black antennae quivering with greed and malevolence. David stared at it for a moment in dismay, and then rose to carry the creature out of doors, when the walls of his hut began suddenly to creak and shudder. From the western horizon, a roaring, grinding sound arose and rapidly approached. This was an earthquake, and not a small one.

He and the sugar bowl were out of doors in less than two seconds, and after that, he forgot for quite some time about *Dictyoptera blatteria.* The earth was swaying and rolling beneath him, with a noise as if large rocks were being torn asunder down below. The parsonage groaned on its foundations, and he watched while his prized pavilion cast off its moorings and lurched away in a southerly direction. The sun was shining brightly on his window panes, and he saw that glitter suddenly arrange itself in concentric circles that buckled in and out, convex at one instant, concave at the next. Then they all shattered with a loud report, sending daggers and shards of glass in a deadly shower over his bed. He gazed on all this as if in a trance, then lost his footing and stumbled, righted himself for a moment, but tripped again and fell heavily to the ground. The Dresden bowl flew from his hands, landed on lava rock, and exploded.

As soon as the earth had settled he ran to the church. *Deo gratias*, it had survived! One of the front steps had come loose, and above the altar there was a crack in one of his new window panes; that was all. Even the tall front doors with their massive hinges still opened and shut without difficulty. The sea below was calm, with no sign of the tidal wave that might be on its way after such a convulsion. He stood for a time at the top of his hillock, listening for any untoward sound and searching for smoke. All was quiet. Though he knew that other, lesser shocks were likely after this, he decided to make what order he could in the vicarage, and began by bloodying his hands in sweeping the broken glass from his bed.

To David's surprise, Captain Hawkins himself rode down the hill that evening to inquire about his welfare, and said that he would send a man to help retrieve the porch that David called his pavilion. Richard Cornwall and several other parishioners stopped by the following day. Each of their homes had suffered damage, and he was touched by their concern for him. Not only that, but Harold Lopaka arrived unexpectedly at his doorstep the second day after the earthquake. The village was unharmed, he said, although the sea had gone out quite a way at first and then had come back to flood some dwellings. He had not climbed the pali, however, only to deliver that news. David waited patiently to hear the real reason for his visit. Lopaka remarked at some length on the weather. He admired the parsonage and the church, he quoted Scripture, and he handed over the small traveling mirror that had belonged to Maile. Would David return it to the *haole wahine* some day? David said that he would, and the two shook hands on it. Still he was waiting to hear what was on Harold's mind; and then, as if by afterthought, Lopaka remarked that he would like to attend some services at Grace Church. And so he did, and from that time on was a loyal member of the congregation.

Several days later David decided that his wound had healed well enough so that he might shave his face for the first time since his injury. As he went to the cooking pit and made a fire to heat some water, he found that fragments of the Dresden bowl lay all around him. The sugar had been discovered by regiments of industrious ants; over hill and dale, grain by grain, they were carrying it away. There would be feasting and celebration, no doubt, for weeks to come in some giant ant-metropolis nearby. Dozens of the busy creatures were swarming in one spot, struggling over what appeared at first to be a small lump of lava. But it was not; it was the empty carapace of *Dictyoptera blatteria,* and David turned it over absent-mindedly with a stick.

Just at that moment the sun was rising over the mountain, and a shaft of golden light touched something that glittered beside him in the vegetable garden. When he had separated it from earth and pebbles, sugar and ants, he saw that it was a bit of metal, irregularly shaped. He put it into his pocket and went indoors to shave. That was not an easy job with a rather old, dull blade, and after such a long hiatus. But he persevered, for although many clergyman wore beards in those days, David Wilkinson considered them a temptation to vanity, and so had always been clean-shaven. Viewing the results in Fiona's looking-glass, he did not see any signs of madness or sorcery; he only saw a sunburned, black-haired man with a livid scar on his jaw.

He went out again to empty his shaving-bowl, and his eye was caught by another gleaming object in the soil. A strange sensation came over him then, as if he were standing up in a schoolroom, being questioned on a subject he had failed to study. He stared at the horizon for a time, wondering, and then looked back to see whether the gleam was still there. It was. So he picked it up, and cleaned both of the two strange objects he had discovered. They were both octagonal, handsomely adorned with a design of ribands on one side, and on the other, a bird of prey. An eagle, in fact. He remembered then having heard in San Francisco about a form of currency called an eagle. However, the San Francisco "eagles" were made of gold, and no such thing had any business in his garden. Yet a little later, scratching in the dirt, he found another of the same.

Now he searched the entire area systematically, beginning to understand what must have happened. Herr Lindt had been a cautious man, fearful of being robbed. He had no family left, when his wife was gone. He had liked David – or at least, had been grateful for his help and ministry. Therefore he had decided to leave the little hoard of coins to his attending priest. After every crevice for yards around had been inspected, and all the plants and grasses combed to their roots, David had a total of eleven gold Eagles, without the least notion of what they were worth.

He was sitting on his doorstep washing them in a basin of water when Harold Lopaka stopped by again. "I suspect that someone has left me a valuable gift," he told Harold. "Either that or some absent-minded pirate has buried his gold amongst my cabbages. Have you noticed any Spanish buccaneers here lately?" Harold replied that he had never seen either a pirate or a coin as fine as these.

David left the following day for Honolulu, and once ashore, walked directly to Charles Bishop's bank. There he found the proprietor himself seated in a dim back room, poring like a wizard over his books. After the usual courtesies, David asked for help with a bit of alchemy; for he urgently wished to see eleven California Eagles transformed into one good gray Hawaiian horse.

26

The little seaport of Lahaina, Maui in those days was a sultry, muddy, swarming, insect-ridden place with a history of violence and debauchery. American seamen, whalers and adventurers had helped to make it so, but at the same time, the primary "civilizing" influence in the town during the early eighteen hundreds was also American. By mid-century, pious Protestant missionaries from New England had fought for thirty years to impose their habits of thrift, hard work and harsh morality upon the local residents, both native and foreign. Thus it is not surprising that some inhabitants of the town were astonished and outraged by the appearance of a gentler version of Christianity when the Anglicans arrived.

"I thought you'd never come!" were Scott's first words when David Wilkinson reached the shore in Maui. His next were not, "How long can you stay?" or even, "What happened to your face?" but – with a desperate glance, "Did you bring the money?"

David had not envied Scott Partridge his posting to Lahaina, and now he saw the effects of it plainly written on his friend's face. Scotty was gaunt and hollow-cheeked, pale as if he had never stepped out of doors. But that was not the worst of it; the misery in his eyes suggested that this young priest, for some reason, believed he was a ruined man. By contrast, David felt like a jolly nabob, for he was carrying a small fortune with him in California gold. Charles Bishop had assured him that each one of his Eagles was worth fifty American dollars. He had ten of them in a small leather sack that the banker had given to him, and the remaining coin had been set aside for the purchase of Mr. Gray.

With a brave show of enthusiasm Scotty took him to see his church, which was rather nice, and the vicarage, which was not. Then they walked to a nearby school for young Hawaiian girls that was kept by Anglican nuns, cheerful souls with devotion to God shining in their faces. The children stood up and sang a touching little song for them:

The tempter comes with guileful art
To snare me in some thought of sin;
I breathe in prayer the Blessed Name –
Jesus – a place to hide me in!

O hidden life with Christ in God,
Let me thy blest abiding win!
The shadow of God's lovingness –
Jesus – a place to hide me in.

The sound of their innocent young voices was angelic, and David prayed that the world would be kind to them. Clearly they were in good hands now, for Scotty was in charge of their religious education, while the Sisters taught them hygiene and the domestic arts. "They grow up so quickly here!" one of the nuns whispered to David. "They are women already at the age of eleven or twelve! Can you believe it? We fear for them night and day."

A sudden rainstorm came pelting down as they departed. Scott began to run, and called out, "*Pau hana!*" ("No more work!") When David caught up with him, Scott said with a bleak smile, "Come along, a fine bottle of claret awaits," but their libations were peculiarly cheerless all the same. After a simple dinner that he cooked himself, Scott launched into a tale of woe that was obviously agonizing for him. David interrupted, and poured the 10 golden Eagles out on the table. "Say no more," he told Scott. "Simply take whatever you need, with my blessing."

Without touching the coins, Scott stared at them miserably. Then, with a deep sigh, he continued his narrative. The gist of it was that he had been a fool, trying to refurbish both the church and the vicarage when he arrived. The two buildings had been in ruins, he said. He himself was no carpenter, and the cost of hired assistance had been appalling. The meager allowance he received from the GSBE was hardly enough to keep body and soul together. Before realizing it, he had found himself badly in debt; then had come the new and terrifying experience of owing ever-rising amounts of interest on money that he could not possibly repay.

"The family, you see," he said, "– oh Wilks, this is so embarrassing! But I realize now that I've always fallen back on them; they don't mind, and the truth is, we're all rather lax in money matters. About interest on a loan, I hadn't the foggiest. Still, this is my own fault and I know it. For sheer stupidity I ought to be shot."

"But did you say that you've received funds from the Society?"

"A pittance. A mere £50 thus far."

"Interesting!" David decided not to mention that this was £50 more than he had received; but, to his surprise, Scott already knew it.

"Well you see, the Bishop told me. You know how he talks of everyone's private business. He said you were a special case. No need of salary, since the legacy you had received was quite grand." Seeing the look on David's face, he hastily added, "Wilks, I am sorry, but I believed him. Honestly, I wouldn't have appealed to you otherwise."

A small silence fell between them and then Scott remarked,

"Did you know, by the way, that His Lordship was once quite enamored of your mother?"

"Albert Coldwell? My mother? No! How could he ever have known her? She never told me such a thing."

"He said she was an extraordinarily beautiful woman."

"True, but what business had he…?"

"Doting upon her? I don't know. He offered no excuses. He did remark that it was a pity you turned out the image of your father instead. I had to agree with him on that!" Scott grinned wickedly as he poured himself another glass of wine. David laughed, if only because it was heartening to see Scotty at last more like himself. Still, he was troubled by his friend's freedom with the wine-bottle, and it struck him that this was an extravagant way for a pauper to entertain.

"It was a gift," he said, pushing the coins toward Scotty. "Unexpected and undeserved. So take what you need and don't try to explain. No more wine, thanks. What I need is sleep."

Scott consigned him to a comfortable sofa in the parlor, with a *pulu* pillow in the native style, and a lace-edged, embroidered and monogrammed counterpane. As he lay there counting mosquitoes on the walls above him, David could see his friend still at the table, with the light from a kerosene lamp sculpting his features. He thought, "That is how Scotty will look when he is old."

"I despise money!" Scott cried, just as David was nearly asleep.

"Well don't. It's only a convenience, after all."

"Until it is needed," Scott said bitterly, pouring the last of the wine. "Then the trouble begins."

*

All of the coins were gone in the morning, and so was Scott Partridge. David looked for him at the church, but he was not there. Instead, he found a young girl kneeling alone by the altar. Hearing his footsteps she looked up, then rose and approached him.

"Aloha," she said. "I see you visit the English school. You like the singing? I am glad. Mr. Partridge is your friend long time?" She was a winsome child, perhaps 14 or 15 years old, and surely with that olive skin and those great black eyes, partly Hawaiian. Her cotton frock was fresh and crisp as if it had just come from the laundry. He recalled now having seen her helping the nuns at the school. They chatted for a few moments and then she said, very quietly, "I want to tell you something."

"Yes, of course."

"Only one thing, but it is important."

"Then I shall listen carefully."

"My father is not a bad man. He does not mean to hurt." And, having made this odd remark, she turned and began to walk away.

David followed her, saying in some confusion, "But I don't know your father. Excuse me, what is your name?"

The girl looked at him in obvious disbelief. "Everyone knows my father," she said coolly, and left the church.

*

"What ever happened to your jaw?" Scott asked when he returned.

"A horse tried to kill me. Nearly succeeded. Is the first time you've noticed?"

"Quite honestly, no." he replied. "I mean to say, yes. But it could be worse. At least I can still recognize you."

"I'm glad to hear it."

"Well bless you, David. Just now, you look to me like a saint. I've taken care of the worst of it, and I'll pay you back if it's the last thing I do. So come along," he continued in rising good humor, "let me show you the town!"

In breathless heat under dark gray skies they passed by shops filled with seafaring goods, looked into taverns and noisy saloons, inspected the grim little prison, and caught a glimpse of the American missionary school high above on a mist-shrouded mountain. Then their time was up. Scott handed him a covered basket. "Some edibles for the journey," he said, "and a letter. Burn it when you have read it, please." David watched him on the dock, growing smaller and smaller as the ship moved away. The basket was filled with expensive cheeses and fruits imported from America. Alas for Scotty! The missionary life was never designed for a man who does not know how to be poor. The letter read:

My dear friend,

You are such a good chap, dozing away on my sofa, I can't let you go without knowing more. What I told you tonight was not so much false as irrelevant. I've made a mess of it, yes, but the most serious accusation is simply not true. The father of a young girl here claims that I've taken indecent liberties. Not so! The man in question is an American well known as a bully & a blackguard, looking for ways to disgrace our Church. He promises silence for a price.

The girl is ½ Hawaiian, only 13 but looks & seems much older. She is afraid of Papa, as well she might be, for he is haole scum, and has entire control over her. The Hawaiian mother has run away, for which I do not blame her. I can tell you I've been in Hell's own torments. Have of course appealed to my parents, omitting the worst, but no reply as yet. They are in Venice now, I think. Part of the agony is, I can't speak out without injuring an innocent — thus have been pinioned, unable to defend myself or Mother Church either. Whatever happens, NONE OF THIS MUST BE KNOWN! Not a hint, not a whisper. I trust you more than anyone on earth. Forgive me, I beg you, for my stupidity, and other faults abounding. By all that is holy I swear to improve myself and make up the debt to you.

227

Your friend ever, C.S.P.

*Late night thought. Perhaps Hawaii herself is a lovely
maiden, courted by too many lying, self-serving suitors.
What will the end of it be? Not that the truth – the whole
truth – will ever be known – C.*

David read the letter over twice, burned it carefully and
tossed the ashes into the sea. Upon his arrival in Honolulu,
however, he found that the coconut telegraph had outdone
itself. All the town was buzzing over Scotty's predicament.
One version had it that he had debauched a student, to all
appearances a white girl, though she was really part Hawaiian,
from a noble clan. In another, he was the would-be seducer of
a virtuous young American maiden who refused his advances,
and the father threatened to take him to court. The worst
account claimed that a Hawaiian girl was now with child by
Scott Partridge, and that he refused to marry her. Much of
David's visit to Honolulu was taken up in Scotty's defense,
with vigorous denials of it all.

He was there at the time, however, in response to an urgent
summons from many of the town's leading citizens, on behalf
of the Anglican Church. A meeting would soon be held for the
signing of a resolution that rejected Bishop Coldwell's
leadership, and warned him not to return to the Islands.
According to Theophilus Davies, copies of this document
would soon be sent abroad to Coldwell himself, to the Bishop
of Oxford's Committee, to the Gospel Society of the British
Empire, to the Bishop of London, who was in charge of
foreign missions, and to Archibald Campbell Tait, Archbishop
of Canterbury. David Wilkinson had responded at first that
such a document was no business of his. Davies had replied
that they intended to make it his business; therefore he ought
to attend.

The meeting was planned for half a week after his arrival,
so that David found time to spend a pleasant afternoon with

Dr. William Hillebrand in his garden. With the help of a strong young native boy, they dug the ground, transported rocks and sifted soil to plant a young almond tree (*Terminalia catappa*) that had come to Hillebrand recently from the Indies. It was perfect Honolulu weather that day, with a sky of blazing blue and tempestuous trade winds surging down the Nu'uanu Valley to cool them as they worked. When the tree was in place, Hillebrand gazed at it proudly and said, "What could be more beautiful? The Jews have a fine toast, you know: *L'chaim*, meaning simply, *To Life!*"

"*L'chaim!*" said David, "and this tree, no doubt, shall outlive us both!"

"Yes, and to these branches birds shall come to build nests, generation after generation. A tree is a great work of art. Sometimes the human body, I think, by comparison is a mere dandelion!"

When their young helper had departed he asked David, in low tones, "Have you ever seen leprosy? A terrible disease! But not so terrible as the opinion of certain sacred ignoramuses that leprosy is sent by God as punishment for sin." David said that he did not know such a God, nor did he believe that one existed. Hillebrand replied that the Hawaiian youth would never see his parents again; they had been sent away to die on the island of Molokai. The boy's father had contracted leprosy, and his faithful wife of 40 years had refused to leave him. Whether or not she became infected, she would remain in that desolate place for the rest of her life. There was no civil order there, he said, nor any medical aid, nor hope of release from the leper colony. It was a hell on earth, but for the efforts of a single, saintly young priest named Father Damien who risked his life to serve the colony as best he could. "And yet some people – some find it in their hearts to criticize that man, and whisper filth about him!"

"Yes, I have heard it. Because he is Roman Catholic?"

"Ach – Roman, Calvinist, Mormon, pagan, it does not matter. Because some people are damned fools – pardon me, David – who think only with their genitalia. One day" he continued furiously, "science will find a cure for this. Some herb or berry that even now may be growing – something simple as that, I tell you, it will be found. Let the world judge then who has sinned – the suffering, the dying, or those who despised them! Where is the Will of God in this? I ask you, does not Holy Scripture teach us that God is Love?"

David told him that he might preach at Grace Church any time he liked.

*

The wind dropped at sunset, and the humid air closed down around them like a woolen blanket. In the wooden "pro-cathedral" David Wilkinson was asked to lead the assembled company in prayer. Only then did he notice that he was the only clergyman present; the others were foreigners prominent in the community, and lay leaders in his Church. After the last *Amen*, Theophilus Davies rose up with his broad forehead glistening and read the resolution: a bold document that told the plain truth.

It began with a brief history of the Anglican Mission: how King Kamehameha IV and Emma, his Queen, had requested a chaplain from England to minister to them and some interested foreigners. England had chosen instead to send out an elaborate Episcopal establishment, including a bishop newly elevated to that post. Since then, the Church had spent vast amounts on land, buildings, furnishings and adornments, but the spiritual needs of the people had not been met. Anglicans from Britain, and American Episcopalians as well, wanted simpler services, less formal ritual, and far better pastoral care. They wanted a leader who would stay with them, not be constantly traveling abroad. They wanted to live in peace with members of other nations and denominations in the Islands, but Coldwell's behavior had made that impossible. The present situation, the document concluded, was intolerable. Therefore no further support for the present regime would be provided by the undersigned residents. The Anglican experiment had been a disastrous failure under Albert Coldwell. It was time for him to go.

Nothing in this surprised David Wilkinson, except for the fact that it had been put into writing. The real shock was to come, for in the final paragraph, he heard his own name. The resolution ended by asking that no more bishops be sent out from England, for they were not needed here; and it called for the Rev. David C.P. Wilkinson to serve the Royal Family as chaplain and the Honolulu congregation as rector and priest-in-charge. If this were permitted by the higher authorities, a stipend for Wilkinson's support was guaranteed by the undersigned in the amount of £300 per year.

He was astonished. It was far beyond anything he had ever dreamed or imagined. He looked in amazement at the earnest faces around him, for as well as Theophilus Davies, William Green and Archibald Cleghorn were there, and Charles Harris, and a dozen other civic leaders, both English and American. As they waited for his response, he imagined the little church in Kona neglected and abandoned – and then remembered Emma. "But how does the Queen…?" he began. "Does she …?" Before he could finish, he saw in their faces that Emma knew, and wanted it so. He bowed his head then, and promised to serve them as best he could.

In a daze of bewilderment and excitement he returned to Kona, feeling that everything in the world around him had changed. Never had he loved his little home in the wilderness as much as now, when he thought of leaving it. The rough hut that served as a parsonage suddenly appeared to him as a charming little retreat in a blessed neighborhood, where angels awaited him on the doorstep. The church, with its homely fragrance of beeswax and sawdust became a mighty temple now, filled with power and splendor. These sudden transformations affected every aspect of his daily life: the shambling gray horse that came to live with him was fine as any Arab steed; even the humble cabbages in his garden glowed like jewels, and the very weeds among them stood up boldly, proclaiming their integrity and worth. Nature itself became benign; a flowering vine that had mounted toward his window ventured in now, reaching out fine tendrils to embrace him as he slept. One morning a small gray field mouse dressed in velvet came to his hand for crumbs, and stayed there to eat them, regarding him fearlessly. So might a man feel, David thought, when he awakened in Paradise – or else here on earth, when the hour of his execution has been named. Perhaps, he told himself, we are meant to live this way always: spending each hour so near to the gates of the Kingdom, sensing the fiery breath of God in all things.

*

In time, quite naturally, this rapture died away, and he was an ordinary country vicar once again, going about his chores. He rode as soon as possible to the camp of the "prophet" and was turned away by armed guards. He conducted services, taught classes, visited the sick, wrote sermons, polished the candlesticks, swept the church. He rode to the "prophet's" camp again once, twice, three times and was always refused entrance. Peering in through the shrubbery one day he saw some of the villagers idling about while a youth in white robes harangued them, and then, to his amazement and disgust, saw that the preacher was none other than young Kimo Lopaka, Harold's angry son. After that he consulted Sheriff Kildare, but was told that there was nothing to do but wait.

After a time he cut back the intrusive vine and weeded his cabbage. The mouse was gone, having vanished, he supposed, into the craw of their meditative neighbor, *pueo*. One dark November day he buried the Cornwall's infant son, and built a cairn for him. Far too many children in the district went to their graves that winter, and David grieved as he came to understand that the cause was cholera. Little Ricky Cornwall's suffering had been brief, but terrible, for there was no defense in those days against the disease.

No further word came from Honolulu, and he tried not to think of it. On the 6th of December he carried Melissa

Hawkins, in agony with an inflamed appendix, through the surf to a ship's longboat; from there she was brought to the Queen's hospital in Honolulu, and Hillebrand drained the infection in time to save her. Having stubbornly ignored the seriousness of her illness, Soper Hawkins attacked the priest furiously for "interference" in the matter, and this enraged David so that he actually told the Captain to go to Hell. A terrible, reprehensible thing for a clergyman to say, as he well knew; and later, he had bitter reason to regret it.

On a happier occasion, a handsome young couple came to the church and asked to be married. They were decked with flowers for the occasion, as were all five of their children. That day, David took it upon himself to change the Order of Service somewhat, and after managing a solemn wedding and a rousing baptism of five little Hawaiians, he stood up and read the General Thanksgiving, that delightful bit of liturgy supposedly written by Queen Elizabeth. In gratitude, the couple came back the following week bringing him a fat pig on a tether and a large basketful of yams. Even though he had no money. David never went hungry that winter, for parishioners shared their produce, and he had taken to fishing frequently with Harold Lopaka. As they made their way up and down the Kona coast in Harold's canoe, he taught David the Hawaiian way of catching fish with spears and nets, while the priest introduced Harold to the mysteries of Anglican theology. He was training his native friend as a lay reader for Grace Church in case he himself was suddenly called away; and this was a pleasant task, for Harold was quick, intelligent and sincere.

It was Advent by now, and the coconut telegraph hummed with the news that Emma Kaleleonalani would be coming to Kona at Christmas. On her account, Grace Church would be filled to overflowing, for natives would come from far and near for a glimpse of their beloved Queen. Homesick Americans, too, would come to Grace Church for a taste of the season, since their own pastors refused to celebrate the birth of Christ. In their stern, Calvinist opinions, this was a degenerate, pagan holiday!

And now David began to yearn in a hapless way for home, where snow would be in the air, and holly trees would be wearing bright berries, and oaken logs would be crackling in kitchen fires. Mincemeats were being assembled these days at *Green Gardens*, while kegs of good Yorkshire ale were brought to the back door and rolled into the buttery. Katherine Wilkinson, wearing an apron, was lifting plum puddings up to the highest shelves in the larder, where they would steep in brandy, later to be set aflame. Then, on Christmas Eve, his father would bring an evergreen tree into the parlor, and Mama would deck it with candles, ribbons and bells – a quaint foreign custom to be sure, but one of the better gifts brought over by the German who had wed Queen Victoria. David had decided by now that he would never marry, and that it would be for the best. After all, it was true that he generally preferred his own company; and now he celebrated the coming season by singing loudly as he rode on the flanks of Mauna Loa, *Christmas is acomin'; the goose is getting fat! Please to put a penny in the old man's hat!*

It was cool at those heights almost as Yorkshire, and one day the faithful Curate actually stepped on bits of ice. Some of the low mountain shrubs beside the trail bore handsome red berries, and David was thirsty, so he tasted them, finding them strangely delicious: both sweet and sour, unlike any other fruit he knew. He told himself repeatedly to save them all for decorating the church, but he could not resist eating quite a number before coming home. That may have been a mistake, for that night, for the first, last and only time in his life, David Wilkinson walked in his sleep. Walked quite a distance, in fact. *Wake up!* said a woman's voice ringing with laughter, clear as a bell beside him; and that brought him to his senses. It was long after midnight, and he found himself standing in the church facing the altar in his nightshirt. He knew that he had been looking for something, but he could not remember what it was.

27

Fiona Cameron: Journal   PRIVATE!
Hilo, Hawaii – 10 November 1867

New notebook, new beginning. Bethy disapproves – says I've changed & that makes her unhappy. Damn! I should have known better than to confide so much, even to the dearest of sisters. So I might bow down now – beg forgiveness, say that I've been an impulsive fool – but NO! Better hold my course and see what develops. Thus, these new pages, that I plan to fill with things she would rather not hear.

19th Nov. – I eat and sleep, heedless as a cat or a cow. Thought I'd enjoy having more flesh on me, but instead, I find it a bother. Don't know quite who I am any more. Used to think of myself as something like a bowstring, pulled taut to its limits – or else at times, an arrow in flight. Now I am suddenly lumpy, sad, tender, uncertain. Alive, yes – very much so, but irritably. Sick to death of these timid little pictures I keep drawing. Well then, burn them! If you don't like them, F. C., God knows who else will.

20th Nov. – It's all useless. The more I criticize myself, the more I'm unable or unwilling to progress. I urge myself forward only to retreat. Hunger at the oddest hours. Strange sensations in the pelvic area. Can't button the camisole now – but look here, never mind that. Stop worrying about your appearance, of all things. The fat will melt of itself one day –

or if it doesn't, soon enough my girl, you yourself will be a wicker basket full of bones. Her epitaph: Spinster, Dreamer, Idler, Unbeliever – or, just as likely – no one notices that she is gone.

10 December –Farewell to Hilo! In a flash yesterday found myself on the deck of a sailing ship with cape for blanket, saddle for pillow – hurrah! Missy to be brought over the mts. to Kona for me by a nice young native boy. Present fit of joy brought on by a splendid letter from Q Emma demanding my presence at her side.

She misses me – will be staying at the Kona palace for Christmas – also says D. is by far the best of the English missionaries! Riggs has gone home, Russell to follow – and of Truckle & White, no mention. Scotty Partridge it seems is in dark trouble of some sort in Maui. She says nothing about His Toadship, & that in itself tells a story.

In Kona, she wants to show support of David's work, teaching native children along with the whites quite brilliantly – a fine little parish brought to birth out of nothing – oh, she is proud of him! But I must meet her for a few days first at the Hawkins' estate. "The parsonage," she says, "not suitable" – how I smiled at that! And wondered what she may have heard!

So now, 2 days later, beating southeast against the trades – the sky a bitter blue, the sea tumultuous, all aglitter with flying, dashing spray & my heart soaring. It's all foolishness, I know – thinking of him – and all that can never happen – & yet, and yet! We are tilting wildly now, first one way then the other – I can scarcely write. But not sick in the least – feeling fine, in fact – though I did slip and fall down rather badly this morn on a mucky place where an Englishman had just vomited.

16 December   *Kihapai O Ekena.*
Here in this gloomy house, awakened by something at 3 a.m. – a mewing or a moaning, animal or human? It has stopped now but I am sleepless, in misery, thinking again & again in terrible lightning flashes of the time on the terrace last night, just after dinner. David's face looking at me, then looking away, out to sea – brown now, almost as a half-caste & suddenly older than before – that strange scar on his face, the line of the jaw that was so much too perfect, now marred. Of all things, an accident with a horse – after I had offered a careless word on the subject to Bethy.

Not meaning to wish it, surely, and I'm not superstitious enough to believe that a thought of mine was the cause.

The evening began well enough – a pretty scene on the lawn at sunset, when D. somewhat late in arriving, dashed up the road on a big gray horse. "Young Lochinvar rode out of the West!" cried Queen Emma. Then a gently teasing remark or two from D. to me – and on to the dinner table where a half dozen light and dark brown children sat scrubbed & starched, bored to distraction – later fussing & squirming so that they were sent off without dessert. Social wastelands ensued, of the sort that always make me want to tickle someone or shout something rude. Capt. Hawkins, that pillar of the Church, more than half drunk & peering down my bosom, where the white dress was suddenly, alas, too tight. His dark, pretty wife either mute or terrified. For the better part of an hour nothing but scattered remarks, no real conversation. My own small offerings consigned to darkness, Emma, with polite smile firmly fixed, looking beautiful, David brooding & glooming far down the table – staring at me from time to time – no relief in sight.

In desperation at last I burst forth with the story of my Jacobite cousin Annie – the most outrageous thing I could think of. Told them how she was called "Colonel Anne" at 20 – clever, beautiful, audacious – and how her husband rode off one day to fight for the English. So she called up the clan, armed them and led them out for Bonnie Prince Charles!

"Looking for trouble, was she?" Hawkins remarked, picking his teeth. As usual with him, it was a statement – not a question.

"Oh no," I told him. "Following her heart – or it could be said, doing her duty. She was a Highland lady, after all! She was a Mackintosh!"

"Her duty? And never mind her husband?" said Hawkins, sneering.

"Well I rather think she didn't like him very much," said I with a smile as sweet as I could make it. But Emma was suddenly looking stricken, and I promised myself to behave from now on. No one spoke as the dishes were changed between courses – by an elderly Asian man – his hands shaking – the candles all burning straight up – a silent, windless night. I was thinking about D. in a dreamy, childish sort of way – when almost as if he knew it, he suddenly said, "Lady Fiona, I believe there is more to that story."

"Yes," I said – not of a mind to tell it. But he turned to the children and said most gravely, "Lady Anne was captured, and the English put

her into prison."

"Well of course," I said, "But they let her out soon enough."

"Because they all fell in love with her!" said D., lifting the wounded chin. "She charmed them all foolish, as I heard it."

"Quite unintentionally, I assure you," I told him, "But there is more to it —" by now I couldn't resist — "because you see, two years later, Lady Anne went to a ball given by the King of England's son — the same one who had imprisoned her, and defeated the last Stuart prince. This time he bowed politely and asked her to dance. 'I have danced to your tune,' Annie told him in her saucy way. 'Tonight, will you dance to mine?' He agreed to that, and invited her to give orders to the musicians."

Emma's eyes were sparkling now. "And pray tell us, what tune did she ask for?" she asked.

Again David spoke, solemn as ever. "As I heard it, Ma'am, she told them to play 'The Old Stuarts Back Again' — and that, of course, was a scandal."

Emma laughed heartily.

"No, no," I told him. "Actually, it was 'Who Should be King but Charlie?" Emma remarked that my impertinent relative might just as well have chosen "Charlie is My Darlin" — an old favorite of her own. Hawkins through all this was baffled, but David turned to him & said kindly, "These events took place in Britain more than a hundred years ago, you see, Captain. But they are still rather vividly remembered by all concerned."

"Well, thunder!" the Captain shouted. "A century ago! Then this is all gossip! Not one of you knows what really happened!"

But Emma was fascinated. "And there they were, the two enemies at a royal ball with everyone watching! Oh my! Was he a handsome prince, I hope, and a marvelous dancer?"

"No," I said. "He was ugly, and clumsy, and mean."

"Oh! Oh! But did she dance with him — did they dance?"

"Aye, they danced," said David, looking darkly at me. "They danced."

Then to the terrace again, David just ahead, moving slowly across the soft, grassy spaces, looking at the sea. I was following in the white dress — slightly staggering, with a strange loosening of my limbs that I'd been noticing all day. I was ablaze with sunburn — flowers in my hair —

believing myself, for once, almost beautiful. Just then the Queen, who had been walking behind me, put her hand softly to the small of my back – I turned & she gazed at me – said nothing, but stayed even closer. As we gained the outer reaches of the terrace where the torches are, she quickly took off her shawl & placed it, not around my shoulders – but lower, so that it rested on my hips. There with a merry smile she tied it gypsy fashion to one side – then put her arm about me. I felt loved, I felt safe. But David looked at me with a closed face – indecipherable. It was a Chinese shawl – bright blue, with silver embroidery & silken fringes.

"Blue is for Truth," D. said solemnly, as if conveying a secret message.

"Yes," said Emma. "And so it becomes you, Fiona, very well. You must keep it please, but it is time now for you to retire. Yes, yes, I insist my dear – right away. You must lie down and rest. You have come so far – a hard journey. Rest now, and we shall see you in the morning."

I felt crushed – like a bad child, being sent from table. I looked at David – he turned away again – "Are you all right?" I asked that interesting, ruined jaw of his. No response. Had he heard me? Possibly not. Looked around at Hawkins & wife – made my manners – stumbled over one of their stinking dogs that were always nosing at my privates, excused myself & fled.

Not until I came to my bedroom did I see the wet stuff oozing into my satin slippers. I tore them off & scuttled across the floor – leaving red footprints. The shawl was untouched, but the back of the white gown was stained with it. Dreaming of romance, I'd sat in a puddle. And now I realized all at once that I was not hurt or ill, that this was a part of something quite ordinary and horrid – something that I must live with from now on, whether I liked it or not.

But how? And why? Why now, after so many years? "Count your blessings, child," Dr. A. used to say– that pious old plum. How he loved to peer, and prod, and measure, and press his cold little fingers into my flesh! "The Lord has given you a gift – compensation perhaps for the unfortunate malformation of your spine. For as you are now, you shall be always – young & lovely forever – so pure, so delicate – and the Curse & Pollution of Woman shall never touch you! And God grant that I shall always be here to care for you!" The smarmy bastard. My shift underneath was ruined, so I've torn it up to make bandages. But really, this, every month from now on? Vanquished, without even a battle? Yes, Fiona –

and unless you are very lucky indeed, some day a wee pink worm will gnaw its way into your tenderest inmost parts & cling there, feeding & growing larger & larger until you die, trying to get it out. It's something women have to do, and very often it kills them – it's called a Blessed Event!

But I refuse to allow these thoughts – I utterly dismiss them. The night is nearly over – the stars are fading now, morning is near. In another few hours I shall face them all with my head held high at the breakfast table. No matter what they have seen – even David. Was that why he was so strange? And the lascivious Hawkins. And those vile sniffing, prodding dogs!

19 Dec. But there was no need. Instead, the Queen came to my room in her dressing gown, hair streaming down over her shoulders – carrying a tray with tea, fruit & biscuits. "Are you all right?" she asked – I said yes, of course – & we laughed like conspirators, which in a sense I suppose we were. She knew that this was the first time for me – & had been nearly as amazed as I was. She had assumed that whatever had kept me quiescent – in a sort of neutral mode thus far – must be a permanent affliction, due perhaps to an accident of birth. She told me to rejoice, but I was hardly in a mood for that.

Even so, we sat up in bed together for half the morning talking & giggling like schoolgirls over all the forbidden topics. I told her things that I've told no one else – even Bethy. Nothing about D., though – or the dreams. The silliest was my story about the first time I ever saw a man's privates – when Uncle drew a large piece of meat out from his trousers & used it to piss with – what a shock that was! Oh how we laughed. Then I told her the old Scots saying, "Every little bit helps, quoth the wren as she peed in the ocean," & we laughed more.

After this, Emma explained the mystery of the Bishop's visits. She is in torments – he refuses to let her remarry, a passionate suitor! Why? Because the man in question is the present King, her late husband's brother. He's madly in love with her – sent de Varigny to propose for him, he was in such terror of being refused. Emma spoke with Bsp. Coldwell, who said absolutely not, citing Book of Leviticus.

But Emma knows her Bible too – at least as well as he does. She countered with Deuteronomy, where it says a man is <u>obliged</u> to marry his *brother's widow if bro. has left no offspring – which in this case is true. Her own feelings are not like the King's – not with darling Alex and Baby waiting for her in Heaven! Still she is deeply fond of him – and another child is desperately needed for the sake of the Monarchy. She is so terribly afraid that they will all die out – the Royal Family sickly these days & no likely heirs. This was the anguish when I first arrived. Emma knows her History, as well. She said to Coldwell – your wicked King Henry 8ᵗʰ only fell back on the Leviticus rule because he lusted after Anne Boleyn! He used it as a way of shedding his wife! For shame! And you want me to abide by that? It is clear to me (she said) that Deuteronomy is better, on purely moral grounds.*

The Bishop – when he heard this – was apoplectic. Shouted that Queen or no Queen, she was far out of her depth. If she did not obey him, the little Hawaiian Kingdom would lose England's favor & protection – did she want that to happen? Did she want that on her conscience? In the end, being Emma, she has submitted. Soon, she says, very soon, it will all be over. Either England or America will rule Hawaii from now on. So her solemn, sacred choice has been the British Empire – not America! Not those people! On that, she and her brother-in-law agree.

"But even to think of bearing another child – what courage!" I said. "Must you listen to this dreadful clergyman? Sorry, I can't abide him. And what about God's kingdom – is that only for people who go by Church rules? I don't think that's what Jesus taught!"

"You should marry David!" said Emma, suddenly bright with mischief. "I suspect him of being quite as mutinous as you."

"Hah! No chance of that. I'll never marry."

She was amazed. "But darling, why not? You are still young – we all need love – and you two might have a splendid family."

"No thank you." I told her then about Mum when baby Hal was being born – the look on her face when the screaming finally stopped – & they closed her eyes for her – & took her away. How I ran after them & then lost my mind or something near it, after Papa shot himself later that same day – walking in my sleep weeping & sobbing through the garden night after night, looking for someone or something. Love, I suppose, or safety – or some way out of that terrible reality. "Oh my dear," she said, and that was all – but in her great black eyes, I saw a kind of crucifixion. I began to tremble & shake – at first only a little, & then –

uncontrollably. Covered my face, couldn't bear it, I was so ashamed. There I was complaining of my own miserable, insignificant life, while she grieved for the loss of a Kingdom – & the beautiful land & the beloved people.

"It is not easy being a woman," said Emma Kaleleonalani. Then she put her arms around me & held me close for a long time, while we both wept.

28

I f the summons had not come from Queen Emma herself, he might have declined the invitation for dinner at the Hawkins ranch. As it was, David managed to arrive somewhat late, and after leaving Mr. Gray at the stables, walked reluctantly out to the terrace. To his astonishment, the first person he saw there was Fiona Cameron. She was seated in a bamboo chair, holding a white fan and dressed all in white. There she was – his lass, his Highland lady. He bowed over her hand and murmured, "Your name, please?"

She gave him a bewitching smile, and replied, "You know all of my names, David – every one of them!"

"Take a look at that sunset!" shouted Hawkins, but for the time being they did not obey him.

"Come here, young Lochinvar, and talk to me!" said Emma Kalaleonali, and so he did. A little later, in the softening, greening light of dusk the early stars appeared, while the Queen and her entourage moved slowly about the terrace in their long, swaying dresses, and the Hawkins children came out to frolic on the lawn. Almost, David thought, it could have been a scene at home in England, with sheep in the distance and swallows gathering, after the tea trays are carried in. But there were no sheep, no swallows, and no tea trays; and then, quite suddenly, it was night.

As they came into the dining room, dogs were barking and poor Chin Wong Lo, looking wretched, was being chastised by the Captain for some misdemeanor. The dogs were unusually restless tonight, and in trying to quiet them, David managed to knock down a shotgun that had been left propped carelessly against a wall. All in all, he thought, not a promising start for a dinner party! Then he saw that the seating plan had been badly done.

Queen Emma was not given the place of honor she deserved, but instead was placed far down the table beside David himself, while Fiona was made to sit twelve feet away at the right hand of the host. At least David had the privilege of watching her from afar, and now he saw that she had changed yet again. Tonight she was neither the ailing spinster nor the wayward sprite he had seen more recently; now she was all softness and radiance, a virtuous maiden in full bloom. *Rose of Sharon*, he thought, *Behold, thou art fair!*

The Queen praised him warmly for the excellence of his mission work, and then began to speak of Archibald Campbell Tait. She was thrilled, she said, to learn that he was now Archbishop, for he was a good man, who had been extraordinarily kind to her when she went to England. He and his wife, too – both most agreeable and sympathetic. They had given a lovely garden party for her at Fulham Palace – he was still Bishop of London then – and she would never forget sitting on a crimson sofa beside the River Thames that day while all sorts of distinguished people were presented to her. There had been the most elegant refreshments, and at the end of the afternoon they all sang *Auld Lang Syne* and *God Save the Queen*. (Which queen, she had wondered – or both?) But it was good to know that the Taits were deeply in love – anyone could see it. Thank God for that, she told David, with sudden tears nearly brimming over – because only a few years ago they had lost <u>five</u> children, one after another, to scarlet fever! Five little daughters! All in the space of a single month, the youngest an infant, the eldest ten years old. Can you imagine? No one, she said, who had ever spoken to her of her own terrible losses – no one had known the anguish and the agony so well.

As the second or third lot of dishes came in, Fiona made some witty remarks about a cousin of hers during the old wars between England and Scotland, and finally, at this rather solemn party, there was laughter. But David hardly noticed what it was about, for he was studying the stranger across the table who had once been Fiona sleeping in his arms, then Fiona blushing and laughing as she rode away. Never before had he wanted to court a woman, and he was wondering how to do it. In this case, he told himself, it should surely be managed with great care: gently, patiently, systematically. Above all, he should do nothing to frighten her. But in assembling his portfolio of ideas on the subject, he found it meager, borrowed mainly from the Renaissance poets and a few operas he had seen. Of course there was always the *Song of Solomon* – which was not, he believed, about the passion of God for his Church.

After dinner they moved out to the terrace so that the men could smoke, but David had not brought his pipe with him. Looking up at the starry sky and out to sea, he knew that Fiona was close behind him, for there were magnetic forces moving between them. But, was she aware of them? He thought not. Turning back to look at her again, he saw the Queen tucking a brilliant blue shawl about his lady's waist while Fiona stood with her eyes closed and her head thrown back, looking like anything but a virgin. Amazing! Suddenly she was a hot-blooded gypsy wench. What next? Tomorrow she might wake up as a consecrated nun. Undoubtedly it would cost him a lifetime to learn all her transformations and disguises. However, that thought did not bother him much, for then, he had a lifetime to spend.

"Blue is for truth," he said aloud to himself, but Fiona apparently heard him. To his dismay, she immediately turned and left the party. He slept little that night, and when he went back to look for her in the morning, he was told that she could not be disturbed. He had a difficult sermon to write, and so went on his way downcast. Later in the same day he climbed the hill again, and found her this time, sitting alone on the terrace. She had been making a small sketch of some sort, but she put it away as soon as she saw him approaching. The face that she lifted to his gaze was wan, stern and commanding, under the wide brim of an elegant hat he had never seen before. Today, evidently, she was a princess – and for some reason, a sad one.

"I have decided to go to Borneo," she remarked, and added politely, "Have you ever been there?"

He thought for a moment. "No, But I am going to disregard that statement, since it is not to my liking. Tell me, please, about your drawing."

"No."

"Then may I see it?"

"No, you may not."

"Pray tell why not?"

"Because I do not wish you to see it."

"Then we are at an impasse." He sat down beside her. "Shall we begin again? Did you sleep well?"

"No, I did not."

"Nor did I. There, you see, something we have in common. I was disappointed last night, Fiona, when you left so suddenly." She sighed, and he saw that she had a handkerchief at her wrist. He wondered if it might be one of his, but decided not to inquire. She turned a resentful face to him then and asked, "Why did you look at me so strangely last night, and say, *Blue is for Truth?*"

"Why? Is that something that offended you?" He saw now that there were shadows under her eyes and that her eyelids were swollen. A sad princess, indeed! There was silence between them for a time while they both looked out at the ocean. Then he said, "You are unhappy today, and I believe I know the reason." Her shoulders went up, and she began trying to rub a small ink-stain from her right index finger. "It is nothing," she said, "but tell me, if you like."

"You are unhappy because you are a princess, and you have

been captured by a boggard. Do you know what a boggard is? A sort of ogre, or bugaboo. One that lives in boggy places, hence the name. The worst of the boggards always have castles, and in this particular boggard's castle there are many large, barking dogs, and dastardly weapons in the dining room, and damp, dark dungeons underneath. But nowhere, anywhere, is there a sign of a feather bed with soft pillows and silken sheets befitting a noble lady. And so, I think you have been awake in the night with something – not a pea, but a kukui nut, because this is Hawaii – under your mattress. And this outrageous object has given you a nasty bruise on your delicate skin."

She looked at him as if she might weep, but burst into laughter instead, "Oh David – oh! That is so –" Then she was overcome by laughter, throwing her head back so that the hat slipped from her head. She caught it and skimmed it across the lawn, where it dipped and circled, then fell into a stand of white ginger.

"Oh David, I am so glad to see you!"

"Then marry me." So much for cautious courtship!

She scarcely hesitated before saying lightly, "I am going to disregard that remark."

"It is not to your liking?"

"Come now, tell me what you have been doing, instead."

"Doing? Nothing in particular. Living, and so on. Living in a Paradise that no longer pleases me because you are not there." She began rapidly tidying up her pens and inks, that were kept in something like a shoe box. He retrieved some fallen papers for her and said rather sharply, "Fiona, don't go away!"

"I wish," she said with a sigh. "I wish for so many things that can never – ever –"

"Tell me one wish, and I will make it come true."

"No. I wish for impossibilities."

"For example?"

"For example? Oh, just now I suppose I wish that we were children playing in a wood, by the side of a little rambling beck or burn, with grasses and ferns around the edges, and the cool water running over our bare feet. A magical place, you see – unreal."

"Of course, but my dear, I know the very spot. It's not far from here, less than a day's ride. It's quite secluded, a beautiful place for bathing, with a pool and a waterfall."

"For bathing?" She was amused, and a little shocked.

"Well, we'd be children, so it wouldn't matter."

"David, and you a priest!"

"All the safer."

"I doubt it. I doubt that very much." But she said this without emphasis, absent-mindedly. The sun was descending now in a sky that was almost white with brilliance, and she put the back of one hand to her eyes. "I ask you to remember," she continued, "that I am at least half a century older than you."

"Nonsense! A matter of months, I'll wager. And you are just beginning to live. You have been reborn lately; I've seen it happen."

"Seven years," she said.

"Well then, I am an old man by comparison, since I've been out in the world on my own since the age of fifteen!" She smiled at that, and asked him to please fetch her hat, for the light was dazzling. He thought to himself as he rummaged in the flowerbed that courtship was not so difficult after all. In fact, he was rather enjoying it. On the strength of that, having put her hat back on for her, and helped her to adjust its ribbon, he stood up before her with his hands in his pockets and told her that his situation had changed. He had reason to believe that he would soon be in Honolulu with great tasks before him, earning a far better living. He also hinted that this advancement had come to him because his superior gifts, etcetera, had been recognized by large numbers of powerful and respectable people. But the point of it all was, he said, that in only one more year he would be in a position to –

"David, don't!" she cried, but he continued. "Stop, please stop and sit down!" When he saw that her eyes had actually filled with tears, he ended his argument, but remained standing. "Don't say things that you shouldn't and then hate me for it later," she pleaded, and then commanded him again, "Sit! Sit." This time he obeyed her. But then she surprised him again, for she knelt down beside him in the grass with her arms folded tightly before her, rocking back and forth in her anxiety to find the words she wanted. She was wearing a white blouse and a drab, conventional skirt in some dark red material, heavily belted at the waist. He had never seen this costume before, and thought it unbecoming.

"I would only disappoint you," she said at last. "And that is the truth of it."

"Now that is a real impossibility."

"No, I am not what you think. If I am newborn in your eyes, that is because you yourself have imagined me, invented me as you would like."

"You say so? You imagine this, and therefore it is true?" She did not answer.

"Fiona, you said that you are going away now. Why, and when and where?"

"Borneo. A place there called Sarawak."

"And when will you return?" Again, she did not answer, and he knelt on the grass beside her, saying, "Give me your hand! No no, don't fear. This is not another unwanted proposal. Come, I won't hurt you – which you ought to know by this time!"

She unclenched her arms and held out not one, but both of her hands to him. He took them in his own, committed them to memory, and then turned them over one at a time. They were trembling, but only a little. A more accomplished lover, he supposed, would have kissed each rosy fingertip and written her a sonnet. But Fiona's hands were not rosy, they were brown and strong, so he put his palms down on hers, to see how they measured. His were somewhat broader and thicker, but her fingers were equally long.

"We are a good match," he said, and then stood up. "Come, let's walk for a bit." He helped her to her feet, and then without touching one another they promenaded the lawn while she told him in a gay, determined way why she had always wanted to go to Borneo. She had a yearning for wilderness, she said. Civilization was a trap of sorts, it locked people in. Hawaii was far too civilized already, with all of its manners and formalities, all its secret rules and political alliances. She wanted to understand the truth about life in a place where things were perfectly simple – where it was all made plain – unfettered, undistorted.

"An ambitious desire," he said. "I rather doubt, myself, whether there is any such place. But what will you do in Sarawak, simply ramble about looking at things?"

"That's it, yes," she said. "I am used to being alone, you see. I am really rather selfish. I've always been a private sort of person. I suppose I don't see things the way most people do, and that is why I need so much time to think. And I'll make some more drawings – only for myself, of course, because they help me to understand what things really are, and perhaps even why they are that way."

"And who will look after you?" he almost said, but caught himself. "Where will you stay? Only, that is, so that a person who wanted to might send you a letter?"

"I expect at the Palace. It's a sort of Sultanate, you see, privately owned. My parents knew the Rajah."

"Rajah? Oh, another boggard – a Sarawakian boggard, no less."

"No, no!" she laughed a little, exasperated. "He is an Englishman, named Brooke. He owns the little country of Sarawak, and so he is known as the White Rajah."

"An ordinary, run-of-the-mill boggard, then, who bought himself a country?"

"Bought it?" She was astonished.

"How did he get it, then? Go in with gunboats and steal it from the natives?" She wheeled about angrily, then studied his face and said in a haughty fashion, "You are jealous! Yes, you are jealous of James Brooke! I don't know exactly how he got it. But I do know that they invited him in, and were glad of his help, and asked him to manage the country for them. He has done a great deal for the natives – many, many good things to help them. David, you help people – how is that different from what you do?"

That stung him. "Well then, behave yourself out there, my lady."

She was instantly furious. "I will do no such thing!" she cried. "Haven't I just told you that I utterly refuse to be civilized?" As she stood there quivering with wrath, in her fashionable hat, and her long skirt that was puffed out with petticoats, and her pleated blouse that was like that of an unfortunate schoolmistress who had once tried and failed to teach him French, the full comedy of her situation struck David. There was pathos in it, to be sure, and he should have taken that into account. In fact, at a moment like that, a wise suitor would have covered her face, or the hem of her gown, with kisses if he could think of nothing better to do.

Instead, David pointed his finger at her and laughed, saying, "Look at you, in your garden-party hat, and your petticoats with lace on them. You? Not civilized? You can't help yourself. I can see you now, buttoned up to the chin, giving a tea party in the jungle."

"Don't – you – dare to make fun of me!" she said in a low dangerous voice. And then David, who had never before been in such a situation, made it worse by resorting to logic. "But Fiona, Fiona love," he cried, "we have already laughed at one another so much! Have you forgotten? You seemed to enjoy it well enough, I must say, when we were together on the mountain!"

In even icier tones she replied, "If you ever, ever mention that time – or that place again – or anything – anything at all about what happened there, I will kill you." David was stunned, with sheer admiration. She meant it. And he remembered then that she always carried a knife.

"Fiona, I love you," he said, quite solemnly and sincerely. "I have loved you all this time, since the first day we met."

"Hah!" said she. "Don't be a fool. You know nothing about

me, and you never will. Go away! Go preach yourself a sermon!"

"Oh Fiona, lass," he said with a grin, "Come now – believe me, I <u>know</u> you."

She went crimson, and her hands became fists. Just then, his glance fell upon a stray piece of her drawing paper in the grass. He bent to retrieve it, and saw that there was a picture in pen and ink, on the back.

"Don't you dare! That is private! Give it back to me this instant!" David heard her, but only as if from a distance. What he held was a small portrait of a man's head, finely done, with a strong, sure touch. It was an exquisite piece of work. Furthermore, he saw that the man bore a startling resemblance to someone he knew – in fact, to himself.

"You have no right!" she cried.

"Sorry, too late. But this is excellent! I like it very much."

"Give it back! Then go away and leave me alone!" She held out her hand, but David did not see it; he was staring with increasing wonder at the drawing. Now he began to understand that Fiona had been sitting on the terrace when he arrived, making a portrait of him from memory. And there he was, vividly himself, with the wound he had received quite noticeable on his face. She had never said a word to him about his disfigurement, but she had drawn him faithfully, fearlessly, scar and all. With wise and loving hands she had included his wound as if it were a significant, even a rather attractive part of his being. She had done that – his Fiona!

"So, you have seen it. Now go away! And don't come near me ever again!" She snatched the drawing, crumpled it, tossed it beyond a hedge of scarlet bougainvillea, and then in a whirl of skirts and petticoats, stalked furiously away.

He was after her in an instant, and chased her across the lawn, catching up with her beside the fragrant ginger. He took her by the shoulders and she stopped, breathless and trembling, but violently resisted his attempts to turn her around. Not to be thwarted, David seized her in a rude, unchivalrous embrace, and planted his mark and seal upon the back of her neck. A little later she turned in his arms and swayed, and sighed, and pressed herself against him with the same plaintive moan that he remembered from their night on the mountain. The *Song of Solomon* had nothing sweeter than that moment. By then he had his hands in places where they should not have been, and passion might have blinded both of them entirely if Chin Wong Lo had not suddenly appeared on the lawn. Gazing at the pair he stood transfixed, and cried out in a language that may or may not have been Chinese.

Without a word, Fiona fled into the house, while David moved toward the intruder with solemnly murderous intent. But Lo did not answer when spoken to, and his eyes were so vacant and wild that David soon relented and put an arm around the old man's shoulders. "It's all right, Lo," he said. "Don't worry – everything will be all right."

Unfortunately, that was not to be the case. When he returned the following morning, David found the house strangely silent, all but abandoned. Chin Wong Lo was nowhere to be seen, and Queen Emma and her entourage had departed. Soper Hawkins was not there, and his horse was absent from the stables. When he asked for Fiona Cameron, he was told by the grinning stable boy, "Lady gone 'way."

29

I t was long past midnight under the faint light of a waning moon when he heard hoofbeats approaching the parsonage. For a moment in that pale, unearthly glow, he imagined that the rider was Fiona, hastening back to say that she could not bear to leave him after all. Instead, it was Richard Cornwall at a gallop, evidently on some desperate errand. In a flash, David was taken back to the night of the barking dogs and the furious cannibal at the native village. What now? Cornwall had scarcely flung himself from his horse when David saw that he was closely followed by the sheriff. In that dim light, Kevin Kildare looked more menacing than ever, with a whip in his hand and a shotgun across his saddle, as well as the usual pistol strapped to his belt. For a moment of confusion, David asked himself *Good Lord,* w*hat have I done?* And then, the two men were at the door while he still fumbled with his shoelaces.

Richard Cornwall was pouring sweat and wild-eyed as if he had met a demon on the trail. He wiped his face on his sleeve and began, with a stammer, "I am sorry, sir. It seems that I am always coming here with trouble. I don't like it, but something terrible has occurred up at the Hawkins place. So bad, In fact, I don't know if you will believe it."

"He'll believe it," said the sheriff bitterly.

"What on earth?" David asked, but Cornwall was apparently unable to reply. Kevin Kildare was staring at him silently with something that David mistook at first for contempt. With rising resentment, he asked the sheriff, "See here, what is this about?" But as he spoke, David realized that he had been mistaken. For all his courtliness, Kevin Kildare was a hard man, and his face was distorted now because he, too, had been shaken to the core.

"Monstrous!" he cried. "A desecration! What has happened to Christian charity, Christian kindness? And so to mistreat a newcomer to our shores!? Oh yes, this has been a murder most foul, a criminal act of the most vile, unseemly sort!" David saw it all in an instant: the lecherous eye of Soper Hawkins upon her, a violent encounter, her white gown torn and bloodied, her life ebbing away. It came to him only by slow degrees that they were speaking of someone else – someone who had been slain in a manner that was apparently unspeakable. But the man who had done it was indeed Captain Soper Hawkins, esteemed citizen, man of property, Pillar of the Church. And the poor old Chinaman, Chin Wong Lo, they told him, was the victim.

After his preliminary outburst, Kildare was all calculation and icy curiosity. When and where had David last seen Soper Hawkins? Had Hawkins come to the parsonage at any time since his disappearance 24 hours ago? Where might he have gone to escape the law? Who were his friends? But David had no idea. Friends? Hawkins was the sort of man who did not have any. Servants and sycophants, yes. Comrades, no. His wife trembled before him. As for running away, David could not imagine it. When caught in the wrong, Soper Hawkins would stand up and sneer. Yet the same man had come more and more regularly to church, and sat in the front pew. After the earthquake, he had come to call and then had sent his own men to help David repair the parsonage. How could all these things be true of the same person? "But are you certain that Lo is dead?" he asked. "There are times –"

They looked at one another. "Dead and buried," said Kildare. "We have only just finished digging him up again."

"Buried already? When? By whom?"

"Tossed out like rubbish, he was," said the sheriff. "A dog would have better treatment. And it was the dogs that found him."

"There are witnesses," said Richard Cornwall dimly, after clearing his throat. "Many witnesses to… all that was done to him."

"Done to him?" David shouted. "What are you telling me, man?"

Cornwall shouted back, looking as if he might burst into tears. "Now hold on, sir. Please, I wasn't there! I've not been near the Hawkins place for months. I never knew a thing."

"No one tells a sheriff what he needs to know," remarked Kildare, "Until too late."

David sat down suddenly, hot with shame. "But I was there myself, only last week," he said. "I saw that things were not right. Chin Wong Lo was looking ill and troubled. So what did I do to help him? Nothing! Nothing."

"Now then," said Kildare kindly, but David continued. "And when he came to me some months ago and complained of mistreatment, I sent him back to his master. I was such a fool that I actually believed Hawkins would be kind!"

"Now then, Father, surely you meant for the best. And there is the law, after all. You can help the cause of justice by serving at the inquest. Doubtless you'll be called to witness at the trial as well. As I live, there will be one! Yes, before the highest court, and the Captain will be punished. Unless the bastard has blown his brains out in remorse, which strikes me as improbable. Or else fled the country, which would be good riddance, but also – forgive me, Father – bloody unlikely. We'll find him! I've deputized Cornwall here, and we'll form a search party in the morning."

"But what did he do? Something indecent, you said." Self-loathing swept over David then, as he saw himself once more in the garden lusting after Fiona, and then approaching poor old Lo with murder in his heart. When neither man answered him, he insisted, "Look here, I'll find out soon enough. Tell me! I need to know how, and when and where he was struck down!"

It was the sheriff who answered him coolly, "He was not struck down, sir. He was hung up. He was hung by the hands for three days, and beaten slowly to death in Captain Hawkins' bedroom."

When David could speak, he asked, "And where was – Maria – all this time?"

"Well, it seems that Maria Hawkins no longer shares the Captain's quarters. Has not done so for quite some time. As she told me just now, she moved to another part of the house quite soon after she and the Captain were wed. There she habitually locked and bolted her chamber door. She heard nothing. 'Tis a strange story, but I have reason to believe it. You married the two of them, Father, rather recently, I believe?"

"Aye, that I did, God help me."

"Six months ago, she told me. Time enough I suppose for a man like Soper Hawkins to become more than a trifle irritable." He gave a deep sigh and walked to the door, where he stood looking up at the goblin moon.

*

A sea of dark faces awaited him when David entered the Hawkins' parlor. He had never seen so many Hawaiians together in one small space. They were everywhere – men, women and children – sitting quietly on the furniture and on the floor, while Maria Hawkins stood before the fireplace in a long yellow gown. She was a delicate woman, with lustrous eyes, and her hair was done up in a braided coronet.

"Thank you for come here, Mr. Wilkinson," she said calmly. "We do not know where is my husband. Will you have coffee?" Her voice, that he did not recall having heard before, was gentle, pleasantly accented. Two of her older sons stood protectively at her side. Melissa, he knew, was still at Honolulu, in Queen Emma's care. As he sat down with Maria Hawkins to speak a few words of sympathy, a small figure scrambled through the crowd and threw herself at him. It was little Noni, who had left his classroom to go with her parents to the "prophet's" camp. Here she was again, gazing up adoringly at David Wilkinson. "Oh Pelekane!" she cried. "You are here! So now you make everything good! "

At the next moment, Noni's older sister, Kualani, came across the room and knelt at his feet. There was something expectant in her manner, and this puzzled David. He did not learn until later that the "prophet" had claimed the ability to resurrect the dead. In this instance he had refused, saying that he would not waste his powers on a yellow infidel.

Why, David wondered, was he the only *haole* in the room? Where were the other neighbors, and what connection had Chin Wong Lo to this native gathering? Now he saw that Harold Lopaka was there, and some of the people who had nursed him in the village during his illness. One he remembered well was Leilani, a striking young beauty with a mane of dark hair, who wore a garland today of red lehua blossoms. "This is my sister Leilani," said Maria. "You know her from before?" Leilani embraced him without a sign of self-consciousness, and he found her such a soft, marvelously comforting armful that he was reluctant to release her. He knew that an unendurable sight awaited him in the Captain's bedroom. On Maria Hawkins' orders, this was where the remains of the murdered man had been laid out on a rubber sheet. As soon as possible they must be inspected by all participants in the inquest, including himself.

"Mrs. Hawkins," he said, "I did not know that Leilani was your sister!" Maria smiled and said, "We are all family here." He looked around the room and came to the conclusion that this might be quite literally true. "I am glad to see that many of you have come back from the camp," he told them. "You have been sorely missed!"

"This is my *ohana*," said Maria softly, tears welling in her eyes. "They never go leave me long." Now she introduced him to another sister, this one called Pua, who carried a newborn infant. Radiant as a young brown Madonna, Pua proudly held her baby up for him to view. *This is all very strange*, he thought. *Why does it feel more like a birthday or a baptism, than a wake?*

"A beautiful child," he announced in his most professional manner. "Boy or girl?"

Rather than answering, Pua opened the infant's loincloth and showed him what was there: a tiny, triangular, wrinkled bottom supporting an enormous set of male genitalia. "Oh thank you! Very nice!" said David, and hastily covered him up again.

*

The wounds of the dead man were so many and so grievous that he could not count them, and the evidence of suffering was far beyond his ability to measure. Anticipating the legal procedures to follow, he tried to think calmly, logically about the hideous sight before him, but again and again he was overcome by rage and pity so profound that he wondered how he would manage to behave rationally in court.

That was the day and the hour when David Wilkinson began to think differently about certain teachings of his Church, for he sensed in the presence of the horror on the rubber sheet that Chin Wong Lo was not destroyed, and could not be destroyed, even by the vilest of human brutality. Despite his sins and rascal ways, despite the fact that he had not been converted to the One True Faith – nor was he baptized, nor had he ever, to David's knowledge, gone to a Christian church – this ignorant, lowly Chinese pagan was now at peace with Christ in Paradise. David felt sure of it, and he knew why: The despised and tormented one had been called as an honored guest to the greatest of all Feasts: *For the last shall be first. For the Lamb which is in the midst of the throne shall feed them, and shall lead them unto living waters: and God shall wipe away all tears from their eyes.*

David returned to the parlor in silence, grim and dry-eyed. When he saw the young Madonna weeping, he lifted the infant from her arms and said, "Come, let us go outside." Pua followed him to the terrace, as did most of the others. Maria Hawkins sat in the same chair where he had found Fiona drawing his portrait. "Good people," he said, "a very terrible thing, an evil thing has been done here, but we must not soil our hearts with hatred. *Vengeance is mine, saith the Lord!* Never ours, never ours."

"He only want to see the baby," said Pua in a small voice.

"What was that?" David asked. "See the baby?"

"When he runned away. He only want to help us, bring some money. But the Captain catch him before he…" and there, in tears again, she halted. David was puzzled, and looking down at the baby in his arms, saw something he had not noticed earlier. This child was rather light-skinned for a native Hawaiian, and there was a delicate fold of flesh covering the outer corner of each tiny eye.

"Then this baby belongs to…?" he asked the young Madonna.

"Is mine," she said firmly. "My baby."

"Good for you! He is a fine little lad. And the father, who is he?"

She looked away. David glanced around the circle of people and sat that he was the only person present who did not know the answer to that question. Still, he was struggling to believe it. "How old is your son?" He asked.

"Two week."

"And what is his name?"

But he was deliberately interrupted now by Maria Hawkins, who launched into what may have been the longest speech of her life. "Oh, Mr. Wilkinson," she began, with sudden vivacity, "I tell you something. It happen in the night because Lo run way again. It was cold, it was raining, so later he came sick. Captain was *huhu wela loa*, very angry, because Lo steal money – he take two dollar from my husband's desk. Captain say he going kill the bastard this time. He kick the door down, say he going beat him dead. I hear this myself but never believe. This is only temper. Captain always like show who is boss. But then he say same thing me all the time and never kill me. Never even beat me till our wedding day."

The last remark made David instantly furious. "Mrs. Hawkins! Am I to understand that your husband struck you – that he beat you, on the very day when you were joined together at Grace Church in the bond of holy matrimony?"

"That was first time, yes."

"I believe we should speak more of this later, in private," he said. But the faces around him showed no surprise; it was obvious that they knew the story – that they had known it all along.

"I got nothing for hide," said Maria. "I didn't do something."

"What man in his right mind would strike his wife just after solemnly vowing in church to cherish and protect her?"

"It was the *ohana*," Leilani explained. "Too much family come that wedding day. Too much people here, big party, make him crazy." Several others nodded in agreement.

"Yes," said Maria, "Captain my husband is very proud man. When he see so many people love me, he feel shamed. He got plenty land, plenty big cattle, horse, pig, but nothing more. He got no *ohana*, he got no heart, nothing inside." At this moment David looked up and saw Captain Hawkins in the doorway, whip in hand, staring at the people on his terrace. Hawkins' face reflected a sense of bewilderment rather than anger or dismay. Perhaps he had not heard the words just spoken.

After giving Chin Wong Lo's infant son back to his mother, David stood up and asked, "Captain Hawkins, where have you been?" There was no answer, although Maria Hawkins repeated the question. But in another moment Hawkins began to shout, "Where in bloody hell do you think I've been? Up *mauka* after the cattle, chasing the goddam strays, that's where! Two days and two nights of it, in the rain. It was goddam cold up there. What have you been doing, Mrs. Hawkins? That is the question! Here in my house, in my absence? Entertaining yourself? Having a party?"

"Soper," Maria began, her voice trembling as she approached him, "Last night you see, last night the dogs – they find –" But by now he was livid with rage. "What is this?" he shouted, "a funeral? A wake? Well, I'm not dead yet – too bad Maria, sorry to disappoint you. And I am still master of this house. So, avast, all of you! Get out of here! Go! You are not wanted on these premises!"

No one moved. "Maria, tell these people the party's over! They can get out, *wiki-wiki! Go!*" Still, no one stirred. After a pause, Maria said softly, "No, I don't say so. This is my *ohana*, Soper. And this is my home, where I live. So I think I have got some right."

"What did you say?"

"I got some right," she whispered.

"And before that, what did you say to me?"

"I say, no."

"You said what? Louder! No one can hear you!" Hawkins gave a ghastly laugh, and several things happened now very quickly. He lifted his whip to strike his wife. David rushed forward and seized the Captain's forearm as it descended; then they both fell to the ground. When David rose to his knees, he saw Hawkins lying on the grass, with his right arm broken.

"Mr. Wilkinson!" said Harold Lopaka. "Are you hurt?"

"No," said David, "but I don't understand what happened." And in fact, he did not understand it fully until many years later, when he studied the martial arts of Japan. "I saw that," said Harold. "He did this thing to himself. You only stop him."

"I saw too!" cried the lovely Leilani, "You never touch him, never even touch!"

"Not so, Leilani – although it is rather a mystery." David took out his watch and listened to it, glad to find it still running. Maria was kneeling at her husband's side now, all sorrow and sympathy, though no one else was paying him any attention. Serenely, Pua began to suckle her child.

*

Before he set Hawkins' arm for him, David gave him a mercifully large dose of laudanum, but received no thanks for it, nor curses either; in fact, during the entire procedure the Captain said not a word, nor was there any change in his distant, preoccupied manner. He was a man, it seemed, who had very little comprehension of pain; in fact, it may be that he himself never experienced it. Nor did he have anything to say when Maria, in tears, asked him what had happened to Chin Wong Lo. Evidently, the subject failed to interest him.

30

The trial took place five weeks later. A panel of Kona men, four American and five English, had viewed the corpse and heard the statements of witnesses. Their judgment of the case was sent on to Honolulu, stating that "The Chinese servant Chin Wong Lo came to his death on account of blows and cruel treatment inflicted upon him by his master, Captain Soper Hawkins." After this, Hawkins was taken briefly into custody by Sheriff Kildare, and released after posting $5,000 bail. As the date of the trial approached, Richard Cornwall and David Wilkinson traveled to Honolulu together in case their testimony would be wanted.

The new courthouse on Fort Street was a stately structure made of stone with broad steps leading up from a portico that was flanked by classical pillars. The interior was equally imposing, with high ceilings and massive walls that were penetrated at intervals by deep, shuttered windows. Through these the daylight filtered, and the breeze as well, when there was one, but wiser visitors brought fans with them to stir the humid air. On the wall beside the spectators stood a majestic clock with a mahogany case and a long brass pendulum, and during the trial, the silence in the courtroom was sometimes so intense that they could hear its whirring motions and the delicate click of the minute hand as it darted forward.

In front of them, at a dais swagged with flags and royal finery sat the judge, a keen-eyed gentleman of middle age and part-Hawaiian ancestry. In death at least, poor Chin Wong Lo had a noble defender, for his case was summoned under the title: *The King vs. S.D. Hawkins.* On the other hand, the trial would not proceed without prejudice: because the accused was an English citizen, a special jury had been empaneled, consisting of twelve Englishmen selected by Hawkins' own attorney. This made David uneasy, but Richard Cornwall said he trusted them to be fair. After all, Cooper, Brewster, Anderson and Sparks were members of Grace Church, and all were apparently honorable men.

As his pastor, David had tried repeatedly to visit Soper Hawkins since the crime, but had always been told either that he was "out" or "busy." When Hawkins was ushered into the courtroom, David searched his face for signs of shame or penitence, but was able to find none; in fact, Hawkins appeared to be simply rather bored and preoccupied. When told to respond to the charge of Murder in the Second Degree, he seemed not to have heard, or else not to have understood the command. He was reminded twice that he must stand up and speak before he obeyed, and then he pled *Not Guilty* in the manner of a man who is interrupted by some minor annoyance. This was all quite strange, David thought, especially since someone convicted of a far lesser crime had recently been sentenced to a crippling fine and two years at hard labor.

An interpreter was sworn in, since a great part of the testimony would be given either in Hawaiian or Chinese. Next, fines were levied by the Court upon a number of witnesses for the Defense who had failed to appear, while those present were moved into an anteroom under the surveillance of the Marshal.

Now the trial began. The prosecuting attorney made a brief statement of fact and then called in the first of seven witnesses to the crime. Of these, the first gave the most detailed and extensive report. He was a Hawaiian resident of Kona Kailua town who had come to *Kihapai O'Ekena* to sell a basket of fish. In going around to the back of the house he saw Captain Hawkins run after a Chinaman and knock him down, then kick him and beat him with his fists. Hawkins was wearing heavy boots. The Chinaman was small and frail, said this witness; he did not protest or try to defend himself, but sat on the ground afterward "gasping and shuddering like an animal ill-used." Then Hawkins shouted at the man to go back to work, but the Chinaman laughed at him; whereupon Captain Hawkins flew into a passion and kicked his servant in the small of the back. The Chinaman fell to the ground choking, while relieving himself at the same time in his trousers. The Captain dragged him toward the house after that, and threw him in head over heels. A few moments later the witness heard the sound of lashes, and heard the victim wailing. He went away quickly after that, because his daughter was with him, and he did not want her to see or hear any more.

The second witness was the daughter, a girl of perhaps 20 years, who testified in a faint voice without looking up either at the King's Counsel or the jury. The judge asked her several times to speak a little louder. The girl reiterated her father's testimony, and said with some embarrassment that the Chinaman, when kicked on the spine, had "dirtied himself." Then she added that she had looked into a window after hearing the sounds of whipping, which she said consisted of about 20 blows. She saw a bedroom inside, where the Chinaman had been stripped naked. He was tied hand and foot, hanging from a hook by means of a rope that secured his wrists. Hawkins was standing before him with a heavy iron bar in his hand, and seeing this, she had run away screaming to her father.

The third witness was another Hawaiian, one of Hawkins' servants, who said that he was called the same night to his master's bedroom. There he saw the Chinaman hanging, partially conscious, with his hands and feet "swollen nearly black" from the pressure of the ropes. He asked the Captain to let him take the man down, and bring him food and water.

Hawkins said no, and began beating the Chinaman with a heavy iron rod, while blood flew through the air. As he did this, he told the witness to bring in the other servants so that they could see what would happen to them if they should disobey him.

The fourth witness was a Chinese cook who had been at *Kihapai O'Okena* for only a few months. He told of seeing Chin Wong Lo laughing at his master, then being kicked and thrown into the house. That same night, he said, the other servants had been taken into the Captain's bedroom one by one, to see what would happen to them if they were disobedient. Hawkins was "in a passion" all the time, beating Lo first with the handle of his whip, then with an "iron" he said "of the kind that is used for prying stones out of the ground." Chin Wong Lo, covered with blood, made no sound, but appeared to be partially conscious.

The fifth witness, another manservant, told of seeing the Chinaman lying on the master's bedroom floor the following morning. He was naked, with wrists and ankles tightly tied. Although the night had been cold, he lay there without any covering. The Captain's clothing was stained all over with blood, both his shirt and his trousers. He sent the servant away to wash these garments. When the servant returned, the Chinaman was hanging up by his hands once more, quite silent, though apparently still alive. The Captain began beating him again, first with a heavy iron bar and then with the handle of his whip, jabbing the end of the whip into the Chinaman's ribs. The witness expressed surprise that although he was a feeble man, Chin Lo did not die for another day and a half of this treatment.

The sixth witness was a farm worker employed by David Wilkinson's neighbor, Edward Anderson. This man had seen the body of Chin Wong Lo before its burial. Captain Hawkins, he said, had sent for Anderson to ask him his opinion; Hawkins claimed to be puzzled by the Chinaman's death. "What do you think caused this man to die?" he had asked Anderson in the presence of his employee. Hawkins admitted freely that he had administered "discipline" but said that it had not been too severe. Then the farm hand, in a voice that shook with rage, described the condition of the body.

The seventh and final spokesman for the Prosecution was Kevin Kildare, who reported his discovery of the grave. Thanks at first to servants' gossip, and then to the Hawkins' dogs, the body had remained buried for less than two days. Sheriff Kildare had found it lying, unwashed and unclothed, in a flimsy box in a shallow grave. Glaring at the jurymen, he added some vivid details to the previous testimony: the color of the corpse, he said, was nearly black, with tongue and eyes protruding. It looked, he said, "like the body of a skinned animal that had been flayed alive."

Several ladies had left the courtroom hurriedly by now, and one had apparently fallen, or else fainted, in the portico. A half-hour recess was called for by the judge, and duly taken. When they reassembled, Counsel for the Defense promised to prove that there had been no killing at all. The Chinaman, he said, would not have died unless he had been already ill.

Manuel, the Captain's chief *paniolo*, was the first to appear for the Defense. He stated firmly that Hawkins was a kind master, that he never used a crowbar for punishment, only a whip or a bamboo cane. The Chinaman had been sickly from the time when he first came to *Kihapai O'Ekena* from an Englishman's yacht, where he had not given satisfactory service. The Chinaman had been given light work only, yet he was disobedient and mischievous. He had run away more than once, and when found, had defied his master. Manuel had seen him after the whipping, and said he "did not seem to be suffering much."

Manuel stated further that Captain Hawkins had not been in a passion of rage. He had never seen his master in a passion of any sort. If the Chinaman had been kept naked in the Captain's bedroom with his feet tied, that was to keep him from running away. On the morning when he died, the Captain had called for Manuel. "What is the matter with this man?" he had asked. The servant was lying still, but he still had a pulse, and then Manuel saw one of his eyelids twitch. "I told the Captain," said he, "that he was only pretending, for I know how false and deceitful these Chinese are!"

To David's surprise and dismay, the second witness for the defense was none other than Edward Anderson, who had voted with the rest of the Kona panel for Hawkins' indictment. Anderson testified in a grim but sturdy fashion that Captain Hawkins was a good man, a kind boss, a person who never lost his temper, and never asked more of his servants and laborers than he asked of himself. "The Captain is a very religious man," said Anderson, looking directly at David Wilkinson. "He goes to church. He knows the Bishop, and many other important people. If it was not for Captain Hawkins' generosity we would have no English church at all on our island!"

Anderson finished by saying that he had changed his mind about the indictment during the past few weeks, after talking several times with Captain Hawkins. He now firmly believed that the Chinaman's death had been caused by his own ailments, and not by anything Hawkins had done. Anderson claimed that he had been mistaken earlier, after being pressured by certain people (whom he did not name) toward a different view. He resented their interference, and was glad today to speak in support of his distinguished friend and neighbor, Captain Soper Hawkins.

The third witness for the defense was an Englishman from Honolulu who said that he had known Hawkins for six or seven months and was favorably impressed by his character, which he said was "uniformly courteous and manly."

The last two witnesses were also Englishmen, one a physician. Both testified that they had spent time living in China, and therefore knew the Chinese character very well. "Chinamen commit suicide on trivial occasions," said the doctor. "In one place where I practiced medicine, thirteen of them killed themselves in one week." At this, Cornwall and Wilkinson exchanged an ironic glance. The second Englishman said, "Suicide is an everyday occurrence among Chinese. They make away with themselves to avoid some evil, either real or imaginary. Truly, you can never tell what these people will do."

And there, the Defense rested.

Now the King's Counsel rose with flashing eyes and named the death of Chin Wong Lo "a crime of utmost horror and brutality." It cried out, he said, to heaven and earth, and to the conscience of mankind, for justice and due punishment! This man's eloquence was impressive, and the spectators were visibly moved by it, while Soper Hawkins continued to look blandly unconcerned.

When he had finished, the judge spoke to the jury at some length. To begin with, he said, while it might be a common custom to punish servants by whipping, this habit was not tolerated by Hawaiian law. Such behavior in fact ran contrary to every decent notion of liberty, humanity and justice. Secondly, it was not an acceptable defense to claim that the deceased had been ill already; for if blows or cruel treatment had helped either to cause or to hasten the man's death, then Hawkins was guilty and must pay the penalty. Here he cited laws of Britain, Europe and America, and mentioned in particular a landmark decision by an English judge, one Baron Parke. Thirdly, he told the jury that they had the right to return a verdict of Manslaughter, although the charge was Murder in the Second Degree. If Hawkins had beaten his servant to death in a sudden unreasoning passion, without malice aforethought, then the law might punish him with a lighter hand, in recognition of our common human frailty.

After this he turned a stern eye upon the jury of handpicked Englishmen, and commanded them to put all individual feelings and considerations aside. No claim of friendship, neighborliness or common nationality must intrude upon their decision. The cause of justice was a higher one, he said, and justice must be served here and now, or else civilization itself would suffer. With great solemnity he dismissed the jury with instructions to consider the case carefully, deliberately, without regard to any personal opinion or prejudice, in a morally responsible way.

The men of the jury filed out of the room, and for a quarter of an hour, the clock's minute-hand ticked impassively forward. Then they returned, all broadly smiling, to report their unanimous verdict: *Not Guilty!* After a stunned silence there were gasps and groans from the audience, and David Wilkinson was on his feet before he knew it, crying out, "Shame! Shame!"

"Quiet!" barked the judge, signaling his Marshal. "Order! There shall be order in this court!" He glared at David and then, perhaps because he was a clergyman, hesitated for a moment. That was enough for David to shout at the grinning jurymen, "You think that no one will know! That no one will care! That no one will remember what you have done here today! But the Lord God of Hosts knows what you have done here, and He never forgets!"

"Marshal! Marshal!" called the judge, wielding his gavel.

"And the people of these islands shall hear it!" David went on at the top of his voice. "England shall hear of it! The world shall hear! This vile, cowardly travesty of –" But this was as far as he was allowed to go before being hauled unceremoniously from the courthouse and left to cool his temper in the blazing street. Richard Cornwall hurried along after him and then put an arm around his shoulder, saying, "There now, sir – there now, best say no more!"

Captain Hawkins came out of the building alone then, looking neither to his left nor his right, and without speaking to anyone. He passed closely by Cornwall and Wilkinson without any sign of recognition. After this he seems to have gone directly home to Kona, but the rest of his story has only been pieced together from a few meager reports and some circumstantial evidence. Apparently, when he came back to *Kihapai O'Ekena*, he found no one there, neither his wife nor his servants, nor his children, except for the oldest boy. This was a lad of 16 who refused to serve him and then defied his father openly for the first time in his life. Harsh words were spoken, a rash blow was struck by the son, and returned by Hawkins with more of the same. Then the youth saddled his horse and rode away to visit a girl he knew in Ka'u.

Three days later an empty bottle of port was found on the dining table, beside some remains of roast beef that had been attacked by regiments of cockroaches and ants. The candles had all burned down to jumbled pools of wax that lay like islands here and there in the vast expanse of the koa table-top. Apparently, after dining alone that night, Soper Hawkins had gone into his bedroom with the intention of hanging himself; but before the rope could finish its work, he put a pistol into his mouth and shot off the top of his head.

It was Manuel, the faithful paniolo who discovered him, having come back from Honolulu by a later ship, and then being led to his master's window by the bawling of a cow that was frantic to be milked. He took the Captain's body down and tried to arrange it decently. Then he realized – *Ave Maria!* – that this was a case for the authorities. He rode to the parsonage, and finding no one there, went on to find the Sheriff.

Kevin Kildare was delighted to hear the news. It proved to him, he told David, that there is moral order in the universe. Besides, it saved him the trouble of blowing the bastard's head off some other time. David was amused by the sheriff's vehemence, but he took a different view, arguing that one man's pain will not cancel out another's; and furthermore, that God cares for us all, including persons thoroughly disliked and disapproved of by Wilkinson and Kildare.

"At least he showed some remorse there at the end," said the sheriff grudgingly. But David could not agree with him there, either. He saw Hawkins' suicide as vindictive – not as a gesture of penitence, but as the act of a man sunk in self-pity and injured pride. "A wise man once told me," he said, "that a suicide usually wants to leave his skeleton in someone else's closet. In my opinion, the issue in this case was power, pure and simple. Soper Hawkins refused to live in a world where he was not obeyed."

As it happened, the dead hand of Soper Hawkins reached out from his grave to strike David Wilkinson more than once.

After he had buried both men, Hawkins at his ranch and Chin Wong Lo beside the parsonage, he was assailed by thoughts of what he should have done differently. He saw now that he had failed the Captain as well as his Chinese servant. He told himself that he might have understood Soper Hawkins better had he seen more of himself in that man – his own infirm humanity, reflected as if in a pool of troubled waters. He asked himself: if truth be told, have I not the same base instincts? Have I never, ever acted upon them? Have I not whipped a defiant horse, and lusted after an unwilling woman? Have I never looked upon a lowly Asian coolie with murder in my heart? Have I not wanted to beat Captain Hawkins, and that many times? Worst of all, did I not tell him once to go to Hell? And did I not, more recently, publicly, call down destruction upon the spineless liars and sycophants who had set him free? Yes, and some of those were my own parishioners.

It was a time of great sadness, for the little family of Grace Church was split now, riven apart, between those who had supported Hawkins and those who had testified against him. People who had been friends before could no longer look one another in the eye. Edward Anderson's sympathetic farmhand had been fired for his honesty in court, and sent packing. Richard Cornwall wanted nothing further to do with the Andersons; the Coopers and the Cornwalls were no longer on speaking terms; and after the public position David Wilkinson had taken, the other local jurors did not come to church. Throughout the neighborhood, natives and foreigners looked upon one another with new suspicion. The Chinese people of Kona, David thought, would never forgive his countrymen for what had happened here. The malevolence of the great landowner lived on; his death settled nothing. It would take generations to mend such a wound, if indeed it could ever be healed.

Here I am, Lord, he thought, in a land that my betters said was Eden. How mistaken they were! Hawaii lost its innocence when the earliest of humans came here, bringing their sins with them. The Hawaiian himself was never a noble savage, but a cousin of mine with all the usual family failings. The rest of us have compounded the problem, year by year. The American missionaries came here on the most barbaric of terms: obey us or be damned! We English have been kinder, but in other ways just as mistaken, for we have entertained ourselves with reveries of perfect bliss and liberty here in these isles, even while bringing with us the meanest of our political, financial and military ambitions.

These were some of the melancholy thoughts that weighed upon David Wilkinson during a season when it seemed that he was always burying his neighbors; when no word had come, either from Honolulu or from Borneo; when his classroom and his church were emptier than ever; when the "Mad Prophet" flourished in Ka'u. There came a turning point at last one morning at dawn when he had spent another sleepless night questioning his faith and his God, wondering whether life was worth the pain and sorrow that it brought, yearning for some sign that he himself was not a ruined man. Then the first rays of light came over the mountain to greet him with a touch so tender and gracious that he knew all at once that the universe was in the care of a Sacred Being far greater than any he had yet known. He walked out of doors in his bare feet, and saw a cluster of native canoes starting out on the blue immensity of the ocean. The old moon was not yet down, and already they were on their way, risking their lives as they did each day to perform the humble tasks that fate had put before them.

"Resign!" the Bishop had said in his letter, but David knew that this was exactly what he must not do. He would stay where he was for the rest of his life, if necessary. Should every neighbor and the Church itself abandon him, he would still have his little hut, his prayer book, and his cabbages. Richard Cornwall would stand by him, and Harold Lopaka, too. That was enough. He would keep the school open and hold services even if no one came to them. Nothing would dislodge him – nothing less than death, or a summons from the Archbishop of Canterbury himself! In the meantime, he would feed himself with fish from the ocean and vegetables from his garden. And then, when his day's work was done, he would rest in the shade of the pavilion, smoking his pipe and looking out to sea.

31

JOURNAL - PRIVATE   Singapore – Feb ? 1868
F. Cameron

*A tiger swam over the Straits of Johore last night, marched into town
& devoured 2 or 3 Malay natives – so they say – before being shot by a
policeman. All this not 60 yards from me! I heard zoo noises & a bit of
uproar, but coward that I am, put a pillow over my head & went back to
sleep.*

*Crushing heat – nothing whatever like Hawaii. No escaping it, even
in the night. When I waked this morning a brown hairy spider the size of
a teacup sat beside me on the pillow, taking my measure. I thought
perhaps I should put him into a little cage & train him to live on
cockroaches.*

*Still it is pretty here – the plush green lawns of the Cricket Club – the
glittering palms, the frangipani, the government buildings like wedding
cakes melting in the sun. But oh! The silly band playing oom-pah 3
afternoons a week on the Esplanade, w. the Naval officers looking all of
15 – the older Englishmen in their very pink flesh, packed like sausages
into their clothing. Their powdered little wives promenading in serious
gowns, all taken up & pleated over the rear – Heavens, what new form of
prurience is this?*

*A rich person might starve in Singapore, if unwilling to eat curry. But
then, there is always gin, whisky, brandy, rum etc. – I never saw people
drink so much. If I lived here I rather think I'd lie all day reading in a
cool bath & never do anything at all. (Time's winged chariot hurrying by!)
A tremendous effort here, even to think – then to find the right Chinese*

tailor who with small, clever hands has made me instantly a half dozen tunics in silk, w. matching trousers – narrow, to tuck into my boots when I go to the jungle. My own design – not scandalous, I trust, only pleasantly unfashionable. It's lovely cloth – I touch it with my left hand now as I write – strong & supple, close- woven, gossamer-light. I found some good forest colors: dim shadowy greens and browns, so that I may be very nearly invisible.

Brother Hal here for a week to see me, looking dreadful – gaunt & spent at 25, emaciated almost as much as the old men smoking opium in the Chinese quarter. Smells like a mouse's nest. One tooth missing in front – doesn't care what people think. Won't let me help, not a penny. Poor sweet lad, God help him.

God?

*

Sarawak, 1 wk. after

A dreamlike voyage, sliding between sheets of fire, the sky ablaze, the ocean dazzling, perfectly motionless. Anything metal far too hot to touch. No other sound for hours but the roar of engine. Centipedes & scorpions aboard – but the old, bent, blue-eyed sailor vows that they are not poisonous at sea!

A smudge of coast – then little islands – uninhabited, green to the water's brink. Or else with a tiny fringe of golden sand. Oh to be left alone in such a place, for three days or a week. What would one do? What would one not do, that is worth doing?

Turtle eggs for breakfast today & now the vast blue mountains rise to embrace us – majestic yet soft, sweetly enfolding – the Matang range. I shall feel safe here. Sarawak itself is a sort of island – mountains on 3 sides, sea on the other.

Entering the river's mouth – low, swampy growth on either side – mangrove & nipa palms rooted in mud – snakes & crocodiles, no doubt. Proboscis monkeys, lithe & comical, leaping above. Further on, taller, prouder, even more primitive jungle – shimmering, dark & solemn – utterly primeval. No birds nor animals here to be seen, as if not yet invented. I wanted it never to end. But after miles & miles, a thicket of

277

masts ahead – small boats at anchor & here is the town, partly in water itself. That is, on pilings, running ¾ mile or so along either bank, 2-3 houses deep ashore. On a little hill above, the Rajah's flag (St. George's cross, half black, half red, on a yellow field). And a church tower – and the palace, the Astana.

We're on the Rajah's ship, so people come running – beating gongs, shooting guns & firecrackers by way of welcome. If we had him with us, what would they do? Where'er he walks, I've heard that they actually hold a golden umbrella over him!

*

10 Feb. '68 – The Astana   *Sarawak, Borneo*

Dearest Beth,

I am sure it is my own fault that I haven't heard from you in so long – for as you see from above, I've been traveling again. I trust you and your dear ones are all quite well. You may tell the young rascals that I finally saw a pirate. No cannibals as yet, for which I humbly apologize – and the pirates not very near – still, I think we may check them from the list. Their ships are called prahus & we spotted 3 of them with a spyglass – close to the horizon – as we came in from Singapore. Not at all threatening at that distance – they look like flattish pin-cushions afloat, with dozens of oars & riggings & masts & banners sticking out. They're said to be fast, though not to match our sleek little steamer the RAINBOW – which is very speedy indeed & well armed for protection, with guns both large and small.

My stay in Singapore was brief & uneventful except for seeing darling Hal, who sends love. He thought it unwise for me to come to Australia – his mining camp too rough, he said, for a lady. The nearest town called "New Eden" it seems is rather a joke. He is working hard – doing well – and was amazed to see me so strong and fit. So I'm safely here – for a month or so in this little capital – formerly called Sarawak like the country, but now Kuching – which in Malay means cat. Why I don't know – having believed that every cat in the Pacific lived in Honolulu! I have a nice bungalow to myself – a latticed nest where I am raised on posts in the native fashion – so that a breeze may touch me if it chooses. There's a splendid view across cocoa palms, arecas, gardenias, hibiscus, jessamine – and over the river to the Malay campong across the way.

You'll want to know what is an Astana – & the word means palace, but this one serves partly as a residence, partly as seat of gov't for the Raj. It is actually a modest, rather Chinese looking structure of two storeys, made of wood. The lower part is relatively cool – which is to say, only at the simmer, not the full boil. It's quite spacious, with a well-appointed dining room, several offices & domestic privacies attached. The upper floor has a large drawing room – wrapped round with a verandah – thus a fine view of the town, the river & the great blue mountain where the sun goes down. Also, comfortable chairs – books – journals & newspapers from home. And, to let us know that this is the domicile of an English gentleman, various deadly weapons – plus native arms, war cloaks, blowpipes, etc. hanging in decorative fashion on the walls.

I learned only upon my arrival that our parents' friend James Brooke – the one who devised all this – is mortally ill in England – and sad to say, I won't meet him – he's being nursed at this moment by Angela Burdett-Coutts at Torquay. The magical Angela, wherever she is most needed! The White Rajahs here must be special pets of hers, for I'm told that she has given lavishly to this little country – and has provided such rather expensive toys as the gunboat RAINBOW for old Sir James.

Actually it was a necessary toy, for in years past, pirates roved this coast at will – devastating native villages – robbing, burning, slaughtering, capturing slaves by the hundreds, whom they treated abominably. But thanks to years of policing by the Brookes – with the help of a Captain or Commander Keppel & his fleet – all is in order now. In case anyone asks you, Bethy, how James Brooke got control of this country, he came here when they desperately needed his help – & he saved them. As a result, the people want to obey him & in fact, adore him to the point of idolatry.

My host today, instead, is his nephew Charles – one of several Johnson relatives in Britain who've changed their names to Brooke, in hopes of inheriting. Old James it seems did not care for women & had no offspring – except possibly for a dubious youth he claimed as his bastard & adopted late in life. One enterprising chap actually changed his name to Brooke Brooke – a bit much, wouldn't you say? But that didn't work. Charles is the heir – known as Tuan Mudah – meaning Young Lord or Crown Prince – and he knows the country from years in the bush.

279

I know what you're thinking now – is he handsome? – brave? – kind? – rich? etc. Well, fair inquisitor, my answer to all that is: (1)not really, unless you like your men small, dark & muscular w. eyes rather close together, a thin upper lip – a pouting lower one & a visible layer of fat under the chin. (2) Is he brave? I'm not sure yet, though I've heard a great deal – from him – about his exploits. Is he kind? I very much doubt it. Rich? Definitely not. It seems that most profit collected here goes to the Borneo Company, not to the governors – so Charles no doubt will be wanting a rich wife. I rather think that is a pattern – that the sort of men who come out to live in such places actually prefer one another to female company – and don't often marry unless there is serious money involved.

As to my safety, chaperonage, etc. – you see how well I know you sister dear – be assured that there are a dozen servants hovering at all times & numerous armed guards watching our every move – Malays in dashing uniforms – tight blue jacket, red sash – white trousers & enormous knives with jeweled handles, known as Krisses. Add to that several earnest missionaries who stop in for tiffin – half a dozen European ladies rattling around – & another guest who only just left, the Hon. J.R. from Moreton-in-Marsh. The latter kept a close & curious eye upon me all last week when he was not off in the jungle killing beautiful birds or baby orangutans that had done him no harm.

I did so hate leaving Hawaii, but it was time. I'll end this now, hoping to find word from you when I return to S'pore. Tell the young, please – for their lessons – that the products of this land are: timber, sago, rice, coal, antimony, diamonds, quicksilver, gold, gutta percha, wax, rattan & a kind of edible bird's nest that I'm sure they are longing to taste. Shall I bring one home? We might dip it in chocolate. Love to dear Wm. And yourself. As ever yr. devoted – F.C.

*

JOURNAL CTD.   *10th February, SARAWAK*

Head hunting! I had forgotten – but of course it actually happens here, tho' strongly discouraged by Rajah & Tuan Mudah these many years. Mrs. Cruikshank – the Resident's wife – says the natives crave it as children do sweets – carry the rotting heads around with them affectionately

& firmly believe at least one such trophy to be necessary before man courts bride. Today in the market saw a baby bear offered as pet – 20 cts. & I sadly declined, hoping not to see him next in a stew. Why is food always so much on one's mind when traveling? Felt a craving today for chocolate – none to be had of course, only a steaming mile of other things all stacked & jumbled together: bananas of at least a dozen varieties, plus every other fruit imaginable, wild pig & deer meat, spears & swords, poultry both dead & alive, fishes of all colors in dazzling arrays, mats & baskets made of straw, live parakeets, cockatoos, little mouse-deer alive in cages of rattan, all kinds of cloth, tobacco in bins – all this through the colonnade by the river – where canvas is hung between pillars, for protection from the glare.

Shopkeepers mainly Chinese – customers a few shy Dyaks in from the forest or the sea – a scattering of Hindus in turbans – but many little Malay men in their cleverly twisted head-scarves embroidered in gold, their brightly-colored jackets & plaid sarongs. The tiny Malay women are often beautiful, with long, gleaming black hair – some with jackets open at the front & nothing under. Far more fetching, I must admit, than my own costumes – providing one wanted to fetch.

Their teeth, though – filed into points & black from chewing pinang – somewhat mar the seductive impression. I'm told they think people with unfiled teeth look like animals. Interesting! Charles Brooke's #1 Malay MISTRESS – NEVER (!!!)TO BE MENTIONED above a whisper – is said to be with child, due this July.. Does she think Charles resembles an animal – & if so, which one? Charles does not trust me as yet – says I may not go upriver into the jungle alone & he has no "boys" to offer as guides just now. Why don't I just pop round & visit the ladies? Hah! Why indeed? I told him I did not come all this way to sit in a parlor drinking tea with Europeans – & I rather think he liked me better after that.

*

20ᵗʰ February, 1868   *The Astana, Sarawak*

Dearest Majesty,
The name of Emma Kaleleonalani is known and honored even in this

remoteness! My host, Charles Brooke, who is heir to the Rajah, sends greetings & I expect you'll have official notice directly. As you see I am safely here – and yet, how I miss you! The Astana is nothing to your lovely Summer Palace – or your winter one, either & the climate is nothing to Hawaii's – yet I think you would find ways to enjoy it. For one thing, you'd find an Anglican church here, made of stone & very large – too vast, I expect, for the wee number of Christians here. Let us hope the same thing does not happen in Honolulu – I know how you worry about costs! The local Bishop McDougall is on his way now to England & retirement – but unlike the one who causes you grief, he only left after many years of faithful service – a grand sort of warrior priest in the old style, who once got into an actual battle and apparently acquitted himself quite well.

But oh dear friend, wise confidante, I had thought I'd write you a sensible letter about the look of the landscape, the gardens, the mission, etc. – but I can't today because something so bizarre & unexpected has happened. The very thought of you makes me feel there's no stopping it – pour it out I must!

First to explain that I've been dining most evenings, and alone most of those, with Charles Brooke the Crown Prince, apparently soon to become Rajah number Two. Dozens of servants about, of course – and sometimes, another guest or two. But for 8 nights now we've been stuck together like bread & butter (neither of which they have out here, by the way!) – and I can't speak for myself, but C. Brooke is NOT one of the world's great conversationalists. When one has heard 6 versions of the Rebellion of 1859 – when he led a Dyak army against the poisoned blowpipes of the Kenowits – things tend to sag a bit. It helps if a man is present to ask, for example, why the Dyaks don't raise pepper (they won't have oxen or bullocks, won't use ploughs!) – or to discuss the management of silkworms at his new mulberry farm, which I am not allowed to see. But he never bothers to answer my questions – & plainly thinks women are idiots. I suspect he also suffers from a paralyzing kind of shyness, either inborn or resulting from his years in the bush.

So imagine my surprise, if you will, when last night after dinner he called for a bottle of whisky & two glasses – lit up a Manila cheroot & sent the servants away –then told me that there was something for us to discuss! After this, with his elbows on the table, he suddenly said, "Lady

Fiona, it's time I was a married man. I am thinking of making you an offer. You may well believe it's time you were married yourself!"

As you see, dear – toujours la politesse!

"Come now!" he said when I made no answer. "You're not a determined spinster – not a perpetual vagabond, are you? No! I know more about you than that. You came here with certain rather splendid references, and not just from Angela. Think about it. You might like to stay here part of each year. You'd be Ranee – Queen, don't y'know, and all that – not so bad. Plenty of girls would jump at it. Do what you like – go where you like, the rest of the time. You seem to take an interest in this country. More than that, you understand the problems – the responsibilities – of owning property."

"Oh," I said – "Do I?"

"Well, your castle in Scotland, for example."

"Oh, that –" said I.

"I know I'm not good company for a lady," said Charles. "I have no illusions on that score. But I wouldn't bother you. I'm hardly the man to run up to the Highlands and make a damned fool of myself chasing grouse. You're an independent sort. Good! You run your place – I'll run mine. I need to be here in Sarawak, and when I am here, I want to be out of this town that bores me to fits – out in the jungle with my Dyaks. My work – this country – these people I care for – this is my life."

Well, that was remarkably honest of him I thought – & even rather touching. Though it may have been one of the oddest proposals ever made, I began to see Charles Brooke in a new light. Even his narrow eyes – the rather small hands & wrong sort of chin began to look better. As you know, darling Emma – so well – men's feelings are far more easily injured than ours – and when making almost any sort of offer, they are often far more tender than they seem. So I thought quite carefully how to respond. Seeing me hesitate, he said, "You are a man's kind of woman – that is to say, aren't you? I mean, despite…"

"Despite what? Oh, the independence? The trousers? Or, what do you mean? Oh I see – I'm sorry, I didn't understand. You want a breeder! We don't have to live together, but you need me to get you some nice, white, legitimate heirs."

That embarrassed him horribly. I thought – poor man, I must get this over. So I said – I was sorry to disappoint him, but the castle in question is no more. I had it taken down stone by stone – after Uncle died – because I so very much disliked it. All this was expensive, of course – an entire village of workers, wagons by the dozens, etc. I'd also given away the dreadful old furniture, the hideous tapestries, etc. – thus a major blow to my inheritance. "So you see, Charles, I am rather homeless just now & not very rich after all. Didn't Angela tell you?"

He was appalled. That in effect, was the end of the conversation. I went home to my bungalow pleased at first – then furious with myself. Of all the sins in the world that I hate, the one I most despise is lying. What a crashing bore to find that I'd done it myself. So I went back and confessed, first thing in the morning. I'd expected him to sneer – to storm at me, or heaven knows what – but he only said, "You were very convincing, you know. You should seriously consider a criminal career."

Then he said – perhaps truthfully – that he had only been thinking aloud last night, playing with an idea to see how it sounded. Surely in my response I had done the same? "That's allowed, isn't it?"

"Within limits," I said, "yes. But about the castle, I was perfectly sincere in saying that I loathe it. I have tenants there now, but tearing the damned, beastly thing down is something I've always wanted to do."

"Then do it!" he said with something like a smile. Arthur Cruikshank, the Resident, came in just then with a little ape on his shoulder. Quite as if I were not there, Charles told him, "I didn't know what to make of this lady at first – we've had so many queer ones." Arthur sat down – we were having coffee on the verandah – & the baby moa, with soft little moans of pleasure, petted him about the shoulders while the two men launched into reminiscences. First, about a Miss Doome or Coome, quite elderly, who had descended upon Kuching in a beribboned opera cloak of yellow satin, lined in pink. She flounced around town, they said, desperately flirting – and when rebuffed by everyone, began keeping pigs on a leash.

Another of these ladies said that she simply must go & find God in the jungle. Charles said very well, but mind where you put your feet – which she did not – & came back howling, covered with leeches. But oh, the third! She was a stiff, formidable teacher of middle age who came out to work in Kuching – fell madly in love with a stern young missionary 10 years her junior – & to everyone's amazement, married him! Soon afterward, they were seen walking into the sea hand in hand for a bathe *one day, in native costume – which is to say, in nothing at all. The lady suddenly grew 10 years younger – made him laugh – mended his clothes, put crystal on his table & he adores her. Not only that, they said, but he became a much better, far more compassionate priest – and people are now saying that he will be the next Bishop of Sarawak! Emma dearest, every word of this is true, by the way – & I've met them and they are charming. Chambers is the name.*

I must stop, but not without telling you quickly what happened next. That same morning, without a glance in my direction, Brooke said to Cruikshank, "I'm thinking of taking Fiona with me to help with the doctoring." Then, to me, "If you're coming, be ready at dawn tomorrow. I'm going upriver to look after my Dyaks. They've been having some cholera."

Tomorrow! At last! And so, dearest of all ladies – I bid you farewell for now and send you aloha nui loa. Be well, be happy always, and know each day how much you are loved by your ever grateful & devoted – Fiona.

32

The long drought of the winter had been merciless; thus by Lententide of 1868, the fields of Kona lay bleached and scoured, in places, white as bone. The nights were incandescent with fiery stars, and the sound of the surf during those hours was an insistent, throbbing roar. At last one day the sun rose up clothed in the sheerest of cloudy veils, and David felt the earth quiver beneath him, not in a threatening way, but gently, as if it were a soft little gesture of greeting. "Aloha, Madame Pele!" he said aloud with a smile, before remembering that this remark was unsuitable for an Anglican clergyman.

He and the Curate had spent the previous week on a pastoral pilgrimage from one far-flung ranch and farmhouse to another, bringing a message of peace and reconciliation to members of Grace Church. His remarks on forgiveness and brotherly love had been well enough received so that he was in a hopeful mood today, and decided to pay a visit to Harold Lopaka. He turned toward the path to the native village, but for an hour or more afterward was so lost in thought that he did not notice the landscape around him; and then another tremor struck, with such a strong swaying and undulating motion that Mr. Gray was badly frightened.

David dismounted and tried to soothe him, but the horse would not be consoled, and then David suddenly realized that he had lost his way entirely. He was in an unfamiliar landscape now, as if he had come to a place high on the mountain amid the steaming, volcanic rain forests. Giant tree-ferns loomed around him, while a vine nearby displayed white blossoms of a flaring, conical shape that he had never seen before. Above him in a haze of golden light stood the great ohia trees that were sacred to Pele, and the lavish odors of damp and mould rose up from the forest floor, mingling curiously with the fragrances of spring and new life. This, he thought, was all very strange. He did not feel like his usual self; was he awake or sleeping? Had his reverie delivered him into some bewitched or enchanted realm?

Behold! I show you a mystery, Saint Paul had written. *We shall not all sleep, but we shall all be changed; in a moment, in the twinkling of an eye...* And then, as he stood musing upon those enduring mysteries, he heard an unexpected sound nearby. It was a charming rill of laughter that was not quite human, but rather more like the chuckle that a freshet of water will make when thrusting among pebbles and reeds. He looked around him, and spied a slender figure standing in the shadows of the wood. It was a woman, a young one, he thought. Her feet were bare and her clothing was made of some silken cloth that was dusky green or brown, and thus nearly indistinguishable from the forest around her. On her dark, luxuriant hair she wore a wreath of scarlet ohia blossoms. Who she was and why she had come there, he could not imagine. He called to her twice but she did not reply. Then she vanished down a narrow path that led deeper into the forest.

Powerful waves of emotion swept over him: curiosity, wonder, fear, desire. When he turned to look at Mr. Gray, he found that the troubled horse had disappeared. He did not come when called several times, and David finally shouted, "Look after yourself, then, faithless beast!" Without another thought, he plunged into the forest. There were no visible footprints, nor as much as a crushed leaf or a broken twig that might have hinted at human passage. Was she a nymph, a dryad, a forest sprite? He was tempted to imagine that he had been transported to a sacred forest and that she was its guardian, or custodial spirit. That was nonsense, of course. More likely he had imagined seeing her, or else she had simply been a local maiden on a private errand of some sort. After a time he was more lost than ever, and no longer knew in what direction he was moving. There was an uncanny stillness all around him, so that he began to be alarmed, and ran as much as he walked for another mile or more.

Finally he stopped to listen for any sound that might help him. He heard one distant bird call, and then another. After that there was nothing except for a silence so profound that the throb of his own pulse, and the clamor of his laboring breath, seemed to resound through the forest. Gradually, as he quieted, he began to feel certain that there was some other being, either animal or human, quite close by.

A shaft of sunlight pierced the forest dusk, and he saw it glint for an instant upon flesh: a bare brown arm flung out, lying upon moss. He made no sound, but silently drew near. Then in the leafy shadows he saw the single, rounding and brown-tipped breast of a woman, equally bare. *Venus Aphrodite!* he thought – but did not dare to whisper the name. He took another step forward and saw that the bed she lay on was not moss; it was made of her own hair that was spread as thick and wide beneath her as a pelted carpet. As he stood trembling beside her, she opened her great, dark eyes and leveled a glance at him that told him immediately what his fate was. Without another thought he fell to his knees beside her, and then with his next breath, fell from Grace.

The afternoon was long and the night was longer, while every craving of his lonely life was measured and met with passionate completion. He slept at last, but only for a frantic moment. When he awakened at last she was gone, and he found himself shivering in a dense white mist that swirled like smoke around him. With her musk still on his hands, he was lying in a crude detritus of pebbles, sharp as small swords. A cluster of brilliant *ohia* blossoms lay beside him like stained glass, crushed. Without a word or a sigh, she had vanished. Beyond the mist was the soft, forgiving light of early dawn; and beyond that he could hear the solemn threnody of the sea.

He remembered two things then: first that he had lost his horse, and second that he was a clergyman. He was on his feet before he realized, in a thunderclap of horror, that he had just spent the better part of a day and a night in the vile depths of lust and debauchery. However, a man with one leg into his trousers does not stop long for sermonizing, and so he bent his will, for the time, to the humbler task. After this he set off at a brisk pace toward the sea; the trees thinned rapidly and the mist began to disperse. In a very few more minutes he stood at the rim of the *pali*, where he saw his Curate contentedly grazing. "Oh comrade!" he cried. "Oh good, gray, gelded Puritan!"

As he grasped the horse's reins, the earth gave a violent shudder, and this time it lasted much longer than usual. David made an instant decision: from now on, he would be a vigilant observer and recorder of such events, for the benefit of science and mankind. Very little was known about volcanology then. It was still an infant science; but on Saturday the 28th of March, 1868, David Wilkinson began to make the meticulous notes that were published later, not only in Honolulu, but in the best of the London scientific journals. With his watch and his diary constantly in hand, he became the only man in Hawaii to produce a comprehensive account of the most violent series of earthquakes ever recorded in human history, and the greatest volcanic upheavals of his time.

*

When he came to the village, Harold Lopaka was sitting under his usual coconut palm, staring out to sea. "Too much quake," he said to David. "Someday one monster wave come in, then *pau!* House, tree, canoe, dog, people, all gone!"

"Shouldn't you leave before that happens?" David asked.

"Come to the church if you like, and bring the others to stay safely there. How many are left?"

"More now. Leilani is back, and her sister with baby. They all sleeping. Some men and boys out in canoes. Kekei all back home, all but one. They tired of the Prophet! They play go fishing now, say they going catch something big."

"Which one is not back?"

"Kimo. That son of mine thinks he is big man. No respect. Always angry, always fighting. I fail with him, never know why."

"These things happen, Harold. He may change as he grows."

"Time passes," he said. "I pray, I wait. So now we talk story, yes? You have something to tell?"

"Story, yes, that's it. As a matter of fact, something astonishing has happened, and I need to discuss it with you. Something very disturbing, something quite shameful, I am sorry to say, has happened to a man I know."

"This man your friend? What kind this man?"

"What kind? I am not sure. Just an ordinary man, I suppose. But I think it's fair to say that he has always tried to help those less fortunate."

"People have hard times, yes." said Lopaka. "So he bring food and so on?"

"Food of a sort. Food for the heart and soul. And he always imagined that he might – well, slay a dragon or two, save a kingdom, rescue maidens in distress, all that sort of thing."

"You say dragon. Where is this kind? Why is this maidens in distress?"

"Well, it's a part of the old story, you see."

"Ah," said Lopaka. "This is Pelekane story – English kind?"

"Exactly. But then one day something happened. The man found himself in a forest, and that was odd, because he had not known that there was a forest in that place. He had lost his way, and everything around him was so different from before that he thought he must have been bewitched, or put under a spell."

"Witch? Under a spell? So this was a heathen, your friend. He did not know Jesus?"

"He knew, he knew. But he forgot. And then he met a dragon. At least, it may have been a dragon, but he is uncertain, because this one appeared to him as a woman."

"A beautiful woman?"

"Yes."

"Ah! I see. And so, he did not slay her?"

"No."

"And was this woman in trouble?"

"No, not in trouble."

"I think I understand this," Harold remarked, faintly smiling. "And when he met this woman, what did they do?"

"They did, Harold, what a man and a woman do when they don't know any better – that is to say, when they are not civilized."

"So, I see. This was in Hawaii Nei?"

"Yes."

"And the woman, did she tempt him to do this thing?"

"Yes and no, She looked at him in a certain way. But after that, he did what he did."

"Ah too bad, he make mistake! So now he is sorry for this wicked fornication? He tell you he repents?"

"Yes and also no. He does not understand that, either. He simply does not know what any of it means. He asks himself, what have I done? And he has no answer. If she was a dragon, then he was bewitched. And if she was so dangerous as that, then he has escaped with his life, in which case, he is obliged to rejoice and give thanks."

"Pelekane, what kind of woman this?"

"He does not know what she was. Something more than a woman and also, something less. She was a wild creature of some sort. She did not seem to care or even notice who he was. She was like a force of Nature, and she wants to do only this, she must do this thing. He begins to think that she may be a creature made by God for this one purpose. And when it is done, then there is nothing, there is no one. She has vanished."

"Oh – oh – oh – oh," said Lopaka, shaking his head.

"It's true, Harold. She simply disappeared."

"Not good. How did she look, this one. What did she say?"

"Nothing, never a word. She seemed small at first, and young. Then older, darker, deeper, more mysterious. She never tired, and late in the night she rose up until she loomed above him with her hair flying – flashing out like lightning – and in her eyes, he saw fire."

"Fire!" cried Lopaka.

"Yes. At first he had been afraid of hurting her. Then he began to fear for his own life, that she might actually destroy him. It seemed to him finally that he had made his way into the heart of the world, and witnessed there something dark and terrible, cruel beyond measure. But as soon as he closed his eyes for a moment, she was gone. And there was nothing left but smoke and waste, and silence, and the sound of the sea."

"Oh!" cried Lopaka. "Ah!" He sat motionless for a long moment. Then he said softly, not looking at David, "Pelekane, it is dangerous to speak of this thing."

"Well yes, I should think so."

"You were frightened, yes?"

"I was. I admit it."

"Very frightened?"

"Yes."

"Good, I am glad."

"Then help me, Harold. What happened? Who was she? What does it mean?"

"I tell you this is not new to me," said Harold Lopaka. "Long time ago in these islands, all men know this one. She make and she destroy, yes. She is born for this. But in the old days she was different – I think, not so dangerous, not so angry, nothing bad."

"I don't understand."

"I speak of the time long ago, Pelekane, the time before the wars that stain this islands with their blood. All men remember long ago the time of the glad new day, the time of innocent and holy. They know this in their heart, and they dream it in their dream."

"Ah," said David. "The dream of Eden. Even here?"

"Yes, yes," said Harold. "Here in Hawaii Nei. Long ago, the time of the great canoes, the time of the hunters in the sea that find this land and plant it with good things. And the world was new then, and the man and the woman both was new. He was strong then, and she was also strong. She did not hide, or want to hurt someone, or make someone afraid. This was the day when woman walk the hills in the glory of her flesh, and every man is king."

"But Harold, is that truth or poetry? As well as we know human nature, can there ever have been such a time?"

"Truth or poetry? Only one? But poetry is true, or else no good. You never dream true? No, I will not believe that. All men do. Good and true is also in the heart – not only this danger, this darkness."

"Darkness, yes, that is the worst of it. Darkness and unknowing."

"Tell me David, did you never see in your dream one great canoe that take you far away to a beautiful land, a secret island in the sea where you will be king? And there the woman of your heart and soul awaits for you to love, and food is on the trees and in the sea, more than you can ever need?"

Tears came suddenly to David's eyes, and he could not answer. "Come, this is enough," said Harold Lopaka, "Come, walk to my house. I give you something to drink, something to eat. You want *poi*? You want *ono*? I tell the boys, get some."

"Not *ono*, thank you," said David. "And please tell the children to come away from the tide pools. I am afraid it is not safe for them there anymore."

*

At Harold Lopaka's dwelling David recorded several light tremors and one sharp one between 1:28 and 2:57 P.M. Harold had cleaned his hands and face for him as if he were a child, and now they sat cross-legged in his hut, facing one another over a calabash of savory three-day old poi. Harold seemed lost in thought, and David was quiet, not wishing to disturb him. At last Harold said in a meditative way, "Leilani is beautiful woman."

"Yes," said David.

"I see you notice that some time."

"Well, yes."

"Leilani goes up *mauka* for flower to make her leis. Sometime stay all night up Mauna Loa."

"But this was not *mauka*, and it was not Leilani."

"You are sure? Very sure?"

David groaned. "I don't know where I was or how I came there. I am certain of nothing now, except that it was not Leilani."

Lopaka pondered for a moment, then said gently, "The one you love, the *haole* lady who gone away. Maybe she come back, look for you?"

"No, impossible."

"Ah, David, you have met someone else."

"If so, I am not proud of it," said David bitterly.

"Proud? Proud is a rope to hang yourself. Listen, you are good man. You have good *mana*. I watch what you do. You go quiet, but you win some day. Now this time you are lucky and unlucky."

"How so?"

"Unlucky to find her, lucky you still alive. I tell you, I think you have met the Goddess. Do not smile! She does not like that."

"Sorry, but I don't believe I hear you say this. After all our studies, what makes a good Christian like you believe that there is such a thing as a goddess?"

"Same thing make you afraid!"

David had no answer for that. After a moment Harold continued, "Listen, David, this goddess is not good and she is not bad either. She is only what she is, no other. And she is here. She lives at this island."

"Surely, you are not speaking of Madame Pele?"

"I never say that name. I will not say it."

"Why not?"

"I am Christian."

"Now you confuse me, you distress me, Harold. When it comes to this goddess person, what do you believe?"

He drew himself up and thundered, "I believe in one God, the Father Almighty, Maker of heaven and earth, and of all things visible and invisible; and in one Lord Jesus Christ ..."

"My dear, dear friend, I know that you do. But there is nothing in our creed about goddesses."

Lopaka's chin thrust forward. "*All things invisible* it says! Invisible unless God make a man to see them. I see these things sometimes – so do you! Listen, I read my Bible. One this kind, she is in the book."

"One this kind what?" David asked, with a sense that English grammar was beginning to fail him.

"Goddess," said Lopaka. "In the Bible. Listen: *Wisdom hath builded her house, she hath hewn out her seven pillars; she hath killed her beasts, she hath mingled her wine; she hath also furnished her table. She hath sent forth her maidens: she crieth upon the highest places of the city!* Proverbs chapter nine! David! This is the goddess called Wisdom. And she is worth more than gold, the Bible says! So of course, all men desire her!"

"Oh, but that is a manner of speaking. Not a goddess, Harold. Only a way of expressing an abstract – that is to say, invisible – idea."

"Yes, yes!" said he. "Invisible!"

"But she is only an idea, not a person."

"Not? And she builded a house, and she hewn out seven pillars?"

"But you see, we in our Church believe that this Wisdom figure in the Bible is a concept, an abstract idea – if you will, a sort of prefiguration of our Divinity."

"Just what I say!" cried Harold. "Figuration! So we can see her. Then we believe what is right. Take more *poi* now, David, and tell me some about your English dragons."

*

They stood together later by the shore, calling the children in from the tide-pools. Lopaka blew on a conch shell, and the canoes began to return from beyond the reef. Mauna Loa's heights were still discreetly veiled, but on the western horizon, cloud-castles were building. Soon they would be lofty citadels with shining domes and battlements of gauzy, rose-lit gold – *Camelot!*

"We must pray for rain," he told Harold.

"Rain, yes," Harold replied. "Not today I think, but soon. Come, walk with me, tell me something. The story you make, this man with sorrow and fornication. Will he give thanks now, or will he repent?"

"Both," said David. "Most humbly and fervently, both. But Harold, what more can you tell me of this goddess – this female creature you so vividly imagine?"

"All is so change, Pelekane," he said slowly. "Before missionaries come I love many girls, many women. We did not know this is base and sin, we did not know fornication, so we never call it bad. But I believe our gracious merciful Lord forgive us."

"Of course he does."

"You understand. The light had not come to us then. The *ali'i* had power like gods, times were hard for poor Kanaka. All that war-time, power-time is bad for man, but worse for woman. I think Goddess go away then, hide up *mauka*. She send forth her maidens to stay down here, so that was when ships came – men from your country."

"Captain Cook?"

"Yes, English like you. And my grandfather see him killed."

David made a quick calculation. "But Harold, the death of Cook was 89 years ago. Are you certain that was your grandfather?" The Hawaiian looked at him reproachfully, and told him that the ancestor in question had been at Kealakekua Bay during the events that led to the murder of James Cook.

"It was a mistake, Pelekane. Something happen wrong, you know? Captain Cook was good man, they do not like to see him die. But when it happen, they take his bones to clean them. This is for *ali'i*, old custom here for great man. But I know something. They did not get his heart!"

"What do you mean by that?"

Lopaka smiled broadly. "I know it. What happen to his heart? Well I tell you something, he did not give it to a woman! Captain Cook was not like other men. He never take a woman, never even look."

David thought of mentioning that James Cook had a wife at home in England, but did not like to interrupt. "Now the heart," Lopaka continued cheerfully, "the heart of Captain Cook! Listen, this is good story and it is true! My own grandfather took the heart away to keep it. This was his wish, to save the *mana* of this man who is so great. So Grandfather hang the heart up in a shed to dry, and he go away one minute, maybe two. But some keikis come that time, some little girls very hungry. Two of them. So they ate it."

"God in heaven!" said David. "Is this true?

"True, yes. But not so bad, Pelekane. Calm yourself! This is mistake. Listen, I tell you they did not mean it. They did not know any better. They saw it, they tasted it, they thought it was the heart of a dog."

*

Before he left the village, Harold Lopaka embraced David for the first time since they had met. Just after that a sharp tremor shook the earth and David made another note in his diary. Harold told him, "You won't stop her, making those numbers."

"I know," said David.

"My friend," Harold said, "I tell you something. Last night Leilani went *mauka*, and up Mauna Loa she saw fire. Look up there! What you see dark is not rain coming, it is smoke from the volcano. Something more I think will happen soon. Maybe something big."

David said, "I must get back to the church. Please come if you wish, and bring the others. Only tell me, Harold, one more thing about Cook. About his heart. Is it possible that Queen Emma knows this story?"

"Ah well, does Queen Emma know what happen to the heart of Captain Cook? Of course she knows! Kaleleonalani knows everything. She is a saint."

They walked together to the pali, and before turning back, Harold said, "Be very careful, Pelekane, after this thing you have done. When a man wake up and his eyes are open, sometime he see Goddess everywhere."

33

JOURNAL
PRIVATE – F.C.

Hurrah! We embarked today in a sort of sampan, Malay boys laughing & chattering as they poled our way slowly, slowly upstream in the amazing, punishing heat of early morning. The town soon vanished behind us & then we were captured by magnificent jungle – mute, inviolate, impenetrable. Trees embracing one another with branches intertwined, the most tremendous ferns of every sort & a bewildering network of lianas tangled in everything. Very few flowers to be seen – but oh! once a garland of blooms flinging itself from tree to tree – blue orchids!

Farther up a narrowing stream, now with little waterfalls & rapids here & there. Quite exciting, I should think, coming down – a green pool below each fall w. crocodiles lying in wait! More & more slowly we went & water at times flew into the boat, so I found a tin & bailed with it – then narrower yet, with vines & branches meeting over our heads. Even now blazing hot as the sun slipped through the leaves, dappling & flashing on the water – my eyesight blurring, wavering – my hair dripping onto my shoulders in salted points. Chas. perspires easily, happily it seems but the Malays hardly at all – I wonder why. But no more jokes & laughter after the second hour – we were all captured by the silence of the forest.

Then a few rather shocking villages, ramshackle houses like sheds, quite high on poles with ladders leading up, or else a tree-trunk with steps cut into it. Natives here not yet felled by cholera, but quite unhealthy looking. Men almost entirely naked, short & squat, each with a large knife called a parang at the waist – women in petticoats w. heavy rings of brass wrapped round from hips to just below the bosom, which is left bare. And I believed we would not see corsets in the jungle! "How on earth do they get them off?" I asked – "They don't," said Charles with something of a smirk.

Then the procedure: Chas unpacking the medicines – explaining to the Dyaks in rapid bursts of their own language – then lining them up, while I was to sit on a stone & dip one dose with a silver spoon into each approaching mouth. I smiled until my face ached & spoke to each in as friendly a tone as I could muster. They accepted my presence without interest or curiosity, though they all gazed at Charles Brooke with dumb adoration – trying to come close, to touch and stroke him as if some of his magic might rub off – while he walked slowly among them with a secret smile.

Charles was using an old physic of Mrs. Bishop McDougall's – a solution of camphor in brandy, with a bit of sugar & aromatic cajeput. If this didn't work, the blessed lady used to dose them with laudanum & castor oil, which no doubt ended their problems entirely. In any case, 'twas better than being treated by the local witch-doctors, whose regimen for inflammation of the bowel was commonly to apply a mix of animal blood & their own spittle – then do sleight-of-hand, producing the "demon" supposedly responsible.

Under their houses, piles of refuse & a frightful stench – where all the garbage & litter go, with pigs & chickens constantly rooting around in it. No wonder they have disease! How can they live like this? Chas. says never mind, some of the filthiest families have escaped both cholera and small pox year after year – he does not know why. Against pox he has been doing inoculation, but says it makes no difference –and 1,000 of his Dyaks died of cholera last year.

Coffee & boiled eggs for tiffin, then a quick wash, up to my neck without undressing – upstream, where the water was fresh & clear. Afterward, a long trek through a bog to another village. Butterflies everywhere – a few tiny striped squirrels, very shy – a great blue kingfisher on the wing – dazzling! – and a chattering group of monkeys, shaking down leaves & twigs. No large carnivores here supposedly, though they say if we are lucky, we may see leopards. Trunks of trees had been set on the ground end to end for great distances to walk on – very slippery indeed. As I attempted them in some hesitation, Charles shouted orders & I found myself suddenly tucked up as baggage upon a strong young Malay back, his arms under my knees – as I used to carry baby Hal.

We had a bonfire that first night & ate broiled python, which tastes rather like chicken. That was after plucking off our leeches – of which I had by far the fewest & stopped the bleeding instantly with my little vial of cayenne-pepper paste. Charles was agog – I told him I never travel without certain small domestic aids & conveniences. Then I looked at him – saw him admiring me quite frankly in the firelight, and a great silver moon coming up over the mountain. All very nice – together with a good feed & fireflies darting about. So I thought, well, here we are, & you are not such a bad man I suppose – but how I do wish you were someone else!

From time to time he was poking the fire & barking out orders to the Malays, who were singing through their noses in a strange, droning style. I thought I'd try once more for some civilized conversation, so I asked him, "What do you think is the true difference between animals & humans? Only a matter of degree? Or craft in survival, as Darwin implies?"

He appeared at first not to have heard me, but said after a time: "That other fellow was here, 10 or 12 years ago. Not Darwin, but Wallace. Odd chap – not a word to say for himself – just went about collecting things."

"Which reminds me," I said, "what ever happened to the lady who kept pigs on a leash?"

"I didn't say leash. Kept 'em in her room – that was it," he said vaguely.

"Oh I see. Well, after all, the poor dear. I suppose she desperately wanted something to be fond of."

He yawned and bade me good night. Then, as he departed, "Alfred Wallace had a large collection of flying frogs."

"And you have a large collection of Dyaks," I almost replied – but for once, held my tongue.

We slept that night on cots in an abandoned fort. Then 2 days moving about, doing much the same – except that later villages offered people down with cholera. Most were women – not surprising, since I'm told that their lives are harder here than the men's. From girlhood they do heavy labor & carry supplies for miles. If only they would boil their water before drinking it! A desperately ill baby reached up from its mother's arms – snatched a lock of my hair & sucked on it. "Charles" I said – "Surely it is salt that they need, as much as anything." But he answered that they had plenty of salt if they wanted it – & we must move on. If they had cholera now, they would die in any case.

*

Another day, with a different sort of Dyak tribe & Chas. says these will not need medicine. First fruits of their harvest are now being celebrated – I've come at a lucky time of year – otherwise they'd be off somewhere else on the jungle, working their rice paddies. As it is, we are to have a feast. "I trust, Lady Fiona, that you like your chicken charred quite black & cooked in all its feathers!" – I said, "Of course."

So up from the forest floor we came, climbing a sharp rise – a hands & knees ascent, in the usual suffocating heat. Over a rocky chasm on a narrow, swaying bridge w. only one railing – & that one not to be trusted. But then – oh then! – a sound of water gushing & splashing nearby, invisible among palms & plantains. A few more steps and at the side of the path a bamboo conduit suddenly appeared – a rest stop of sorts, with a shelf for people to sit on while the blessed water pours over them, after cooling itself on the way down from a height of 10 feet. Bliss! "Thank God for water!" I cried – not to Chas, who'd gone on ahead – but to the Anglican missionary, Smithers, who had joined our party. A lean & angular youth w. a long untidy beard like spun red wool.

"Amen" said he – "Church of Scotland?"

"No," I said. "Just an ordinary heathen." He looked so dismayed that I took pity on him and added, "Please don't feel obliged to convert me – I'm sure you have enough on your plate as it is."

"Just look over there!" he said in gloomy tones – "They've left offerings for their spirits." Sure enough there was a little tray beside the path, surrounded by flies & filled with rotting fruit.

Atop the next hill, a dwelling like a warehouse on poles, known as a "longhouse" – w. dozens of Dyaks living in it, above the usual piles of *refuse & the usual pigs. Inside, the human population crammed into tiny compartments – each one completely open to the long common space – a sort of covered verandah. A certain expression on my face may have suggested that I would not care for such an arrangement myself, and Charles laughed at me. "Ada bikit, ada paya" he told me – which he said means in Malay something like, "To each his own."*

Naked men young & old strutted about looking grim wearing various bits of brass jewelry. Old women sat grinning in petticoats with dangling bean-pods for breasts – the younger ones of course quite beautiful in that same deshabille – Chas plainly enjoying himself over it. As for furnishings: mats & platforms, metal cooking pots – some cheap crockery & dreadful Dutch or Chinese jars – kept, I was told, as a sign of their wealth & some believed to have magical powers. Tucked away under the eaves were spears, knives, tools & utensils, plus several clusters of ancient skulls. Animal? No, human. Cooking fires were blazing on the verandah & children, in that blistering heat stood round one of them roasting mice on skewers – evidently a great treat.

"Come walk this way," Chas. told me – "You can look into all the apartments & see how they live." But I sat down on a mat & refused to move.

"What's the matter?"

"If I lived here, I should not like people coming in, peering at me. I do not consider myself an exhibition." So he & Smithers went about together inspecting, greeting people who seemed both pleased & frightened, or in awe. I thought of Chas' remark one night that it is important for Church & State to work together closely – their aims being much the same, in relation to the natives.

A tiny naked boy child came over to inspect me & we flirted a little – then he ran back to his Mama. I wondered how soon that smile would be gone from his face. A little later at the banquet table I was dodging the black, burnt chicken to taste some rice – steamed in small bits of bamboo, quite sweet & delicious – when I could not help noticing on the same table a human head. Rather freshly removed, it would seem, from its owner. It was prettily decorated w. leaves & ferns – and had a lot of food stuffed into its mouth.

No one I knew.

"Have you met the guest of honor yet?" I asked Charles.

He was livid with fury when he saw it. What a temper! Made the most enormous fuss. Name of the Rajah invoked – law of the land – severe punishment, a heavy fine for the chief etc. etc. Hartley Smithers stood beside him during all this, looking like waxworks under the red beard. "Charles, what happened to ada bukit, ada paya?" I remarked as he walked by – no answer. But my eyesight went off just after that into its worst pinwheels, stars & blind spots – & I fainted – but only for a moment, hating myself all the way down.

Charles was still scolding the Dyaks, but Smithers brought me a cup of water with salt in it & a damp cloth for my head. Horizontal as I was, and not God knows at my best, I did remember to ask for the water to be boiled, and he obliged – then knelt beside me, taking my pulse at the wrist. "Where did you study?" I asked him & he said, Canterbury. "Did you know David Wilkinson?" He said of course, D. was one of the best – so bright, won every prize – sang like an angel – so attractive, everyone loved him, etc. I feasted on this & wanted more – but then came the most unearthly shriek, like an animal in extremities of pain & terror.

Chas. explained, smirking, that this was the signal for the evening's entertainment to begin. It was growing dark – torches were set ablaze casting wild shadows on the ceiling & the Dyaks mostly naked but for their gleaming, jingling ornaments began parading back and forth in rows, flexing their knees & tipping their feet in a curious manner, rather as if they had uncomfortable new shoes on. A terrific pounding of drums & smashing of gongs served as accompaniment – and that was it – and it went on for the next 3½ hours. Easier to appreciate, I'm sure, if one has consumed a great deal of arrak (native brew) – however, Smithers & I were drinking coconut milk – & I dared to put only a small tot of whiskey into mine.

Our Malays were nowhere to be seen & Charles disappeared after a while – with a girl, I suppose, or on some private errand. Hartley Smithers and I walked out to the edge of the verandah where a very old man was relieving himself through a crack in the flooring – plop, onto the pigs below. "I may become a Muslim some day soon & stop eating pork altogether," I told Smithers. "Or else, a Jew."

Alas, he was not amused, so I tried again – "I'm sure it must be lonely for you, out here. Will you marry one day, do you think – or stay forever under the stern taboo of St. Columba's?" His answer was puzzling: "A wife would be of no use in a place like this. She would only be in the way. What a man wants in the field is a sister." I guessed that meant he didn't like making love to women – but whatever it was, the dam was broken. Out poured a tale of struggle and misery, all in a passionate rush. There were too many missionaries in Kuching, he said, serving too few people & having a grand old time of it there in town! He was the one doing the hard work of mission – out in the jungle on his own – and he had just had the most crushing blow. The little chapel he had built was flooded, then carried away entirely, during a recent cloudburst. So he and his 5 converts – all young Dyak boys – must begin over again. It was heartbreaking. It helped him tremendously, he said, to see Charles Brooke – even more, to be seen with him in the district. That showed the natives that Government and Religion were hand in hand.

"But you cannot imagine" he said, "how difficult it is to explain Holy Communion to people so primitive. They were convinced at first that the English killed a man every Sunday so as to eat and drink his flesh and blood. They are so low and dull that they have no understanding of the spiritual – and as for teaching them the Doctrine of the Real Presence – well, it is enough to drive one mad.

Just then Charles Brooke came up the ladder. "Ah Fiona," he said, flailing with an excess of arrak. "Lady Fiona Something-or-other Cameron Stuart! Mr. Reverend Hartley What's-your-name Smithers! Complicated people! Civilized people! Far too civilized, my friends! Look around you! What a night – what a glorious night! They have the secret of it here, I tell you! – they understand that life is simple, gloriously simple! And these poor ignorant people are clever enough to know it! I tell you, Fiona – don't look so sour! – these natives are much, much happier than we are!"

"Oh?" I said. "Are they now? And if so, whose fault is that?"

*

2 March '68

Charles & I have had – since coming back to the Astana – what I suppose will be our final conversation. It began last night at table. The Resident & wife were there, the Colonial Secretary, several missionaries & a new guest – a young American, out from California for the shooting.

During the soup we heard of the battle of 1863 when Chas. led 15,000 Dyaks against the Kayan tribe, etcetera. During fish it was, in some detail, the horrible tortures the pirates liked to inflict on their captives. As curried pork came in he began a lengthy thesis on the necessity of inter-breeding in places like Sarawak. Anglo-Saxons, he said, could not endure the climate here for long – their women died in childbirth, or shortly after – & their children died if not sent home to England by the age of 5 or 6. His own officers left him, the missionaries left one after another – the Bishop himself had now gone home. The English ought to face facts and be rid of their racial prejudices! The only answer for it was a new lot of humans – a mixed race, that would have in their blood the superior Anglo-Saxon intellect, conscience and will, together with the physical strength of the Southeast Asians.

I put my fork down at last – the silver & crystal glittering on the table – the Malay guards rigid in the background – a faithful Dyak beside each one of us, wielding a fan – and I said, "Charles, if this is so, wouldn't it be a fine thing then for a child of mixed race to be the next Tuan Mudah – one who would then inherit Sarawak? Some local woman's child – perhaps of a liaison, not necessarily a marriage – with an Englishman? There you might find the strengths – the powers that you say are needed here, both mental and physical, yes?"

I paid for it, of course. The rest of the evening was ghastly – empty chatter alternating with sinister silences. When he spoke to me privately in the morning, it was to say that I had been nothing but trouble to him from the first. I was indiscreet, insulting, supercilious, a fraud, a flirt, a liar, etc. & had no understanding of the real world. Furthermore I had made a nuisance of myself by fainting at the sight of an amputated head – was obviously suffering from nerves as well as heat prostration & must be sent at once to his "sanitorium" in the hills, at Santubong.

I made him a counter-offer. What I really needed, I said, was a dip in the ocean – a nice refreshing little bathe in the sea. Would he be so kind as to send me with a guide or two out to the coast for a week? After that I would go directly away.

"Where will you go then?" he asked – thinking, I suppose, of what to tell Angela.

"I have friends in Hawaii," I said.

*

So I left with two men – Piti, the youth who had carried me so valiantly through the swamps – & an old man named Magro, silent, smiling & kind. In less than two days we were there – made camp on the beach & I crept into the water that evening – oh, blessed peace, silence & a sky that went on forever, with great blazing stars. I floated about for the better part of an hour while Piti & Magro were singing at the campfire, then dressed myself again & fell immediately asleep.

When I awakened at dawn a man was standing over me – a strange sort of man with no eyes. That is, he had eyes, but the expression was flat, black & empty as if there were nothing inside – no brain attached. I was prodded then, with the point of a kris. I leapt up shouting, but it was too late. Magro's head was gone, bleeding on the sand. The man picked it up & tossed it to his comrade, who stood nearby with a gun. Piti was being led away at the end of a rope, toward the ocean. A ship had come in during the night – oars, masts, banners, tip-tilted riggings. Pirates!

"The Rajah shall hear of this!" I cried. "The Tuan Mudah shall –" but I was struck on the face then, knocked to the ground and dragged away – first to a small boat, then quickly to the ship – where all was in hasty preparation for leaving. Piti had been tossed in on top of me & was weeping profusely. When we came to the ship, he tried to fight them – I heard him give a great shriek – a shot was fired & a body fell into the ocean. At least, I thought, he won't have to die by inches, as a slave. I was being carried now to a cabin at the back.

I did not scream, since that would be of no use. Knowing that I must save my strength I crouched in a corner at first – the captain's cabin, surely – for there was a great high bed – velvet hangings, a looking glass, a heap of maps. If this man had authority, I could appeal to him – make a bargain, offer ransom. I stood when he came into the room, but it was the same one again – the man with death in his eyes . He was the captain.

When I tried to speak to him, he struck me in the mouth & tore my silk tunic in one quick motion from collar to hem. Then he backed off a bit – watching me – threw his jacket & his jeweled kris onto the bed. I could hear the oars creaking & felt the ship beginning to move. Now he came closer – & still without a word, opened his trousers. Motioned impatiently for me to undress – took out the usual instrument, licked his fingers – & wet the bulging end of it.

Did I pray then? Yes, if prayer can be the one word only – help! It was said in the silence of my mind, but the connection was instant, to Someone or Something that was there with me, beside me, in the cabin. I felt it as a perfect circle of light enclosing me in perfect safety, signaling me to take courage. I knew then that I was not alone, and knowing that, it did not matter so much whether I died or lived

But I thought I should very much like to live, if possible. Therefore I smiled sweetly & put my hands together in the polite Asian gesture of submission – the gesture that is in itself a sort of prayer. And I bowed low before him, most humbly – and lower, more humbly still – until I could reach the top of my boots. Then I pulled out my knife & killed him.

I was lucky – very lucky, of course. Caught him by surprise. Also I happen to know exactly where the heart is. He scarcely had time for a single cry before falling down very hard on the knife – face to floor – and then shuddered silently for perhaps half a minute. After he stopped moving I could not bring myself to touch him – so, alas, Mother's little pearl-handled knife is gone forever.

As soon as I dared I ran from there, dodged behind a door – a heap of sailcloth – a cannon – & then slid quietly into the sea. The sky had turned black – a deluge of rain was coming. But for safety's sake, I dove down deep & swam beneath the surface of the warm, salt water, almost all the way to shore.

BOOK FOUR: ARMAGEDDON

.

34

When David returned to the parsonage, Nancy Cornwall was waiting at the door with a basket full of newspapers and letters for him. Her face was troubled, and her voice trembled as she greeted him. "Come in, sit down," David told her. "What is it, my dear? Too many quakes for you? I've already counted nineteen today."

"It's not that," she said, "It's Richard. I'm afeared for him. He's been gone so long now, and still no word. That's not like my Richard at all. I don't know what to think. And the new stone wall went down all over our vegetable garden this morning, after he worked so hard on it. "

"But where did he go?" David asked, looking rapidly through his letters and finding one at last written on the familiar, pale blue stationery. Three days earlier, Nancy explained, her husband had gone on an errand for the law. There was a writ of trespass that he was supposed to deliver for Sheriff Kildare, into the "prophet's" hands. The camp was no more than a half day's ride, but Richard Cornwall had not been seen or heard of since. This morning, the Catholic priest from Ka'u had stopped unexpectedly at her door. Over a hasty meal of tea and porridge the little Frenchman had told her of riding past the "prophet's" camp, hearing sounds of riot and gunfire. Nancy had begged him to fetch the sheriff, and Pierre Armand had hurried away to Kailua town. As she told the last of this story, the ground gave another jolt, and then a long shudder that sent the old Pierpont teapot and one of David's four china plates crashing to the floor. At the same time, a slim crack appeared in the seaward wall of his hut, and he thought for a moment that he saw fire beyond, but it was only a final ray of brilliance from the setting sun.

*

While he secured the rest of the breakables, Nancy swept up the fragments of his shattered treasures for him, and now her tears began to fall. "The worst is, I can't go looking for him," she said. "We have a cow ready to drop her first calf, and the chickens and dogs are all gone bedlam with this quaking. Oh, Mr. Wilkinson, what shall we do?"

"First things first," he told her, and the two prayed together for Richard's safety. Then, over cups of cold coffee, he said what little he could to comfort her, and promised to ride out himself early the following day to search for Richard. When Nancy rose from her chair to leave, he noticed for the first time the depth of her blue eyes, the sweet curve of her upper lip, and then he felt the tender weight of her breast as she swayed against him for an instant. *Heaven help me! Goddesses everywhere!*

As soon as he was alone, he lit his lantern and read:

20 Feb   *Sarawak*

    My dear David – I'm moved to write, after hearing your name most kindly mentioned here in the jungle, by one Hartley Smithers who knew you at school, and said such nice things–

Continued: 4th March   *Singapore*

    Something rather disagreeable has happened. I am on my way back to Hawaii, hoping that I may talk with you about it, and about a few other things as well. Expecting to stay with Q. Emma again, but if not, she

will know where to find me. Please if at all possible come to Honolulu.
We will be sensible this time, yes? You never had a sister, did you? Then
perhaps I may be allowed to apply for the post.
    F.C.

Why was Smithers, of all people, speaking well of him?
David was annoyed. He had never liked Hartley Smithers; in
fact, he had found the man detestable, a perpetual complainer.
The rest of Fiona's letter was equally disturbing. What could
have happened? Puzzled, David began to pace about the little
parsonage. Then quite suddenly, leaning against the seaward
wall, he fell fast asleep standing up. He had noted a small
tremor at 9:01 P.M. and had closed his eyes for no more than a
second or two before he found Fiona in his arms, bitterly
weeping. She held a small, pearl-handled knife in her hand, and
he feared that she might try to stab him with it, so he wrested it
away and hurled it into the water. They both fell down heavily
then onto wet sand, while great, transparent ocean waves rolled
over them. Her dark, serpentine hair lashed itself about his
throat, and then floated away; it was only seaweed after all, and
when he saw her poor, bald head so pitifully cold and bare he
covered it with a paisley shawl, and took her trembling hands,
and drew her to his bed.

All this time he had been firmly convinced that he was
awake. Now he thought – this cannot be! – and forced his eyes
open, only to find himself in his bedroom at *Green Gardens*.
Jenny Miller had left one of her stockings on the floor and he
was afraid that his mother might see it; so he crept down the
creaking stairs to the kitchen-garden and climbed into his tree-
fort, where he stood up nude as a pickle before a well-dressed
congregation and preached a brilliant sermon on Theological
Dilemmas in the Book of Job. After that, amid enthusiastic
applause, he and Fiona sailed away to Japan, where he suddenly
became an archbishop, carrying bagpipes and wearing a kilt.
Fiona wore a pale blue silk kimono and a necklace of edible
jade that tasted like almonds, but the Ten Erotic
Commandments of this diocese were all so indecent that he

tied a handkerchief over her eyes, so that she would not see what they were doing.

"God help me, this is Sunday!" he cried aloud as he waked for the third time, only to find himself lying amid splinters on his parsonage floor in Hawaii. His watch read 9:07, and he felt most marvelously refreshed. The diary, still in his hand, reported 24 earthquakes since morning, ranging from the barely perceptible to the dangerously violent and prolonged.

For only the second time since its founding, Grace Church had not held Sunday services, for its wretched vicar had been up *mauka*, breaking his vows.

*

Long before dawn David packed his saddlebags and set off in such haste that he forgot to bring any water. On the way back for it, he was shaken by two more rather sharp tremors – one at 6:11 and another at 7:18 A.M. – and now Mr. Gray grew annoyed. He was tired of this, and made it clear that it was all entirely David's fault.

At 7:32 he found Harold Lopaka sitting on the church steps reading Morning Prayer to a small cluster of local people, both English and Hawaiian. Those from the seaside village had brought various bundles with them, evidently preparing to settle in. David spoke to them briefly, led a prayer, gave a blessing, and galloped away again. This time he brought bread, fruit and water as well as his papers and letters that were still unread.

Now he was suddenly in high spirits again, imagining from time to time that Fiona rode beside him: a new Fiona, willing and compliant; a devoted Fiona, determined never to let him go. The southern trail offered a splendid view of the ocean that day, dark under the sheen of a sky that glowed like the insides of mussel shells. The dim, bitten wafer of a quarter-moon rode aloft among milky clouds that shimmered with the promise of rain. All the air smelled of life: earth-scents of moss and fern, stirred by his horse's hooves, mingled in David's nostrils with the mist of a pungent, salt sea-spray. Wild heliotrope shone silver amid the taller grasses, and golden *ilima* cast its gleaming net on the lava shore below. A little after 10 A.M. he dismounted and slowly ate a succulent Ka'u orange, licking its juices from his fingers while admiring the curve of a *pali* a few yards ahead of him on the trail. It arched above the shore in a graceful way that reminded him of the soft green turf above the white cliffs of chalk at Dover. Then as his thoughts idled and strayed agreeably toward home and England, the ground lurched, this time so violently that he lost his footing and nearly fell. The earth continued to shudder and shake as he watched the lovely hill tilt seaward until it detached itself approximately 20 yards ahead of him. Slowly at first, it carved itself away from its adjoining meadow and then suddenly fell, crackling and crumbling all at once; and after that, with a great rush and a monumental roar, it plunged in chunks and slabs of rubble into the sea. The dark waters parted to receive it, then churned powerfully skyward again. From a fall to his certain death, David had escaped only by stopping to eat an orange. *Father in heaven, hallowed be thy name.*

Yet a few minutes later he found himself pacing about feeling peevish and resentful, as if some primeval covenant had been broken. "What is the meaning of this?" he cried aloud. "Will you destroy this whole island ? Do away with it all? Every living thing – all this beauty? And the animals, the people, the land – all of your own magnificent handiwork? Lord, how could you?" As if by sentient and purposeful reply, the waters of the bay hurled themselves more furiously than ever against to the shore below; and now a violent gust of wind came in from the sea, flattening the grasses and shrubs beside him, flinging dust and pebbles into his eyes. David heard his answer in the whirlwind: *Where wast thou when I laid the foundations of the earth? When the morning stars sang together, and all the sons of God shouted for joy?*

He fell to his knees in the dust, and forgot to record the great quake until the following day. It was a very powerful one, commencing at about 25 minutes before noon, and continuing

313

at its climax for longer than a minute. Afterward, as if a matter of some vast importance had been settled, the earth was perfectly still for the rest of that day.

*

Skirting the fractured rim of the *pali* he continued on his way, but found no sign of Richard Cornwall, and met no one who had seen him. In fact, he met no one at all except an elderly couple with baggage-laden mules riding helter-skelter toward Kailua, where they said they would take the first ship to Honolulu. From there, they would make their way home to Ohio as soon as possible, for they could bear no more of this.

Actually, there was less evidence of destruction along the seacoast than David had expected, although he saw stone walls laid low, and cattle wandering. Early in the afternoon he found himself approaching the "prophet's" camp, whose location was newly marked with white rags tied to bushes and posts. He paused at the entrance, where a rough trail led toward the ocean, dismounted and turned the Curate out to graze.

The slim young guard today was none other than Kimo Lopaka, wearing the tattered remains of a robe that had once been white, and holding a large, old-fashioned rifle with its barrel pointing up. "Go way! You no come here!" was his greeting. The sandy soil beneath them looked as if it had suffered a recent drenching, and in the distance, a sagging canvas tent stood among a number of low hovels made of sea-drift.

"Aloha, Kimo," said David. "Careful with that weapon!" He reached for the rifle, but the boy quickly drew it away. "Kimo, tell me, has Richard Cornwall been here?"

"Who want to know?" the boy replied. "Who care?"

"I do, and so should you. Have you seen him? Answer me!"

"No matter what happen him, you stupid – don't you know – the end is come! Tribulation time! Today is the last – the last!" His youthful voice cracked with emotion.

"Come now, don't be afraid," said David. "The same

person told you that the world would end on the eleventh of February, and it did not. The world is not going to end tomorrow either. But in the meantime, Kimo, you may hurt someone, or hurt yourself seriously, if you are not more cautious with that weapon. Give it here!"

He took the rifle, wrenched it open and threw the bullets away into the branches of a *pandanus* tree, wondering at the same time whether the people here had been reduced to eating *pandanus* fruits, which were generally considered edible by humans only in famine. "That's better, Kimo," he told the boy. That is much safer, both for you and for others. Now tell me please what you know about Richard Cornwall. Has he come here?" The boy refused to answer, and some of the camp's inmates began to crawl from their huts and move toward them. He was shocked by their appearance, for he had never seen filthy Hawaiians before; as a rule, the natives were cleaner than either the British or the Americans. These were sickly-looking lads of the most derelict and pathetic sort, all dressed in rags. He saw almost no women among them, and no young children at all, for which he was thankful. Several canoes were drawn up on the pebbled beach, and tremendous waves were cresting high enough to block the sun, then roaring in foamy torrents to the shore.

"I come in peace," he said, holding up his prayerbook with the sign of the cross on its cover. "Peace be with you! I need your help. Where is the man you call prophet? I must speak with him – now!" At this, several of the young men approached, rattling small gourds and beating on drums, while a ragged woman whirled about in a frantic barefoot dance.

"Tell me," David shouted, "Have you seen the man called Richard Cornwall? Has he been here?" Now several youths picked up stones and faced him with clearly murderous intent, though only a single stone fell at his feet, as if tossed half-heartedly. Looking around for the person who had thrown it, David saw something else: Cornwall's familiar chestnut roan, without saddle or bridle, tethered near the canvas tent. It occurred to him that his friend might be held prisoner there, and at the same instant, for the first time, he thought that Cornwall might be dead.

Holding up the prayerbook, he strode forcibly through the crowd. A small stone struck his shoulder, but did no damage. Another flew toward him as he reached the entrance to the tent, and followed him inside. There it rolled another few yards before stopping beside the body of Richard Cornwall.

"Another messenger from Satan!" said a fretful voice nearby, as David knelt by the body. He was indeed dead – brought down, it was plain to see, by stones and a bullet to his throat. David made the mark of the cross on Cornwall's forehead and took the cold hands in his own, crossed them over Richard's breast and began to say, *"I know that my Redeemer liveth…"*

"Quiet! He is only sleeping!" said the voice of Lorenzo Scuppers, alias Billy Smith.

"Be quiet yourself!" David replied. "This man is dead, and you are the cause of it." He turned to look at his adversary and saw a nondescript creature with a straggle of beard, sitting on a muddy straw mat. His feet were bare, and he wore a filthy robe and one gold earring.

"No," said the creature. "Not dead. I shall wake him if and when I please. Stay here and you will see it happen. Yea verily the Lord God Sabaoth will come in from the sea at dawn tomorrow with all of his heavenly hosts and legions. And so the world will end, and all the world's people will die and go down to eternal damnation, except for the favored few who believe in me. And you will see my people taken up into a cloud of glory, and Jesus himself will carry them to heaven."

"Stop talking nonsense! Look at this man!" David cried. "See what you have done! This is my friend, my brother in Christ, one of the kindest, truest souls ever to live on this earth. He has been murdered, and you are responsible. Believe me, Lorenzo Scuppers, I shall make you pay for it."

Scuppers pointed a bony finger at David and intoned, "This evil messenger brought a letter to me from Satan. For that he was crushed, but do not weep for him. I can bring him to life again whenever I like, for I am greater than Satan."

Just at this moment David noticed a sturdy length of bamboo nearby, and considered breaking the man's knees with it. Then he looked down at Lorenzo's neck and remembered how at *Green Gardens* a decapitated chicken would sometimes run a crazed path through the kitchen-garden before expiring in support of Sunday dinner.

Amen, he said to calm himself, and then again, *amen,* for he knew that he could not do such a thing to any human being. "Are you human?" he asked Scuppers. "Have you a heart? A soul? Do you care anything at all for truth? For justice? For decency? Where have you come from? Are you a man or a ghoul, a fiend, a demon, a slave to Lucifer and Bealzebub? If you are human, damn you, then stand up!" When Scuppers did not move, David hauled him roughly to his feet and shook him. "You may be insane," he said, "but you are also clever and vicious, and blasphemous, and you are a murderer. You have gone too far this time. It's not the jail or the madhouse for you now, it's the gallows!"

Lorenzo Scuppers began to laugh as if he were enjoying all this. David, enraged, shook him again, this time violently enough to make Scuppers bite his own tongue. As he whimpered and spat blood, David shouted, "Stand up and admit what you have done! You and I are going out there to tell these poor, frightened people that you have deceived them, robbed them of their faith, their dignity, their worldly goods, all for your own vile sake!" He pushed Scuppers ahead of him, out of the tent.

The few people left at the camp were milling around in confusion at the center of the compound. Grasping Scuppers firmly, David cried out to the crowd that they had been deceived, that their leader was a liar and a wicked man. Angry shouts were the response, so he decided to appeal to higher powers and told them, "Your royal monarchs the Kamehamehas and the government of this kingdom have decreed that this shall be a civilized nation! Civilization demands law, justice, truth and responsibility. You have none of these things here. You have only a criminal leader who controls you by claiming that the world is about to end. I am here to tell you that the world is <u>not</u> going to end tomorrow, or any time soon, for that matter. Furthermore, you will be held to account for the death of a fine man, my wise and noble friend Richard Cornwall. I intend to take his body home with me now for a decent Christian burial, and the Sheriff of Kona will be here very soon."

At this, Scuppers broke free and dashed toward the nearest of the beached canoes, but before he could launch it, he was surrounded and captured by his own supporters. Shrieking as if they would tear him apart and devour him, they pressed around him so closely that David could not see what was happening.

"Stop!" he cried, and began to run toward them, thinking to prevent a massacre, but then realized that he had been mistaken. The madman's followers were not bent on killing him; they were in a frenzy of fear that their idol might escape. When they caught him, they fell to their knees in an ecstasy of worship, desperate to touch the hem of his robe, to kiss his filthy feet.

35

L ess than an hour later David Wilkinson lay in a thicket outside the camp, bound and trussed like a Christmas goose. There he waited with what patience he could muster, while the sun sank slowly behind a rank of gold-rimmed clouds, then doubled its size and turned the color of blood while careening the last few inches to the horizon. The faithful Curate came to snuffle at his predicament, and dripped saliva sympathetically over his face, but was not otherwise helpful. The knots that held him were beyond his ability to undo, and so he said his prayers and then composed himself as best he could for sleep.

Immediately after sunset, in a brief spell of soft blue semi-darkness, David began to hear an interesting sound in the distance. Something or someone was approaching on the same trail by which he had come; it was a four-footed beast but not a horse, and therefore, not Kevin Kildare. By rolling to one side he was able to see a small person in a dark garment jogging along in his direction, and then he heard him merrily singing: *Gaudeamus igitur! juvenesdum sumus...* It was his Catholic friend, Fr. Pierre Armand, riding his usual gaunt, fleabitten mule and carrying a pistol as large as his forearm. David began to shout.

"Oh, mon ami!" cried the Frenchman when he had drawn near. "Qu'est-ce que s'est passé? What do these devils make to you? And where is Monsieur Cornwall?" He jumped from his mule and began to undo David's bonds.

"Richard is dead. They've killed him."

Armand crossed himself quickly three times and bowed his head. Then, seeing that David could hardly speak for thirst, he ran to fetch some water. A full pint later, David told him, "They have all gone mad in there! I demanded Richard's body for burial, and they refused. Can you imagine? Then they tied me up and threw me out here."

"I was coming to look for you! Le bon Dieu be thanked something is not broken," said Armand, gently rubbing David's arms. When David could stand, Armand made a little bow and handed him the pistol.

"What on earth?" David asked. "Where ever did you find this thing?"

"Good, eh? You like? Very old, I think, very valuable antique. I get him from a man I know and bring for you."

"Did you see Kildare? Will he be coming soon?" David asked. "Is this thing loaded? I am in a mood to shoot someone."

Armand hung his head. "Je regrette, mon ami. No bullets. But David, you are strong. I think you use it to break a man's head, if you like."

＊

They made camp together on a rocky hillock nearby, but remained as quiet as possible and did not light a fire. They were close enough to the camp so that they could hear the inmates calling to one another and beating on drums. "Today Kildare finds the men with the guns and the horses," said Pierre Armand. "Early tomorrow he comes with the posset."

"Posse."

"Oui."

"You know," said David, "I made a discovery some time ago. This wretched fraud who calls himself a prophet is also a murderer. He came ashore from a shipwreck last year, telling us that his comrade had died of natural causes, and that he had drunk the man's blood for his own survival. But there was a bucket of it in the boat, and my friend Dr. Hillebrand tells me that blood does not run out so freely as that unless the heart is still beating."

"Please, mon ami, my nerves."

"Unless you hang him up like a duck and let him drain. But he cannot have done that in the open boat."

"Please, I have the migraine," the Frenchman whispered, "already two days. When the earth shake, I am crazy waiting for the next."

"I know what you mean. I am feeling a bit crazed myself. I was afraid a while ago that I had lost my prayerbook, but it was here in my pocket all the while. Now it seems to have gone missing again. Tell me please if you think I am going mad."

"Sleep, David," he said. "I pray for you. Excuse me for mentioning, but I speak to Saint Joseph and the Blessed Virgin for help to you, if you don't mind."

David did not mind, but sleep refused to come. The drumming continued, and Nancy Cornwall's face rose before him in the dark. What would he say to her, how would he comfort her? He had assured her that God was watching over Richard. Had she taken that statement of ultimate faith as quite a different sort of promise? Had he failed them both? Then in a hideous procession came every sin he could remember having committed, beginning with a blueberry muffin stolen from the pantry in 1849. He had considered lying about that one, and did not only because he thought it beneath his infant dignity. He told himself now that pride, greed and lechery had filled his days since the days of his early youth. Thus, when a sharply punishing earthquake struck at 1:38 A.M. he was ready to believe that he deserved it.

The sound of this one approaching had been the most frightening part: a dark, muttering roar in the distance, then a powerful vibration in the air, as well as the ground, while it rushed closer. At the finish it sounded as if the earth were being torn apart and then liquefied, stone by stone, directly beneath them. He began to fear that a rush of blazing lava might erupt just there.

The Frenchman sat beside David, softly tumbling his beads. "How are you?" he asked. "Better now? Myself, I am worse."

"Worse. All my devils are marching tonight." The stars had vanished; the air had turned sultry and ominous. The drums were still beating in the camp below.

"Cher ami," said Pierre Armand, "You made angels to me one time on my ceiling. So beautiful! I thank you again. But where angels go, I think always come devils too. It is the way of the world, n'est-ce pas?"

"What do you do, as a Roman Catholic, when you are out here in the wilderness and cannot go to Confession?" David asked. Armand was silent for a moment, then gave a deep sigh, and replied, "You will forgive me for mentioning, my friend, but I think the Roman Catholic is the religion of civilization, the religion of city, town, village, and so on. Some time I say to my Bishop, this life of too much alone is not good for us, not good for Holy Mother Church. This place, I tell him, this place so waste and sauvage, it will make Protestants of us all."

David laughed heartily. "Well, you are forgiven. Any man who will ride 20 miles on a mule to bring me a valuable antique…"

"Unless we are saints, *bien sur.* There are saints among us, but I am not one of them. I lose the proprieties. I become the child. I complain, I am rude, I quarrel every day with *le bon Dieu, tête à tête.*"

"A savage land, you say – and terrible? Then you too are sometimes lonely and discouraged?"

"*Mais oui.* I am lonely, I am discouraged all the times, and I am sinful too. And to speak the truth, this too much earthquake and volcano make me lose the reason. I sometimes think the world will stop next time, as the 'prophet' say. Then I am nervous almost to insane."

"I don't care much for the tremors myself."

"But you have the courage, David, and you have the head that is hard like the mule. You are so English! I never like an

Englishman before. But for you, I make exception."

After this, the two men entered into conversation about the controversial question of priestly Confession and Absolution. During this discussion, two more violent earthquakes suggested to the men that their days, and indeed, their hours might be numbered. Under the circumstances, David gratefully confessed all the sins he could think of to his Catholic colleague, and Pierre Armand confessed to the Protestant a touching and rather surprising history of his own. The thorny question of Absolution still remained, and here the Anglican and Roman traditions even more strongly disagreed. However, by that time a large tree had fallen almost on top of the two men, and so they hastily forgave one another and decided to hope for the best.

When morning came at last, the earth was sublimely still under a sky that was rinsed in the first pale tints of a lime and silver dawn. This is the hour of love and mercy in the Islands; the world is renewed once more, fresh in its innocence as if each leaf and blossom had come moments ago from the hand of the Creator. This radiant time of beauty may linger for a silent hour or more in the wilderness places of Hawaii, as the sun rises majestically over ocean and shore, over mountains that loom to the sky, over grasslands and forests with hidden streams and waterfalls, and over beaches without a footprint in their sand.

Silence reigned now, even in the "prophet's" camp. The drumming had finally stopped and this was the last day: the time of utter destruction had arrived. Shafts of early sunlight had reached the top of the canvas tent, and illumined the transparent waters beyond. Either an angry Lord God Almighty would come now from the sea, and they would all die immediately – or else he would not, in which case, they would be obliged to go on living.

Nothing happened. Minutes went by, and then more minutes; still nothing at all. Finally there was a sound of murmuring in the camp, and the murmurs rose and grew louder, then louder still, culminating in wild, tormented howls that reverberated in the morning air. Then a single gunshot echoed in the hills. Soon it was followed by several more, and David leapt to his feet. He called for his horse, but Armand put a restraining hand on his arm and said, "No, no, David! When the posset come, then you go *la bas*. Not yet!"

He was right, of course. The Frenchman was tired to the bone, but he insisted on riding out to the western shore immediately to see whether his little church was still standing, and to bring what comfort he could to his miniscule congregation. He said that he would return with provisions the following day; in the meantime, David solemnly promised to wait, concealed among the branches of the fallen tree, for the sheriff and his men to arrive. Still, as he watched Pierre Armand ride away, David wondered sadly whether they would ever meet again.

*

One hour and then another went by. He shared the last of his mountain apples with Mr. Gray, and sprawled on his back gazing at the immense vault of heaven. There was neither a cloud nor a bird aloft, and the vast blue sky looked as innocent of meanness or malice as the visage of Richard Cornwall. He could hardly believe that his good friend and neighbor was gone, and he wondered whether Richard might be watching him now from the void above, rejoicing in his new capacity as pure spirit: Essence of Richard, healed, cleansed, unencumbered.

A silent quiver deep in the earth rocked him gently back and forth at 9:28 in the morning, but he wrote it down without paying it much attention, for by now he had remembered to open the mail he had brought with him. There was a letter from Scott, and he was stunned by the message he found inside. It was written on a scrap of paper, evidently torn from the back of a book, in a hand that was so cramped as to be nearly illegible:

Dear Old Comrade,

You'll be hearing that I am a rat and deserter. Truth is, there isn't enough money in the world to satisfy my accuser. He talks, + now it is all over Lahaina. My American neighbors are sneering openly, crazed with joy over one more blow to our sacred cause. For the sake of Ma Church + my own sanity I am resigning, leaving for England next week. Pray for me that I'll find some other way to serve. Something inside me is dying, or perhaps has died already – but I haven't forgotten what I owe you, and I never will.

God bless,

C.S.P. / Honolulu, 22 March

As he finished this, he heard another gunshot from the camp. Afterward, silence. On the trail from the north, no sign of anything stirring. He must wait! And now, Scotty gone too – and again, nothing he could do about it. Again, he must simply wait.

A soft breeze was stirring, and shadows lengthened over the mountain. Perhaps it was already raining up there: silver sheets of it falling, splashing into the steaming caldera. Fresh rivulets running on the ground, ferns and blossoms lifting their faces to the wet. Poor old Scotty. He was innocent, of course. And yet – and yet, for some reason, David suddenly imagined his friend barefoot, in his shirtsleeves, embracing a young Hawaiian girl: the same one who had been kneeling before the altar in Lahaina. She had said that her father was a good man – that he did not mean any harm. And now David heard gunfire yet again – five shots in the camp below, with a long pause between them, as if someone were firing with great deliberation, and then stopping to reload.

*

They came at last in the afternoon: more than a dozen men heavily armed on horseback, moving along the trail in a nimbus of yellow dust. He stood up, shouted and waved his arms, but no one saw him. A bloodbath, he thought, unless I am quick! For once he did not stop for the saddle, but leapt onto his horse and rode him straight downhill. It was a foolhardy thing to do in such terrain, but the trusty Gray did not fail him. Kevin Kildare was riding at the head of the column, and as soon as he saw David, he signaled a halt.

"A very good morning to you, Father," he said cheerfully. "And what do you say to all this?"

"I say it is afternoon," David replied, "They are all gone mad in there! They have killed Richard Cornwall, and I don't know how many others."

"Killed, did you say? Cornwall? He is dead?" Kildare was astonished.

"Yes, murdered. Slaughtered, with stones and a bullet. At least two days ago. And they refused to give me his body for burial."

Kildare looked at him in anguish, and David knew that he would never forgive himself. Indeed, the sheriff's next words were, "God forgive me! I should never have sent him down here alone."

"You had no reason to expect this."

Kildare crossed himself and said with deep sadness, "Ah, David, the good Lord keep him. Many a man will live and die before we see another fine as Richard Cornwall." David bowed his head, and could not speak.

But now Kildare became brisk. "You were in the camp, you say. What arms do they have? Did you see any old people, any women or children?" When he had heard David's story, he called his men to gather around him. They were all looking fit and grim-faced, more than ready for a battle. David told them what he knew, and added, "Please hold your fire if possible!" Then, riding five abreast, they moved forward, with all weapons at the ready except for the Frenchman's antique, that David had left in their hideaway on the hillside.

There was no guard at the entrance this time. David called out, first for Lorenzo Scuppers to show himself, and then for the people. Finally he called for Kimo Lopaka, but he was answered only by silence at first, and then by confused sounds in the distance. Kildare shouted that he was the sheriff of the district, with a large party of armed men. They were coming in! No one in the camp would be harmed if they put down their weapons and obeyed his orders. Then he lifted his hand, and on his signal the men of the posse all moved forward, three by three at first, then two by two, on the narrowing path toward the shore.

Great curling waves were thundering down in a haze of glittering spume, and then withdrawing. Nothing else moved; no human being was in sight, and the inner areas of the compound were apparently abandoned. Some of the huts had been taken down; their remnants lay on the sand, together with a hand-painted sign that David had not seen before, reading, *Come Jesus!* Empty barrels, tools and fishing nets were scattered about; faded clothing flapped idly on a sagging line between two trees. There was nothing to betray the nature of the camp to a casual observer; yet, to the initiated, there was a sense that something malignant had been there.

Then all at once they came upon one of the strangest sights that David had ever seen. Five bodies lay on the ground, four men and a woman holding hands in a circle, all quite dead and beginning to attract the notice of insects. All were decently clothed. None appeared to be bruised or mutilated. Apparently, each had died from a single gunshot wound at close quarters. Fragments of bone and flesh, pools and spatterings of blood lay here and there for yards around. There was no sign of struggle, and those who still had their faces looked remarkably serene.

Some of the men dismounted, and one was sick into the nearest barrel while the others looked away. David Wilkinson and Kevin Kildare walked together to the canvas tent. Both called again, but no one answered. Then, as they were about to enter the sanctum, several things happened at once. A ghastly howl arose from the water's edge, and when they looked in that direction, they could see an outrigger canoe being

327

launched, with considerable difficulty, into the surf. Several men of the posse ran that way, firing their weapons overhead. At the same time, David heard his name called from close by – *Pelekane!* He and the sheriff turned back as Kimo Lopaka and several other youths leapt at them from the shrubbery, shrieking like demons.

The two men were almost overcome before they could react. Kimo was wielding the same rifle that David had once emptied of its bullets. Kildare raised his pistol and took aim at the boy. There was no time for explanation; David reached forward and thrust the pistol aside, so that it discharged harmlessly. Kildare stared in astonishment while David made an awkward dive for Kimo, and managed to catch him by the knees. "You fool!" David was shouting as they went down together, with Kimo's comrades tumbling over them. He was trying to extract himself from the tangle when Kimo's rifle exploded just beside his ear. That temporarily deafened him, while putting a crease in his scalp that he did not notice until the following morning, when he tried to comb his hair.

At least one good thing came of all this immediately: they forgot their terror of the earthquakes. Kimo's comrades ran to the waterfront, where a violent struggle was taking place between the camp's inmates and members of the posse. Kildare took charge of the Lopaka boy himself, and bound him up with ankles together and wrists behind his back. In the meantime, David Wilkinson sat on the sand, contemplating the various woes and afflictions of mortality. He had imagined that Kimo's gun was still unloaded.

"Father Wilkinson," said the sheriff in his usual courtly way, "While I appreciate your moral intent, and the energetic style of your approach, would you kindly stay out of this from now on?" David said humbly that he would. Kimo lay face down beside him without making a sound while tears coursed down his cheeks. "No one will hurt you, Kimo," David told him. "Only be patient. And while you wait, you ought to think carefully about what you have done here, for I guarantee that you will have to answer for it."

As he finished speaking, there came a ferocious booming and roaring noise from directly underneath them, as if a great sea-monster had turned in its sleep and awakened in a rage. Lava rocks heaved by the shore, and the sand on all sides began to undulate wildly, so that strips and sheets of it were torn away by the wind. A moment later the ocean drew back rapidly from the beach by some 20 yards, leaving fish and crustaceans floundering, and carrying away with it three canoes, two of which had people in them.

Kimo began to shriek, "Pele! She is come! She is here! Help! Don't let me die." Beside him, David Wilkinson was consulting his watch and his diary. It was 4:43 P.M. and he decided to mark the tremor "M" for moderate. "Be quiet!" he told the boy. "You will only tire yourself with all that noise."

Half an hour later, twenty-six of the camp's inhabitants were roped together under the guns of the posse. None had been killed or badly injured, although some in a crazed state had run out to sea, trying to collect the stranded fish. Those people were brought back forcibly for their own safety. Of the three canoes, one had foundered and forced its passengers to swim ashore, while an empty one had floated away. But where was the third canoe, and where was the "prophet"?

Like water in a pail that is swung first this way and then that, the ocean soon came back to flood the beach. It ran quickly uphill a little distance, with people scattering before it, but harmed no one. At sunset, both the wind and the waves grew suddenly calm. David covered Richard Cornwall's earthly remains with the only decent bit of cloth he could find, which was Mr. Gray's blanket, and then searched the area without seeing any further signs of the "prophet." He did, however, find two more dead bodies, young Hawaiian women shot and tossed into the shrubbery. Both were exquisitely formed, and naked in their beauty as young goddesses.

As the sun dipped below the vast blue bulk of Mauna Loa, Kevin Kildare stood up on a stump and announced that a ship was on its way to receive the captives. They would be delivered to the Marshal in Honolulu, where they must face arraignment and trial for trespass, disturbance of the peace, assault and homicide. "Pele going get you!" one of the captives shrieked. "Pele going burn you alive!" said another. Ignoring this, Kildare said that they must build coffins in the morning for the eight people they had murdered. At this news came uproar, with each person claiming that his neighbor had done the killing, or else that the "prophet" had done it all. Kildare did not respond, but merely doffed his hat, looked carefully at the inside of it, then put it back onto his head and stalked away.

Following him David asked, "What happened to the third canoe?" Without slackening his pace, Kildare replied, "The bastard was in it, and he got away. Well, well, Lorenzo Scuppers! Quite a history there. I saw his record recently in Honolulu. His first arrest in these Islands was for larceny and fraud. He's fond of opium, it seems, and will do anything to get it. He was a salesman in those days, claiming to be a gentleman from New York. At his next arrest he was done up as a preacher, charming and respectable as you please. That time it was theft from the church treasury and corruption of the young. Unfortunately, they neglected to hang him then. I saw the maggoty son of Belial just now climbing into the third canoe with a sackful of loot. He's taken their money, of course, and any valuables. Tell me this, Father. Do you Anglicans believe in Old Harry and his lot ?"

"Oh yes," said David. "The Devil is part of our pantheon. However, in our day we speak more often of a *demonic influence* …" But Kildare interrupted. "I'll warrant you," said he, "this son of a bitch is a plain everyday devil of the old fashioned sort. He's clever, I grant you, but mark my words, I'll have him at the end of a rope one day."

"What happened after Mailelani caught him?"

"Oh, those fools in Honolulu! First he charmed the judge. Then he convinced his jailers that he belonged in the madhouse. Once there, he persuaded them that he was a sweet little old crock that wouldn't hurt a flea. So they took off his chains and he was over the wall and away before dinner."

36

A major eruption might happen at any moment, said Kevin Kildare, and the camp was directly in the path of a likely flow from Mauna Loa. Still, they must wait for the ship that would take their captives to Honolulu. The bodies of the slain had been wrapped in lengths of canvas cut from the tents, and they would be carried away at the same time for proper burial. There was no sleep that night; members of the posse paced about the campfire while the prisoners kept up a steady jibber-jabber of discontent; and the sheriff sat on a stone beside David Wilkinson with his pistol on his knees, indulging in a lengthy reminiscence about his boyhood running barefoot in the hills of Connemara.

As the night wore on, a shroud or pall descended upon the mountain, made of a dark substance that was denser than ordinary air. They could see no sign of flame within the pall, but shortly after midnight they began to notice a foul, metallic odor.

"Sulphur and brimstone, if I am not mistaken!" Kildare remarked, "the very scent of the devil himself." He bent down and began to untie Kimo's bonds.

"Why you do that?" the boy asked scornfully.

"We may be moving out quite suddenly," Kildare told him.

"If so, you'll need to walk – or to run, as the case may be."

"I know what happen now," said Kimo. "Pele come down, kill us all dead. Why did Prophet go way? He was afraid?"

"I expect so," said David. "He knows that he has lied, and cheated people."

"Yes," Kimo admitted. "But he didn't do all the killing. Only *Kanaka wahine*, two that were his wives."

"How gracious of him! Only killed his wives! Kimo, tell me if you know, how did Richard Cornwall die?"

"He come with paper say we trespass, say we must go. People throw stones at him, he fall down. Prophet say, kill, kill!"

"And then?"

His voice trembled, but he looked bravely at David Wilkinson and said, "I have the gun, I shoot Mr. Cornwall."

"I didn't hear that!" said Kildare instantly. "Come, up on your feet! That's the boy! How old are you, sonny?"

"Thirteen," said Kimo, looking quite a bit younger. The sheriff raised an eyebrow at the priest and walked quickly away. This, evidently, would be on David's plate.

"Listen to me, Kimo Lopaka," said David. "Every one of us may be dead by morning. It is not good to die without being at peace with your Maker. Are you ready to tell God that you are sorry, and ask forgiveness?"

The boy made a smart grimace and said, "Your God can make no peace to me, Pelekane. I never believe this one you teach. Prophet say different. Mr. Shadbolt say different too."

"How so?"

"Shadbolt say *Kanaka* people no good. Prophet say same. Hell and damnation coming down and all us bad folks going burn."

"Kimo, did no one ever tell you that God cares for you?"

"They come, they go," said Kimo. "First one Shadbolt missionary come here, say we bad, say he going save us. Then he go 'way. Then Great Prophet come, say we bad so he going save us. But now he gone, so we got nothing. Look up *mauka*! See! Pele coming down, so now, Pele going kill us all! What do

I know? What do I think? No matter what, nothing left for me. I only laugh! I laugh at you, Pelekane. I laugh at your Church. You English say God so nice, so kind. Maybe nice for you, have house, cattle, horse, plenty men go work for you. So maybe this God come after save me, then he see I am one bad *Kanaka*, so he put me down your kine hellfire. Your kine more bettah? Nice and cool? Plenty *aloha* down there? I don't think so. I live – I burn. I die – I burn. So who care?"

Angels and ministers of grace defend us! David thought. How could he reach the boy? Their time might be very short. Intellectual argument would not help, but perhaps he could appeal to Kimo with a story. And so, with the dark earth muttering around them and the reek of damnation in the air, he told the ancient tale of the Prodigal Son: that foolish youth who went away and wasted all his substance; yet his father forgave him, and ran to embrace him when he finally came home. "You must know, Kimo, that your own father, would welcome you in the same way. He is waiting for you even now, longing for you to come back. And that being so, can you believe that your Heavenly Father, who is so much greater than all of us, would turn you away and condemn you to everlasting suffering?" At this, he thought he saw a tear glittering in Kimo's eye, but he was mistaken.

"What I think? What I believe?" the boy said, "I tell you, this one *Kanaka* here never going believe anything – no, nothing – never again!" He meant it, and his eyes were shining, not with sympathy, but with the icy light of hatred and contempt. At the next moment, that light went out, and David saw before him only a stripling with the vacant, pitiless face of a man who has lived too long already, and has seen more than he can bear.

*

A little later it began to rain. There were a few light, preliminary showers, and then, at one o'clock in the morning, the heavens opened. Such a downpour had not been seen on the Kona Coast for more than a year. The quick and the dead, the just and the unjust were all drenched to the skin immediately, while the earth continued to heave and shudder beneath them: by noon the following day, David Wilkinson had recorded 30 distinct quakes in a period of 24 hours. Members of the posse had departed at dawn; the ship came in soon after, and left again as quickly as possible with its miserable cargo. David was alone once again on the shore, under a darkly threatening sky, with the flanks of Moana Loa above him hidden by clouds the color of rusted iron.

Through pelting rain he rode to the fallen tree on the hillside, hoping to find provisions there and a message from Pierre Armand, but there was no sign that his Catholic friend had returned to their bivouac. He retrieved his saddle, his saddlebags and the antique pistol, but thought it useless to leave a note for Armand in such weather, and turned toward home. His oiled-cloth coat had failed him by now, and his boots were a pair of saturated bogs. Yet he told himself not to mind – to be glad, in fact, since the long drought was broken at last. New life would come now to the thirsty land and all its creatures.

In less than a quarter of an hour he stopped to record a light tremor at 2:41 p.m., and then decided to change his mind and his direction. He could not bring himself to leave the area before looking further into the district of Ka'u. He was worried about the little Frenchman; Pierre Armand was not a man to break a promise. If he could look over the next valley but one, then he might have a glimpse of the little Catholic mission still standing.

Reining in his horse at the top of a rise a few miles farther on, he found spread beneath him a magnificent view of a long, gently sloping valley that held some of the richest pasture lands on the island. Large flocks and herds of livestock were quartered here in Wood Valley, cattle and sheep by the hundreds, and horses, too. Many of these animals were eagerly browsing now, despite the rain, while others stood patiently clustered under small groves of sheltering trees. It was a place of deep soil, and David knew that this made all the difference in Hawaii between an inhospitable environment and a land of plenty. The grass that grew here *(Cynidin dactylon)* was marvelously nourishing, prized by the natives as *manienie*, and when David saw it that day, after only a few hours of watering from heaven, it was already beginning to turn green. The idyllic scene below him included a scattering of herdsmen's huts among stands of breadfruit, bananas and coconut trees. An occasional hillock raised itself above the valley floor, crowned in green foliage, while a veil of transparent mist lay softly over all.

"Thanks be to God!" he cried aloud when he spied a small steeple rising at the farthest end of the valley. The handiwork of Fr. Pierre was not destroyed; the priest himself was almost certainly safe, and had merely been delayed for some good reason. He feasted his eyes in silence for a few more minutes, then turned his horse's head, saying, "Well done, old friend – and now we are on our way home!"

At the next moment, something happened that his mind failed at first to grasp. It began with a fearful sound, less like thunder than a tremendous explosion nearby, and continued with the sensation that a terrible accident was still taking place, or as if earth's inner works were in the grip of a wild convulsion. Something essential had been badly hurt, he thought, or else destroyed, in the workings of the planet.

In another moment he was hurled violently from his horse to the ground, which in itself was not so surprising as the discovery that Mr. Gray was also down, some distance from his rider. And now the calmest, most amiable of companions was seized by a fit of hysteria, shrieking and thrashing like a colt in a burning barn. David came to him as soon as he could, crawling along infant-fashion, grasping at stones and grasses all the way, but was not able to offer much comfort. There was no question of walking, or even of standing upright, in such chaos.

A blue cloud in a white sky loomed above them – dark blue cumulus, roiling, pulsing, electric. The sun was nowhere to be seen, but the rain had either stopped or else was falling upward. The ancient trees around them no longer swayed before they snapped, but simply exploded. The tumult increased to a deafening pitch, adding the cold, ghastly, factory-shriek of steel upon steel, and the grinding of iron gates and locks to its rhythmic roar. A vivid, scalding substance leapt all at once from a new crevasse nearby, filling the air with crimson and purple steam; with this came a powerfully repellent and nauseating stench, as if a tomb had opened and legions of the dead were coming forth.

When David Wilkinson presented a report about this event long afterward at the London Geological Society, he was asked whether he had thought at the time that the world was ending. He told them that he had not. It did occur to him, however, that the orderly revolution of the globe might have stopped somehow, and then suddenly reversed itself, with disastrous results. And later, as reason abandoned him to pure feeling, he sensed that the earth itself was in some terrible agony, casting off its own flesh and blood. However, there was not much time for contemplation under the circumstances. He prayed, of course, but at the height of his terror, he felt suddenly that God was not so much outside of him as inside, using his eyes to look out.

When the shaking had eased a little, he rose to his knees and leaned against the Curate's flank, for poor Mr. Gray had fallen into a trance and lay still now, evidently only partially conscious. David's hands were bruised and slippery with mud, for he had been clutching at the ground gibbering nonsense, like an ape-child clinging to its mother as she flings herself from tree to tree. Meantime, the boiling stream he had seen earlier had grown to a river, resembling nothing so much as the bright blood of a pierced aorta. The earth itself was bleeding, bleeding! A mortal wound had been opened somewhere deep within. Before his eyes the red river became a torrent, and then a mighty cataract, soaring high into the air and falling some 100 yards forward on the slope before meeting the ground again. He watched then as the cataract became a surging, steaming,

ever-widening flood of devastation that raced with unbelievable speed down the hill below him, and plunged, savage
and heedless, into the valley below. Speechless with horror, he
saw a river of death travel three miles in three minutes, to the
edge of the sea.

Then he thought of two words only: *Jesus wept.* Cattle and
horses, people, dwellings, goats, bullocks, trees, insects, grasses
– all things innocent, tender and aspiring that dwelled in that
beautiful valley were overcome by the boiling flood, choked
and scalded by it, drowned and embedded in it, utterly
destroyed. And in another instant, amid a tremendous, rising
tower of red and brazen gold, the torrent poured into the sea.

*

The man and his horse slept in fitful snatches through the
night that followed. When the sun rose the following morning
it looked to be flat, rather small, and made of metal: copper,
perhaps, or brass. The air was filled with a fine, scarlet dust,
and where the sea met the shore below, 1/8 of a mile or so of
it was filled with a ghastly, churning, blood-red foam. On the
valley floor there was no sign left of human habitation, and the
steeple of the little Catholic mission had vanished. Small green
hillocks here and there raised themselves from the flood with a
few animals moving slowly about on them, but David knew
they would not live long. There was no way for them to be
rescued, and in the heat and the fumes, without water to drink,
they would perish soon and painfully.

A great darkness had fallen upon him after the catastrophe,
so that David was for many hours unable to walk, and could
not see very well either. It was a physical shock to the muscles
and the nerves, he supposed, that had damaged both his bodily
strength and his eyesight. Fortunately, the worst of these
effects were temporary. Mr. Gray had lumbered to his feet
during the night, groaning and complaining, and turned out to
be physically unharmed but for some badly bruised fetlocks. At
first light they limped cautiously, side by side, through the

wreckage of the forest. Both of them desperately needed better air to breathe, and a drink of good water. In their stunned and grieving state these took a long time to find, while further disturbances of the earth – 36 in the next 24 hours – were almost unendurable.

It was not until the following afternoon that they made their way down at last to the stricken valley. Creeping as close to the scene of the catastrophe as they dared, they found no sign of any living creature. A pair of hawks, high above the devastation, drew random circles in the sky. Everyone, everything else was gone.

David bent down to touch the stuff of the disaster, which was still warm and malleable, then took some of it up in his hands, and found that it was something like ordinary mud. Later, no doubt, it would harden into something resembling sandstone or a poor grade of concrete; later still, it would disintegrate and disperse. He had guessed by now that it was not lava after all, for this had been a somewhat unusual volcanic event. Apparently, this rosy, gritty, powdery sort of dirt had been mixed in the depths of the earth with boiling water, and had then burst forth in an explosion that had torn off the side of the mountain. The worst of all the recent devastation had been caused, in fact, by a boiling flood of clay: stuff of Adam's birth, ground of all human life, sign and symbol of his own pedigree.

How many humans had died? He could not imagine. Several hundred cattle, the Honolulu newspapers said later, and "31 persons – all natives." *But what were their names, please?* Far across the steaming river at sunset, with a mile-wide swath of destruction between them, he saw several human figures far away on horseback, evidently surveying the scene. This told him that he and the faithful Curate were no longer alone with the disaster, and yet, across that trail of desolation, living creatures could not communicate.

So weak and miserable that day as to wonder whether he might be permanently crippled, David turned his thoughts once more to his church and his parishioners in Kona. He was extremely anxious to get back to them, and yet, at the only pace he could manage, it would be a very long journey indeed. Mr. Gray was in no condition to carry him; therefore he divided their gear into two parcels, and set about carrying one of them himself. Alas, the splendid antique pistol had to be abandoned, but he hid it well and promised himself to retrieve it someday. He could do nothing for Pierre Armand at present except to hope and pray for him. A few steps at a time, the two survivors began to make their way north again, and David wondered how they would stay alive. Hunger and thirst assailed them, and the air was foul with smoke and fumes. How could they continue to breathe it and survive?

They became nomads after that, wandering about like their most primitive ancestors, now up to the hills, now down to the sea again in search of life's necessities: air, water, food. They were often lost, sometimes for a day or more. They learned to breathe carefully, and to rest for a time after every effort at moving. They slept side by side, with David's head often pillowed on the horse's flanks. They ate seaweed, when they could find it. Now and then there were berries in the woods or edible shellfish on the black and rocky lava shores. Once they found bananas, and had a feast. When it rained, David collected water in his hat for Mr. Gray and sucked on wet leaves, or else on his own wet clothes. For thirst, it helped at times to keep a pebble in his mouth. He ate grass alongside Mr. Gray when there was nothing else.

The days and nights went by, sometimes too fast and sometimes too slowly for easy reckoning. David kept his mind somewhat in order by continuing to note each tremor and jolt of the earth in his diary. Still, it must be said that some things happened during that journey that he told later only to Fiona, since he did not expect anyone else to believe him.

Once, for example, when it seemed that they would die of thirst, David saw ahead of him the tall, striding figure of a woman, her long hair flying, her lithe young body surrounded with light. She vanished suddenly, and immediately after that he came upon an orange tree laden with young green fruit that turned golden-ripe as soon as he touched it. Another time, as he stood trembling and hungering by the sea, a great silver fish swam up to him and died on the sand at his feet, after asking in a calm, sweet voice to be eaten.

These, some would claim, were traditional Christian miracles of an ancient sort; others would call them the work of an even more ancient Goddess. Many, of course, would insist that they were merely illusions of a lunatic mind, the product of shock and hunger.

David Wilkinson decided in the end that such events were not his to judge, but rather to marvel at, and be thankful. Fiona said that it was definitely the work of Madame Pele.

To wonder at the inexplicable is perhaps the beginning of wisdom. As for the catastrophic earthquakes and eruptions during the weeks before, during and after April 2, 1868, their records are safely stored in archives of the Honolulu newspapers of the day, thanks to the observations of a meticulous Anglican clergyman. There also remains the historical fact, curiously enough, that a stream of fresh water began rather quickly to issue from the hideous wound in the mountainside. It had sprung out from the new crevasse, soon after the boiling mud-flow ended. According to reliable witnesses, the stream was clouded at first, amber in color, and steaming hot. It soon cleared, however, and when David Wilkinson left Hawaii for the last time several years later, the little rivulet was still flowing, quite cool by now, and mercifully refreshing. He saw it himself one day in June of 1872 as he rode to the bedside of a dying child, and drank from it gratefully, as did his old gray horse.

37

F. CAMERON: *Private*   *Honolulu, 28 March '68*

O God, what have I done? Burnt all my little drawings, every one!
Desperately sorry afterward, of course – but nothing had come out the way
I intended. Ran to Emma for scissors then, wanting to cut my hair off –
after it had grown so nicely! Wisdom prevailed – hers, that is.

30 March
   Emma's unhappiness has changed her. She moves more slowly,
deliberately & carries the hint now of a second chin. But oh, the eyes are
the same – yearning & sorrowing with the sort of dark, liquid brilliance
that cannot be caught by art. Waves of sadness pouring out – yet she is
perfect as ever, the perfect Lady, perfect Dowager Queen & finally looks
that part. Even the King fades before her – shifts & shuffles in her
presence like a schoolboy.
   Went with E. to her ladies' sewing circle today – made a botch of it.
The poor beggar who must wear that pair of drawers may wish that clothes
had never been invented. She was reading some of the politer psalms aloud
– but where in Scripture can I find the One who was there with me in the
pirate's lair? Much of the Bible is so dreadful that I can hardly bear it,
and as for church – horrors! I doubt they'd have me anyhow, esp. because I

refuse to call it a He or a She either – only a sort of blazing O at the back of my mind – the silent presence, the secret connection.

Emma frightened me today by saying – as if delivering it with silver tongs – "There is something you should know, dear, about David Wilkinson." Promised to tell me later – then over tea said only that I worry her, I am so thin and pale these days. Thought for a dreadful moment that she would tell me he's gone & married someone brown and fat. But then she handed me a newspaper cutting – amazing!!

A CALL FOR MR. WILKINSON

It was to be expected, we suppose, that the Anglican Bishop of Hawaii (now on holiday, as usual, in Europe) would continue to offend the citizens of Honolulu, even in absentia.

In the latest outrage, he has inflicted upon us a new "Dean" of his non-existent "Cathedral," whose views and practices are so extremely, elaborately Ritualistic and Romanist as to be illegal in the Church of England at home, and here, a public scandal.

Our question is this: What has become of the urgent message that was sent from our shores many months ago, to the ecclesiastical authorities in London? To our knowledge, it was signed by many of our leading citizens.

Dare we suggest, from our humble position here in the Mid-Pacific, that there is, in fact, a God west of Cape Horn? Have England and Lambeth Palace decided to ignore us entirely? Or is the new archbishop there uninformed, or does he not yet understand our situation? We have heard, and want to believe, better of him.

The substance of our message was that the Episcopacy of Bishop Albert Coldwell does injury to the sacred cause of Religion on these shores; that the Anglican Mission in a greatly simplified and purified form should instead be placed in the care of an appropriate minister.

We have named a sensible, moderate, highly respected clergyman, already well known and well liked in these

Islands. His name has not been mentioned heretofore in the public print; but the time has come for interested parties to declare that the man we desire to lead us is Mr. David Wilkinson of Grace Church in South Kona.

2 April

Flat on my face this afternoon as I was being blissfully mauled & pummeled, a most astonishing jolt! Followed by soft rumblings below – rather like casual household rearrangements. Just as we thought it must be over, a giant picked up the whole building & shook it gently sideways. My first earthquake – rather delightful!

3 April

Something strange is happening. The sun came up today like a great torch blazing, in a sky streaked with brilliant red! By noon we were all coughing in red dust, & everyone has a different idea about the source of it.

4 April

A ship in today with prisoners from Kona – tales of a riot & numerous earthquakes there last week. Then a whaler from Lahaina – the shock of 2 days ago was felt powerfully there. Must have been tremendous! The dust continues – blows this way & that – sticky stuff, falls on everything. When it's damp, as on perspiring skin, it turns almost to paint – hard to get off, then dries to something like clay.

5 April

We are going to Kona! A most terrible, horrifying disaster there & in Ka'u. The Eastern coast of the island inundated by tidal waves – many villages destroyed, many, many people dead. Louise de Varigny says King has met with Cabinet & it is decided – he'll go on a rescue mission. Some objected because of danger to His Maj, but Lot Kamehameha boldly insisted. My estimation of his character soars!

Emma everywhere today, with me & Keanani at her side loading baskets & calabashes w. medicine, money, clothing, food & supplies for the people over there. The de Varignys are both going over – also,

Monsignor Maigret, the R.C. man who has missionaries there. Now I must find a way to be on that ship.

20 April

No time, since I last wrote here – so I will recall it all as best I can. To begin, the voyage – in a chartered steamer w. the royal ensign at the mast. We plunged almost instantly into a chaos of heaving waters, darkness & smoke, volcanic cinders everywhere – could hardly see a thing. Mauna Loa evidently in full eruption & perhaps Kilauea too – lava pouring down. Off the coast of the stricken isle the 2nd afternoon, towering, billowing domes & plumes of darkness ahead – all shot through with bolts of blue lightning. How could anyone survive this?

For David, I was frightened more than I had ever been. The King stood beside me on the deck at his vigorous best – the Kamehamehas, it is said, never like to be idle. "Lady Fiona," said he, "Thank you for coming with us today. This is a great tragedy for my land and my people."

"How does your Majesty explain it? Is this all Pele's work?" He looked at me as if judging my weight & seriousness.

Charles de Varigny intervened, "We may be sure that the steadying presence of the King will more than counterbalance any superstitious pagan influence!"

But I had heard it whispered that Lot Kamehameha is extremely superstitious himself – has no use for Christianity, except in a political way. On important matters they say he regularly consults an old Hawaiian sorceress.

"I have seen the Goddess," I remarked to the King – who again made no reply, but moved toward me listening intently – as de Varigny, obviously miffed, moved away. I told the King then of the night I had spent on Kilauea – the splendid young woman who vanished – the crone who saved me – the white dog, the sacred berries and the rest.

"This is most unusual for a visitor to our land," he said. "In fact, my dear young lady, you have been fortunate – and I think, very likely for some special reason. What can that be?" Then he looked at me for a long moment, until I thought something invisible moved between us. It's strange – the more I think of D. the more I see other men differently. If the King had suddenly kissed me then, I would not have been either insulted or surprised. Still, I am glad he didn't.

We came in from the east — toward South Point the other side from David's church. There was no seaport left where it had always been — no pier, no shelter — nothing but broken cliffs & rocks. Every dwelling gone & coconut trees all smashed to bits by waves that must have been terrible. Twilight at 3 in the afternoon — a bubbling sea as if horror underneath. Things one did not want to see, in the water.

A bonfire was burning on the hill above & people gathered around it waving.

"Look!" said Louise de V. — the coconut telegraph, still working!" They had put bamboo stakes with banners on the beach, to show us the best way in. The King & I went in the first small boat — he lifted me out, into the water — then strode ashore. An old Hawaiian man came to him & bowed low — but Lot took the man in his arms & embraced him. No wonder his people love him! Then others came to kneel at his feet.

All Hawaiians here — & all so deeply shocked that there was almost no conversation. Few were badly injured, it seemed — though some were dressed in scraps & others, only in their dignity. Quickly, lumber was brought from the ship — the men put up a shed for supplies with amazing speed, then raised a tent for the King — who soon sat there with chair & table, lantern & a map. De Varigny said his Maj. was planning how best to give his own land away to those who had lost everything. My admiration grew & grew! I glimpsed him there later, the lantern shining upward on his face — this ugly, beautiful man — saw his great soul clearly at last & thought, Rembrandt could have caught that.

Monsignor Maigret was looking for a horse — Louise gathered the women to help her cut cloth & they all began sewing — I fled. Went among natives who were sitting on the ground or lying down, poured water for them, passed out food, cleaned & bandaged a few minor wounds, but could not think what else to do. Wanted rather desperately to hold & caress them — esp. the children — but since I am white & don't speak their language much beyond aloha & mahalo — was afraid to try. Then one very dark, gnarled old woman took both my hands & kissed them — at which, I wept — & she comforted me!

Next day, horses were found — Maigret departed — then Lot said that he & his men would go by ship to the next village. They would come back & fetch us in a few days, on the way to Kailua town. Both the de Varignys and their strong, helpful son were going inland — where people said a mountainside had been torn apart by boiling mud & they wanted to see it. Also, reports of a ruined village on the heights – with people there in the toils of a crazed "Prophet" of some sort. The man had just arrived there, but quickly took control – said they must obey him or they would not be "saved" – so they did not dare to come to us for help! Not even to their King! Chas de V. was furious – took a pistol with him – and said if he could find the scoundrel, he would arrest him on the spot.

So they all left, except 3 of the King's men, a few natives & myself – I had a horse by now & a plan of my own. Just as I was packing up the next morning – the sun had risen, though barely visible through smoke – I looked up and saw a very strange sight. Beyond the next point of land, billows of steam were rising – lava evidently falling into the sea. But silhouetted in front of it all was a very small man emerging – slowly walking toward us – leading a donkey, or a mule. It was a Biblical scene – even more so, when I saw that a woman was half reclining on the animal – and when they came closer, I saw that she was a young native girl.

"Bonjour, Madame," said the little man. "This young lady has trouble. Please, will you help?" Then he collapsed on the sand at my feet so suddenly that I thought his heart had stopped – but he had only fainted.

I helped the girl down – & seeing that she was, indeed, in trouble – tried to make her comfortable on my bedroll. After I had washed the man's face & given him water to drink, he whispered, "Enceinte – comprenez? Baby inside – coming out now. Where is the King? But you are here, thanks to le bon Dieu!"

So it was true, as I had thought – I felt my shoulders begin to shake – "But the King is gone, Monsieur – and Mme. de Varigny also – there are no women except – je suis seule! Alone! Je ne sais pas – I have no idea what to do! Is this your wife?"

"Mon Dieu!" said he, and closed his eyes – "Madame, I am a priest!" So there I was, alone with a half dozen men I did not know, on a narrow strip of beach – in the midst of a volcanic eruption – and a young girl, whose language I did not speak, was about to give birth! I went to the King's aides, who were standing about looking helpless – & shouted, "Make a fire! Quickly!" I was thinking – heat water, tear up sheets – what next? My brain refused to work, for I was already hearing my mother's screams & the sound of Papa's gun, echoing through the castle.

346

I cannot do this, I thought – God, forgive me, I will do all things in the world – anything, everything else – but this, I cannot. No, no, no! Help! I prayed as I had done on the pirate's ship, but this time, nothing happened.

The girl was gasping from time to time, but made no other sound. Sweat stood out on her forehead & I wiped it away – but she did not want to lie down any more – instead, got up & walked slowly around in circles, holding up her swollen belly in both hands. There were a few native men under the shed, still asleep. I ran to them – "Can you help? Look! A baby is coming – there is the mother – tell me, what does she need?" The two men sat up – looked impassively at the girl, then at me – & entered into a long, thoughtful conversation in Hawaiian.

"What are they saying?" I asked the Frenchman.

"Kalo lauloa and niu," he said. "This is the native way, for the birth. You scrape this two and mix with the pounded uhi, while you make prayer to the powers and spirits. Next you take the soft slime of the hau which is something I think like the Chinese hibiscus, and then –"

"Bloody hell! We have nothing like that here! What shall we do?"

"This is only for the pain," he said with a shrug – then took out a rosary and began plying his beads.

I walked with the girl, round and round – my arm around her – thinking, this at least I can do – but my teeth were chattering – I was shaking from head to foot – my head was in a vise & eyesight suddenly filled w. black spaces, pinwheels & jagged bolts of light. The headache would come soon, I knew, and I had no herbs with me. Someone stood before me then in the gloom & dazzle – the old crone I had not seen since she had embraced me. Both of her hands were filled w. morning-glory leaves – from the sort of vine that grows on the beach. Slowly, carefully, she counted out 12 leaves from her right hand to the girl, who took them and ate them immediately. They exchanged a few words I didn't understand – then the crone chewed another lot of 12 from her left hand. This she did not swallow, but spit into her palm – then lifting up the girl's gown, rubbed the green mess over the great, bare, pregnant belly,

After this, the girl knelt down on the sand with her knees apart & fell into seizures of hard labor. She gripped my wrists until they were numb – her eyes rolled back – sweat poured from her body. Still, she did not make a sound. The old crone was squatting behind her, moaning steadily – but holding her, bracing her, with surprisingly powerful hands.

I reached down, trying to draw my shawl underneath – to protect the baby – saw the swollen vulva, hideously stretched – palpitating, beginning to tear, blood & water spurting out with each convulsion. Suddenly could not help myself – let out a wail & began to sob uncontrollably. The crone shouted something at me, but I could not understand it.

"What does she say? Qu'est qu'elle dit?" I cried furiously to the little priest, who was still mumbling over his beads. He answered in French – said, would I kindly excuse him for mentioning it, but I was making a mess of things. There was a rule about such matters among Hawaiians – if in emergency, without proper medicine, someone else can take on the pain. But with all my woe and misery, I was interfering – because, I was not the one!

Still, I did not understand.

"Alors, voyez vous," he said – "this is not yours to take – it is already taken." The girl, he assured me, was hard at work, yes – but without suffering. The old crone was feeling it for her. They had made an agreement when they chewed the leaves together. I was only the attendant, the midwife's helper, in this. All I had to do was catch the baby when it came out.

At this pleasant thought I vomited, then felt better.

But the worst – most frightening part of all was yet to come. After what seemed like hours more of straining, w. fountains of blood – mucous – urine & feces all mixed together – a small, soggy head tried again & again to burst through. Then one last, monumental heave thrust a blue, slippery, wriggling fish into my hands – one that to my horror, I nearly dropped into the sand. But the strange little creature was all caught up round the neck – with a tight mess of umbilical cord – "Quick! Get me a knife!" I shouted. The priest leapt up & handed me his shaving knife from a small, ivory case. I got it open – managed to cut the cord in two or three places without committing another murder. The little fish began to gasp – then turned quite human – pink & brown & definitely alive – a boy.

The old crone came round, sucked the last of the mucous from his tiny face & spat it onto the sand. At this, he began to howl like a champion – the mother let out a great animal yell of triumph – then began laughing and screaming with joy. All the men were madly cheering, except for the little French priest who was crossing himself over and over again, with tears pouring down his face. I tore away part of my red paisley shawl to wrap the baby in – & a short time later the placenta slipped out quite easily. The old woman took it & chanted over it – something very solemn – as she placed it carefully in the fire.

38

The Hawaiians were chanting now – prayers, it seemed to be, or else thanksgivings. It was obvious that this baby would not belong only to the mother, but to the whole clan. Even the King's aides, who were mostly native, joined in. It was late in the day now, with a dark red glow on the horizon. The earth gave a lurch & a quiver beneath us – but I scarcely noticed it. Less than a mile away, torrents of red & purple steam were rising with a terrific rush & roar – but after this, I thought that nothing could frighten me ever again.

At the water's edge the gnarled old woman lifted the baby in a grand ritual gesture as she sang the same word over and over again: "Hokule'a!"

"Hokule'a!" said the French priest, approvingly. "Very good name – good for luck! She introduces now the child, you see – to the powers and the spirits – to the world!"

"Hokule'a?"

"Star of Gladness."

I felt like a star myself just then – soaring in gladness, lighter then air. "Who is the old woman?" I asked him. "Were they praying just now?"

"Bien sur, Madame," he said.

"But, to what god? Something pagan, I think – at least it didn't sound Christian to me. Do you mind? Does it disturb you?"

"Oh yes, Madame, oh yes. I am only a small human being, you see – so I am always troubling for my faith. But God does not worry, I assure

350

you. Le Grand Seigneur who rules over all the universe? Oh no – he is much too great for that!"

"And you aren't worrying for the natives – afraid for them, if they are doing things in the heathen way?"

"Oh yes, I trouble, I trouble. But one must not force these things. I speak for them each day to the Blessed Virgin, and she always understands." He asked my name then, and told me his – but I forgot it right away, so startled I was when he stared at me, repeating my name and then saying, quite suddenly, "God bless you my child!" – as if he knew me already, and cared for me.

"I'm sorry Father, I was terribly frightened, and I made an awful scene."

"Pas du tout!" he said, smiling sweetly. "I have done some time worse already, Mad'moiselle – much worse myself." Then he lay down peaceably on the sand & went to sleep.

*

The young mother's name was Mailelani – same as the one in David's village, though quite unlike. She was curled up contentedly now, calm and beautiful, half-asleep with her babe at the breast. The old, old woman was walking by herself – apparently deep in thought, at the edge of the sea – so I didn't like to intrude. I rinsed out the remainder of my shawl & spread it out to dry – thinking that I should give it to Mailelani before leaving. Perhaps she and her child might like to have some small – though worn & tattered – bit of Scotland in their lives.

At dawn I was soaring still, as if intoxicated – drunk & drenched with joy & thankfulness. Decided to ride west – around the southernmost point of the island – that ought to bring me to David's church & parsonage before very long. The haze in the air was thinner now – and a bit of breeze was blowing. A path soon appeared, going the right direction – & climbing nicely above the place where lava was pouring into the ocean. That bit had emerged quite near to the seaward cliff – and was now oozing & crunching along quite fast & purposefully – black w. red lights in it, till it came to the cliff & tumbled over. There it fell in clouds of steam to the crest of a little, smoking, cone-shaped hill that it was busy building in shallow water. Perhaps – I thought – at the very beginning, before there were any people – or plants, or animals– all the world had looked like this? Watching it I felt shy, like an intruder.

Rode on for a bit & then saw someone on the trail ahead – a bent old person leaning on a stick. A woman – perhaps the one who had helped with the birthing? I followed her, wanting to thank her for all she had done, but whether my horse was at a walk or a lope, somehow she always stayed ahead of me. At last – at a turning in the path – she disappeared & when I rounded the same corner, she was not there.

What I saw now was quite a different person. She was standing beside a small, green lagoon – an old fishpond, perhaps – back a little way from the sea. She was tall as I am, with a regal stance, wearing a long cape. Quite a distinguished look – neither old nor young, for her dark face was quite smooth & unwrinkled, though she had masses of long curling & shining silver hair. She was watching me calmly – I had dismounted & was tugging my horse along on a short rein. When I came nearer I said, "Aloha!" – & she did not answer, so I spoke again – "Can I help you?"

"What do you want of me, haole woman?" she asked in a rich, melodious voice – with an accent that did not sound Hawaiian.

"I thought you might want something," I said, feeling foolish. "Water – food – or help of some sort, since you are alone."

She studied my face, then said "It is you who are alone."

"Who are you?" I asked. She did not answer, but asked me instead, "What were you looking for in the garden?"

"In the garden? Oh – but that was long ago and far away, in Scotland."

"I know," she said. "Look at me! Now do you know who I am?"

She was not my mother – I knew that much. Then I remembered the night at Kilauea. And I looked at her again and told her, "Yes, and I owe you a great debt of gratitude! You saved my life, that terrible night on the mountain."

"Wrong!" said she. "That was not a terrible night. That was a beautiful night. And you owe me nothing. I do not keep accounts of that sort." She gave a little sigh of impatience then – & said "It is late now, Fiona Cameron. Tell me, will you be going back to find at long last what you have been looking for?"

"But that is impossible!"

"Nothing is impossible. You must only understand that the garden

belongs to you. The garden is yours, child, and everything in it is yours. That is what I have come here to tell you. Do you understand?"

"No, I am sorry – I don't," I said, close to tears.

"Never mind. You will when it is time. I must leave you now, but I am always nearby – especially when you do not know it." Then she held my hands in hers for a moment, smiling at me with great tenderness, before moving quickly away.

My horse had been fretful through all of this – and now bolted off with me as I was remounting. I lost a stirrup – fought to retrieve it & gather in the reins. By that time the strange woman was gone & I knew it would be useless to look for her again.

*

An hour later I was riding through a darker, more menacing landscape, with jagged tumbled rocks & twisted trees – like a place that the sun had never touched – or a dream from which one might never awaken. Still, for some reason, I did not feel much afraid. But oh, the agony of the land was all about me – destruction everywhere & patches where all had been burnt – smoke & fumes drifting, walls & fences down. The first house I came to had lost its chimney, and a stone wall had toppled over into its vegetable garden. No one was there. Nearby it, a small building where three trails crossed, its door bolted – windows shattered – tins & boxes inside, fallen from the shelves. A neatly painted sign in front said CORNWALL'S PLACE. No one was there either. Another farm also abandoned – chickens pecking in the dirt – a dark swale behind it, where the earth had been wrenched open. Quite a wide rift, but my dithering horse managed a small run & we leapt over it. I looked up then and glimpsed far above me a thin red line looking like satin –or a sort of spangled glitter – that came rapidly snaking, sizzling, down the mountainside – and that, I soon realized, was caused by trees catching fire ten or twenty at a time – each lot passing instant death down to others below them. Horrible! And yet I could not resist watching, it was so beautiful.

Familiar terrain began to appear now – the path to the seaside village, the cliff invisible in mist and smoke – but there was the little parsonage, still standing! Had it been moved? I thought so at first, remembering that it had been raised up on a sort of hillock near the church – but now there seemed to be a larger hill behind it – and he was not there, or anywhere near – where was he? By now I felt real terror at what might have happened to David.

But no, there was his church, evidently still intact – and touchingly forlorn – wild guava grown taller than before *&* on the front steps, a child's muddied cap – a gardening trowel with handle broken – a wet wicker basket with a few purplish, withering mountain apples inside. I took one *&* ate it, tho' it did not taste good. Then crept into the church, bumping against pews in the dark. Despite smoke in the air outside, the fragrance in there was still of safety, sanity, health – beeswax candles and rough-cut wood.

I closed the door quickly behind me and then knelt by the altar, leaned against it – tried for the longest time ever to make a proper prayer *&* failed entirely. I am simply not meant for this sort of thing. And yet, when I stood up to go out again, I felt something happen – a sudden, subtle, elliptical connection, a pale reflection of what happened when I begged for help in Borneo. Felt myself very strongly then as part of a closed loop – invisible, crackling, electric.

The dark hill behind the parsonage turned out to be another flow of lava that had come rather appallingly close – the distant parts of it still bejeweled, the nearer flows quite warm as human flesh. One of those had swerved away as if courteously just a few yards from the parsonage, on its way down to the sea.

The door to the little hut did not want to open – I persisted – stumbled over things on the floor – then found a lamp and oil to fill it. When I finally had some light I could see that David had been away for quite some time *&* the little house was badly shaken in his absence. Everything there was in a mess, most unlike him – and quite beyond me to sort *&* tidy.

A barrel outside was filled with rainwater, and so I stripped off my filthy garments *&* bathed myself with great pleasure *&* relief – listening all the while for horses, dogs, humans. None came. But David will come tonight, I thought – or else in the morning early. He will find me here – I'll be sleeping in his bed. No, not be sleeping – and not in his bed, either. That would be excessively bold.

I watered the horse, brought my bedroll inside – *&* promised myself to stay awake, for he might arrive when least expected. I will lie here quietly, I thought, on the floor that David made – & try to remember everything about the old woman – and once again I heard the King saying that I must be here in Hawaii for a reason.

What did it mean? Surely this woman was a Power, one of a benign and helpful sort. On the other side of the world I had heard of such beings – when I was a child, stories of a mysterious woman called Maeve or Morrigan, Bridget or Bride. She could work miracles, it was said, and often did. Those were my favorite stories – the thrilling tales I heard at night in the servants' hall. Uncle scorned them, of course – said such myths were only for peasants and little children.

But I was too tired to make better sense of it all, and so certain was I that David was on his way to me that I put the lantern on the windowsill to guide him – and then, just for a moment, closed my eyes.

39

One desperate afternoon while he was still lost on the slopes of Mauna Loa, David thought to search again at the very bottom of his saddlebags, in case there was any crumb or morsel of food left there. He found nothing to eat, but he did discover two damp and crumpled letters, both unread and forgotten since he had left the parsonage so long ago. One was written in the generous hand of his Uncle George Merryman, and the other came from some unknown person in Honolulu.

My Dear Davey, his uncle's letter began, and went on to say:

I trust this finds you safe and well, which is always our hope and prayer for you. Your Mama asks me to write this for her now while she recovers from recent events and so I deeply regret it is my solemn duty to tell you that your beloved father has left this world at 10 oclock in the evening of the 12th inst., most peacefully here at Green Gardens. He was taken ill of a sudden three weeks ago, and old Doc Witherspoon has come round either once or twice each day to care for him, as well as the nursing of your splendid Mother who was with him night and day and would not hear of leaving his side. Also you will like to know that the new vicar, a nice old chap from Leeds retired, brought the Sacraments and told us that he had never seen a person's mind better prepared.

When I came myself this week to bid the dear man goodbye, he was resting comfortably and said many times he was grateful for his long & happy life of 63 years, that you were his & Mother's chief delight and he had only one regret, namely not seeing you once more before that Heavenly Kingdom where we shall all meet again. I asked if there was any special message for you & he said no, only his love, for you are a good boy, in God's hands.

Gentleman to the last, when the angels came for him he asked them to wait while he thanked your Mother for all their years. Then he told her they were very close, and the brightness of their wings was 1,000 times greater than the sun, and after that he smiled & breathed his last.

Carriages have been coming up and down the drive all week with people wanting to bid him farewell and hear last words, and I reckon the church will be filled to the rafters and then some for the services tomorrow. Everyone loved Charles Wilkinson that ever met him. Only themselves will ever know how many he helped and comforted in their hour of need. Always in confidence, never said a word. Gentleman of the old school, that was your Papa. God rest his soul, I never knew a better man. Never fear for your Mama, she is strong. Elizabeth and I will stay as long as she wants, and I will see to the finances.

With most afft regards, deepest sympathy &c &c
   I remain as ever
    Yr. Loving Uncle, George Cecil Merryman
    Green Gardens, 14 January, 1868

After he had read this once, twice, and three times over, David dried his eyes and opened the second letter, too tired to weep more. This one was a haughty message of rage and scorn from a man he had never heard of, announcing his recent arrival to take charge as Dean of the Anglican Mission in Hawaii. "I am well acquainted with His Lordship Albert Coldwell," he wrote, "and it is beyond either his ability or mine to understand why you are still here in these Islands, when your Bishop desired your resignation nearly a year ago!"

According to this letter, David Wilkinson was unwanted, disobedient, insubordinate and ecclesiastically felonious in some unspecified way. In a furious postscript, threatening disciplinary action, the Dean ordered the Rev. Mr. Wilkinson to appear before him in Honolulu no later than a date that was already two weeks past.

After reading this letter, David began to laugh. Honolulu? Was there still a place by that name, or had it fallen by now into the sea? He had not seen the sun for so long that he could not tell east from west, north from south. All he knew now was uphill and downhill: *mauka* and *makai* – Hawaiian directions that made perfect sense, providing a man could still walk. He laughed and laughed more as he gazed around him at the smothering pall made up of cinders, dust, smoke and fumes from volcanic action on every side. According to his diary, it was now the 7th of April. Five days had gone by since the great explosion, and the earth still heaved and swayed beneath him so frequently that he could scarcely tell where one earthquake ended and the next began.

Later that same day he heard a sound like that of a great waterfall or else of heavy surf breaking on a nearby shore. Then he realized that trees and bushes were catching fire not far from him and saw the red glitter of lava oozing rapidly along the ground, heading for the sea. Following its course as closely as he dared, he came to a place where the flow turned away into a gully, and there a sudden breeze swept in, revealing a flat expanse of rough grass and thorny weeds just ahead of him. This area was already marked by earlier flows of lava that were just now drying and hardening. Several hillocks here and there rose above the black flood, crowned with trees whose leaves were dry and burned by the heat. On one of these mounds he thought he saw people – human figures moving about, waving, and perhaps crying out for help. Immediately after that they were obscured by smoke. Had he imagined it? No, he was certain now that he heard someone calling.

What was he to do? There was no question of taking Mr. Gray over such ground, so he left the faithful horse at the edge of the meadow, and instructed him to wait. The outer edge of the lava flow seemed firm enough to bear his weight, but he knew that the same might not be true of the deeper portions that must lie ahead. The people were now clearly waving and shouting to him: one tall and white-haired, and one small – a child. David cut a long, pointed stick to help him walk and to test the lava on his way. Then he gathered some of the meadow grasses that were still green and tied them in bundles under his feet for protection against the heat. Next, he took off his shirt and tied it around his nose and mouth as a shield against the fumes; and then he started to move cautiously toward the hillock.

His progress was slow at first, for after he had gone a little way, the lava crust began to buckle and sink a little more under each footstep, while the pointed stick came back to him with its tip red and smoking. At more than one thrust of his stick, the crust was broken away enough to reveal a fiercely hot, brilliant river of scarlet moving rapidly underneath. At the same time, sulphurous fumes threatened to overcome him, and his feet told him that his boots were being scorched. Now, in fact, David had to make a choice: either to go faster toward the hillock at greater risk of death in the blazing river, or else to go slower, at greater risk of destroying his lungs and his feet. He chose the faster method, and arrived safely in good time at the hillock. Still, he was not quite soon enough, for the white-haired old Hawaiian man tried to speak and then fell down dead. David could only close his eyes for him, and say a quick prayer; nothing more was possible under the circumstances.

His small companion turned out to be a two or three year old child who was still very much alive, a pretty little thing with fat, sturdy limbs, a mass of glossy black ringlets and great dark, shining eyes. She fought him vigorously, shrieking, coughing and pounding him with her small fists when he picked her up and held her. "Now then lass," he told her. "Tha's a feisty bit. Hush thyself, my dear, hush, I'm doin' the best I can." All the way back across that black and smoking river of death he prayed for her, soothed and petted her, and began to wonder whether he might keep her as his own – that is, if no one else should make a claim. Surely he might care for her as an *ohana* parent, since that was an old Hawaiian custom. As they reached safety the little girl stopped crying at last, and nestled against him with a soft little sigh of content, and choked on that little sigh, and died.

He broke down after that and howled like an animal, cursing his life and his fate, and he cursed Pele and all her works, and the heat and the fumes, and his thirst and his weakness, and the death of the child, and his good father's death, and the Anglican Church and the anger of the Dean and his Bishop's life of spiritual waste and selfish insolvency.

"But you did not curse God?" the Archbishop of Canterbury asked him when he heard a rather more polite version of this story many months later. This was Archibald Tait, and the two men were sitting in his office at Lambeth Palace together on a dreary November day, while gusts of sleet lashed at the window panes. David told him truthfully that he had not, for such a thought did not occur to him. Then he said in an offhand way that after all, God was in it too. Tait raised an eyebrow at this, and asked rather dryly, "Tell me now, Mr. Wilkinson, did Our Lord reveal his presence to you at that time?"

David thought and thought again before replying, "I am not sure, Your Grace." That won him an appreciative glance and a nod, as the Archbishop turned to another subject. The new chief prelate was not a man given either to mysticism or to personal disclosure. Yet he was no innocent, either, for he had lost five little daughters of his own.

*

Finally, on an evening not very different from the others, David looked down through a dark wood and saw a phantom floating in the air far below: a single window, softly lit. Suddenly, all that was strange in the landscape became familiar again: the Hawkins house was above him and his own must be hidden away below, where it was too dark to see. But now he knew at last that his church was still there. That hovering, flickering yellow lozenge was the twelve-paned window he had labored to fit above the altar on its eastern wall so long ago; and now it brought him lurching and sliding down a steep slope between trees, with Mr. Gray thrashing along behind him. Someone was in the church, for the door was ajar and a cluster of candles burned on the altar; and a moment later, Fiona was in his arms.

"You taste of fire and smoke," he told her.

"So do you" she said.

"Fiona Cameron! What in God's name are you doing here?"

"In God's name," she said, "I am guarding your church!"

"Water!" he croaked, and she quickly brought him a large bottle of it, and then poured more into a basin for the faithful Curate. "Poor thing!" she said, "Where is his blanket?" David decided to answer that question another time, and instead, lay down on the floor, closed his eyes and went instantly to sleep.

The next part of the evening was something he might have dreamed or imagined, except for Fiona's presence, and her assurances that it was all quite true. When he awakened after the better part of an hour, there was a feast prepared for him on the altar. Linen napkins were neatly folded beside a pair of china plates and crystal goblets. A silver platter held a whole roast chicken, and various baskets held mangos, apples and bananas, biscuits and pastries and a large loaf of bread. A bottle of fine French wine stood beside the goblets, and on the front pew, Fiona Cameron lay half asleep. What a woman! How on earth had she managed this?

But all he said was, "No doubt you forgot the bottle opener?"

"Certainly not!" She opened the wine expertly, and poured it. "But David, I am sorry, no forks or knives. We must manage without, and your hands need washing. Wait, I'll do it." She washed his hands and face for him, and gently applied a creamy lotion that must have been her own. Hawaii faded away, England vanished; he was a Prince of Egypt, or else a Turkish pasha, or an Oriental grandee.

"You have a cut there that bears watching," she murmured, stroking his brow.

Fiona, marry me! He wanted to say; instead of which he asked, "Where is your knife?"

Looking straight at him, she said coolly, "I left it in Borneo." After that, they tore the handsome fowl limb from limb and feasted. In a passion of joy and relief, David poured himself glass after glass of wine and devoured everything in sight. Fiona ate in her usual manner, neatly, quietly, steadily, with obvious enjoyment, and then rather abruptly stopped. He was looking at her, admiring the way her shining golden hair now fell straight to her shoulders, and thinking: *That head, that perfect head shall lie on my shoulder tonight.*

"David, something dreadful has happened," she was saying. "I have a confession to make. It is something that I have done, and I must tell you."

"Well, my love, it so happens that I have something to tell you, as well. Bad news has come from the Church in Honolulu. Very bad, but I refuse to think about it at the moment."

"But tell me, please. Not so bad as mine, I am sure. It couldn't be."

"I'm sure that it is."

But she said gravely, "David, it can't wait any longer. And I will understand if you never wish to speak to me again."

"Don't! Not now, Fiona!" He did not care what she had done; she was the love of his life; she had been his from the beginning. They were fated to be together for the rest of their lives, beginning tonight. The bottle was empty now, and he was embracing her, and searching for little buttons, when she took his hands in her own, kissed them, and held them firmly in her lap. He noticed then that she was wearing her emerald ring again, and heard her say, "…sorry I burned it down."

"My darling girl, burned what down?"

"Your house," she whispered.

"My house?"

"So careless of me, can you ever forgive me?

"Think nothing of it, my dear. What house was that?"

"Your parsonage."

"Oh my. Well, never mind."

"By mistake, of course."

"Of course." Both of them were still whispering. "You couldn't help it. I suppose you touched it – like this – and this – and then, it burst into flames."

"David, stop! I am afraid that you are not quite sober. Have you heard me? Do you understand?"

"Of course. My house is gone. All of it?"

"Yes."

"Everything in it as well?"

She nodded.

"And the bed," he mused. "And the chairs and the spoons and the spiders. And your own little looking glass! And the Pierpont teapot – but no, that was gone already. And the diabolical sewing machine?"

She nodded again.

He burst into laughter. "Bravo! Fiona, you are a wonder, you are a marvel! By heaven, you have done me the most enormous favor. This is perfect! Now everything is finished and done with. Gone. Everything. And for you and me, this is a glorious new beginning!"

"You are mad," said she, but without conviction. "Oh David, it was dark – terribly dark that night, so before I lay down, I put a lamp in the window for you – I knew you were coming, you see –"

"The Bridegroom cometh. But I didn't right away, and still you waited. This is all very Biblical, you know."

"And then there was another earthquake, after I thought they were all over –"

"And I thought all this time that you were safely in Honolulu."

"No, I came here, and I was in your little house where I had no right to be –"

"No right? Not so. But you fell asleep. Well, of course! And the lamp fell down, and the house caught fire. Why not? Perfectly logical sequence of events."

"There was nothing I could do," she said. "When I opened my eyes, it was already too late. I had to leap from the window. The flames were enormous – and before that, I had been so deeply, deeply asleep – dreaming – dreaming I don't know what." She shivered. "So many strange things have happened."

"Yes indeed," said David wisely. "All very strange. Too bad, but never mind. Now we have one another, you and I. And that is all we have. And that is a very fine thing to have, and to celebrate. So come, let us finish the last of the wine and go for a little walk together under the stars. "

Of course the wine was gone, there was not a star to be seen at the time, and he was tottering as he spoke. In fact, a dark shadow descended upon his brain just then, and did not lift until the following morning, when he awoke and found himself on the floor again. This time he was lying under a blanket beside a woman who was wearing something soft and green. "Oh God, what have I done," he groaned, and struggled to his knees while Fiona – for of course, it was she – turned over and stretched like a cat.

"Good morning," she said calmly. "You were very extremely tired, and you drank nearly a whole bottle of wine, for which I do not blame you in the least. Then we talked for a bit and you fell asleep in my lap."

"And that was all?"

"Nothing else worth mentioning," she said with a small, private smile. "But I must say you are very heavy to move."

"I am the world's worst fool. Where is my shirt?"

"You tore it off, I think, and threw it somewhere during your sermon on Heavenly Love."

"Fiona, I am deeply sorry and utterly ashamed."

"Actually, it wasn't at all bad," she said, "as sermons go. Quite a lot about the theology of Incarnation, which has always rather interested me. But look, David this is not our blanket. Where did it come from? What mark is that?"

He looked again at the blanket and found an embroidered

crown, and some words in Hawaiian. It was the royal seal.

"Oh, I see!" said Fiona laughing gaily. "The King has stopped by! How nice of him to tuck us in."

*

This incident made a curious little tale that came back several times to David in Honolulu later. Still, neither his own name nor Fiona Cameron's was ever attached to it, and this, he thought, said something significant about the King.

It seems that Lot Kamehameha had been on his way from *Kihapai O Ekena* back to his rescue ship quite late one night. Although the little Anglican church was dark as he passed by, His Majesty noticed horses tethered and grazing there, and so he took a lantern and went in. To his surprise, he found a pair of lovers sound asleep under the Cross, as if offering themselves up in a gesture of pious devotion. As to clothing they were decent enough, and they lay nestled together like a pair of matching spoons, or an old married couple innocently dreaming the night away. The lonely bachelor king was greatly moved by the sight and told his aides not to disturb them.

There was a chill in the air, and so he sent a man to fetch one of his own blankets. When it was brought, he drew near to cover the pair himself. At this moment he evidently recognized them and smiled, but did not divulge their names, either then or later. Instead, he raised his hand and gave the couple his royal blessing: a solemn *pule* in Hawaiian that is said to have been both pagan and Christian, calling for joy, peace and honor for all such devoted lovers in his realm. After this. Kamehameha V went quietly on his way down to the sea. This is a story that David treasured ever afterward, particularly because he found reason to believe that the King, at the time, was more than a little in love with Fiona.

40

He breakfasted on fruit, bread and remorse, while Fiona, in a tense, excited mood, tidied the church and tended the horses. Then she said there was something else that she must tell him now, for something "quite tremendous" had happened while he was away – in fact, something so astonishing that she did not know quite how to tell the story, and yet, he must hear it immediately. David, certain of nothing just then beyond the fact that he was still alive, asked humbly to hear it and sat at her feet as she prepared to speak.

She began with a nonchalant "Oh, by the way… our lovely feast of last evening came, not from guardian angels as you may have supposed, but from Maria Hawkins' kitchen." The Hawkins house, she said, had suffered little damage from the quakes, since – like Grace Church – it was flexible, being made of wood. They learned later that most of the stone buildings on this side of the island had been demolished.

"How is Maria?" he asked.

"Worried about you, but otherwise very well indeed – in the absence, that is, of her delightful husband. Quakes or no quakes, the terrified look is gone. She actually smiles now, and looks at people, and says what she wants to say."

"And the others? What of the village people?"

"David," she said. "Something has happened to them, and that is what I must tell you. How to begin? Well, let's see. All right, it was the middle of the night, two nights ago. And down in the village by the sea, the Hawaiians were all awake as usual – eating and drinking, talking and singing – and the little children, too. And they didn't know it – they had no way of knowing – but a terrible, terrible thing was about to happen. Because a massive, a truly tremendous tidal wave was coming in just then from the sea. It had started because of the earthquakes, and now it was moving very fast in their direction. A monstrous thing, coming in at a terrific speed, directly toward the village."

"What? A tidal wave? Where? When did this happen?"

"David, wait, I am telling you. It was the same night I burned your house down. Night before last. And the huge wave was on its way toward them, an enormous wall of water heaven only knows how high. But it was black as ink outside, so no one could see it coming. Every one of them would have died. But just before it reached the bay, someone in the village looked up and shouted FIRE! And then they all turned to look, and they saw at the top of the *pali* great flames leaping up into the sky – and clouds of bright red smoke – and someone cried out, 'Look! It is Pelekane's church! It is burning! Quick! Let us go and help him!' And then they all began running, running – away from the ocean and up the trail to the top of the cliff. And as fast as they could, they all came up here – every one of them – and then –"

"Fiona, is this true? Did this actually happen?"

"Yes, yes it happened, just as I am saying. They all came up here to help you save your church, simply because you are a good man and they love you. So that's how they themselves escaped. A whole village of people – safe now, and alive, who would have been killed, every single one."

"This is a miracle," said David.

"I don't know about miracles," she answered, "but I do know that something tremendously strange and beautiful has happened."

"Fiona. Look here, my lady, you are a heroine. By setting my miserable hut afire you have saved an entire village."

"No, no, no, no, no! It was you that saved them – don't you see? Because they care so much for you and they wanted to help. That was the only reason. And so it wasn't me, it was love that saved them."

"Then love is the marvel," he said. "love is the miracle."

"I am sure that it is."

"Yes. But I'll spare you further remarks just now on the Theology of Incarnation."

"Spare me or spare me not, sir, as you wish."

"But all of them got away, you say? And Harold Lopaka? And the children?"

"Yes, Harold is fine. All forty-two of them, safe and accounted for. As for the children, they led the way, scrambling up the hill. Except of course for the wee Chinese babe – he came up in his mother's arms. There's a little charmer! I held him and he laughed and kicked for joy and cooed at me. He loved the fire! Where, by the way, did he come from?"

"The Chinese baby? A long story I'll tell you another time."

"Well, it was a tremendous, unforgettable sight, you know – your poor little cottage roaring in the wind, exploding with huge flames and sparks flying up and walls pitching down like so much kindling. When they saw that it was the vicarage afire and not the church, they were terrified at first that you might be in there – but I told them, no. And they wanted so much to help, and so did I. But there was nothing – almost no water, no buckets or hoses – so we could do nothing at all. We just had to stand there and watch."

"Yes. Yes, I see. Of course. And the village itself, what happened there?"

"Completely destroyed. Demolished. Nothing is left at all. We heard it when the water came thundering in, a most terrifying sound. High as the tops of the palm trees it must have been, and smashed everything to bits – everything. Trees, houses, canoes – all that they owned, swept away to oblivion. The dogs are gone too, alas, and the chickens. Even the beach was taken – the sand and the shells and all the beautiful tide-pools."

"But the people were saved. Where are they now?"

"Up at the Hawkins house, camping on the lawn. They are already planning their next village. One somewhat farther from the sea, I trust."

"Fiona my dear, give me your hand," he said. She did, and he took it solemnly in his own two hands and kissed it.

*

He had been gone for so long by now, in such dangerous circumstances, that most of the people waiting at the Hawkins ranch had stopped expecting him, believing that he must have died. On their way up to the house Fiona said, "When they see you, they will all stand up and cheer!" But this did not happen; instead, they stared at him in astonishment mingled with fear, as if they thought he might be a ghost. The first to approach was the lovely Leilani, who touched his arm as if it might vanish at any moment, and whispered, "Pelekane?" Next, the youngest children came shrieking and climbing upon him as if he were a tree, while Harold Lopaka pounded him again and again on the back, shouting something triumphant in Hawaiian. Just then the earth gave another powerful jolt, shaking them all back and forth again, and everyone laughed. Everyone, that is, except Harold, who said, "Do not laugh at her, or you will be sorry!" And then, quietly to David, "Two days from now is Easter. You remember maybe? Or you forget?"

"Lost my mind for a time there," said David. "But here I am again, and we must have a celebration, yes?"

"Celebration, yes, truly so. Pelekane, this is very good that you come back now. So much is lost all around us. These folks here need the bread and the wine that bring us life. Will you give?"

David had been following the letter of ecclesiastical law thus far in his ministry, abstaining from Communion until a bishop should arrive to make the act official. Now he said, "Will I celebrate? Holy Communion? The Eucharist? Offer it to these people, who are not official members of our Church?" Little Noni was clinging to his knees now, and all eyes were upon him. The room grew very quiet as he continued. "This is not allowed, Harold, I am sorry to say. Members of the Anglican Church must be examined by the authorities and confirmed in their faith by a bishop before they may receive the holy sacraments. I am already in trouble with my superiors in the hierarchy – my bosses, that is to say. If I should do what you ask it is doubtful that I would be allowed to continue as a priest in the Church of England."

Here he paused, smiling down at Noni, then looked around the room and said, "Little children are not supposed to receive Holy Communion in my church either. Those are the Church of England rules. And now, what was the question again? Will I give Communion to those who desire it the day after tomorrow? My answer is yes, good people, of course I will. Young and old, every one of you will be more than welcome to receive. Come to Grace Church Sunday morning and we will give thanks together for the miracle that has spared you from the sea. I have always known that God loves you, and I am his servant, not your judge."

Nancy Cornwall came across the room to him then, with such pain in her eyes that tears arose in his own. "I am so sorry!" was all that he could say. "Richard was an extraordinary man, Nancy. I loved him, and I shall miss him all the days of my life."

*

Later that afternoon Fiona was in the kitchen beginning to sketch a regal portrait of Maria Hawkins in her crown of braids, when David came to join them. As the three chatted companionably, the room suddenly swayed, and pots began to dance on the stove. Then came a sound as if a dragon strode through the woods nearby, devouring rocks and trees. "*Pahoehoe!*" said Maria, and it was indeed the slick, viscous sort of lava that tends to move quite rapidly. "What shall we give her?" Maria asked. We have almost nothing left. But wait – there is some milk, and yesterday I made a cake." She looked at David Wilkinson and asked him shyly, "Shall I bring?" For a moment he wondered whether he might find himself involved in an antique pagan ceremony, propitiating the volcano goddess with food and drink. The thought made him smile, even in the midst of keen anxiety. Fiona stared furiously at the lava flow without uttering a word.

They ran to the terrace together and saw that this flow was moving rapidly toward Grace Church. *So now*, David was thinking, *it will be the long grass first – and then the shrubs – and finally, the church itself will explode in a fiery holocaust.* Yet to his surprise, he heard himself saying quite calmly, "If the church is destroyed, we must hold Easter services here in the garden. While we still have voices, we can raise them in song. We can still pray together. If we have no bread and no wine, we can celebrate our love for God and one another with cake and milk instead. We need not try to please the volcano goddess. She will do what she will do. The important thing is to know that the greatest God of all is with us here and now, suffering and rejoicing with us, and he cares for us, and he understands."

Amen, he thought, *so be it*. He was unspeakably weary, but he was still sentient, he was fed, and he was even rather strangely content. What he wanted just now more than anything else was a bath, a clean suit of clothes, and some time alone with the woman he loved. Before leaving Kona he would baptize the Chinese infant, and do what he could to comfort the bereaved. He would send messages to Pierre Armand; and he would remind Harold Lopaka of his duties as lay reader and prospective deacon in the Church. Last of all, on his knees, he would ask Fiona Cameron to marry him. She would say yes, and he would put her own emerald, for the time being, on the fourth finger of her left hand. Then he would go to Honolulu, submit himself to the authorities, and be sent back to England in disgrace.

He sat down now in the same chair where he had once found Fiona drawing his portrait, and closed his eyes. Despite pain, confusion and fatigue, the depth of his reverie grew deeper and finally dipped, not quite the full distance into sleep, but as far down as the private sanctuary where he abandoned reason, reclaimed forgotten dreams, and offered them up to the God whose face he did not know and might never see.

*

It was the beautiful Leilani, after a time, who ran to him first with the news that the lava flow had circled the hillock safely and then plunged away toward the sea. "Pelekane," she whispered, "I think the Goddess love you! Look how she save your church!"

He followed her to the edge of the garden and looked down the long slope below. The handsome little wooden building was apparently untouched. It had not caught fire, nor had the nearest shrubs and grasses. However, its hillock now stood between two tumultuous assaults of *pahoehoe*, one on either side. The charming little *kipuka* he had chosen for his home, his church and his ministry stood isolated now in the only remaining space between two deadly flows, the recent one still steaming. As he watched in weary numbness, he saw his heart's pride transformed into a ghost building on a dying island of temporary safety, and the island itself now threatening to vanish, as it appeared to lurch and quiver in volcanic heat. The latest assault of the volcano, as if deliberately, had made it certain that Grace Church would not serve as a gathering place for many years to come. By then, no doubt, the structure itself would have crumbled to dust. In fact, the work of his loving and hopeful hands was lost forever, marooned in the midst of a vast and glittering ebony sea.

BOOK FIVE: PALACE

41

L ondon: November, 1869. A fitful wind came in from the east, scattering the last of the autumn leaves across the footpaths in St. James' Park, casting foamy scuds of spindrift against the banks of the Thames, and driving pellets of icy rain against the leaded window-panes of Lambeth Palace, across the river from Westminster. Dusk was already descending at four o'clock in the afternoon, and within the relatively new domestic wing of the ancient building, Archbishop Archibald Campbell Tait was kneeling on a Persian carpet, trying to adjust a stubborn damper so that the fireplace would not smoke.

He was feeling poorly today, but that was not unusual. Ever since a violent attack of rheumatic fever twenty-one years earlier, he had suffered from annoying, occasionally crippling pains in his chest. In 1848 his life had hung in the balance; his colleagues had paced the courtyards of Rugby by the hour, listening for the bell that would toll their headmaster's death. Yet, wounded and flawed, canny, tenacious and determined as ever, he had survived.

Tait had been vigorously active in his younger days, but now he set about changing his way of life entirely. He decided to cultivate repose as if it were a garden for him to live in. He vowed that he would never worry about anything after midnight; that he would never run again, nor lift anything much heavier than a prayer book. And since he was a man of quiet disposition and resolute will, he never did. If he found himself at the bottom of a hill, he waited for a vehicle to come and carry him up. If he was late for a train, he deliberately missed it. By way of comforting others with similar afflictions, he often said "I have done the hardest work of my life since I have had an incurable heart disease." Firmness in self-management was the key to it.

Today, after grappling briefly with the rusted iron damper, he decided that this was unwise, and summoned his aide, who sent word in turn for assistance from below. The Archbishop spent the interval that followed studying materials from a file box labeled: *HAWAII (Sandwich Isles): Anglican Mission, 1860 – Present.*

Archibald Tait had been born in Edinburgh of Scots Presbyterian parents in 1811. Due to a congenital deformity of the feet, he spent his infant years wearing metal "training" shoes that were exquisitely painful. His mother died when he was three, and this was a desperate blow, but he learned in time to console himself with the love of a father, a brother, and an affectionate nurse. In the years that followed, he distinguished himself at the University of Glasgow, then at Balliol College, Oxford, where he won a First in Classics, was made Fellow, and in due time, entered the priesthood. After the headmastership at Rugby, where he was well liked despite his rather dull sermons, his star began to rise.

Tait was made Dean of Carlisle in 1849, and in 1856, Bishop of London. Finally, in 1868, he attained the highest office in the worldwide Anglican Church, as Archbishop of Canterbury. Those who envied him – and there were many – said that he would still be in Carlisle if it had not been for the intervention of the Queen. While mourning the death of her adored husband, Queen Victoria heard of Tait's anguish over the loss of his five little daughters, one after the other, from scarlet fever. She spoke to Lord Palmerston, who managed his appointment to the London See.

He did well in that demanding post, for Archibald Tait was a rare combination: a devout, deeply private man who was also a formidable politician. Throughout the turbulent ecclesiastical times of the mid-nineteenth century he served the Church with quiet brilliance as a peace-maker and reconciler of opposing forces, with the result that he made enemies for himself on all sides. Throughout those controversies there were many who forgot what Tait knew very well: that the Church of England's ultimate strength lay in its ability to embrace a wide variety of souls and several different styles of worship.

Today, he opened a file marked *Wilkinson, The Rev. David C.P.* just as a stout and rumpled, rather breathless janitor named Twigg was shown in, still buttoning up the jacket of his uniform. Tait was pleased, for this was one of his favorite members of staff. From time to time he invited Harry Twigg to take a seat in the office and deliver his own opinions on matters of Church and State. Twigg had never consented to sit down in the Archbishop's presence, but with encouragement, he was willing to speak his mind.

"If you have time, Mr. Twigg," said the Archbishop in his usual calm and courteous manner, "before you go, I should like to hear your thoughts on Hawaii – the Sandwich Isles, that is."

"I should of been called in sooner, Your Grace. Here's a nasty situation! I'll send up the boy to fetch these cinders double quick, else we'll be having a fire in the chimbley." Then, as he manipulated the damper, "The Sandwich Isles, is it? Oh well sir, I hear that's a terrible wicked place. You wasn't thinking of going out there, was you? Don't do it, Your Grace. If the lions and tigers don't devour you, they say the natives will. It's a bad lot, out there!"

"I see," said Tait. "But should we not try to improve these natives, try to make Christians out of them? The Americans have sent missionaries already, but I doubt their motives, as well as their religion."

"Let the Americans have it," the janitor replied. "'Tis no

place for civilized folk."

"But consider this argument," said the Archbishop. "If we have been endowed by God with greater blessings, and a purer, truer faith, and if we fail to share these benefits with men less fortunate, are we not seriously at fault?"

Harry Twigg settled thoughtfully back on his heels. "Well, since you put it that way, Your Grace, I'll admit it's a vexing question. But surely the Lord knew what he was doing when he made savages. So I ask myself, why did he put 'em over on t'other side of the world if he wanted us to mess with 'em? Why not just back off and let 'em be?"

"At risk of their immortal souls? And let <u>Satan</u> – and let <u>Death</u> have dominion over these poor, misguided folk?" At the mention of death the Archbishop's eyes began to flash, and his long, pale face looked very Scottish, and very Presbyterian.

"Well now," said Harry Twigg with great gentleness, thinking of the five little girls, "Well now, Your Grace, the Lord looks after his own, don't he? 'Deed he does, under the shadow of 'is wings. But what I mean to say is, you won't find me out there looking for trouble, seeing as I have got enough at home."

"Ah yes. Yes. And how is Mrs. Twigg? Any better?"

"The same, thank you. The same. And now, Your Grace, I'd better be leaving you in peace. I'll send the boy later and he'll finish up."

"Harry?"

"Yes, Your Grace."

"Your wife's Christian name is Nora, is it not?"

"Nora, yes Your Grace."

"Good. I have been praying for her."

*

David Wilkinson's dossier consisted of old school records, a small collection of letters, some cuttings from various journals and newspapers, and a few notes in the Archbishop's own austere, rigorously masculine hand. He began with the letters. Those from Lord Henry Chatham were quickly set aside; the man had no judgment. Despite the best of recommendations and an excellent family tree, Chatham had turned out to be a drunkard and a philanderer who had caused no end of embarrassment to the Church. The C.F. Truckle reports were far more reliable. In June, 1867 Truckle had written that David Wilkinson was *"able, independent, may cause trouble."* Tait began to skim now through material that was already underlined: *"Almost immediately upon arriving, Mr. W. had words with Bsp. Coldwell, evidently about his stipend. Contrary to Bsp's instructions, takes up with natives."* (Here, Tait drew a small, neat star.) *"Whilst building a church in South Kona, at his own expense"* (and another star.) *"Dines tête-a-tête with Queen Emma, who appears favorably inclined. Bsp is enraged by W's deportment, calls him an 'arrogant pup.' W's continuing friendship with Mr. Partridge perhaps ill-advised."* Here a note on the margin in the secretary's hand: *"See Partridge file on scandal, blackmail etc."* But Tait did not need to look at that; he remembered it.

A later message from Truckle mentioned David Wilkinson's good impression on the civic leaders of Honolulu and their desire to have him lead the Mission if the present Bishop were removed. Here Tait added another star, and began a small list for himself on the side. The young man's preaching, it seemed, was much admired – though not by C.F. Truckle who found it "emotional" and "bordering on the visionary." At this, the Archbishop sighed. While racked with fever during his worst illness, he had heard the wings of angels pulsing violently in the air around him, and he had been horrified. As he was drawn, willy-nilly into a hot white light, he had begged, "No visions, please! No visions!" What happened next he could never remember, but during his convalescence, his spiritual life had regained its customary balance and serenity. Christianity, to the Archbishop, was not merely the business of the Church; it was a steadily glowing force within, a calm assurance of the belief that had been with him since childhood: that the supernatural realm lay very close by, and yet would never violate or overwhelm him. The Archbishop winced at the thought of emotionalism; above all, he hated to see a man make a fool of himself over religion. Women were different, of course. His darling Catherine was a dreamer, a romantic, a mystic, and Tait fiercely and protectively loved his wife.

But back to Wilkinson, according to C.F. Truckle: "*Enclosed find W's reports on the great Haw'n quakes & eruptions, much admired when published in Honolulu newsp.*" To this, more clippings were attached, as well as a letter from a Hawaiian sheriff citing Wilkinson's courage during a row with some madman claiming to be a prophet, who was taking advantage of the natives. What concerned Truckle most was the indiscriminate character of Wilkinson's relationships. Among his friends and supporters were three Americans, including Charles Harris, the Attorney General who was clearly a leader in America's conspiracy to take over the islands. There was also a German physician named Hillebrand and a dubious French Catholic priest, one strongly suspected by his own people of having Unnatural Tendencies. In addition, "*W. seen several times with a Lady of uncertain age, Scottish, eccentric, wears trousers, travels under an assumed name.*"

My, my! thought the Archbishop. These modern women! The description reminded him of an alluring, red-haired cousin of his who went unchaperoned to Zanzibar and rode upon an elephant. Truckle's report concluded, "*3rd June 1868. Unconfirmed rumor of violent quarrel with the new Dean. Appearing despondent, W. left Hawaii today by steamer. Would not say whether dismissed or resigned.*" To this, a personal note from Truckle to the Archbishop was attached, still in its envelope that was marked MOST SECRET & CONFIDENTIAL. Tait opened it and read it for the second time:

Your Grace: The Americans continue to conspire toward possession of these Isles, pressing their men into high Gov't posts, not only Chas. Harris but many of their former missionaries. Meantime our unfortunate Bishop has aroused such anger & enmity that it is only the loyalty of Q. Emma & the good work of a man like Wilkinson that allows us to be tolerated at all. I must respectfully ask by whom might Mr. W. have been properly dismissed? There is no ecclesiastical authority here. Before His Lordship's latest departure, he refused to appoint a President for our Synod, thus by the statutes, we have no powers. Bsp. Coldwell does not answer his correspondence. At the moment, no one knows where he is. After stopping the larger part of our funds from reaching Hawaii, the Bsp then sequesters another part for building of the Cathedral, while his missionaries go hungry. It is common gossip here that the Bsp travels in luxury & the ornamental stone from England cost in excess of £4,000. Some of us, by God's mercy, have other means to survive, else we were beggars in the street & a scandal to the Church. Russell's health failing, he will soon be home after Riggs. That leaves only 3 of us, all quite new. The young Rev Peregrin White is reduced to running a dancing academy. Your kind generosity to me is ever deeply appreciated. With constant supplications for your Grace's continued health I remain your Grace's most humble, ob't etc etc. serv't. - C.F.T.

*

Well before the hour, the small brass carriage-clock on the mantelpiece chimed five times in rasping tones, reminding the Archbishop that it needed repair. This was his second year in the Palace, and he still had a sense that things in the dear old place were slightly askew. A fresh blaze flickered now among reddening coals, but it would be some time before the temperature of his private office improved. Still, Tait preferred to stay here for personal interviews like the next one, rather than repair to the grim Gothic and Jacobean formalities of the drawing room.

A small bit of paper slipped from the files as he put them aside, and fluttered toward the fireplace. Tait left his chair to retrieve it, and saw a few scribbled words: *The Bishop of Natal has been converted by the Zulus!* He was not amused. Some wag was commenting on a genuinely distressing situation. He had tried his best with Bishop Colenso of Natal, but the man was a dangerous nuisance, a loose cannon on deck. Colenso tolerated polygamy among his converts, he challenged the wording of the baptismal and confirmation rites, he publicly denied the truth of the Creation story and the entire Pentateuch. And all this, after finding himself unable to answer the questions of an intelligent Zulu to his own satisfaction! Tait tore the paper neatly into small pieces and consigned it to the fire. Just then there was a soft knock at the door, and the missionary from Hawaii was ushered in.

42

David Wilkinson was equally as tall as the Archbishop, with sun-darkened skin and powerful shoulders pressing against the seams of his shabby parson's jacket. There was a long pale scar on his face, suggesting that he might have been in a duel. His hair was black and apparently unvisited by any recent barber. This man, thought Tait, did not look either particularly young or particularly English. There was something bleak and feral about him, inappropriate to his years. A castaway from the Spanish Armada, or a Jew perhaps, had got into his family tree. His features were finely drawn, and he was immaculately clean-shaven, but the lower lip had a sensual look. Something alien and provocative had come into the room with him; and as this rather shockingly handsome young man looked him squarely in the eyes, Tait remembered with a pang that he himself had once dreamed of being a missionary.

"Your Grace!" his visitor said, with a quick, courteous bow. When bidden, he seated himself without hesitation. A small silence ensued.

The Archbishop cleared his throat and began by saying, "I understand, Mr. Wilkinson, that you have been hard at work in Hawaii."

There was no response, and so he continued, "I am also informed that you distinguished yourself at your missionary college, and that you spring from a fine old Yorkshire family."

The instant reply to this: "We fought for the Crown at Pontrefact!"

Tait suppressed a smile, for it had been said in a broad Yorkshire accent, with a quick lift of the chin that he remembered well from the days of his own youth.

"A splendid legacy," he said mildly, turning over the papers that remained on his desk.

"Aye, but we lost," said Wilkinson. He was looking now at the casement windows, that were beautifully glazed and adorned with multicolored coats-of-arms. The curtains should have been drawn, for it was quite dark outside; the aide had forgotten.

"There was honor in losing," said the Archbishop. "That was a cruel siege, as I recall. There was honor, and something of justice, on both sides. That is, of course, the tragedy of civil war. But tell me, if you will, your view of the present situation in Hawaii."

Wilkinson looked directly at him again, and almost said something, but then stopped, and was silent. The Archbishop had met many a missionary returning from the field, and they were all strange in some way. Still, thought Tait, he had never seen more anguish in any man's eyes.

"You may speak frankly here," said Tait. "You are quite safe, I assure you, in saying anything that needs to be said." But the young man known in Hawaii for his courage and eloquence had, apparently, nothing at all to say to his chief prelate at home. The Archbishop waited.

"Lamb's Harbor!" said his visitor at last.

"What's that? Oh – Lambeth. Yes, the word *beth* or *byd* meant *harbor* long ago. It's a fine old place. I hope you saw some of it on your way in. The gallery? The portraits? I am hoping to bring some small improvements to the chapel while I am here."

Wilkinson shifted about in the chair that was too small for

382

him, leaned forward, and remarked politely that he had met a previous Archbishop long ago at Canterbury. That would have been John Sumner, he supposed. His father, he said, had dearly loved Canterbury Cathedral. Never cared so much for York, although it was so much closer – and also beautiful. Why? Well, that was an old story. One of his father's mother's ancestors had his head put up on a pike there at York, looking out from the city walls while it rotted away. "Took quite a time," Wilkinson said. "People tend to remember that sort of thing." Then, to the Archbishop's surprise, the young man laughed.

Tait tried the subject of Hawaii again, and when nothing more was forthcoming, rang for tea. Then he pulled at the bell a second time: his signal for biscuits and jam. He had never met a returned foreign missionary who did not relish the sight of an English tea.

"Sustenance," he explained. "It will be along shortly."

"They have asked for bread," said Wilkinson in a low voice. "We have given them stones."

"Ah!" said the Archbishop. "The Hawaiians."

Wilkinson nodded, looking at him intently.

"Pray continue."

"A fortune for stones – thousands of pounds sterling to decorate a cathedral where, I fear, no one may ever wish to worship. What can I say? I tremble for their souls – the Hawaiians, that is. And for ours, since we have set them such a poor example."

"A poor example?"

"Our Hawaii mission is a failure, Your Grace. Worse than that, it is a disaster. I have nothing to say for myself, except that I was part of it."

"A disaster," the Archbishop said calmly.

"Yes. And we have had help in that. The Americans have been out there for two generations ahead of us. Many of them have meant well, I am sure. But the damage they have done may be irreparable. I have seen too much to believe otherwise."

"Can you be more specific?"

"Yes. For one example, the natives have lived well enough with their volcanoes for centuries, but during the latest eruptions, they were ready to believe that the world was ending, that this was Armageddon. The Americans have taken them part way there; a criminal mind did the rest. A man commonly known as the Mad Prophet, and yet they believed him."

"Then the American missionaries, in your opinion, are not to be admired?"

"Your Grace, I have thoroughly admired some of them as hardworking, courageous individuals. In the practical sense, they have done much for the Hawaiian people. But any man who takes his morals from the Old Testament, and his theology from the Book of Revelation, is in serious trouble if you ask me.

"Mmmm" said the Archbishop.

"Trouble," said Wilkinson. "And will lead others there. I have always suspected that a belief in mankind's hopeless depravity is one step from moral chaos. Now I have seen proof of it. Chaos, terror, brutality. Many deaths, the worst being the death of spirit in the young. But perhaps you have not heard about last year's earthquakes and eruptions in the Islands. They were unusually violent and prolonged."

"I have read your own reports, Mr. Wilkinson. They are admirable. Quite an astonishing piece of work, under the circumstances. A credit to you and a credit to the Church."

"You see the Honolulu newspapers?" Wilkinson was astonished.

Archbishop Tait paused for a moment, then said carefully, "Whatever pertains to the Church Abroad is seen in time, both by me and by the Bishop of London. But because of the rather special circumstances, I have also arranged for some private sources of information, there in Hawaii." David Wilkinson's reaction to this, thought Tait, would tell a tale about his character.

Nothing happened for a moment. Then a radiant smile

began to flood the young man's face, a smile that utterly transformed him. Joy, wonder and relief flowed from his eyes with such an extraordinarily beautiful effect that Tait thought: *The girls will be falling all over this one!*

"Thanks be to God!" Wilkinson was saying. He had sprung up from his chair. "There is so much I was not willing to say – not behind a man's back. But of course, you know it already!"

"And what might that be?"

"You know that the new Dean is a traitor to our cause, and you know that the Bishop of Hawaii is a liar and a fool!"

"Well now," said the Archbishop, "you may as well sit down again, Mr. Wilkinson. Here is our tea."

*

"Are you quite all right, Your Grace?" Only a few seconds could have elapsed since he had put his cup down rather unsteadily upon its saucer, but the lad from Hawaii was already hovering over him, looking stricken. "Of course I am all right," said Tait crossly. It was humiliating when these spells came over him, but mercifully, they were always brief. They had been speaking of Wilkinson's experiences during the great earthquakes, and then of his long, circuitous journey home. He had served for a time as rector of the Episcopal Church in San Francisco, and then had spent nearly a year in Ohio, or Iowa, or some such outlandish place, working as a carpenter!

"I was afraid," said Wilkinson, "that I had spoken too freely, and that had troubled you."

"Not so!" said the Archbishop. "I asked you to say what needed saying, and you did. Sit down and finish your tea. I have a question or two." He reached for his list and could not find it. "What was your argument with the Dean?" he asked as he searched, for he already knew the answer to this.

"Not precisely an argument, Your Grace. The Dean was angry because some people said that I should be leading the Mission instead of himself. He showed me a recent letter from Bishop Coldwell claiming that I had been sent away a full year earlier. Dismissed, it said, in 1867. The Bishop had written that he could not think why I was still in Hawaii. The Dean wanted to know what I was doing there."

"My goodness," said Tait. "Mr. Wilkinson, please have another scone if you like, and help yourself to butter."

"Are you sure that you don't – ?"

"Yes, yes. Only tea for me, at this time of the day. But had your bishop in fact dismissed you?"

"No, Your Grace. He sent me a foolish letter last year, which I thought best to ignore. I know the man. He was in a temper, dared me to leave, said that would prove me a traitor. If I had left then, he would have said that I deserted my post. In fact, I hear that he has been saying as much since his deputy sent me packing. I kept his letter, of course, but it was lost in the fire when my parsonage burned down."

"Ah," said the Archbishop, who was beginning to feel quite weary. "Yes, I understand what you are saying, and I find it distressing."

"Beyond all that, sir, there was a question of honor on the part of the Dean. To put it plainly, if I want a Roman Catholic service, then I may visit my Roman Catholic friends. I do not expect to find it in my own church, and I told him so."

"That was what you witnessed in our church in Honolulu? The Roman Mass?"

"Yes, sir. The whole Order of Service. It was not ours! I have brought you a copy of it." He reached into his pocket and handed a small booklet to Tait. The Archbishop had already received a copy of this publication six months earlier, but he took it without remark and asked, "You confronted the Dean about this matter?"

"Yes, Your Grace."

"And his response?"

"He flew into a rage. Claimed that Bishop Coldwell had given him explicit instructions that the Catholic service would be acceptable in Honolulu. Said that he and Coldwell are both members of a Society here in London that wants to bring the Anglican Church back to Rome, and they thought Hawaii was a good place to try it."

"Oh my," said the Archbishop. He was silent for a moment. "This is all very sad, Mr. Wilkinson. But we must be thinking now of what is best for the Church, and for the people in Hawaii who want and need us, even if they are only a few. Are you aware that the Dean has since resigned?"

"I heard such a thing, but did not know whether to believe it."

"Well, it is true. And the fact is that some people in Honolulu have asked us to send you along as their chaplain, and rector of the new cathedral. We have been looking into the matter. It seems that these are men of substance, quite serious in their intent. We are considering their request. But before acting in haste we should like to know more about you and your churchmanship. In particular, we need to know about your style of worship. This is evidently a controversial issue in the Islands, as it is indeed, alas, here at home."

"Do you mean that you are willing to consider – ? Are you saying that there is a chance that I might go back?" Wilkinson's face was aglow again, but Tait chose not to pursue that question, and silenced him with a gesture. "Style of worship," Wilkinson said. "The various arguments between High Church and Low, the Anglo-Catholics versus the Evangelicals?"

"It is the price we pay for freedom," said the Archbishop. "All this fuss."

"Why, I am neither, I suppose – though perhaps I am both. As for elaborate vestments, I have none; not only do I dislike them, but I cannot afford them. As for candles, I have always used them when I could get any. Quite frankly, I should sorely miss candles if Low Church prevailed. No incense for me, however; the fragrance of the Islands is sufficiently sacramental. My choir is not surpliced because, in the first place, we have no surplices, and in the second, there are times when we have no choir either. As for example when the coffee comes ripe. That is a very busy time in Kona. I wish you could see the coffee trees, Your Grace, when they are all in bloom. It is like the lightest of faerie snowfalls, with a most haunting, delicate perfume."

"I should like to visit Hawaii one day," said the Archbishop "and partake of the sacramental fragrance you describe. Have you a Prayer Book with you?"

"Yes, sir. Do you want it?"

"Read to me the beginning of the Preface, if you please."

Wilkinson opened his Prayer Book and read aloud: *It hath been the wisdom of the Church of England, ever since the first compiling of her Publick Liturgy, to keep the mean between the two extremes, of too much stiffness in refusing, and of too much easiness in admitting, any variation from it.* Shall I go on?"

"No, that will do. Only, keep it in mind. Your conscience, I take it, is quiet as to the Thirty-Nine Articles?"

"My conscience is never quiet."

"Mmmm. And as to the Doctrine of the Real Presence?"

After a pause, Wilkinson said, "A delicate matter, Your Grace. There language itself may be inadequate. I have some difficulties with it, and some questions."

"You are expected to have difficulties," said the Archbishop. "You are allowed to have questions. In our Church, we do not remove people's brains when we baptize them. How do you stand on Confession?"

"Confession is a private matter, in my view. I confess to my friends at times, but I know that I am lost unless God forgives me."

"And He will, and He does," said the Archbishop. "That is His gift to us, and that, in so many words, is the message of the New Testament. Take that gift and feed on it in your heart, and be thankful. Cultivate repose, Mr. Wilkinson – cultivate repose and you will live longer. I should like to see you here again in about a fortnight. My secretary will send word, so be sure he knows where to find you. Thank you for coming in. You have been most helpful."

He knew that he was being abrupt, but it had been a long afternoon, and in many ways a miserable one. He wanted a nap, he wanted to pray, he wanted to talk with Catherine. A small fox was beginning to gnaw at the hollow of his left shoulder: one of his old acquaintances, suddenly returned. He thought that he had better not stand up just now. "Mr. Sandford will show you out," he said.

But David Wilkinson was already standing, smiling at him again in that extraordinary way, as if his face were filled with light. For a dreadful moment The Archbishop imagined that the young man was actually going to kneel before him and ask a blessing. But instead, he bowed in a quick, courtly fashion and left the room without a word, quietly closing the door behind him.

Archibald Tait gazed into the fire that was now brilliantly glowing. The Honolulu debacle was too appalling to contemplate at the moment. He must write to Wilberforce, he must speak to the Bishop of London. That pathetic letter from poor Queen Emma must have an answer. It was all heartbreaking, yet he must not allow his heart to break. Work to do, work to do – quietly, quietly. *Lead kindly light. In Thee, O Lord have I put my trust. Cast me not away in the time of my age: forsake me not when my strength faileth me.*

He looked at his bookcase, and the treasured volumes that had always sustained him: Tertullian, Cyprian, St. John Chrystostom, Justin Martyr's <u>Apology</u>. There was Hooker's <u>Ecclesiastical Polity,</u> that had got him through many a bad night. There was Darwin, close beside one of Tait's own books: <u>The Harmony of Revelation and the Sciences</u>; there were the sermons of John Donne, and the elegant poetry of George Herbert. It had been said of Tait, he knew, that he "lacked poetry" but this was not true. In fact, he had even written some poetry himself. He was simply cautious about it, because he was so vividly, keenly aware of its power that amounted at times to wizardry. He marveled, for example, at what can be done by a man like Herbert with a few simple words:

Love bade me welcome; yet my soul drew back
Guilty of dust and sin.

But quick-eyed Love, observing me grow slack
From my first entrance in,
Drew nearer to me, sweetly questioning
If I lacked anything…

I shall go and find Catherine, he thought. I shall hear her sweet voice, and kiss her tenderly, and hold her in my arms all night, tonight. Yes, I shall do that. He left his desk without clearing it, and this for Tait was unusual. Then, as he was walking slowly down the corridor toward their private chambers, his heart seemed to throb suddenly against his throat, for he remembered when it was that he had last seen his remarkable red-haired cousin, that first of his many secret loves. In childish dreams he had often claimed her as his own. At one moment she had been a legend, riding an elephant in Zanzibar – and at the next, she was standing in the rain in Edinburgh, at the bottom of Prince's Street. He had been a boy or five or six at the time, still struggling with the agony of his feet. There she was, unexpectedly, and he was frantic with shame; someone was lifting him just then over a gushing culvert; he did not want her to see him being carried. Fascinating, frightening, outrageous creature, she had kissed him once on the lips! But she was standing that day under a bright blue umbrella, laughing aloud on Prince's Street – laughing in great ringing, chiming peals as the rain poured down – and she was leaning at the same time with her whole body against a tall, dark-haired, extraordinarily beautiful young man.

43

A pale blue envelope addressed to David Wilkinson had come to Lambeth Palace more than a year earlier, after traveling first from San Francisco back to Honolulu, and then to London in a packet for the Archbishop from the Hawaiian Queen. After that, no one had known where to send it. The Archbishop's aide, Mr. Sandford, gave it now to Wilkinson with his apologies. A second, smaller envelope was handed to him at the same time, but David only glanced quickly at that before putting it into his pocket. Then he stared as if transfixed at the handwriting on the blue envelope.

"Will you be walking back to the City, sir, in this weather?" Sandford inquired. They were standing just out of the wind and rain, at the entrance to the Palace. David asked quietly whether he might stay there for a few moments, to have a look at the long-delayed message. "Ah," thought Sandford, "a woman!" but curbing his curiosity, left the Archbishop's visitor on a bench inside the Guards' Room, under the eyes of Harry Twigg.

Then, by torchlight on a stormy evening in London, David read the only words he had received for the past eighteen months from Fiona Cameron:

11 May 1868
Honolulu Harbor

David – I am sorry, but I simply had to leave you when I did. I am going back to Scotland to begin my life anew. I cannot trust myself with you now – there must be some distance put between us, and I shall do it. You must sort out your own life while I try to do the same for mine.

In the meantime, there are things we must think about quite seriously, and decisions that must be made. For example, have I no right to give you a new suit of clothes, after so carelessly destroying all that you had? Can you accept nothing at all from me? Why should you decide that I want to "manage" you, simply because I allow myself the pleasure of giving you something you need? Any woman who thinks she will rule your life is far more a fool than I am. Let me assure you that such a project does not interest me in the least – I have enough trouble managing my own. Furthermore, were you not obliged by Christian courtesy to accept such an offering, if only for my sake? Have you forgotten how you sermonized over the fish I brought you from the Hawaiian village one day? How you said the Hwns understand Giving and Receiving as a sign of Grace? But in my case, no, it's a haughty imposition. Where I am concerned, you must demonstrate your male powers of independence I suppose – in other words, your damned pigheaded obstinacy when a woman tries to help. You would have reacted differently no doubt – had I been a native! It seems it is quite permissible for Emma's maids to look after you – I saw them washing those ragged clothes of yours! But then, they are no threat to your dignity, you are so far above them – Hah!

And furthermore – I am not through with you yet – there is precedence in that favorite book of yours. Let me ask you this! Did Adam and Eve insist on going forth from Eden in the same old tattered fig leaves – or did they gladly accept the new clothes God gave to them – all made with lovely fur! And by the way, why do you assume that God is a man? Have you never questioned that? It says that he made those garments himself. Sounds to me as if the Old Testament God is either a very clever woman or else a Chinese tailor, take your pick.

Yes I freely admit that I was distressed & may have made a disagreeable remark or two – but I hardly behaved as you said like a Medea – or was it a Medusa, with snakes in my hair. What a thought!

Simply by expressing a bit of displeasure, do I suddenly become a dragon in your eyes? I sometimes wonder – often wonder, in fact – what sort of women you have known before me. And I do most truly & sincerely hope they are all dead.

Ctd. 18ᵗʰ May, at sea.

Shall I ever send this? Yes, of course I must. In the first place I am incapable of staying angry for more than an hour at a time – it is simply not in my nature. One day you may like to remember that.

In the second, there are things you should know. Last week, the dinner party you refused and I attended – at the Palace, I met Theophilus Davies – a good man, I promise you, even if he is quite rich. Need I say, Achilles, that you were missed – sulking in your tent! There's a battle going on now, among the Powers and you are needed. Davies says the Church can send you away but it won't stick, not if the people here want you – and they do! These men can well afford to pay you directly, and they're more than willing – they simply refuse to give any more money to this awful Bishop and watch it disappear. Theo Davies holds the title now to that bit of land under your church, since William Green went bankrupt. Did you know that? It's clear that he wants to turn the land over to you – even though he will never give another sixpence or a square inch of soil to this corrupt administration!

Another thing, David – I am worried about Emma. She is near to despair over all the anger, malice and indignity in the Church. The new Dean may resign, she says – he is already so unpopular, brutally criticized. She does not care what his style of worship is, she likes him, and if truth be known, she quite likes the fancy dress, the genuflections, the Catholic Confessional, etc. She is so bereft, the Church is her whole life now – and she sees it crumbling before her eyes. Please comfort her if you can – she has been Mother, Sister, Friend to me & I know she is very fond of you.

Also – on my way to the ship I saw that miserable Truckle person snooping about the waterfront – you know, the soft, egg-shaped little man who used to hang like a watch-fob upon your Bishop – and I am convinced that he is some sort of spy. He looked me up and down in a curious manner and asked how you were. How dare he? I stared him down at my iciest and said not a word.

Another serious point of difficulty between us, David, I'm afraid is religion. When you began questioning me so closely the other day about mine – my family's, rather – no doubt you thought me careless or flippant in my response.

The truth is, this is a painful subject for me, one I cannot easily speak of.

However, I believe that I owe you an explanation – so here it is. For centuries we were all Roman Catholics, though I don't suppose there were many saints among us. Then my father killed himself in a crazed state, mad with grief. Mother had just died horribly in childbirth – he felt responsible – they were desperately in love. The priests told us Papa was going to Hell & refused to receive his body or bury him or hold any services. There were even remarks about how suicides ought to be buried at the crossroads – with a stake through the heart! That did it. We'll never go back. And that is why my darling Pa, a man who was Kindness and Chivalry itself, with a brilliant career ahead of him – is buried on our property with the dogs.

22 May: San Francisco

Which brings me to the worst of it. Having put 3,000 miles between us, I find courage at last to tell you what has been worrying me – to the point where I could think of little else for the past few weeks. And this is painful – but you may as well know the truth about me. In any case, you'll discover it sooner or later and it must be dealt with. The awkward, difficult, embarrassing fact is – David, I am very rich. Quite terribly, in fact. Not an Angela Burdett-Coutts – I won't be buying any gunboats for the White Rajahs this season! But enough, now that my Uncle is dead, so that I must face it and learn to cope. If you refuse any small gift or comfort that I may offer, even when I clearly owe it to you – then I am truly at a loss, and must assume that you will despise me for every bit that I own more than you. Even I didn't know how much it was, when we first met.

I had thought of appealing to you for the loan of your Uncle George, who sounds like a wizard, for management advice – but neglected to do that before leaving. In any case, here is my truth. There are investments, but they are entailed – not for me to control, only to use the income. So it's mainly a matter of a castle to get rid of – rather a large one, with an abandoned village beside it & an old marble quarry, some neglected farmland and forests badly tended in recent years. The castle was left to me alone, the rest to be divided. I said something rude to you once about my uncle – you looked shocked & must have wondered – having such a lovely one yourself. As trustee, mine supposedly managed everything for our benefit – that is, for my sister, brother and me. Actually, he stole as much as he dared & then committed the worst sin possible, by shipping our faithful crofters – tenants & friends for generations – off to Canada & bringing in sheep.

Still he was not satisfied but leased the forest, dwindling as it was, to English nouveaux riches – merchants & industrialists of the sort who like stalking about the woods in fancy dress, shooting birds by the thousands. One of those idiots, I imagine, will buy the castle outright & live happily ever after, playing at being Scottish nobility. What a gift your little Queen Victoria has been – with her Balmoral theatrics – to the pull-the-wool-over-your-eyes industry in my country! No self-respecting Scot would be caught dead hunting in such garb.

But you see, while Uncle was alive, I was the one trying to keep our substance intact. Beth married in Edinburgh, Hal ran off to Australia. There were papers Uncle wanted me to sign – & I had no power beyond the power of refusal, which I almost never dared to use. David, you would not have recognized me in those days, so subdued and secretive was I, hiding from life in every way possible. PERFECT MANNERS & PERFECT OBEDIENCE were Uncle's rules & I lived by them so literally that – in the end – I neither winced nor shed a tear while I watched him die with a fishbone in his throat. Just sat there at table, while he choked to death, politely pretending not to notice.

So I needed to shed somewhat more than a few names when I came to Hawaii, and I've done some of that. But the problem remains between us – for when it's all sorted out and I am free at last, I'll still be a heathen in your eyes, and a richer, more objectionable one than ever. These are the reasons why – despite our strong feelings for one another, which I am frank to acknowledge – I could not accept your proposal of marriage, as being unwise for us both. I shall always care for you David – I am certain of that – & it should be clear, from all I have confided here, that I count upon your friendship absolutely.

So now I'll sell what I can and give the rest away. Then I'll buy a really good horse – and after that, I'll learn how to paint with oils, for that is what I want more than anything. We'll meet again some day, I am sure – no doubt when we least expect it. This has been much too long – I am sorry. And so, goodnight. F.C.

25 May: San Francisco

This will leave by steamer tomorrow morning, so it should reach you quickly – but first I must say one more thing. You have given me so much, shown me so many kindnesses – and I haven't thanked you. I need to do that. And so let me thank you now with all my heart for everything – beginning with our first conversation on the ship, so strangely intimate – when I trusted you instantly, without knowing why. And for the way you came inquiring after my safety during the storm, yet never intruded. Also I recall with appreciation the fact that you did not scold me when I came to invade your tiny parsonage – and I thank you for protecting me at the mountain cabin, with the dear old German and his sugar bowl. And for the day when you made me laugh so, telling me about Boggards – then chased me like a Satyr through the garden. And yes, the night when we slept curled up together after you preached that splendid sermon that neither of us can remember – the one about Incarnation.

We were not really wicked, I think – just captured by the Spirit of those Isles – the beauty of the place, with the sense always of unknown forces – mysteries pressing against each present moment there. The King once told me that the true history of Hawaii has never been told & never will be – it is a secret reserved for the royal family. I can believe that. Oh, but the rest of us do hear things & see things in those Isles that connect us unexpectedly to the mysterious powers that are always at work in our lives. What would the scientists – what would Darwin say to that? I notice that many people are not too fond of Mr. Darwin. Still, I wouldn't mind being related to apes if everyone else was too – come now, good sir, would you?

You needn't answer that. But when I think of the beauty of it all – the sea, the forest, the high rainbow places where I've gone alone – the light on the snow in the mountains when the sun is just rising – Oh how I dread going back to the other world again, that dingy, mean place with all its grayness, hardness – & ugly facts to be faced about money – property – industry & power – people's fears & ailments – everyone pent up together, scarcely able to breathe!

But I expect to survive, and if I do it will be partly because I'll carry something of Hawaii with me always from now on, by way of an emblem, a touchstone – your best gift of all to me, although I never saw it. What I mean is the enchanted pool in the forest you told me about – the secret place with the waterfall, do you remember? Perfect for bathing in, you said – less than a day's ride away – and we'd be like children again, quite safe. Why did I not go there with you? It's hard for me to believe today that I was such a coward! But thank you, David – for that, and so much more. Au revoir, and aloha – Always, Fiona

When he had raced headlong through the letter David startled Harry Twigg by jumping suddenly to his feet with a loud exclamation in a strange foreign language. Then he clapped the astonished porter on the back and shook Twigg's hand as heartily as if they were the best of friends in the world, before striding hastily out into the dark.

44

The Reverend C. Scott Partridge was in the slums of East London that same night, working in his new capacity as a minister to child prostitutes. As David left Lambeth Palace, Scott was searching through dark, muddy streets near St. Paul's for a scrawny wretch known as Baby, who claimed that she had no other name, no family, and no idea how old she was. Six at most, Scotty had judged at first; with more experience in the district, he came to believe that she was more likely ten or eleven. The homeless poor of the East End were often so wizened and deformed by malnutrition and disease that they looked like a different species of human.

The child with no name had been approached many times by Father Scott, who belonged to the local Anglo-Catholic mission. Her grudging attention had been won by his gentleness, his patience, and the splendid sweets he brought to her from his home at Holland Park. She was an urgent case for rescue, with a rattle in her chest; and he knew that she had been trying recently to attach herself to the ranks of older prostitutes who worked the streets beside the Bank of England. Baby had come to the Mission a time or two, and liked it there, where she was fed, washed and treated with respect. Scott had explained to her that there were nursing

Sisters who would care for her at a pleasant home in the country where a far better life awaited her, if she would only trust him. He promised that he would take her there himself and see that she was taught the skills that would allow her to earn a decent living. The child had no means of support now, except to collect animals' excrement from the streets and sell it for a pittance to leather-workers, or else to service the toffs who came from the West End after dark. In her spare time, Baby was a pickpocket and a thief.

He found her in Cheapside just behind St. Paul's, yet nothing went forward as he had hoped. "Cor!" said Baby, "Go 'way, gov'nor! I tykes care of meself!" When he knelt down and took her by the hand, the miserable child yowled like an injured cat, then broke away from him and scampered off shrieking "Murther! Murther!" as she threw herself into the arms of a tall man walking toward them, carrying something like a sailor's bag.

"What? What is this?" cried the sailor, holding the child as if to shield her. Then, by the light of a nearby street-lamp, Scotty saw that this was no sailor – this was David Wilkinson!

"Wilks! Don't let her go!" he shouted. The child screamed louder, and began to kick and scratch like a small tiger, but David had heard him, and obeyed.

"Oh blessed sight!" cried Scott, as he reached the struggling pair. "But you're supposed to be in America!"

"I was looking for you," said David, calmly smiling. "Isn't your mission close by?"

"Look to your valuables first, old chum!" Scotty told him. David's watch had already been removed from his breast pocket and slipped into the grimy sack that Baby kept tied to her wrist. When the watch was taken from her, she began to shriek again.

"Stop that!" Scott told her. "Look here, this is a priest, he is a good man – this is my old friend Father David. Will you come with us now like a good girl and let us look after you?" The urchin's face turned up to them in a grotesque parody of a leer, and she said, "Oy! Look atter me, will ye? Ho, masters, I'll do the syme for you! Tell you wot, I'll do the bof of you, nice and easy, for a quid."

"What is she saying?" asked David in disbelief, although the lewdness of the message was clear enough. Baby circled the two men in her ragged shift, with her bony arms akimbo and her infant hips thrown forward in a wanton strut. "Oy, masters, y'won't find better! Look – no teef!" She opened her small filthy mouth, and stuck out a tiny purple tongue at them.

Scotty was incensed. He shouted at the child that God wouldn't stand for her wicked whoring, nor her thieving either. She must change her ways! She ought to come along quietly now to the Mission, and accept the help he offered, unless she wanted to die in a ditch some day and go to Hell. A small crowd of street-people had begun to gather, crawling out of the empty barrels and heaps of refuse where they had settled for the night. Inspired by this audience, Baby shrieked louder yet and hopped up and down in a high state of glee, mocking the two young men for their lack of intelligence and their absence of testicles.

Rubbish flew through the air; threats and insults were hurled, until a shoeless wreck of a man cried out that this was the "bloke from the bloody Mission! He means the girl no harm, 'e wants to 'elp her!" Baby herself, by this time, had vanished into the night.

"Well, David," said Scott. "Welcome to the Confraternity of the Blessed Virgin, now that you've met some of our charming parishioners."

*

They sat up together for the rest of that night in the Mission drinking tea, eating cheese and biscuits, hearing the street sounds – human quarrels, curses and laments, the squeak and gibber of marauding rats, an empty tin can skittering over the cobblestones – while they talked of all that had happened since their last meeting.

Since his return from Hawaii, Scott had lived for part of

each week in the palmy luxury of his parents' Georgian townhouse in the West End, at Holland Park. Artists, architects, poets, playwrights and relatively insignificant members of the nobility gathered here in a perpetual salon, where Scott appeared as a languidly amusing young man-about-town who refused to take anything seriously. It was a great source of entertainment for these visitors that Cornelia Partridge brought a parade of eligible young ladies before her son "Scotto Darling" with matrimony plainly in mind, and that he would have none of them.

Later in the week, Scotto Darling disappeared in the family carriage that brought him as far as the Bank of England on Threadneedle Street. From there he walked to work, past prostitutes who never failed to greet him with gross suggestions and raucous laughter, into a milling, shouting, thronging mass of street-people: costermongers, hucksters and hawkers, thieves, tramps, wharf-rats, vagrants and drunken idlers. *"Ho! Ho! Handsome cod!"* cried the vendor. *"Handsome turbot, best on the market, all alive! Alive! Alive O! This way to fine cock crabs, all alive, O! Come and see, gov'ner, you won't find better."* And then the antiphon, from across the street: *"Oy! Bottles and rags! Old chairs to mend!"* and *"This way, this way, cherries ripe, all o' the best, and rushes green, O!"* Fifteen minutes later he reached the mission of the Confraternity of the B.V.M., climbed steep wooden steps and let himself into the chapel that was over a fish-market, with corresponding sounds and odors.

Despite all the fragrance and uproar, the loft was a haven of peace, with its clean wooden floor, its makeshift altar and the fine embroidered altar-cloths, its heavy bronze Cross and candlesticks, and its crates to sit on, since there were never enough chairs. When he arrived, Scotty always began his tour of duty by kneeling before the Cross with a sense of physical relief, putting his burden down there, knowing that it would be carried for him until he could bear it again: the shame, the remorse, the misery. Even his doubts of Christianity were laid down here week after week, in solemn trust that they would be healed.

Some months earlier, Scott had heard Father Matthew Pearl, the director of the Mission, preaching at St. Paul's. A large part of his life had been surrendered on that day, for Scott had found a spiritual leader he could trust. Pearl was a brawny, vigorous, laughing man who loved the derelicts he had chosen to serve, and at the same time, took no nonsense from them. In the meantime, he was under constant attack for his style of worship, which was flamboyantly Anglo-Catholic– very nearly to the point of being illegal. If it had not been for the personal intervention of sympathetic Broad-Churchman Archbishop Tait, this priest might have been arrested long ago, and might even have been sent to jail. As it was, Pearl stubbornly persisted in the effort to save souls in his own way, in the bleakest, most dangerous parts of the city. He loved his work, and he would have walked through fire for his Archbishop.

When it came his turn to confide, David cheerfully admitted that he had been living hand-to-mouth in America for more than a year, and had come back to England again only this week. He had gone to Lambeth Palace to leave some papers off for the Archbishop, and to his great surprise, had been given an audience.

Why, Scott demanded, had he not come straight to Holland Park? Had he really been staying in a waterfront tavern that was filled, no doubt, with verminous whores and stinking sailors, four to a bed?

"It wasn't that bad," David replied. "I slept in a chair, and they gave us coffee and bread in the morning. All this for a shilling a week. But I am suddenly a rich man now, Scotty! I've just seen a saint called Archibald Tait. He fed me a sumptuous tea and wanted to know all about Hawaii. Never said a word about money. But had his aide slip me a note for £100 as I left, with the message that this is <u>part</u> of what I am owed by the Church!"

Scott, who was deep in thought, said off-handedly, "But you did receive what I sent you?"

"No," said David. "When was that?"

Scott groaned. "Oh, but I did! All that I owed you. But of course, it went to Kona, and you had already left. It's lost somewhere! It was a note I made out over a year ago, and I never looked to see if it had been drawn. Mea culpa, mea culpa, David. We are going to be at the door of the bank when it opens tomorrow morning, and I am going to reimburse you with interest."

"Interest! I am not a usurer!"

Scotty laughed. "Good old Wilks, you haven't changed a bit." He knew as he said it that this was untrue. David was as threadbare as Scott had ever seen him, but his physical presence was far more commanding than before. Scott had grown pale and stylishly plump, while his friend had changed from a lanky youth to a powerful, full grown man.

"A decent suit, if you please," said Scott, "must be your first chore. We'll stop at Regent Street on the way home. Cornelia would have the vapors over that one."

"Of course," said David humbly, "you are right. "Who is Cordelia?"

"Not Cordelia! Cornelia is my mother. You met her once at St. Columba's. Now that she's forty-five, she's decided to be young again. I warn you, she's concentrating on romance at the moment. She'll probably take one look at you and try to eat you alive. She's had four lovers already this year that we know of, two since Michaelmas. Well, David, that's London for you – at least, in their circles. Pa doesn't mind, he has his own little entertainments."

Scott's bitterness was so near the surface that he had set out deliberately to shock his old friend. But David did not offer sympathy, or make any comment on the morals of the senior Partridges; he simply said with a grave, appreciative smile, "And here you are, in the slums, trying to help these people. I am proud of you, Scotty."

*

The gray light of dawn was filtering through the fog, and

403

the wagon of an early coster-monger jolted through the street before their conversation lapsed. Scott dozed on a pew while David stretched out on the floor, knowing that sleep would not come to him. Fiona Cameron's name had not been mentioned, but her electric presence had been in the air throughout the night. He would find her, he thought, wherever she was, and he would woo her again, and this time he would win her.

A heavy step was heard now on the outside staircase, trudging slowly upward. Scott waked instantly and listened in alarm. "Something is wrong!" he whispered. A huge red-bearded man in clerical dress appeared in the doorway, filling it with his bulk, then dipped his head and moved into the room. With blinking, uncomprehending eyes, he stared first at Scotty, then at David, as he sat down heavily in the nearest chair.

"Matthew, what is it?" Scotty asked. "Are you hurt?"

"Cut to the bone," the priest said, breathing like a man mortally wounded. "And so are we all. My dear brothers in Christ, England is assaulted, the Church is mauled, felled and sundered. How do you do, young sir? You are welcome," he said, offering his hand to David, and then continuing without pause, "You haven't heard, then. It is our blessed Archbishop! The dear good man has suffered a paralytic seizure of the very most dangerous sort. He is in the jaws of death at this moment, not expected to live. We won't be reading Morning Prayer today, lads. We'll be offering up a Eucharist instead, for the life of Archibald Campbell Tait."

"But I saw him only hours ago!" David exclaimed.

"I have just spoken to my friend Harry Twigg," said Pearl, "who works at the Palace. The Archbishop fell unconscious in the upper corridor early last evening. Harry was called in at seven o'clock to carry him to his chamber. Mrs. Tait has been at the bedside all night. His physician is there, and two nurses. Poor Harry Twigg is beside himself; we must pray for him, too. And for Mrs. Tait. And for the Church and for our country, and for ourselves. God help us all! Well, come along lads, let's go to work!"

Matthew Pearl hauled himself to his feet, then flung an arm

around the shoulders of each of the two younger men as if they were all comrades in arms before a great battle. "Domine Deus, O Lord God of my salvation!" he cried. "Let my prayer come before Thee: incline thine ear to my cry, O Lord, deal not with us after our sins, neither reward us after our iniquities. Bring me my chausible and my stole, Scotty if you please. Prepare the altar and the elements. Come along, boys, we shall storm heaven today! We shall assault the parapets! We shall topple the towers! We shall tear down the gates! What did you say your name was, young man? Does that parson's suit of yours mean what I think it does? Well then, bless you – you have come at a good time! Join us now, please, you are needed. Come, son, will you vest?"

After the least hesitation, David said that he would, and a few moments later, for the first time in his life, found himself wearing silk. The service that followed at eight o'clock that morning, for a congregation of seventeen street-traders, laborers, vagrants and prostitutes had all the high drama that might have been expected on a feast day at a great cathedral. Unaccustomed as he was to such celebrations, David found himself deeply moved by the beauty and generosity of it,

"Well done, lads," Pearl said afterward. "Glory be to the Father, and to the Son, and to the Holy Ghost! Perhaps it is all to no avail, but I have seen too many miracles in my years not to believe in them."

"I have seen a few myself," said David.

"I am badly in need of one," said Scott. "Let's hope there's a small miracle waiting somewhere with my name on it."

Then, as the three clergymen walked out together into the swarming streets, they all thought at the same moment that they heard a costermonger far away, chanting *"Tait is alive, O Archibald Tait is alive, alive, alive Oho!"*

45

"Scotto Darling, how could you?" his mother asked, as soon as she had met David.

"What do you mean, the dreadful suit? We've stopped with Pa's tailor and he's already ticked up for two new ones."

"No dear idiot child," said Cornelia Partridge, patting cream onto her face and throat as she studied herself in her looking-glass. "I am speaking of temptation. You know my proclivities. When you said that David was coming, I thought you meant that horrid little boy who stole all the prizes at St. Columba's. Now you've brought me the young bronzed Hercules, instead."

"Good luck, chum," said her son.

She drew up her chin to inspect her profile in the glass. Cornelia was a beautiful woman, with classic features and radiant skin, looking far younger than her years. "Why do you suppose he is a clergyman, with a body like that? What a waste! I've never understood what turned you in that direction, either – except that you knew it would annoy me."

Scott said nothing, but only smiled.

"But I must say, David Wilkinson seems to lack ordinary conversation. He says almost nothing, and yet, when he does speak up, it is usually to say something peculiar. Whatever the topic, I mean – there it is."

"Well," said Scotty. "Yes dear. There it is."

She was smoothing her skin now with a swansdown puff, drawing the peach-colored satin negligee aside to powder as much of her bosom as she planned to reveal at dinner. "Cecily Bancroft will be here this evening," she told her son, "and I expect you to pay her a great deal of attention. She may not be pretty, but her father is rich as Croesus, and your bank account does not allow you to go on ignoring girls like Cecily."

"Actually," said Scott, "if the truth be known, I am thinking of joining the Cistercians."

"Don't be ridiculous. What ever would they want with you? We'll have a simple little supper in the garden room tonight – cold salmon, salad, strawberries and champagne. Do me up, will you darling?" She had dropped her negligee to the floor and now drew on a slender gown of scarlet silk, with small satin bows at the deep décolletage.

"Mother, don't wear that tonight," said Scott. "Please. It's degenerate. My God, you'll look like a hungry troll."

"I love you too, darling. That sweet little mouth of yours. Your Pa will be at his club again this evening. I shall entertain myself with David Wilkinson, and you may look after Cecily. By the way, you have been drinking far too much lately."

"Yes," said her son. "I know."

As it turned out, the garden room was chilly, the champagne was warm, the rich young heiress was disagreeable, and the dinner party, all in all, was a quiet disaster. Fortunately, Scott was able to collect some bits of dialogue from the evening to use later during his work as a successful London playwright, best known for amusing light comedies such as *The Primrose Path* and *God Forever Waiting*. Cornelia Partridge, feeling more and more irritable, suddenly remarked during dessert that Christianity was "a disgusting religion, when you consider that we all pretend to eat our God each Sunday." To this, David replied quite seriously, "But we are not pretending." There the conversation died for a rather long moment, and then David added – looking with solemn appreciation at Cornelia's bosom – "Surely you have fed an infant with your own body?" She looked at him through lowered lids and replied, "Certainly not! I have always left that revolting chore to a wet-nurse."

"Ah!" said David. "But God is not so fastidious."

*

It is true that the Archbishop was still alive, reduced to his primal essence, scarcely breathing and almost unable to move, lifting a lizard's eye from time to time with an expression that was fearless, primordial and strangely sardonic. If muscles had obeyed, it might have been a happy expression, for he knew that he was alive, and was glad of it, although rational thought had departed, along with the memory of prayers, daughters, wife, palaces and cathedrals, canons and theologies. The spark of consciousness that had remained overnight was nurtured during the early morning hours by an increasing sense that something extraordinarily good was happening: something that he would later describe to Catherine as the assurance of Divinity, the actual presence of Eternal Order Made Small, in the form of an angel sitting on a stone beside him. Hour after hour during the acute phase of his illness the angel was simply there, like a motionless flame, or the bud of a lily, sitting with folded wings quite still, watching over him. This figure, he knew, contained immense, controlled power; he had seen it before, but now it did not disturb him to have it so close by, for he knew this time that it was a real angel, and not a vision.

*

Two men met that morning on the steps of Lambeth Palace, each anxious for his own reasons to know whether or not the Archbishop would recover. The majestic Bishop Samuel Wilberforce was coming down from the domestic quarters just as the ruined Bishop Albert Coldwell was going up. Wilberforce was instantly furious. How dare the miserable

Bishop of Hawaii intrude at such a moment? The man had no sense of propriety whatever.

"Good morning, Bishop."

"Good morning, Bishop."

Wilberforce told his carriage to wait, and when Albert Coldwell had left his visiting card upstairs, the two met again in front of the Palace.

"You have not heard me, sir," said Wilberforce. "I have told you more than once that the Archbishop desires your immediate resignation."

Coldwell replied that he had expressed his <u>intention</u> of resigning half a year ago. But after all, he must know first that he would get another post of equal importance. Having traveled to South America recently, he had decided that he would like to be Bishop of that region. He had put the idea forward in London, without response. Also, he could not resign while his financial accounts were still being audited. He must be prepared, he said, to defend himself against scandalous accusations – some of which, to his great displeasure, were now appearing in the British press!

The fact that they were standing at that moment across the river from the Houses of Parliament may have helped to inspire Samuel Wilberforce's next remarks, for he raised his chin, tucked his thumbs into his waistcoat, stood well back, and delivered himself of the following: "You and I, sir, once discussed a plan: a great vision for the future of the Pacific Isles! It was our intention that our influence, and that of our enlightened religion, should flow easily and naturally from Hawaii, once it was well introduced, to all of the other islands and territories in that great sea; we believed that a firm establishment of our cause in that agreeable kingdom, with its sympathetic royal family, its cheerful, innocent natives, and the sublime beauties of its landscape and climate should be a relatively simple matter; that it should ensure to us a bastion of defense against the dangers and solicitations of Rome. As matters now stand, I have no hesitation in telling you, Bishop, that I am disappointed, grievously disappointed in your performance in Hawaii. A noble cause has been injured, perhaps fatally; a high and benevolent hope has been destroyed; and as a result, this nation of ours may never recover her rightful position in the Pacific!"

"Gracious!" said Coldwell. "There was nothing I could do. The Americans mean to take Hawaii for themselves."

*

Scott Partridge sat at the breakfast table, the morning after Cornelia's dinner party, looking very pale indeed and groaning from time to time, with a cold towel wrapped around his head. "Pack some country clothes!" David told him. "I am leaving for Yorkshire tomorrow, and you are coming with me!"

"Not now!" said Scott. "Can't possibly."

"Yes you can," David replied, "and you must. Tomorrow! With the life you lead here in London, you're in serious danger of growing old before your time. Come to *Green Gardens* and learn to be young again!"

Scott was still hesitant when the morning newspaper brought the news that Archbishop Tait, by the Grace of God, had survived. Not only that, but a full recovery was expected. There was another notice toward the back of the same paper: the London Geological Society had the honor to announce that it would present, at eight o'clock that evening, an address by Albert Coldwell, Bishop of Hawaii. His Lordship's subject would be a first-hand account of the recent earthquakes and volcanic disasters in those Islands.

"First hand!" Scott exclaimed. "Ho ho! We mustn't miss this!"

"Probably," said David slowly, "he got the information from the Honolulu newspapers. My own chronologies and descriptions were published there. The Archbishop told me he had seen them."

"Well then, *wiki-wiki!* Prepare your own address! We'll pop on over at eight o'clock and expose him!"

David smiled. "No need. I'm already writing my own report

for the Society. That should set things straight."

"But this is an outrage!"

"I know. But truth will out, sooner or later. It always does."

"Well, don't you want to go there tonight? Make an appearance? Confront him?"

"Frankly, old friend, I'd rather go home."

*

Curiosity won in the end. The two went that evening to the Geological Society, and arrived as the meeting was being transferred to a larger room, owing to the popularity of the subject. Upwards of forty scholarly gentlemen had gathered, on a rainy London night, to hear the thrilling tale of a Bishop's adventures in Paradise.

For the first few moments David failed to recognize his former prelate, for the man who stood uneasily before them now, fretting with his papers, seemed much smaller, thinner and a good deal older than he had remembered. Lord Hereford, President of the Society, called the meeting to order and opened the proceedings. He was proud, he said, and we must all feel proud, that this most interesting and important communication had been prepared by a Bishop of the Church. He need not say how valuable it was to receive such observations at first hand from our countrymen who so boldly explored distant parts! He knew, from certain unnamed connections, how worthily this courageous Bishop fulfilled the duties of his sacred office. It did honor to the British Government to have placed a man like Albert Coldwell in the position he now occupied!

After a round of polite applause, the Bishop rose to say that he felt it his sacred duty to convey such information to the renowned Geological Society, and that he was gratified to be introduced this evening by so distinguished a gentleman as Lord Hereford. After this he looked at no one, but put his head down and read rapidly from the papers in his hands, that trembled slightly as he spoke. All of his material had been taken directly from the pages of the *Honolulu Mercantile Gazette*, where it had appeared in April and May of 1868 over David Wilkinson's name.

When the speaker had finished, and after much enthusiastic applause, Lord Hereford announced that there would not be time for the usual questions and discussion period this evening, since the Bishop had an important engagement out of town. At this, the Rev. Scott Partridge leapt to his feet, demanding to be heard.

"No Scotty!" David was saying quietly. "Let it be!"

But Scott did not wait to be acknowledged; he spoke in a loud, clear voice directly to Coldwell. "My Lord Bishop, I believe that you owe it to this distinguished audience of scholars to disclose your source of information, since you yourself were not in Hawaii at the time!"

The room fell silent, and Lord Hereford turned a bewildered face to the Bishop. After a brief hesitation, Coldwell answered impatiently, "Why, that is easily enough explained. One of my clergymen, with his diary and his watch at his side, took notes on the nature and comparative violence of the shocks, and he also described some of the volcanic effusions."

Now the entire audience turned to stare at Scott Partridge, while David murmured, "Enough, Scotty, enough!" But Scott continued the confrontation. "And where is that clergyman now?" he asked. "Your Lordship, surely he should have public credit for keeping his wits about him in the midst of such peril, as for his patently obvious devotion to the scientific cause?" Whispering now began on every side.

Coldwell gave a little laugh and then said, after glancing disdainfully at Scott, "Actually the person in question would probably rather not be mentioned. The fact is, he abandoned his post and left Hawaii, very shortly after the eruptions." Then, smiling broadly as he looked around the room, he said, "It is not every man, after all, who has the stomach for this sort of thing. No, I shall not mention his name. And now, gentlemen, I regret that I must leave you."

David stood up, and a profound silence fell over the room as he said, "I am the man."

No one moved or spoke, while the dark-haired, dark-skinned priest with the scar on his face gazed at the Bishop of Hawaii.

"Why, Mr. Wilkinson," said Coldwell at last. "I didn't know. That is to say, I didn't expect to see you here." David made no response to this, but continued to look at Coldwell in the same intent way.

"Thank you gentlemen, thank you," said the President of the Society in the smooth, mellifluous manner for which he was famous. "And now it is my duty, if not my pleasure – never my pleasure – to inform you that this meeting is adjourned."

Still there was not a sound, and no one moved. "Just a moment if you please, sir," said a small, bespectacled man in rumpled tweeds. "I should like to ask whether this gentleman would care to make a statement. Mr. Wilkins, is it? After all, we are a Society dedicated to the discovery of Truth! And it is a matter of importance that the observer of scientific phenomena should be known and identified as such."

After a short silence, David said evenly, "You have heard what the Bishop said."

"Well, well!" said the Bishop. "And now I must depart!" Taking up his briefcase he hastily left the room, followed by Lord Hereford, scrupulous as ever in his role as host.

All eyes turned now to David Wilkinson, who remained standing, and looked at one member of the audience after another without saying anything more. A soft spate of murmuring quickly grew to a roar of general conversation until Scotty jumped to his feet again and called for quiet. "If my friend chooses not to speak for himself, then in the name of justice – in the name of common decency – I cannot remain silent. David Wilkinson did not abandon his post! No! And he is most assuredly no coward. He left Hawaii most unwillingly, after having recorded the information – after having written the very words you have just heard. They were published last

413

year in the Honolulu newspapers, where anyone could have seen them, copied them, and claimed them for his own. Anyone unscrupulous, that is." As the murmuring began again, Scotty raised his voice and finished by saying, "You should also know that Mr. Wilkinson is working even now on a far more extensive, descriptive and analytical report of the same phenomena, which he did, in fact, witness at first hand, despite grave personal danger. I shall urge him to give it, as soon as it is finished, to this Society."

All eyes were once again on David, who spoke at last, but only to say, "My friend is kind in recommending me. And now, gentlemen, I bid you goodnight, Come, Scott!" With that, the two young men departed.

Sir Charles Lyell was in the audience that evening: a giant among the scientists of his day, a friend of Darwin, and himself author most recently of *The Geological Evidence of the Antiquity of Man*. Sir Charles rose wearily now, shaking his great, silver, leonine head. After his cane was handed to him, he remarked to his companions that the influence of the Established Church upon the progress of science was no more benign this evening than usual.

Hear! Hear! said a few somber voices. Yet another, noisier group maintained that a clergyman had no business challenging his Bishop on any issue whatever, and that the work of a priest was the property of his superior, in any case.

To this an elderly clergyman, evidently of the Old School, responded vigorously, "Not done, old chap. Plagiarism! Church or no Church, simply not done."

That settled things for the time being, and the men began to disperse in an orderly fashion, except that the one in tweeds was heard to say, in passionate tones, "By God! I tell you, no coward would have stood up in front of us all and said, 'I am the man.'"

46

When he opened his eyes, a pool of sunlight lay shimmering on the wall across from his bed, and in the midst of it was a painting that David had never seen before: a view of the Alps, or the Welsh mountains, perhaps, in winter. Golden light fell slanting upon snow under a gold and peach-colored sky. It was a pretty thing, he thought, and on further inspection, something more than pretty; the old gilt frame did not do it justice. There was frost on the lawn at Green Gardens that morning, and at the top of his water-pitcher, a film of ice to break before he could wash.

His arrival the night before had been fortunate in its timing. Uncle George Merryman was leaving today for Australia to see about his investments in a mining town out there that was called, optimistically, "New Eden." Aunt Elizabeth, in a daring mood, had decided to go with him. They had both been expansive and affectionate as ever, while David's mother, a stranger for one brief moment, had given Scott Partridge a cordial welcome before turning, blinded by tears of joy, to embrace her son.

Scott was still asleep in his room across the hall when David went downstairs, so that he and his mother were alone over breakfast. "You look so well!" each said to the other at the same moment, and then both smiled contentedly. David had thought that her face was unchanged when he viewed it by lamplight , but in the morning brilliance he saw that the bones were shapely as ever, while the flesh had swelled and softened, so that it was riddled over now with fine lines, like the glaze on well-worn porcelain.

"Mother, the rubies," he said.

"The rubies?" she echoed him, smiling.

"Last night. You were wearing them. I was surprised."

"But it's Advent, dear. And your homecoming."

"Quite frankly," said David, "I had thought they were gone long ago. I believed all this time that you had sold them."

Katherine Wilkinson put her hand to her throat and gasped. "But how could you think – oh, Davey, how could you?"

"To help me with my church in Hawaii, I thought."

"Sold them? David, don't you know that I would never, ever do such a thing?"

He put his fork down and laughed. And laughed and laughed, until his mother's curiosity was almost more than she could bear. Then she actually saw her elegant, well-bred son wipe his eyes on a damask napkin.

"Where is your handkerchief?" she asked him crossly. But this only sent him into fresh fits of laughter, until he came around the table and kissed her, first on one cheek, then on the other. After that he held her head in his hands and looked down at her fondly, as if she were a hopelessly wayward child.

Katherine's cheeks flamed. She drew away from him and said, "Why, I never heard of such a thing! I told you that bit of paper came from a lucky investment with Uncle George. David Wilkinson! It's well over two hundred years we've had those rubies. If we all starve, I must keep them and pass them on some day to your bride!"

David went back to his porridge, his eggs, his bacon, his sausages, his jams and jellies, his scones and crumpets dripping in butter, and said that he didn't expect to starve in the near future. And he was glad to see that she had a cook in the kitchen again, and the hedges nicely trimmed, and the roof repaired.

"Yes, yes, but we must do something about Scotty," said Katherine, lowering her voice. "He is looking peaked. Is he a worrier? Yes? Oh dear, I believe he's been overindulging in spirits. He must have a physic while he is here. I shall put him on a regimen!"

"Mama, I was certain that you would."

"Honey and vinegar every morning," she said. "Plenty of fresh vegetables and fresh air. He must walk several hours each day, and take a glass of good Yorkshire ale with his dinner. Before he goes to bed at night I'll make him a nice warm syllabub."

"And what will you do for me?" asked her son. "Are you tired of me already?"

"Get along, you," said Katherine. "There's weeds in the garden waiting for you, and firewood to be split. And by the way, some very pretty young girls these days in the village!" She wanted to add, "Oh Davey, have you found anyone yet?" But just then, Scott came into the dining room, asking what all the merriment was about.

*

The new vicar was delighted to meet a pair of foreign missionaries, and quite disappointed to find that neither Mr. Partridge nor Mr. Wilkinson wanted to preach, or even to talk informally about his experiences in Hawaii. Yet both came to services regularly, assisting when needed, and their voices added a welcome measure of masculine ballast to the choir.

"Shall you be going back to the Islands?" Mr. Malvern asked one afternoon when he found David Wilkinson sitting, as he often did these days, alone in the church.

"That depends." David replied. "Just now I am waiting to hear from some people."

"People in Hawaii? Forgive me, but I was fond of your father – and he was so devoted to you. I hope the experience abroad has not been discouraging?"

David looked surprised, and considered this for a time. Then he said, "A wise old Hawaiian friend of mine used to say when he was troubled, 'I wait, I pray.' That is more or less what I am doing now – that is, when I am not busy writing a promised article."

"Oh, I see! You prefer not to speak of Hawaii at present because we shall see your impressions in print one day soon?"

"Interesting observation," said David. "Thank you, Mr. Malvern, you have been most helpful. But then, you always are."

"I hope so," said the vicar, and left as puzzled as before.

*

Once they were settled, Scott Partridge found that he was far more deeply tired than he had known. With his usual grace, he obeyed the commands of his hostess, and took to rambling the moors on his own each day while David worked at his desk. David and his mother visited together now in a newly intimate and congenial way, often chatting for an hour or more after breakfast while their visitor slept.

"Tell me," said David one day, "what was your connection with my former bishop Albert Coldwell?"

"Connection?" Katherine, wearing an apron, was on her knees with a dust-bonnet on her head as she polished the brass fender of the fireplace. "With Bishop Coldwell?"

"Yes. He told Scotty that you were the most beautiful woman he had ever met."

"Did he now?" said she. "No connection, none whatever. He came around for a bit, but your Grandpa Merryman soon sent him packing,."

"And why was that?"

"Well, my dear, it would have been impossible. Albert's family were not at all our sort. They were all in trade, you see. In any case, it wasn't me he wanted – it was position and pedigree."

When he had nothing to say to this, she added, "I know what you're thinking. But there are people in every social class who are natural aristocrats, and little Bertie Coldwell was not one of them."

*

That afternoon, when David carried in the firewood, he found her studying the tea leaves in the bottom of a Canton china cup. "I'm reading your fortune," she said, "and I am beginning to think you have found someone. I mean, someone lovely, someone really right for you." She gazed up at him wistfully.

"Yes," he said. "I have found her. And lost her again, but I think only temporarily. I've written to a friend in Hawaii who will know where she is, and I am waiting for an answer."

Katherine bit her lip for a moment before smiling bravely and saying in an inordinately bright, cheerful way, "Oh! I see! Then, she is Hawaiian?"

David could not help laughing. "No, Mama. Fear not. She is a golden haired Scotswoman with an independent turn of mind. She is very fine, very strong, very wise. I am certain that you will like her."

Katherine's eyes filled with tears. "I shall love her," she said, "with all my heart, if she is good to my boy."

*

On the third Sunday of Advent, Scott said that he must be leaving soon. But first, would David come with him for an afternoon's walk? There was something he needed to say. Over hill and dale they plodded for two long hours while Scott said nothing at all. At last they climbed a rough slope that was punctuated by the remains of a sunken moat, and crowned with ancient castle ruins. The view from the top was stunning in all directions. Celtic tribes, no doubt, had dug their ditches and built their palisades in this very spot, long before medieval days. Later a massive fortress had been raised at the crown of the hill, and later yet had fallen. Standing amid its shattered arches and tumbled stones, the two men looked out as their forbears must have done, across a wide blue expanse of northern England. Below them, the River Calder lay glittering in a series of loops over a tranquil alluvial plain. Among the ruins, but for the sound of the wind, it was extraordinarily quiet.

"I have come here often," Scotty said. "It has helped me to gain a certain perspective. I know now that I cannot conceal the truth from you any longer, David. I am most desperately sorry to say, but the fact is that I did it."

"You did – ?"

"What I swore to you that I had not done."

"Oh. With the girl."

"Yes."

"I see. Then tell me about it, Scotty, if you wish."

"She came into my bed one night while I was sleeping. Not to excuse the inexcusable, but she was far more experienced than I. Believe it or not, Wilks, I have tried to keep myself pure, and for the main part have succeeded. I simply wasn't strong enough that night."

"I see. I see. And are you saying that it was just that once?" Scotty groaned, and replied in tones of abject humiliation, "No, more than once – half a dozen times or so before I came to my senses. And then she laughed, and told me that she had learned it all from her father. Apparently he had taught her that this was permissible, even virtuous, simply because it pleased him."

"Now I understand." said David, "That is, I think I understand what she said to me in Lahaina that day. That her father meant no harm. She must have believed it."

"You met her? That was what she said? Meant no harm? Good God, David! They both believed at the time that she might be with child by him. I was to be the mark, the sacrificial goat, while our Church suffered and he came through unblemished. He was a big man among the Americans there, one of the Hallelulia crowd. Sat there grinning in the front pew at their place every Sunday."

"But she wasn't –?"

"No. I waited long enough to be certain. Then I spoke to the Sisters at the school before I left. They promised to help her."

"They did? Then, they understood the situation?"

Scott laughed bitterly. "They had already suspected most of it. Those sweet little ladies know more about life than we might imagine. Also, they are brilliantly strong-minded. One of them told me, actually, that she had fled to the Order at fourteen for the identical reason. Amazing! What beasts men are! But there it is. That was when I began thinking seriously of becoming a monastic. There are some orders for men starting up again, you know, in our own Church, so I wouldn't have to go over to Rome."

"But you found Matthew Pearl instead, or he found you."

"Yes."

"And he gave you your present assignment?"

"Indeed."

"As a form of atonement?"

"I suppose. It may have helped me, thus far, more than it has the children."

"If only you had told me sooner," David said sadly.

"Mea culpa. It seemed the decent thing – I mean, to spare you and shoulder the ghastly burden of the lie. I meant to use that pain for my reform, you see."

"Pride," said David, after a brief silence. "Harold Lopaka says pride is a rope to hang yourself. Don't do it, Scotty. Give me your hand." The two shook hands, looking one another in the eyes, and no more was said. A little later, David remarked, "Weather's turning. We'd better be on our way."

"Can you possibly forgive me?"

"What do you think? Of course I can. Already have. But the more important question is, can you forgive yourself? Look here, Scott, I've had a thought. Let's agree to meet here ten years from now, and compare notes on all that has happened in the meantime."

"I won't last ten," said Scott. "Make it five and you're on."

They walked home in silence as far as the village, and stopped there in a driving rain outside the "Goat and Thistle." Then David put his arm around his friend's shoulder and said, "Come old man, your life is just beginning. Let's go in and raise a pint to that!"

*

After Scotty had left, the darkest part of the year closed down on Yorkshire. This was the time when Viking invaders, on the longest night of all, had lit defiant bonfires on these hills and moors, while Druids prayed at Stonehenge for the absent sun to reappear. The cold was intense; the north winds came prowling over the moors at night and moaned in the eaves and chimneys of the ancient house. In the morning, icy stalactites glittered outside David's window, and the painting across from his bed seemed to glow more intensely than before. On a very dark day a golden pathway blazed near the center of the canvas, while the palest of sunbeams caused the same scene to recede, and made the mountaintops glow softly in shades of mauve and rose. How was this done? On closer examination he saw that the paint was put on thickly, with a vigorous hand, but this did not explain it.

"The new painting in my room, Mother," he said that morning at breakfast. "I think it's alive. It changes constantly. Who was the artist? I don't see a signature."

"It's on the back," said Katherine, "She is only an amateur, and she didn't want to sign it. George insisted, because he thinks it may be valuable one day. There's another by the same person, but I didn't care for it, so I put it away."

Later that morning, mother and son went up the stairs together, and while David took the snow scene down to look at the back of it, Katherine went into the attic to find the second painting. Unbelieving at first, he read the signature aloud: *F.C. Stuart*. Then he looked at it more closely, and studied it again, until hot blood coursed through his every vein. Fiona! What was a painting by Fiona Cameron doing in his bedroom? Then a phrase from her last letter came back to him: "I had thought of appealing to you for the loan of your Uncle George…"

Katherine came into the room with the second painting. "This one is not so nice," she was saying. "But George told me to keep it. A perfectly ordinary, not very handsome man, and that's all." David looked at the painting and felt disappointment at first. The background was dark and indistinct; in the foreground, the light of a single lantern from below illumined the face of a man who was most certainly not beautiful. Yet there was something attractive and appealing, even something compelling about him; or perhaps that was true only of this tender, sympathetic view of the subject. Who was it? Then he knew.

"Mother, this is no ordinary person. This is King Kamehameha Fifth of Hawaii. This is King Lot Kamehameha, a fine monarch and an excellent man!"

"Mercy!" said Katherine, "I had no idea. What ever shall we do with him?"

"I don't know," said David, as he sat down abruptly. He had just remembered that George Merryman was on his way to Australia. And that, in turn, meant that Fiona was no closer than before.

*

It began to snow heavily that night, and he stood by the parlor window watching the whirling flakes as they fell. Tomorrow he must bring in a tree for the parlor, and the next night, carol-singing would begin in the village. But would he ever hear from the Archbishop again? When would Queen Emma answer his letter? His mother had assured him that she knew of no way to find the artist. George had simply brought the pictures to her one day. Come to think of it, he had told her that she must be sure to let David see them, and that was why she had put the one she liked into his room.

Tonight she was sewing by the fire, with her feet tucked up on the gleaming fender. He asked her, "Quite honestly, Mother, have you ever wanted a profession? Any sort of work, or life, that is to say, beyond the usual?"

"A mother, a wife, a widow, a manager in the home," she replied, without looking up. Some day, I trust, a grandmama. That's enough to keep a person busy, wouldn't you say?"

"Busy, of course. More than enough for that. But there are women who – that is, I've sometimes wondered whether you've ever wanted more. Something of your own, a skill or an art, perhaps, that would help you to fulfill your own dreams, enlarge your horizons."

"Well, if you promise not to laugh at me, darling."

"Of course not," he said.

"Only if you promise. It's no occupation for a lady, I know. But I've always liked helping people, and I always hoped to travel one day. It was a long time ago, and foolish of me, to be sure, but when I was a young girl I used to dream of becoming a foreign missionary."

47

Archbishop Tait sat by the fire in his library, peeling a peach. With a cheering note from Angela Burdett-Coutts, it had come in a basket filled with fresh figs, limes, grapes and other exotic delicacies. At this time of year it must have been shipped from Spain, or perhaps from Africa. Still, here it was on a dark February day, and he found himself in a state of pure childlike delight as he held the soft, plush weight of it, while slipping the skin away with a silver knife.

Tait was convalescent now, although still so weak that he was allowed to work only for a few hours each day. Sandford entered the room silently, carrying the Hawaii files. "Another letter from Bishop Kip of California," he said.

"Oh, good!" Tait replied. The dimpled pit of the fruit had retrieved for him the look and taste of a certain sublime peach he had eaten, warm from the sun, in 1837. That had been before his marriage, when he was still a shy young curate, and a tutor at Balliol. He had been standing in an orchard near Oxford, and a wasp had stung him shortly afterward on the lip.

"Fortunately," he remarked to Sandford, "the Honolulu cathedral is not yet built." Then, after a pause, "Unfortunately, on the other hand, the lad we saw here must be prepared to sacrifice himself so that it can be built one day."

"Wilkinson," said the aide.

"Yes. He must agree to silence on all that has taken place. He must take on the burden of it, stand in the breach alone if necessary, and hold it for us against all besiegers, as his ancestors did for the Crown, at that place in the north."

"Pontrefact."

"Yes. You see how it is: the next bishop we send out will want a full grasp of power and a clean start. Young Wilkinson will be popular. Already is, it seems. Also, he will know where all the bodies are buried, so to speak. Therefore, the next man in charge will question him closely and then find some way to get rid of him."

"Is there no possibility that David Wilkinson himself might be made bishop? He is young, of course. But he has a good record, he is apparently honest and energetic, and he knows something of the Islands."

"Wouldn't work," said Tait. "The people there will pay him as chaplain, but the money must come from England for the expenses of an episcopate with all the trimmings. England must pay for what England wants in Hawaii; and the people who pay will demand to have their own man there."

He was looking through the files now, wondering whether he might have missed a letter from Queen Emma. "For Jesus' own sake, do not cut us off!" she had written in that pathetic note to Wilberforce. He winced at the thought that it might have gone unanswered. Emma had turned a sacred key in his heart: the beautiful, sad young widow who had sat still as a statue beside him at Fulham Palace, while people sang to her.

"If I am still around when Wilkinson is sent packing," he told Sandford, "I'll want to do something for him. Make a note of that, please."

"Strike him a medal?" inquired the aide, who had certain privileges. Then he added, because he nearly always knew what the Archbishop was thinking, "But that won't be soon. Surely, Your Grace, we shan't be in a hurry to send out another bishop when they clearly don't want one?"

"Two or three years, at least, I should think," said the Archbishop, shuffling papers. "Let them settle down. Oh my, look at this! I had forgotten that the unfortunate Bishop who has caused all this trouble actually asked for a warship last year to take him back to Honolulu!"

"Perhaps he expected to be fired upon. You are far too kind, your Grace. In my opinion, Coldwell is a scoundrel and a blackguard. Any man who will threaten the Queen!"

"Threaten the Queen?" Tait was astonished.

"Queen Emma. It's there, in her letter to Manley Hopkins, that he sent on to us. Her language of course is gracious as ever, but it's obvious what Bishop Coldwell has done." He found the letter and handed it to the Archbishop, who read:

"...Bishop Coldwell asserts confidently that when he brings home news of the insolent and disgraceful treatment he has received in Hawaii, no prayers however urgent from this place for the continuance of the English Church can ever be granted..."

"Mmmm," said the Archbishop. "And this man Hopkins?"

"Hawaiian consul here. Wrote a book about the Islands. Promises the impressionable young adventurer a veritable Eden of innocence, if only he will go out and help to make it less innocent."

"Mr. Sandford, you sound a trifle bilious today. You are not having an attack?"

"No, Your Grace, I am well enough, thank you. And now, Mrs. Tait has asked me to remind you of your beef broth at mid-afternoon. Shall I ring for it?"

"No!" said the Archbishop. And then, "I am not a good patient, am I? Well then, have it sent up." He had decided that he would write tomorrow to Queen Emma, and that he must see the Bishop of Hawaii himself. If the man was beyond improvement, then he must be tucked away in some quiet place in the country where he would do as little damage as possible.

He thought of Emma and Hawaii again, as he looked out at softly drifting snowflakes and darkening skies; then he reminded himself that winter was nearly past, and that nothing in all the world is more beautiful than an English spring.

*

Dawn touched the skies over Hawaii an hour later, and Emma Kaleleonalani walked in her garden, thinking of the Archbishop. She could not write to him directly, for that would be improper. Yet perhaps Tait would find a way to help her, for she recalled that a warm touch of benevolence had passed between them when they met at Fulham Palace – something like the breath of the Islands, the sacred essence of *aloha*. Tait had a good face; he was a kindly shepherd, a man acquainted with sorrows. After meeting him she had learned that he had gone to comfort people in the slums of London at the height of a cholera epidemic. Such an extraordinary thing for an archbishop to do, it had been in all the newspapers.

This early morning hour was the time of Emma's closest communion with the loved ones who had gone on before. They were her guardian spirits now, her ministering angels that watched over her and lifted her up as she struggled with more sorrow than she could bear. Bishop Coldwell, in a foul temper one day, had told her that he was going to turn his Episcopate over to the Americans. She had asked him, *Is Hawaii a toy? Are we a mere bauble to be passed back and forth between nations?*

She wept as she prayed, and then smiled through her tears, for she felt the first touch of a little breeze that was stirring now, wafting its way up from the shore. To Emma, that was a sign from the Holy Spirit, the wind that bloweth where it listeth, moving every morning up toward the mountains, and every afternoon, down to the sea – a daily reminder of the fact that Hawaii was sacred ground. And as long as she could walk in the garden with her invisible loved ones, she would never be alone.

She forced herself to smile and drew in a deep breath of the cool, scented air. The day ahead would be filled with good works: help for the poor, the sick, the despised, the abandoned, the family of Christ. Yet a few more tears fell later, as she brushed her long, shining hair, thinking of Fiona Cameron. Oh, if Fiona had only married David, surely they would still be here. Why did they both go away? And why did they not go together? She did not understand it, and now he had sent a letter asking for Fiona's address. *But what can I do?* thought Emma. *I must wait for her next letter. I don't know how to reach her either, now that the castle is sold.*

*

The hours of quiet comfort and sweet communion with his wife had left the Archbishop in a tender mood as he summoned the unfortunate Bishop of Hawaii. He was prepared to see a man wholly crushed and humiliated, with his life's work and his reputation lying in ruins about him. Instead, Coldwell came bustling in, cheerful as a cricket, and then, without waiting to hear what his chief prelate might say, launched into a diatribe against the population of Hawaii. It was these crude, ignorant people, said Coldwell, who had destroyed his regime. The natives there were so degraded that they were despised even as servants; the American missionaries who had seized control were heretics and fortune-seekers all; their sons were vulgar, deceitful merchants and tradesmen of the commonest sort, with no interest in higher things.

The Archbishop took out his watch and placed it carefully on the desk in front of him. He would allow no more than ten more minutes for the rest of this interview. The mildness of his usual manner had a certain edge to it as he asked, "It is true, is it not, Bishop, that you have been away from the Hawaiian Islands for more than two of the past three years?"

Coldwell began to explain that he had to be away, in order to raise money. To his surprise, he was interrupted. "You have told me, Bishop Coldwell, that the population of Hawaii is dominated by certain vulgar, deceitful American tradesmen. While traveling abroad, were you able to offer your own congregations a better example of spiritual leadership?"

Coldwell looked puzzled. "My congregations. Why, your Grace, they are all the same. The difficulties in such a place are insurmountable. An Englishmen could not succeed there if he was an angel. And my own clergy have been disobedient! They have dishonored themselves and the Church by maligning me behind my back."

"Bishop Coldwell," said Tait, "the fact is that your mission in Hawaii is a remarkable failure, in a part of the world that welcomed you and the Anglican Church with open arms only a few short years ago. I can do nothing for you unless you come to a better understanding of what has happened there, and take responsibility for it." With this statement, he prepared to rise from his chair. Coldwell was astonished. Apparently, he was being dismissed.

"But your Grace!" he began. "That was not all! On every side, there were plots and conspiracies –" For the second time, Archibald Tait interrupted. Now he said, in tones that few had ever heard him use, "You will kindly spare me, Bishop, any mention of conspiracies. For some time now I have been aware of the *sub rosa* 'society' to which you and your Dean belong, the intent of which is to turn the Anglican Church over to Rome. Say no more to me, Bishop, unless you wish to apologize for what you have already said and done. Before you leave, you should know that I also have the letter you wrote some months ago to Bishop Kip of California, offering your position to him and naming the American priest of your choice who should be consecrated to rule it. If you think so poorly of the vulgar, deceitful Americans, I am astonished that you would betray your sacred office, and the trust of your nation, to them."

"Your Grace, I thought – what I meant by that was –"

"I know why you did it," said Tait. "You wanted it to appear that no English prelate could succeed in those Islands. You wanted to make certain that no other Englishman could go out there and prove you wrong. You were trying to conceal such a multitude of errors and misdeeds that the file in my office is more than six inches thick with them. Now, you shall have the goodness to cease and desist from all such activities. I expect you to be very quiet indeed from now on, to retire from public life, to make no further public statements or speeches that only serve to embarrass you yourself and the Church and your country further. Do you understand me?"

There was some indication, in a confused and wandering glance on Coldwell's part, that the full weight of the Archbishop's message was beginning to reach him.

"And now, Bishop Coldwell, I must ask you to leave. I have no further time for you. Within the week I expect to see a copy of your resignation, which you must write in correct legal form, and send immediately to the King of Hawaii. You were consecrated here for the purpose of forming that See, but it was His Majesty Kamehameha Fourth who gave you leave to enter his country and serve his people. I can only hope that his brother, the present king, does not regret that as deeply as I do. Good day, sir."

The Archbishop knew that he had allowed himself to become dangerously angry. He breathed deeply several times, felt his pulse, and retired to his chambers with a copy of John Donne's sermons under his arm. But Albert Coldwell, who had never before had a vision, was granted a sudden, panoramic overview of his future as he left the Palace. For the rest of his life, he suddenly saw, he would be nothing more than an ordinary clergyman somewhere in the depths of the English countryside, ministering to the commonest of common people while his wife kept goats and bees.

48

When the lad from Hawaii returned, the Archbishop did not recognize him at first. David Wilkinson looked like an Englishman now, with his skin a good deal lighter than before, and quite a decent haircut. The suit he wore was evidently new, and although it was black and plain, the fit suggested the hand of an excellent tailor.

After Wilkinson had expressed relief and delight at the Archbishop's recovery, Tait asked for a report on the population of Honolulu. What sort of people were these? David Wilkinson replied that they were most interesting. There were Hawaiians, Americans, Europeans, Asians, and even a few Africans there: an example of the world's population in small. "And the foreigners who settle there," he said, "often have more than one area of proficiency. One of my good friends, for example, is a German scientist who is preparing the world's first monograph on Hawaiian flora; he serves in the government as well, and he is also chief physician at the Queen's hospital. William Hillebrand, by name."

"I see," said Tait. "And what would you say about the character of the natives?"

"The Hawaiians are a clean and handsome people, Your Grace. An intelligent people, who have not until recently had the power of the written word. What they have done without it is remarkable, but the speed with which they have learned to read and write is even more so. We may thank the American missionaries for that, even while we deplore their theology. Shall I continue?"

"Please do," said the Archbishop.

"The natives are still largely lacking a professional middle class, but your ordinary Hawaiian today is much like your ordinary Englishman. He wants a bit of land to live on, and a garden for his vegetables. He wants a place to go fishing, and a wood nearby where he can hunt. He cares a great deal for his land, his family and his traditions. He is good natured, active, inquiring and much more generous than we are, although – like our own people – not always honest, pure or devout. These, of course, like the English, are islanders; they are makers of ships, explorers, navigators. It is amazing, but true, that they have managed to find their way about in the vast Pacific Ocean without the benefit of scientific instruments. But perhaps I am in danger of boring you?"

"Not at all," Tait replied with a broad smile. "Pray continue. I find this most refreshing."

"All in all, it's the sort of thing one realizes after leaving – with a certain perspective, that is. I was too busy to form such judgments while I was there."

"Yes," said the Archbishop. "It is one of the great joys of travel, coming home."

"Then may I say, Your Grace, in summary that the Hawaiians are much as we ourselves might be if we had their climate, which is superb, and their isolation, which has until recently kept them from the benefits of civilization, as well as its disadvantages."

"A superb climate, did you say? We seldom hear that!" The Archbishop was thinking of the many resignations he had seen, citing the morbid effects of Hawaii's tropical heat.

"Aye, sir, the climate is perfectly made for human health. It is the foreigners and the Hawaiian nobles who suffer from the heat; and that is because they eat and drink too much, and insist upon wearing European clothing."

"I had the great pleasure," said Tait "of meeting Queen Emma when she was in England a few years ago."

"Ah!" said David, with his radiant look. "Her Majesty is the great exception to every rule!"

The Archbishop nodded. "I should like you to leave as soon as possible, Mr. Wilkinson, for Honolulu. I shall give you a private letter to carry to the Queen. Nothing official. Merely a greeting from one Christian to another, across the seas."

There followed a period of instruction, in which David was told in general terms what was expected of him, and, in plain language, how difficult that might be. His duties would be many, his rewards few, and his position in Honolulu might end within a few years.

"Shall you be prepared to submit yourself to the next Bishop of Hawaii?" Tait asked. He told Catherine later that the look on the young man's face at this point was "pure Yorkshire." The reply was stated courteously, but with clarity and firmness: "In all due obedience to Your Grace, whom I have every good and holy reason to respect, my Creator has not made me so that I can submit to any man for the sake of his rank or station, without regard to his character!"

Here is a lad we may lose, Tait thought, *and not to the Catholics!* But he only said, "We shall see."

"I have a question before I go," Willkinson said, "and I hope that it may not seem impertinent." When told to proceed, he said, "If our purpose in those Islands is to convert the heathen, and not to rule the kingdom and take over Pearl Harbor – ?"

"That is not the purpose of the Church abroad," said Tait, somewhat more than crisply.

"– then I am puzzled by our methods. I was told, for example, not to bother with the natives, but instead to ally myself with the English landowners in my district. My bishop gave his attention, when in the Islands, to the royal family, and to people of wealth and station in the capitol. But I came to know ordinary Hawaiians, because they were my neighbors."

"And did you convert any of those?"

"I cannot boast of any great success, your Grace, but the children were making some progress. And there was one person in particular who took our teachings very much to heart. He was a man called Harold Lopaka, and I was training him to be my lay reader and later, I hoped, my deacon. Harold was my friend. He taught me as much as I taught him, and I learned to love him like a brother."

Archibald Tait was touched by this, but remembering the intelligent Zulu who had beguiled the Bishop of Natal, he asked Wilkinson how could he be sure that this Harold Lopaka was no pagan. He rather doubted that Hawaii was Christianized as thoroughly as the Americans claimed. Did not Hawaiian natives, for example, still believe in all sorts of spirits and ghosts, devils, demons and goddesses?

David's face had been aglow with affection as he spoke of Lopaka. Now a different sort of light flicked across his features, before he said in an amicable way, "Well Your Grace, when we have got the ghosts and goblins out of England, and the leprechauns out of Ireland – when our banners, our heraldry and our schoolbooks no longer show Saint George slaying a dragon, then we may see the end of paganism in the Hawaiian Isles!"

The Archbishop laughed aloud, although in such a constricted way that David thought for a worried moment that he might be choking. Then he laughed again quite freely; and this was a sound so rare that it cause his aide, in the next room, to rise from his chair. Sandford shook his head over it, thinking that Archibald Tait's illness had weakened him more than anyone knew.

David Wilkinson was dismayed because he had been on the verge of a solemn confession, in what might well be the last meeting of his life with the Archbishop of Canterbury. With some trepidation now, he described the Communion service that he had given to an entire village of Hawaiians – none of them confirmed Anglicans – after their escape from the sea. Tait said little by way of a response, and what he did say was surprising. He himself had been criticized, he told David, for admitting people to Communion who had not been confirmed. And that, with a few words on the solemnity of the sacrament, was all.

"You see, your Grace," said David, who could not stop now, "I am convinced that conversion should be a matter of persuasion, a matter of wooing, rather than threatening, frightening or overpowering, either a nation or the individual. Quite frankly I have not liked to see the presence in Honolulu harbor of the military forces of many nations, including our own. If Hawaii is a beautiful maiden – as a colleague of mine once said – then Britain ought not to be one of her self-serving suitors. In my view, the winning of a maiden ought not to make her captive, but set her free. Did not Jesus come to set us all free? I find nothing in the Gospels to show that he lacked respect for women, or thought them inferior to us."

A brief discussion followed here, of Christianity in relation to sex, until the Archbishop remarked that David Wilkinson sounded like a man who planned to be married soon. David said that this was true, only that the bride was missing.

"Missing? But, is she pledged to you?"

"In her heart, yes, though she may not know it. There are a few things needing to be settled between us. I hope that I may wait a fortnight or so, before going out to Hawaii. You see, Your Grace, I want to find her and marry her right away."

This was all rather odd, the Archbishop thought. The young man's confidence in his powers of persuasion was extraordinary. He asked what manner of person was the prospective bride.

"A lady," said David. "And very much her own person." Then, remembering the Archbishop's place of birth, he said with a smile, "She is Scottish, you see. And I should like to say that I intend neither to colonize nor to missionize Fiona Cameron, but rather to cherish and husband her as best I can."

Tait was thinking, *Ah – Scottish! The traveler in trousers, the bold one with assumed name – riding an elephant in Zanzibar!* And with that, the proposed union fell into place for him, even though his wife had told him there were never any elephants in Zanzibar – it must have been Ceylon.

"You are in the right place," he told David. "You will need a particular license for an immediate marriage away from home, and the provision of this document happens to be one of my small but agreeable privileges as Archbishop." There was a quick flurry of activity; Sandford was called in to prepare a set of papers, which were duly witnessed and signed. When they were alone again, Tait said, "On your way Mr. Wilkinson, and I wish you success in all your endeavors." David thought the interview was over then, but it was not. Tait had some parting words.

"You will be a controversial figure, of course, but you know that already. It is very likely that people will say things about you in the future that are not true. Don't let that trouble you. Keep to the center as best you can. Hold the balance, guard the center for us like a fortress out there in the Pacific. A public stance embracing both liberal and conservative – a private balance between certitude and humility – is what our Church must strive for, but especially at the present time of ecclesiastical crisis. The world sometimes calls us foolish for it, but never mind. Have good courage, Mr. Wilkinson. Watch your health carefully; sleep and eat sensibly; take some time each day for private prayer. As to those rebellious tendencies of yours, you are young yet, and the great gift of the young to society is their constant pressure against the doors of our cherished institutions. That is good for us. It helps to keep us honest. It causes us to bring about change where change is needed. The law, Mr. Dickens once wrote, is an ass. You may think at times that the Church of England is also an ass. And upon occasion, you may be right. But do not forget that Jesus Christ chose an ass to ride upon when he entered in to Jerusalem."

David was moved by this, and wanted to kneel for a farewell blessing, but refrained when the Archbishop offered to shake his hand instead. As he grasped the firm, cool hand in his own, he wished that his father could have known this man.

And he wished even more that Harold Lopaka could meet Archibald Tait one early morning by the sea, and take him out for a long day's fishing off the Kona Coast.

49

A dense fog was closing down over London that day as David left the Palace with a smile on his face and a marriage license in his pocket. His next stop was at the Geological Society, where he delivered his finished paper on the Hawaiian earthquakes and eruptions. He had struggled over it, trying without success to combine a meticulous factual report with a narrative including the thoughts, emotions and impressions of a witness. In the end, he told himself that personal narrative had no place in a scientific journal; and so, he had tossed those pages away.

With his duty to Science accomplished, he made his way more slowly toward the British Museum. Dozens of faces loomed before him in the mists and miasmas as he walked, and then quickly vanished; but not one was Fiona. There had been no word from her, and nothing from the Hawaiian Queen.

Under the vast, majestic dome of the Reading Room, with the heaped-up riches of scholarly endeavor on every side, David had come to sit quietly several times lately, comforted by the grave, penitential silence around him. Usually, he called for a book and pretended to read it. Today, however, he simply sat down and closed his eyes.

Fiona, where are you?

There was a pencil on the desk before him. He took it up, and without wondering why, began to draw a series of circles in his notebook. The tremendous circle of the classical dome above him, he thought, created a sense of visual grandeur, but it also gave the people below a feeling of shelter. At the same time, it made the circular space below into something like an island. That was where he was sitting, along with several dozen other seekers after wisdom – on an island in space, amid intersecting circles as the round earth slowly made its way around the sun. A central altar? Librarians as priests? What is it, he wondered, that makes a place holy, so that one recognizes a mysterious power in it, as for example, the round pool in the forest, the pool with the ferns and the waterfall? That, he thought, was the place of dreams: the safe place, where they might begin their lives anew. And it awaited them, at this very moment, in Hawaii. *Jesus and all your angels, help me to find her!*

He left the library and began to walk at random through the streets of Bloomsbury. The fog here was noxious, a grimy soup in which people, buildings, trees and vehicles were nearly indistinguishable. If I were Fiona, he thought, then I would know where to look; it would be quite simple, because I would see it from her perspective. Very well, he thought, I shall do it. I shall become Fiona at this moment – I'll put on her clothing, her history, her courage, her fears, her sex.

What happens now? he asked himself. I am still rather tall and strong, though no longer a man, and I am still walking quickly through Bloomsbury. Suddenly that is not so easy to do because I am wearing a tight, boned corset on top of underclothing, and layers of petticoats under a heavy skirt that is dragging in the mud. My shoes are stylish and they hurt. I have breasts that feel vulnerable and a troubling mystery between my legs. What am I thinking? I know only one thing: I must have my freedom! Freedom! Because of all that has happened to me in the past I am frightened, and more than a little angry much of the time. I try to make the best of it. At least I am rid of the gloomy castle now, and I am rich, and that gives me power. I don't know whether I'll ever see David again. I try not to think of him. I can take care of myself! And just now in my life, more than anything, I want to – want to do what? Buy a good horse and paint with oils. *Paint with oils!*

Of course! he thought. *Paint with oils!* Painting is what gives me joy! Paint Mauna Loa at sunrise, paint a Hawaiian king who loved me. Perhaps one day many other things – but now I am still an amateur, not even wishing to sign my paintings. So I must learn how to do this to the very best of my ability, and that means lessons. Lessons. Instruction. Where shall I go for instruction? Not Florence, not Paris – I am not ready. Edinburgh? London? Not Edinburgh. My sister is there, and I refuse to play the role of solitary, aging spinster aunt!

She is here in London, David told himself. *She is here.* But where to look, in a city of more than three million people? Lodging houses? Hotels? No, she will be in a private dwelling. Put a notice into the newspaper? She won't read it. Perhaps there is a school or academy of art here that will admit females. More than likely not. Back to the Library and look it up? No, he thought, that will only be a waste of time. Fiona will not go to school like an ordinary, sensible person. She is far too independent and stubborn. She will find a way to do it on her own.

He hailed a hansom cab and directed the driver to Trafalgar Square. Twenty minutes later he was mounting the steps of the National Gallery. "I am looking for a lady," he said to the guard. "She will be here, I think, with a portfolio, making notes or perhaps copying a painting." The guard did not speak or change his expression, but extending his uniformed arm, pointed to the entrance of a room across the central hall. A sudden chill touched David, as if some invisible, winged presence had swept through the air beside him. Then it passed, and he crossed the hall with his usual quick, impatient stride.

He entered a silent, airless room that was filled with Crucifixions, Pietas, Annunciations – and there she was. In a state of intense concentration she sat before a small easel, with a palette at her side. She had not seen him yet; she was

441

grasping a long, fine brush, straining every nerve to make a precise copy of a miniature painting that showed a unicorn in a circular, enclosed space, surrounded by tiny flowers.

"Very nice!" he said quietly, after he had come to stand behind her. Her hand stopped at mid-stroke.

"Splendid!" he said, "But I still prefer the original works of F.C. Stuart."

She turned and stared at him in a dazed way before whispering, "You! Where on earth did you come from?" In the near distance, the guard began to hover.

"You said it would happen when we least expected it."

"Oh, you remember that," she said coolly, and began to clean her brushes.

"If I am interrupting…"

"No, no. I am finished for the day."

"I have been desolate all this time, not knowing where to find you," he told her in a low voice, mindful of the guard. "I never received your letter until a few weeks ago, more than a year after it was written."

She lifted her eyes to look at him, shook her head slightly, and said, "Oh, I am sorry. That wasn't – wasn't my intention."

"I wrote to Queen Emma immediately, for your address. She hasn't yet replied."

"Sir, if you please! Madam? Madam?" said the guard.

Fiona gave the man a dazzling smile. "It's all right, Mr. Wiggins. I know the gentleman, and we are just leaving now."

They paused together on the steps, looking out toward the crouching stone lions at the center of the Square. Then, simultaneously, the two glanced up toward the place where Nelson stood, triumphant atop his pillar, so high as to be wholly obscured by fog.

"Another dreadful day," she said. "But didn't George Merryman tell you where to find me?"

"Not a word, the old rascal."

"Yes, but he is so *akamai*, and he's been a great help to me."

"Obviously," said David. "I am not the only one in love

with you."

He felt her turn toward him, and considered throwing himself down to kiss her ankles. She was wearing a velvet coat the color of ivory, and he could see an inch or two of flesh above the tops of her fur-trimmed boots. It was stockinged flesh, but still a daring costume. With pearls at her throat she looked like a Russian Baroness dressed for skating on ice. "Are you free?" he asked. "May I give you tea, or something to eat? We have an urgent matter to discuss."

She faced him now and said calmly, "Yes, I am free and intend to remain so, David!" But for her girlish bonnet, with soft white plumes that quivered slightly as she spoke, he had never seen her so armored, so wholly unapproachable. They had not touched one another yet, but now in an impersonal way, he offered his arm. She took it and they paced about the Square as he described his situation: the Bishop had left, and he himself was to have charge of the Honolulu Mission. He must leave for the Islands almost immediately.

She stopped abruptly and stared at him, appearing to be genuinely distressed. With this encouragement, David called for a hack and told the driver to bring them to Simpson's in the Strand. As he helped her into the hansom cab, his hand briefly touched a hard, unnaturally narrow waist. *Not free,* he thought. *Another sort of bondage.*

Over oysters and ale in the restaurant they spoke of Hawaii and recent events, until he took out his handkerchief and wiped a smudge of blue paint from her cheek. At this she laughed so merrily that he decided to take a further step. "I have a proposal to make," he said. She looked away. "Wrong word," he corrected himself. "Suggestion is what I meant. Here it is. Before I leave, I'll be going away for a week to a quiet place by the sea. I need to finish some work I've been doing. I would like you to come with me."

She was surprised, and a little shocked. Then her eyes began to sparkle in a way that he remembered very well. "Why David! Come with you where?"

"Whitby."

"Whitby. Synod of Whitby." She said. "That is something to do with the Church, is it not?"

"It's in the north, not far from the Scottish border. We can be there in a day. You are right, one of the great early councils of the Church took place in Whitby. Your estimable ancestors, the Celts, were battling Rome over such things as which way a monk ought to cut his hair. People came from miles around to dispute the question."

"Not seriously."

"Oh yes. All symbolic, of course, of a power struggle."

"Which we lost, as usual I am sure. But that is not why you want to go there."

"No. Whitby was also the home port of Captain Cook, but that is not my reason either. I have been doing some odd bits of reading lately, and I've come across a report that forty-one unicorns and a merman have been seen recently in that neighborhood. I thought you might like to come along, and bring your paints."

She leveled a swift, reproachful glance at him. "Come now, David Wilkinson. When was this unicorn business?"

"Several centuries ago, I believe. Not so long as we have been parted."

There was a long silence then, and Fiona felt herself beginning to tremble.

"Quicksilver," he said. "Your face. Fiona, I have missed you so. I need rather desperately to spend some time with you before I go away. I'll do all in my power to see that you enjoy it. It's a quiet place, a sort of hideaway that should be very peaceful this early in the season. Clean air, sea breezes, fresh fish to eat."

Actually, Fiona thought, she did need a holiday. Her focus on the historical and technical aspects of her work had become so obsessive as to be nearly self-defeating. Ever since David had come upon her in the gallery she had been feeling giddy, wrenched out of the miniature, controlling dimension into another, so flowing and large that it seemed to lack any boundaries. There was something unearthly about this encounter. "David!" she said. "Why do I sense that you are inventing the town of Whitby and everything in it?"

"Well, I'm not. You'll see. I went there as a child, and have never forgotten it. You need a holiday. It will do you good to get out of London, put some roses in your cheeks. With the weather so uncertain at this time of year, we may even have a tempest! That could be interesting."

"I love storms."

"I shall try to arrange one. And there is another charming story, that in the wildest of gales, a great tolling of church bells may be heard in Whitby. Those are Saint Hilda's bells, at the bottom of the harbor. They never reached the church that was named for her because the ship carrying them went down in a blizzard."

"And who was Saint Hilda?"

"One of your Celtic kinswomen. A distant cousin of yours, no doubt. Like you, a person with a mind of her own, and many talents. Twelve hundred years ago, Hilda was a powerful abbess. She's the patron saint, I believe, of courageous women – or if she's not, she ought to be. So you see, you will feel quite safe there, and quite at home."

"I am touched," she said. "Truly I am. This is very dear of you. But how should we manage? You mustn't be seen wandering about with a dubious female. I don't want to cause you any more trouble than I have already done."

"Trouble? Fiona, I am beyond caring." And having said this, he realized that it was true.

"I could bring my little maid, of course, but she would never do as a chaperone. She is far too young, and very French."

"Others may think what they choose. As far as I am concerned, we shall simply be traveling together. Two old friends who enjoy one another's company."

"Traveling together. In separate quarters, of course."

"Of course," he said. "And by the way, Fiona, it's the sort of place where one may dress for comfort. I still think of you in your riding gear, and that stunning paniolo hat."

"Really? I wonder what I've done with it. But of course, I shall manage my own accounts – that would put a different light on it, for the curious."

"As you wish."

There was a small silence, and then she asked, "If I should come, what would we do, when not out looking for unicorns?"

This was the moment he had been waiting for. He wanted to take her hands in his for the occasion, but decided against it. "My lady, you must do exactly as you like. You shall not be there to please me. I'll be working in my notebooks much of the time, in any case. But if we are both at loose ends we might explore the town, or hire a boat and go fishing, or buy kites and fly them, or simply sit by the fire and read. I know that you are not fond of chess, but do you care for puzzles?"

"No," she said. "But I have never flown a kite. I should like very much to learn how to do that."

"Then I shall be glad to teach you. Only do come away with me, Fiona. Please do."

"For a week, you say."

"Yes, for seven days."

"Then you have a great deal of work to do?"

"Immeasurable amounts," he replied, "But seven is a good number, don't you think?

"Yes, it is lucky number. You've persuaded me. But David, shall I bring Fleur, my petite femme de chambre? I may need her."

"Then of course she must come along. Fiona, I am deeply serious about this. Our pact must be that as long as we are together, you shall do as you please. Nothing more, nothing less, nothing other."

"That is a most chivalrous and delightful invitation. But I think I'll leave Fleur at home." The girl, after all, was quite young and extraordinarily pretty.

*

Before they parted that day, Fiona said, "You have

mentioned research and writing. Are you working on a book?"

"Perhaps. And perhaps only a great lot of nonsense."

"I know what you are doing," she said. "You are writing a book about your adventures in Hawaii."

"Something like that," he admitted.

"Am I in it?"

"Only if you wish to be. You must advise me on that point. Of course, if you prefer not to be mentioned —"

"Oh," she said. "Well, I shall have to think about that."

And so, they went to Whitby.

50

The first day was one of dazzling light and sudden darkness, with tempest clouds racing overhead and distant sounds of thunder over the moors. There were flashes of silent lightning toward the west while David and Fiona climbed the stone steps up to the ruins of Saint Hilda's Abbey. When they walked on the cliffs nearby, her narrow skirt was driven against her body by the wind, and she found it hard to keep her footing. David carried her hat, after it had blown away twice, and told her about his book.

He said that he was trying to write, not the polite, cautiously modest sort of account that was generally expected of an autobiography, but something – for him, at least – far more difficult. What he wanted, in fact, was the truth on every page: truth, pure and simple. That, he said, made it almost impossible for him to write anything at all, since the truth is not pure and it is not simple. In fact, it seems that there are many different truths in this world, and he realized now that his own were often murky, or else quixotic to the point of being scandalous.

"Many different truths?" she asked. "Then you are not a Platonist."

He ignored this and continued, saying that after all, his

intentions had been innocent enough: he wanted to make an honest accounting of one man's life. Something had made him rescue several pages he had thrown away recently, after writing his strictly scientific account of the 1868 earthquakes. "It was Luke, I believe, who said: *the stone rejected by the builders became the keystone.*" Or, he said – to put it another way entirely – it had occurred to him that something important was missing in any purely factual account. Missing in his life, no doubt, as well. Had Fiona ever seen a "magic lantern"? Yes, she had. A stereopticon. Then, he said, she undoubtedly understood the principle involved, in which two slightly different versions of the same scene are shown simultaneously under a brilliant light. The result provides the viewer with a sudden sense of rounded depth and dimension. This was what his book needed: a second voice, a second witness – the voice of imagination and feeling, with a vision equal to his own, but different: the feminine perspective.

At the same time Fiona was thinking: Who is this man? What is he saying? Oh God, this brooding sky, the wind so savage that it whips the breath from my throat! My skirt in this wind – I might as well be naked! Why am I here? This is not the David I know. He had not touched her, nor spoken of love again, nor looked at her as he used to, with honest yearning. When they came to the inn he arranged for a large suite of connecting rooms, with a parlor and a fireplace for Fiona. He handed all the keys to her, saying solemnly, "I believe the lady of the house keeps these in her chatelaine." She had laughed, and told him he was hopelessly old-fashioned. "I have never had a chatelaine in my life!" Still, she kept the keys.

Now he was still talking in his cool, determined and analytical way about the feminine dimension – like someone trying to sew a fine seam, she thought, with mittens on. "Your last letter, Fiona, was very helpful to me. I have read it many times over, and thought a great deal about it."

"Burn it!" she said.

"No, I could never do that. You may have it back and burn it yourself, if you wish. But it was wise and eloquent, and it made me wonder whether you have kept a journal of your own, or whether more of your letters might be retrieved. Our combined observations of the Hawaiian adventure might have a value that neither has on its own."

"Yes," she said. "But you see, I always write indiscreetly. It is my habit, a foolish and a dangerous one, I know."

He looked at her gravely and said, "You have nothing to be ashamed of. Come, let's walk the other way, so that you may have the wind at your back."

*

"There's a pretty pair," said an elderly guest in the inn, after Fiona and David had left the dining room. "That priest and his wife."

"Two priests, I thought it was," said her husband.

"Harry Twigg. You're sore in need of spectacles."

"There in the corner? I saw the two of them, both of a size, both in black. I said to myself, how now! A pair of ravens!"

"For shame!" said Nora. "And she in the latest style, with her skirt drawn up in back, and a ring on her finger would sink a warship!"

He shrugged, and no more was said between them until they had finished, first their halibut, and then their pudding.

"Anyhow," said Nora then, "for sure they're old married."

"What? Those two? What tells you such a thing?"

"Sat there and ate," she said, "the both of them. Never said a word."

He laughed. "Well now, you are an old fox. The change of air has done you a world of good already."

"Would it be that?" she asked. "Or would it be running off like a wild young thing with my sweetheart?"

"You are a dangerous woman, Mrs. Twigg. I fear that I'll be a sunk ship by the end of this holiday."

"We'll see about that," she said, "if you'll get me up them stairs." Very carefully, he lifted her from her chair and gripped her with one arm against his powerful chest, while helping her with the other to grasp the handles of two stout canes.

*

With a rueful glance that night, Fiona had locked the doors between them. David paced the floor in his room, and then tossed in his bed until he heard a distant clock strike three. When she did not appear for breakfast, he toyed with his porridge until the innkeeper's wife asked, "Will the lady be coming?"

"I wouldn't know," he said cheerfully, and left the table.

"Look at that!" said Nora to Harry. "They've had a row!"

"More likely," said Harry, "they're brother and sister. Plenty of Anglican clergy these days are not the marrying kind. They bring the sister in to do the housekeeping."

"There's economy for you," said Nora Twigg.

*

But Fiona was waiting for him at the bottom of the stairs. "Good morning!" she said. "I'd like to do some painting today. Will that be a nuisance?"

"Of course not. Are you breakfasted?"

"Tea," she said. They brought it up – and a biscuit or two. That was all I wanted. But if I go off for the day, you won't feel neglected?"

"Fiona, our pact: nothing more, nothing less, nothing other."

"I want to try something, you see. The light is so different here. I'd better go now, before the clouds gather. But with all this brilliance, I should have brought another tube of white. Where are the shops?"

"Sorry, I've no idea."

"David Wilkinson!"

"Yes Ma'am."

"I should have known! You've never been here before!"

His face lit up in a beautiful smile.

451

"You haven't! You haven't! You and your pretty seaside town! You and your merman and your unicorns! What a terrible liar you are!"

"But it's all true," said David. "You'll see. I'll go with you if you like, and help you find what you need."

"Certainly not. I'll manage. But, really!"

Having started the day with a cold shower, David now felt a need for exercise. He told her that he would work in his notebooks for a time, and then look for a skiff to row in the harbor. So they would meet later for a drink or a meal, perhaps?

She nodded absently and left the inn. Her thoughts were already far away, at the place on the cliffs where she had seen the light yesterday slanting down in a strangely tender, eloquent way to meet the briny mists that floated up from the sea. It was that radiance, that place of meeting and mingling that she wanted to capture, with a mere hint of grass in the foreground, and beyond it, the calm immensity of the sea. Impossible, of course. Still she must try, and launch herself like someone trying to walk on water into that place of pure color, pure light. It had come to her in the early morning hours when she could not sleep – she, too, had heard the clock strike three – that this was the time for it: a daring new departure, with David suddenly present in her life again but not too close, not invading or pressing upon her – yet firmly there, so that for the first time in many months, she need not think about him at all.

Fiona knew that she would never be religious in the ordinary sense, but it was a kind of prayer, she thought, to look as carefully as she did, first at the wrinkling, dissolving glitter of the sea, then at the canvas before her that was blasted by sunlight, sending out little explosions of white wherever the pigment was not. She had often sensed that there was something like a soul begging to be recognized in certain scenes and objects, as well as people. Lately she had begun to feel a keen, almost conspiratorial desire to answer that plea, but as anonymously as possible – wanting like the best of servants to do the work silently, deftly, gracefully and then disappear. If this was how God managed the universe, she could imagine why his presence was so seldom noticed.

She found that she could do without the second tube of Kremnitz White that she had failed to find by using quick dabs and feathery dry strokes that let the surface of the canvas shimmer through. She painted well at first, then badly, then ruined one of the best bits by fussing over it. Rescuing what she could she went on more and more boldly, thinking of nothing whatever for the next three hours, until she realized all at once that she was faint with hunger.

Clouds approached the sun, the light changed, and a small red skiff edged its way into the scene below. She wondered whether that could be David, rowing away – or a message from God, perhaps. Then she decided that a splotch of red at one corner was exactly what was needed on that pale, wild canvas: a hint of humanity, a nice little spill of blood.

*

"It was heaven, David. Thank you," she said when they met in the lounge that evening.

"No need to thank me. I've had a fine day too, and I've even managed to find us a pair of kites to fly. Shall we do that tomorrow?"

Then an awkward thing happened. She stood beside him with a glass of ale in her hand. Turning quickly to express her pleasure over the kites, she saw the windows across the room sliding sideways, then lost in darkness. She reached blindly for him and felt his hand, for a second or two, cupping her left breast. He instantly removed his hand and said, "Sorry. Are you all right?"

She was fine. It had been foolish of her to eat nothing all day and then to drink this lovely stuff that went straight to the brain. They laughed a great deal after that, and their conversation was so animated during dinner that the innkeeper winked at his wife, and Harry Twigg said to Nora, "All bets are off, m'dear. This may be something most irregular."

David was thinking that it was almost as if they were already married. Her beloved face with its new little lines around the eyes was open to him tonight, entirely undefended. They spoke of his future in the Church, and he declared that he was the world's worst missionary. He would serve in Honolulu while he was needed, and then be done with it. Undoubtedly he would end in some obscure country parish in England, planting leeks and cabbages behind the vicarage. He would keep bees, he said, as much for their wax as for their honey, and in his spare time, he would write sonnets in Greek.

"Impossible," she said. "The Greeks never wrote sonnets."

"I know," said David. "That is why I feel obliged to try."

"Believe me, my dear," she said over cheese and biscuits, "you'll be something very grand in the Church one day. I hope you'll remember that I would make the world's worst wife for an archdeacon – or, God help us, a bishop!"

With a humorous eye, but very seriously, he replied, "If that is a proposal of marriage, Fiona Cameron, I accept."

"Hah!" said she, and after that, they were quieter.

*

On the third day it was cold and damp, though not actually raining. David worked at his desk in the morning while Fiona went out to explore Saint Hilda's abbey. On returning at noon she burst into his room, flung herself down in a chair, and vowed that if she burned in Hell for it, she would never set foot in a church again.

"You burn in Hell? I very much doubt it," said David. "But what is all this?"

"Do you know what happened here? Here in Whitby? The innkeeper told me. A beautiful young nun came to the abbey, and they shut her up – walled her in with bricks! To die, to starve, slowly, horribly. All because she fell in love."

"With a fisherman, yes," he said, "I know. And ran away for a week of mischief with him. Broke her vows. But that was a long time ago."

"And they did that – did <u>that</u> to punish her?" The two looked at one another until Fiona looked away.

"How are we to know," asked David mildly, "that this terrible story is true? Why are we to believe it?"

"Because it is true. And I can tell you that Hilda would never have allowed such a thing. It was later, after Rome took charge, and then it was men only. And the men of the Church were mean, and they started killing – burning – torturing people! The Inquisition, remember that? And the Crusades? Blood running in the streets of Jerusalem?" She shot a glance of pure hatred at him, stripped off her muddy boots and tossed them onto his carpet.

David said nothing.

"Something else happened this morning," she said, suddenly grinning. "You may not want to believe this, but it's true. I saw a ghost. Quite a lively one!"

"Ah!" said David. "Ghost of the nun?"

"No, no. Saint Hilda was walking in the ruins. I knew her right away. She appears now as an old, old white-haired woman leaning on a stick. She told me that the unicorns are still here in Whitby – just a few. She cares for them when they are young and then she sets them free. We might see some, she said. Often at twilight they come to the river to drink. So, what do you think of that?"

"I don't know," David replied. "I intend to leave the ghostly population entirely in your charge. But as to the Church, times have changed, Fiona. In any case, you must follow your own conscience. No need to conform."

"But there is!" she said. "I found a Prayer Book by my bed, David, and last night I read the marriage ceremony. It is horrible! Forsaking all others, indeed! Would I forsake Emma? Would I forsake Bethy or Hal?"

"But that's not what is –"

"And as for promising to <u>obey</u>, that isn't decent. For the bride to swear – I mean <u>in church</u> – something she has no intention of doing!"

He laughed heartily.

"I am serious," she said. "Tell me the truth, was it you who left me that book?"

"Fiona, come here," he said.

"Why?"

"Because I want to kiss you."

"No!" she said. "I am not in the mood."

"Then come here because I adore you, and I want to whisper a secret in your ear."

"Certainly not!" she said. "I have secrets of my own."

"Then come to me for mercy's sake, because I shall die before dinner if you don't."

"Stop being an idiot."

"Bravo!" said David. "There you have it. The linchpin, the cornerstone of a splendid partnership: HONESTY!" He came to her and solemnly kissed her forehead. Then he handed her the document from Lambeth Palace.

"What is this? Whose is this signature, C-a-n-?"

"Cantaur. It's the way the Archbishop of Canterbury signs his name. This is a special license that only he can give. It means that we can be married at any time, in any place, without posting banns and waiting. I brought it along in case that was what you wanted to do. Because I myself would like it very much."

"Our names!" she was puzzling over it, bewildered.

"I hope yours is right. We put in everything I could think of."

"Yes, yes, but this is so – I don't know what to say."

"Say what you like. But look here, there are ways of working around the language of the traditional marriage service. I'll be the first to admit that the Church makes mistakes, and you have named more than one of them. But the rest of it, you must admit, is rather good – *to love and to cherish – till death us do part – with my body I thee worship –*"

"Worship?" she said.

"Well, you said that incarnation was something that interested you."

"But David, they can't mean it. Not seriously."

456

"It's always been there. For centuries, in fact."

"But not <u>worship</u>. After all, isn't that a bit —" But she stopped there, when she saw something more than a little dangerous in his eyes.

51

O n the fourth day the wind brought knife-blades of glacial chill from Norway. The herring fleet had stayed in port; evidently a storm was expected. Gulls came in from the sea to keen and complain, then waddled about pecking at the cobbled streets.

To the west of town a single kite rose up, dodged this way and that for a time, and then suddenly went soaring, very small, very high and white against the gloom of the sky. Something of Fiona's heart had gone up with it, so that she felt strangely disembodied down below, holding the tugging, thrumming string. Standing beside her, David sent a second kite aloft, and then stood a little too close by in his desire to be helpful. The two kites met in air, and then came crashing down.

Their owners ran after them, then sat on the turf together, sorting out the wreckage. "David, there is something I must tell you," said Fiona. "I'm sure it wouldn't work, because of the money. You'd resent it, and then, if I wanted to do any little thing for you – well, we've seen already what happens."

"It's worse than that," he replied. "Marriage would make a comparative pauper out of you. Some of it's entailed, you've told me, but by law I would have all the rest of your wealth, and the management of it, in my own pocket."

"That is true, but –"

"No buts about it. The law in this case is clearly wrong.

458

Therefore, we must break it, as I am breaking this string to give us a fresh start on the present project."

"What has brought you to such a conclusion?" she asked.

"Years of living," he said, "with reality. Life as it truly is. I believe that wives ought to have their own money. Not just queens and duchesses, but ordinary folk – and extraordinary ones as well. Must have, in fact, if they are to be safe, confident and free. Which is what I want for you. Therefore, if you had none, I would feel morally obliged to give you an endowment. Which, at the moment, I cannot afford to do. Thus – Q.E.D., I am delighted that you have one. And if we marry, we shall have papers drawn up to make certain that what is now yours remains so in perpetuity."

"Oh," said Fiona, finding to her surprise that she suddenly had trouble breathing. No more was said after that until the two strings were untangled, and Fiona had rolled them up neatly again. David reattached the two kites and stood well away this time, while Fiona launched her own.

*

After dinner that evening, at her invitation, they sat together by the fire in Fiona's parlor. David began reading his manuscript aloud to her, and after a few moments, quite unconsciously, Fiona took the pins from her hair and began quietly to brush it.

"David, don't stop!" she said when he came to a sudden halt. But he was watching her, as she brushed her hair, with such passionate longing that she was struck with shame. "I used to do that for my mother," he said in a muffled way. Her face flooded with color, and David tried to remember whether he had ever seen Fiona Cameron blush before. It was a beautiful sight. She put the brush away, and they sat in silence, looking into the fire.

What was she thinking of? He had no idea, and if he had asked, she could not have told him. Fire, blood, the blade of a pearl-handled knife, the dry, metallic taste of guilt, the ache of fear – as in the teeth when biting into a cold apple, or the savage pang in the throat after swallowing ice – all this at once.

"David," she said. "There is something I must tell you. Something I have done."

"We needn't know everything about one another – if that were possible."

"An act of violence. When you hear of it, you may not like me so well."

"Fiona, confession is not in our pact."

"I tried to write you about it once, but I couldn't. It happened in Borneo."

He watched her struggle, considering new avenues. "I'll put it another way," she said. "I have sometimes asked myself what you would do in a given situation. You say that you want me to be free, and I believe it. But I need to ask what – what you would do if a man were trying to force you – or me – trying to force me, let's say, to do something horrible – abhorrent. Something unbearable, unspeakable."

David responded instantly, "I suppose I should begin by breaking both his legs, and then I'd throw him down a well."

"You!" she cried in astonishment. "You, a Christian – a gentleman – a priest?"

"Aye," he said.

"Oh gentle Jesus meek and mild!" she whispered. Her shoulders began to shake, and she rocked back and forth with interior mirth, before bursting into shouts of laughter.

*

She locked the outer door this time, but not the doors between them. He heard her put the keys down with a clink on the marble top of the parlor table. Brilliant moonlight streamed into his room so that he closed the curtains before lying down to begin counting the hours as usual. Shortly after midnight he heard an incoherent cry, and soon afterward there was a soft knock at his chamber door. When he opened it, she stood there in a long white nightdress, holding a lamp. Her eyes were wild and she was violently trembling.

"Fiona, are you awake?" he asked her twice before she answered, "Yes." She was indeed awake, but nearly speechless with terror. Her hands were like ice.

"Oh my poor love, what is it?"

"Someone was in my room. Not a dream – I don't think so. A man stood over me. He was there. I saw him."

"Come, we'll look together." They went with the lamp, searching from one room to the other, looking into the armoires, under the tables, under the beds, behind the curtains and the chairs. Nothing.

Fiona went back into his bedroom, sat down on his bed, and pulled his blanket around her. "Bloody hell!" she said. "This is so unfair to you." She put her hands over her face and wept bitterly. When she had recovered somewhat she said, "I am not a child, David. I shall not permit myself to behave in this way. I trust you entirely. No one has ever, ever been so good to me. You don't deserve to be unhappy. What I am trying to say is, that if you want me – that is, if you –" She did not finish, but lifted her head proudly and looked straight at him.

He took her in his arms, stroked her hair and kissed her softly. "Oh sweet lass," he said, "Not in payment for kindness. Not in the midst of a cry from bloody hell. Life is not fair. It never has been. We are what we are, you and I. We must keep true to that, and go where it leads us."

And after that, with the lamp at her side, Fiona slept in his bed for the rest of that night, while he slept in hers.

*

David awakened smiling from a dream in which he and Fiona had been children lying together in a mossy glen, engaging in tender mischief of the forbidden kind. As he rose from her bed, he planned to say, "Fiona I have composed a new Article of Faith, an Addendum for the Prayer Book. Let it be said that you and I shall live by this rule: *Submission to all that*

461

is holy, Insurrection against all that is not. Do you agree?

But there would be no time for theologizing this morning. The sun was aloft in a sky of perfect blue, and when Fiona awakened, she was frantic with joy. David was, she told him again and again, the world's kindest, dearest and most splendid human being. She would put on her new gown, and come to breakfast with him, and then they must order a picnic. Today of all days they should explore far and wide, and amuse themselves all the day long, and he must have everything exactly as he liked it.

Five minutes later he found himself down on his knees wielding a button-hook. "So, a new form of devotional discipline!" said he. There were twenty-four small, round, cloth-covered buttons marching down her spine. Each was to be skewered into its matching loop with a silver instrument designed for the purpose. The costume, Fiona told him, had been made especially for their journey: a flowery springtime frock with a matching parasol. But the maid was not here, and without help she could not manage the buttons. Did he mind terribly?

Of course, he did not. However, David's approach to this unfamiliar task was so slow, painstaking and deliberate that Fiona tossed her head at last and said, "Well, I suppose you are used to undoing these for your ladies, more often than doing them up!"

He answered her mildly, "You may imagine so if you please, my dear. But now" – as he stood to finish the task – "between the two of us, we have created an interesting problem."

"And what is that?"

But he only smiled, and did not answer.

*

They hired a pony and trap, and set off into the countryside with bread, cheese and wine in a basket. It was the first warm day of spring, and the animal kingdom was in full celebration.

Fiona was enchanted. Young lambs were gamboling, mares heavy with foal browsed the greening fields, songbirds courted in air. As they passed by an orchard, a drift of apple blossoms came pelting down into the carriage. "Oh, what heaven!" Fiona cried, looking like an affectionate, altogether innocent bride. And this might have been our wedding day, David was thinking.

"Do you know what day this is?" he asked her. "It's the fifth day of Creation, when God made whales for the fun of it."

Just then they came to a farmyard pasture that was filled with thistles, mud, dung, stones and animals. Quite near to the road stood an apparition: a tremendous bull with a ring in his nose, black, gleaming and murderous, ready to kill. But that was not his object at the moment; instead, he stood heaving his massive weight from side to side, snorting and pawing the ground in a fury of lust, close behind a small, glossy female from his harem. The pony slowed, and David caught a glimpse of an immense erection. The monumental grappling and thrusting that followed were enough to shake the earth and toss more blossoms from the trees.

For her to see this, today of all days! David was stricken. And indeed, Fiona was very quiet for a time, but then she said cheerfully, "Looks like Aberdeen Angus there – good stock!"

They paused soon afterward to rest their pony at the top of a long hill. A cloud of iridescent butterflies rose up from the meadow nearby, while the green and silver waters of the North Sea glittered beyond.

"What kind of butterfly is that?" Fiona asked him.

"Um," he said. "A rare variety, I believe. Definitely idiosyncratic. Therefore named *Genus fionamus idiosyncraticus.*"

She laughed, put a finger to his lips, and said, "I love you, David. I have from the beginning. But you know that, don't you?"

The surprise of it nearly cost his composure. But when, at the next instant, she jumped from the carriage and ran into the blossoming meadow, a shadow fell over his heart. Watching her, waiting for her in the carriage, he saw clearly that he himself was the black beast pawing at the ground. Plucking golden blossoms from the green, she wandered farther into the field: a goddess of the Spring, a young Persephone soon to be stolen away and ravished by the Lord of the Underworld – and he was that Lord.

"Fiona!" he called, but she did not hear him. "If she does not come next time," he told himself, "then all is lost; she will never be mine." But before he could call again he saw her running toward him, her face alight, her arms filled with wild irises.

*

"There they are!" said Nora Twigg from her window, when the two came walking slowly back to the inn, late that afternoon. "Look at that, and tell me they haven't been off misbehaving!"

Her husband was lying on the bed in his undershirt, studying the sporting news. After a time he answered complacently, "You're a fine one to talk, Mrs. Twigg."

"I am no tart. I am a respectable married woman!"

"I'd never of noticed," said he, "if you hadn't of told me."

"Bite your tongue, Harry!" Then, turning to her imaginary gallery, "Listen to him!" Peering from the window again she added, "I tell you, that girl has her skirts tucked up halfway to tomorrow, and I'll wager his knees are all over green."

"Well then, cheers for the both of them!" said Twigg. "But that one's no tart – I had a look at her. And I'm thinking the lad is a decent chap, for I'm certain I've seen him more than once at the Palace."

"Go speak to them, then! Find out who they are – what they are doing here!" But Nora knew what the answer would be: *Not the thing.*

"Not the thing," he said. Then glancing past his newspaper he added, "There's a draft coming in there, love. Do you want your shawl?"

"No," she said. "I want my youth back again."

He came and knelt beside her, taking her quivering, distorted hands in his own. "Never you mind. We've had a good run of it, sweetheart. It doesn't get any better than we had."

52

Soon after sunset, wind and rain came in from the sea and assaulted the town. Spring was abruptly ended; orchards were stripped of their blossoms, and more than one old tree, after enduring winter's worst, went down. Seated at his desk, listening to the shrill howl of the gale, David was appalled by what had happened. Their week together was nearly ended, and this day that had started so well had ended in disaster. All of his cautious, carefully considered, chivalrous plans had been defeated in a single stroke by a row of tiny buttons.

She had come to him with her hair down on her shoulders, thanking him sweetly for a perfect day. Then she had asked him to undo the back of her gown. And what had he done? He had said no.

"No? But why?" she had asked, astonished.

"Why? Because it won't stop at buttons. And then I shall be the villain."

"What do you mean? You'll be wanting kisses for your pains?" She said this with a haughty look that made his anger flare. He told her in cruel tones, "It won't stop at kisses either, as you well know!"

"I am aware of no such thing!" she retorted, all dignity and disdain. "Surely you can help me in this simple way without – "

"Without behaving like an animal? Fiona, let me warn you, I am not suited to the bachelor life. What is more, you are no consecrated nun or natural spinster either, so far as I have noticed. The time has come for you to make a decision I shall leave it to you. What is it to be between us, marriage or friendship? A good proper marriage or an improper, wayward, dangerous and mischievous friendship with fornication agreed upon? Yes, I said fornication, and that was what I meant. Fornication is a sin, by the way, and for very good reason. When your decision is made, kindly be good enough to inform me."

He had thought at the time that he was being entirely sensible and reasonable, in fact quite generous, considering the state of his temper. But she had stormed from the room after telling him that he was an object so low, he would stink even in the bowels of Hell.

*

At three in the morning he remembered something Fiona had said: that she was unable to stay angry for more than an hour. Four hours had passed by now. He went to her bedroom, found the door unlocked and opened it. Over the noise of the storm, he could not tell whether or not she was awake. He approached her bed.

"There is a man in your room, Fiona," he said.

"I know," she answered immediately.

"There is a man standing over you at this moment."

"I know," she said again.

"He is a foolish man, and no hero – no knight in shining armor come to rescue a princess. He is a poor benighted human devil of a creature who wants what the black bull wants. Are you afraid?"

"No, but just now I don't wish to be disturbed."

"I may have the instincts of a beast," said David, "but I also have moral principles. And it is my firm belief that any man

467

who takes a woman against her will, or merely for his own pleasure, is a villain."

"I can't give you an answer yet."

"I understand that you might decide to leave me."

"Well," she said, "I am thinking about it."

"I'll help you now with your dress if you like."

"Too late," said Fiona. "It's ruined. The buttons are all over the floor."

"I am sorry," he said.

"We are both sorry. And that, I suppose, is life. So, now will you please go?"

*

After that brief exchange David fell asleep immediately while the storm battered the walls beside him, sending icy rivers down his window-panes. Toward morning he dreamed of music and banners, boisterous crowds of people cheering: a grand celebration of some sort at Bromley Crossing. It was nearly nine o'clock when he awakened, hearing voices in Fiona's parlor, coal rattling into her fireplace, and then the closing of a door. The weather was still dark and wet as he dressed, thinking how strange it was to have a beard, and then to shave it off every day. He was deep in prayer when he heard her calling.

She sat by the fire in a dressing gown with a large breakfast tray before her, on which two places had been set. He looked at her curiously, for today Fiona was clearly a woman of thirty-two, looking her age, pale, composed and dignified: the gracious hostess, very much in command. His heart sank.

"Tea?" she asked.

"If you please," he said quietly, still studying her. It was not until they had finished their porridge, their herring, and their scones in tense silence that she said coolly, "David, I believe we have something to discuss."

"Quite," he said. Obviously, the end had come.

"Yes indeed. Reluctantly, I have come to a decision.

Though I very much regret it, I know that in good conscience I cannot accept either of the choices you offered."

"Choices?" His mind wandered in a blasted landscape.

"Well, yes. I believe you said that we must have either a proper marriage or else a sinful friendship filled with risk and danger. And while I appreciate your concern for my safety, not to mention my non-existent reputation –"

"Fiona, I may have put it badly, but –"

"But it was honest, and that was helpful to me. Especially the part about fornication. Quite truthfully, I had never thought about it in just that way. Very practical of you."

"But Fiona, it isn't fornication if we –"

"Wait. Wait. I told you once that I don't like puzzles, and that is because I am not clever at doing them. So I didn't understand for hours that your alternatives made up a sort of conundrum, a riddle that is impossible to solve because one can't accept the premises."

"Premises." He looked away, seeing for the moment only the ruins of a castle on a hillside covered with thorns and weeds.

"The fact is," she continued. "that if we are to be together, then as far as I am concerned, it mustn't be one or the other, it must be both."

"Both?" He wondered at the sudden tremor in her voice, but he was still groping through briars.

"Yes," she said, "But evidently, in your view, that is impossible. So that is that."

"Nothing would be impossible if you would marry me."

"Marry you?" She spoke as if he had never suggested such a thing. "Why yes, but only if we may include our usual friendship, with all of its mischief and so forth."

He leapt to his feet. "What are you saying?"

"What?" She shook her head, apparently bewildered.

"If we may include! But you have said it. I heard you say yes! Fiona Cameron, as God is my witness you shall have all I can give you. But the point is, woman" – now he was shouting – "will you marry me or not?"

She stamped her foot and shouted back, "Well, of course I will! What do you think? But really David, what was that other nonsense? A proper marriage indeed! A lifetime of legalized boredom? When have we ever done things properly? Why start now?"

"I cannot believe what I am hearing."

"It's very simple. You have only to say whether or not you still want me, under such conditions. Please be quite certain. Do you or not?"

"I do," he said, "Oh yes, Fiona Cameron, I do." And they were both laughing when he took her in his arms.

*

The sun appeared briefly now, in a rainbow glimpse, and the rain turned warm, while the wind continued its assault upon the shore. Soon afterward the wind abated, and a great white mist came in from the sea, masking and cloaking every sign of human habitation. At four o'clock in the afternoon, an aged white-haired woman hobbled slowly through the streets of Whitby, but no one saw her, and so no one knew whether or not she was accompanied by unicorns. The town itself was hushed now almost as if it were Christmas Eve, and the few hardy souls who ventured out soon found themselves lost and wandering in the very streets where they had been born. The curtains of the inn were all drawn shut, and chambermaids tiptoed through silent corridors where every door was locked, only to hear a marvelously sweet, low murmuring in rooms that they had believed to be unoccupied.

Later in the evening the rain began to fall in torrents, and Fiona wakened with a fierce, interior yearning she had never felt before. She cried out, frightened by her condition, and David's response created such a firestorm of passion that they both were shaken with awe. Indeed, for a time they may have lost their reason, for Fiona thought she heard the voice of the Goddess Pele ringing out in gladness; and David was certain that he had heard the bells of Saint Hilda tolling under the sea.

*

On the seventh day they rested, and as they looked into one another's eyes they saw that they had created a new world altogether, one that was very, very good. At last they made their way down the narrow staircase of the inn. Upon entering the common lounge they introduced themselves immediately to Harry and Nora Twigg, and invited them to dinner. The four had a splendid feast together, laughing and talking, eating and drinking with the greatest of extravagance, after which David and Fiona ordered a round of Yorkshire's finest ale for the innkeeper, his wife, the staff, and all of the other guests.

On the eighth day they were married at a waterfront chapel by an astonished young vicar, with the Twiggs as their witnesses. Nora gave lilies of the valley to the bridegroom for his buttonhole, and Harry kissed the bride with a good deal more enthusiasm than custom decreed. "They left out part of the service!" the vicar complained later to his superior. "The man was a missionary priest, with papers direct from the Archbishop. I didn't like to argue with him. What was I to do?"

The Archdeacon shrugged and said, "These foreign missionaries are all mad. They go abroad and learn immorality, indulgence, disrespect. Well, there's nothing we can do. If she won't obey him, they'll just have to sort it out themselves."

*

On the ninth day they went home in a coach and four to Green Gardens, where David had the incomparable joy of seeing his bride lovingly embraced by his mother. Out came the ancestral rubies from the buttery, and a fine bottle of French champagne that had been saved for almost too long.

As they sat together by the fire after dinner, the three spoke less of the present than of the future and the past, and soon lapsed into a companionable silence. Then Fiona gazed at the last of the burning embers, seeing only light – pure light, the seed and promise of new life, while on the same hearth Katherine Wilkinson saw the soft tumbling of ashes: resolution, fulfillment, release. David, shutting his eyes against an excess of bliss, saw great canoes drawn up on the shore of a faraway island: a place of perfect innocence and peace, where love and freedom reigned, where fish could speak, and golden fruit gleamed ripe on every tree.

GLOSSARY OF HAWAIIAN WORDS

'a'ā = a rough, chunky type of lava
akamai = clever
akua = god
ali'i = chief, noble
aloha = love, hello, goodbye
aloha nui loa = much love
'amene = amen
'aumakua = ancestral spirit, guardian
auwē = alas
'awa = a root used for medicinal / ceremonial purposes

haole = foreigner, white person
hana = work
Hawai'i Nei = (all) this Hawai'i, here
Hōkūle'a = star of gladness (Arcturus)
huhu = angry (huhu wela loa = very angry)
hula = Hawai'ian dance, often ceremonial

'i'iwi = scarlet honey-creeper
imu = underground oven
'iwa = frigate bird or man o' war bird

kahuna = priest/expert/sorcerer

Kaleleonalani = name meaning "Departure of the Chiefs,"
    taken by Queen Emma after the deaths of her husband
    and son
Kealakekua = name of a bay, meaning "Pathway of the Gods"
kama'aina = person born in Hawai'i / longtime resident
kanaka = Hawai'ian person
kapu = taboo/ forbidden
keiki = child/offspring
Kihapai O'Ekena = Garden of Eden
kīpukā = hillock or open space surrounded by lava
kou = a tropical tree with orange blossoms
koa = the largest of native forest trees, prized for its wood
kukui = candlenut tree

lānai = verandah
lau hala = leaf of the pandanus tree, used for weaving
lehua = flower of the 'ohi'a tree, sacred to the goddess Pele
lei = garland/wreath
loa = long
lomi (or lomi-lomi) = Hawai'ian massage
mahalo = thank you
māhū = man living as a woman
maile = a fragrant shrub
makai = toward the sea
malo = loincloth
mamo = black forest bird with prized yellow tailfeathers
mana = spiritual power
mānienie = grass similar to Bermuda grass
manō = shark
mauka = inland, toward mountaintop
Mauna Loa = Long Mountain
mele = chant/song
Molokai = one of the smaller Hawai'ian islands
mu'u mu'u = a loose, flowing Hawai'ian gown

Nu'uanu = name of a valley above Honolulu ("cool place")

'ohana = extended family
'ohi'a = tree w. red blossoms, sacred to goddess Pele
ono = a fine, white fleshed fish ('ono = delicious)
'o'ō = Hawai'ian forest bird with yellow feathers

Pake = Chinese person
pali = cliff
pahoehoe = a smooth, fast-moving type of lava
paniolo = cowboy/ranch hand
pau = finished
Pele = Hawai'ian goddess of the volcano
Pelekane = Britain/Englishman
pili = grass used for thatch
pilikia = trouble
poi = paste-like food from taro root
pueo = Hawaiian owl
pule = prayer
pulu = woolly vegetable matter used for pillows
pupule = insane

tapa = cloth made of pounded bark

wahine = woman
wiki-wiki = quickly

NOTE: For simplicity's sake, in the text glottal stops and
macrons are omitted except in cases of isolated double vowels
(e.g. "a'a" and "o'o").

ABOUT THE AUTHOR

The scope of DREAM OF EDEN continues a tradition in the remarkably eclectic body of work developed by writer Sandol Stoddard. She is the author of 27 published books, including best-selling children's fiction, religious anthologies, translations, non-fiction works for adults and various articles published in scholarly journals. From her landmark introductory thesis THE HOSPICE MOVEMENT that launched the concept of hospice care in America, to popular entertainments for the young such as I LIKE YOU, THE THINKING BOOK and TURTLE TIME, to the prize-winning best-seller THE DOUBLEDAY CHILDREN'S BIBLE, her works have been read by millions in English and in foreign translations worldwide. A native of New Haven, Connecticut, Ms. Stoddard graduated *magna cum laude* from Bryn Mawr College and raised four sons in California before moving to Hawaii, where she has lived and worked since 1980.